CHARLOTTE VALE ALLEN

CLAUDIA'S SHADOW

MIRA BOOKS

ISBN 1-55166-245-0

CLAUDIA'S SHADOW

Copyright © 1996 by Charlotte Vale Allen.

Printed in U.S.A.

For some very special friends—
Philomena Plunkett, Angelo Rizacos,
Rudy Hunter and George Koury,
Louis Mainelli, and Jocelyn O'Brien.
My life is enriched by knowing you.

One

Every Saturday morning after breakfast, while still in her pajamas, she cleaned the apartment. She changed the sheets, then put fresh towels in the bathroom, tossing the items to be laundered in a pile by the front door. Donning rubber gloves, she scoured the bathroom before moving on to the small Pullman kitchen. After dusting the living room and bedroom, she vacuumed. And finally, sweaty but satisfied, she added her pajamas to the laundry in the front hall and headed for the shower.

She'd just finished dressing and was about to dry her hair when the telephone rang. She picked up the bedroom extension to hear Ian Hodges say, "Rowena?" and she knew—her stomach went hollow and her shoulders tensed—that she was about to hear bad news. Ian was the manager of her sister Claudia's restaurant and would have no other reason to call except to convey something dreadful.

"What's happened?" She was suddenly, arbitrarily frightened.

"This is very difficult, Rowena," he said, and her fear deepened because she knew he was trying to find words that would lessen the impact of the blow he was about to deliver.

"Just tell me, Ian." She needed to know, to begin dealing with the facts.

"Claudia failed to show up at the restaurant last night. I tried ringing her but there was no answer. I thought it odd but then odd things happen as a matter of course with your sister. When she still wasn't answering this morning, I thought I'd better come round to check. I had the spare set of keys from the restaurant, you see." His voice became heavier as his upset manifested itself. "I'm sorry, Rowena, but it appears she's committed suicide."

"Oh my God!" she exclaimed, while the voice inside her head declared that of the many possible things she might do, Claudia would *never* kill herself. "How?" she asked, as immediately skeptical as she would have been had Claudia herself been calling to suggest an impromptu dinner together. In her entire life Claudia had never done anything without considering beforehand all the possible ramifications and permutations; she was a plotter, someone who never succumbed to impulse but who was always looking to see what possible benefit to her there might be in whatever she did.

"Could you come?" Ian was asking. "I've identified her, but the police would like to speak to her next of kin."

"Yes, of course," Rowena agreed, her brain spinning. "I'll leave right away."

"Oh, good. Thank you."

She hung up to find herself trying to go in several directions at once. She moved to pick up the receiver again, to call somebody but couldn't think who; at the same time she started toward the bathroom to dry her wet hair but abandoned that idea and went for her coat and keys. Her body seemed to want to act independently, according to its own agenda, while her mind was struggling to comprehend the idea of Claudia as a suicide. It was impossible, could never happen.

Hurrying to the hall, she kicked aside the laundry to open the closet door, grabbed the nearest jacket and began pulling it on as she ran into the kitchen for her handbag and keys.

Impossible, could not be, she told herself, locking the apartment door before rushing to the elevator. Inconceivable. Claudia dead. A suicide? Never. Claudia was too tenacious to die, too fixed on sucking the last bit of juice out of life, too young and successful and good-looking to die. Claudia would *not* take her own life. Rowena could imagine someone murdering her sister in a rage, but she would never have killed herself.

Ordinarily the drive from downtown Stamford to the house in Norwalk would have taken twenty minutes. Today Rowena made it in twelve. She sped up I-95 fully expecting to be pulled over, and had a speech prepared about how she'd just received news of her sister's death. But typically everyone was going well over the limit and there wasn't a police car to be seen.

As she approached the house the collection of official vehicles—fire rescue truck, ambulance, police cruiser—parked out front at haphazard angles, and a few curious neighbors gazing over their hedges at the house confirmed what she'd been working to deny: Claudia actually was dead.

The front door stood open and she paused on the threshold gazing in at the uniformed men milling about in the foyer, and at Ian to one side, head lowered, in conversation with a policeman. A very attractive man, Ian, always impeccably dressed; tall and slim, with an interesting face—intelligent, deep-set hazel eyes, long nose, a rather thin mouth, a strong chin. Yet he was oddly sexless as only, in her opinion, certain British men could be. She'd wondered for a time if he might be gay but had concluded fairly early on that he was simply neutral. If he'd been a country, he'd have been Switzerland: appealing, well-maintained, charming, but impartial.

She felt dizzy, dislocated, as if she were standing behind a thick plate of glass that muted all sounds and slightly distorted everything on the other side.

Ian looked up and saw her, their eyes holding for a long, fraught moment. Then he came over. She hugged him, and he murmured, "I'm so sorry, Rowena. This is frightful."

Strange. This man she'd met a few dozen times over the years who had always been the living essence of British propriety with his brisk handshakes and deferential smiles was so rattled that he'd bypassed the usual formalities and was communicating with her in the language of physical gestures. People hugged a lot at funerals. She remembered the way everyone had embraced her and Claudia at their mother's service twelve years before. Formerly reticent friends, both of theirs and their mother's, had suffered a loss of coherency and had to rely on their bodies to convey their sadness. Most of the people who'd known Jeanne Graham had loved her, except those who'd had to live with her, particularly Claudia. What Claudia had felt for their mother was something Rowena could not say with any accuracy. Claudia's true feelings—if she had any—were hidden beneath so many layers of artifice it was rarely possible to perceive them.

"Are you the sister?" one of the officers asked as Rowena stepped back from Ian.

She nodded, her mind like a heavy pudding lodged in the basin of her skull.

"Mr., uhm, Hodges here's already identified her, but if you wouldn't mind . . . ?"

God! She minded! She didn't want to see her younger sister dead, a supposed suicide. But again her body had its own will and was following the uniformed officer up the carpeted stairs to the master suite. Dread made it hard for her to breathe; her legs were heavy. All she'd ever wanted was a quiet life, to be left alone. She hadn't an illusion to her name, hadn't had since the age of twelve or so. But being Claudia's sister meant you were scheduled for drama whether you craved it or not. It was the result of being the only pragmatically rational member of the family, the plain one, the one with small ambitions and no interest in power, no urge to bend others to her will. She'd simply wanted to be able to go to her job and take a trip each summer to someplace exotic. She wasn't even particularly interested in men anymore, not after all the years of Claudia making an ugly game of actively pursuing the few men Rowena had managed to attract. And the thought of having children and subjecting them, no matter how peripherally or infrequently, to their grandmother or their aunt Claudia had made her cringe.

Well, that was certainly no longer an issue. She could start breeding tomorrow were she not too old and lacking a partner. *I don't want to do this,* she thought, aware of her feet moving her along the worn carpet of the hallway, on her way to see Claudia in this house that had scarcely changed since their childhood. Which was odd, considering Claudia's outrageous maneuvering to obtain it. She'd embarked upon a campaign to persuade their dying mother to alter her will, leaving the house and the bulk of the not inconsiderable liquid assets to her. And, through a skillful exploitation of Jeanne's guilt, she had succeeded.

Crushed but unsurprised, Rowena had taken her comparatively small inheritance and invested it carefully in mutual funds, using the interest to pay her living expenses and telling herself that Claudia was welcome to the old family home. They had never been much of a family, and the house had never been a home. Yet once she'd gained possession of the place Claudia had done only what was required to keep it functioning, proving conclusively to Rowena that it had been no more than another prize in another convoluted and incomprehensible game Claudia had played, and won. Twelve years later the house had a decidedly dated air, as if someone well into her seventies had resided here, not a woman of thirty-seven.

Rowena stood in the master bedroom doorway, mouth open, fists shoved deep into her jacket pockets. Claudia lay on the bed, her back to the door. *I can't do this.* The officer had gone to the far side of the bed and was waiting for Rowena to come make her identification, and she felt sick. She would throw up if she had to look at her sister's face in death. Bad enough seeing that too-thin arm bent at the elbow, the deep curve where Claudia's back dipped low at her waist before rising again to her hip. Thin, thin. Claudia's favorite aphorism: You can't be too rich or too thin. *I can't do this.* Fully dressed and under the bedclothes. Claudia would never have climbed into bed with all her clothes on. She had rigid habits, one of which was to remove her clothes before getting into bed. It was a *thing* with her, like so many other *things:* her categoric refusal to do anything on the spur of the moment (she had to have sufficient time to dress appropriately for any occasion); her obsessive concern with her looks (she couldn't resist any opportunity to look at herself, be it in a mirror, a shop window, or the side of a toaster); her bottomless appetite for expensive gewgaws (a Louis Vuitton checkbook cover, a Tiffany money clip, a Cartier key ring); her instant interest in anyone or anything belonging to someone she considered inferior (she considered everyone inferior and thought nothing of seducing a good friend's husband or lover); her need to win over anyone she thought worthy of her attention in order that she could, eventually, prove the person's true unworthiness by playing him or her for a fool. The list was long.

"Is this your sister?" the officer was asking.

Rowena nodded and with a dry mouth said, "Yes."

"Would you mind stepping closer?"

I would, I do mind! She took a few steps, stopped. She could now see the edge of Claudia's face, and had an impression of terrible pallor. The policeman was watching, frowning slightly, expecting her to come right to the side of the bed; expecting, perhaps, to see her display some measure of sorrow. But all she could show was shock. All she felt was disbelief. "Was there a note?" she asked.

"If there was, we haven't found it." He looked directly down at Claudia, as if unable to absorb the fact that such a beautiful woman could really be dead. "But the prescription was hers. She had it refilled a week ago." He indicated the bedside table where there sat an empty plastic vial, a bottle of Chivas Regal, and a glass. "Nothing to indicate anything funny, but we'll wait for the assistant medical examiner to get here. He'll cite cause of death, or order an autopsy. Just the two of you?"

Baffled, unable now to stop gazing at this rear view of her sister, the question failed to compute. Claudia and Chivas Regal? A jarring combination she couldn't consider properly because the man's question was fouling her mental circuitry. Then she got it and said, "That's right. I'm her older sister. We had a brother." Her mouth was running independently now. "But he died a very long time ago." The words dried, her mouth stopped moving, and she felt the pain of that loss—the real pain, the real loss, even after so many years.

Her mother and sister had been like cartoon figures to her, too large for the kind of quiet reality she'd long craved. From a very young age, she believed she'd been born into the wrong family. Cary had escaped early. People might not think death by drowning at the age of eleven could conceivably be good but, perhaps for him, it had been, because he'd been too gentle and good-natured to have survived intact. Even at the age of eight, clad in stiff black serge for Cary's funeral, Rowena had envied her brother, thinking how lucky he was to have managed to get away. She knew somehow that she'd never be so lucky.

"We'll have to wait for the assistant M.E.," the officer said again, mercifully releasing her from having to stare any longer at Claudia's unyielding back. "I think your friend made some coffee," he said when they got to the top of the stairs, allowing her to precede him down.

What friend? she wondered, very confused, then realized he meant Ian. And she could all at once smell the coffee, and followed its homey, tantalizing aroma to the kitchen, the officer right behind her.

With an apologetic dip of his shoulders, Ian said, "I thought I should," as he indicated the coffee maker. "Will you have some, Rowena?"

"Yes, please." She sat down at the marble-topped table, shivering at the feel of her damp hair on the back of her neck. "Do you still smoke, Ian?"

"Would you like one?" He reached into his pocket for a pack of imported Silk Cut 100s and a small disposable lighter.

"Thank you." She accepted a cigarette, and then a light. The first inhalation made her head swim and she sat very still, concentrating on not toppling off her chair as Ian opened one of the cupboards and got a heavy crystal ashtray which he placed on the table before lighting a cigarette himself.

"Guess you folks won't mind if I light up," the officer said with a grateful, conspiratorial we-smokers-against-the-world smile.

"No," Rowena said. "Have some coffee. Sit down."

"First lemme tell the ambo guys and fire fighters they can take off." Authoritative but pleasant, the policeman went to confer with the sundry uniformed men milling about in the foyer while Ian poured three cups of coffee, set them on an enamel tray with cream and sugar, and carried it over to the table. He seemed hesitant, and Rowena said, "Please sit down, Ian."

Searching her eyes, he slid into a chair. "I'm afraid I don't know what to say. I'm stunned. Of course, anything I can do to help..."

"I'm sure there'll be something." She took another puff of the cigarette. If she wasn't careful, she'd be smoking again, after three years' abstinence. "I can't believe this was suicide," she said. "There's no note. She'd have left one. She would have, absolutely." She could imagine the kind of unsubtle recriminations her sister would have committed to paper in a final attempt to control and wound those around her. Claudia liked hurting people. But she was mystified and distressed when the people she'd hurt turned on her or, worse, simply swallowed their bile and walked away without looking back. There was a part of Claudia that wanted to care and to be cared for. But that part of her seemed to have no connection to the one that had to do damage, so that often she seemed genuinely bewildered by the outrage she inspired in people who had trusted her. Countless times Rowena had heard her sister innocently say, "But what did I do?" As if she hadn't fed her latest victim an insidious diet of half-truths, outright lies and genuine affection.

But perhaps Claudia had managed to create a few real friendships. Certainly Ian appeared shattered, though maybe that was due to the shock of finding Claudia dead. Rowena was shocked herself, positively shaken, as if the ground beneath her which she'd always assumed was solid had suddenly turned to liquid and was threatening to submerge her. Claudia dead. An utterly alien concept. "I *can't* believe it." She shook her head, then drank some of the strong coffee.

"I know," Ian agreed quietly, gazing at the tabletop. "It's entirely too sudden, too unexpected."

"She never drank Chivas Regal."

Without raising his eyes, he said, "On occasion she did."

That wasn't true. Claudia disliked whiskey. But Rowena could scarcely argue the point now.

The police officer—Brian Kelly according to his name bar—came to the table, lit a cigarette, and added cream and sugar to his coffee before asking, "Your sister have a will?"

"It's in the top drawer of her dresser," Rowena answered, gripped by the absurdity of all this. Her sister was dead, and she was sitting in the kitchen of her childhood home, discussing Claudia's will. "Why?"

"Formality. We're supposed to ask, in case there are special requests—funeral arrangements, that kind of thing. I'll go get it, if you don't mind."

"I don't mind. She always said she wanted to be cremated." Rowena looked first at the officer and then at Ian, who nodded as if he'd also been told that. She felt cold and very thin, as if she'd lost weight in the last hour. Dead. Claudia. Impossible. If she had any way to locate her father she'd call to tell him. But he'd left them the year before Cary died and no one had known since then how to contact him. For all she knew, he might be dead, too. Sad, sad. What a dismal excuse for a family they'd been! And now she was the only one left.

Officer Kelly came back with the blue-jacketed copy of Claudia's will. "Hope you don't mind," he said, scanning it quickly. "Dated this year, and you're named as her executor, Rowena."

His calling her by name personalized the event as nothing else had. Holding the cigarette to her mouth, she turned her head away as tears, abrupt and unbidden, spilled from her eyes. Poor goddamned Claudia was dead.

Two

The assistant medical examiner, a slight, gray-haired, middle-aged man in slacks and a beige suede jacket, carrying an unlit pipe, spent about ten minutes alone upstairs. He spent a further ten minutes or so up there speaking first to Officer Kelly, then to Ian. Finally he came downstairs, accepted Ian's offer of coffee and sat at the table with Rowena, Ian, and Kelly. He began quickly filling out the death certificate, pausing only to ask for pieces of information—full name of the deceased, age, and so forth—before signing the form with a flourish. "You'll want to call a funeral home to come for the body," he advised, at last drinking his coffee in one long swallow.

"That's all?" Rowena couldn't contain herself. "You're not going to do an autopsy, or investigate?" Couldn't he see that this death was suspicious? And why hadn't he interviewed her too?

"I see no cause," the man said patiently. "Unless you have reason to believe foul play might have been involved. In which case, I'll order an autopsy."

"But I thought it would be done as a matter of course. I . . . It's just so . . . out of character," she said, at a rare and terrible loss for words. "I mean, she wouldn't . . . You'd have to know her, but this simply isn't something she'd do."

"It's a judgment call, and frankly, I see no need. Your sister," he said gently, "died of an obvious overdose of drugs and alcohol. Conceivably it was accidental. But to my eye it looks intentional. I'm sorry," he said again, with a glance at his watch as he got to his feet.

"But . . ." Her thoughts were sluggish, too late. The man was already on his way. She looked to Ian for help but he was also getting to his feet.

Officer Kelly handed her a slip of paper with his name and phone number. "Let me know if you need any help. And thanks for the coffee."

But wait! This was happening far too quickly, and she couldn't seem to think or speak convincingly.

As Ian saw the two men out she helped herself to another of his cigarettes and stared into space, trying to locate her momentum and some thread of logic to her sister's death. It was all wrong, but she seemed to be the only one who thought so. With the exception of Ian, though, none of these people had known Claudia and so couldn't appreciate how utterly unlikely it was for her to end up as a suicide—dead in bed, fully dressed and made-up, with a bottle of Chivas Regal, of all improbable beverages, within reach. It wasn't Claudia's style. She'd have maximized the drama. And she would have left a note.

Ian came back, got the telephone directory from the top of the refrigerator and brought the book over to the table. ''You'll want to make arrangements,'' he suggested quietly.

He was right, she supposed. Horrible, but it had to be done. She'd been through four funerals in the past fifteen months, three of them AIDS-related deaths. Her dearest friend Mark had been paralyzed with grief when his longtime lover Tim had at last died after twenty-five months of suffering. She'd volunteered to handle everything in accordance with Tim's meticulous instructions. So she knew what to do now. She found the number of the funeral home that had organized her mother's funeral, and talked to a soft-spoken man who said he'd have the body collected at once and asked her to stop by the office to go over the details.

Ian sat quietly throughout, lost perhaps to his own thoughts, or listening. She couldn't tell. He seemed dazed, as if from some unseen injury. His aristocratic features were slightly twisted, his eyes glazed.

''I should notify the staff,'' he said when she'd completed the call, ''explain; tell them we'll be closed for a time.''

Hearing the unarticulated question, she was gripped by an almost overwhelming desire to ask what he'd really thought of Claudia. She longed to know, and felt wicked as a result. It didn't matter now what people had thought of her sister. Yet it did; it did. Claudia would quite happily have helped someone else plan his or her suicide; she thrived on internecine intrigue. But if the plan were carried through to completion, she'd have been baffled and repulsed, blind to her contributions. Her sense of cause and effect was critically impaired. Or possibly she'd had a rare ability to remember events in ways other than that in which they had actually happened, always absolving herself from any responsibility. There had been times when Rowena had envied her, wishing she had so convenient a talent for rewriting history, for shrugging off the frequently ugly results of her sister's handiwork. ''Listen to this,'' Claudia had been known to start a phone call, instead of a hello. With a giddy laugh, she'd play back a message that had been left on her answering machine: an anguished voice, asking, ''How could you *do* that to me? I thought we were *friends.*'' Male, female, tears, anger, betrayal, threats, hostility. ''Isn't that *wild?*'' Claudia would ask gleefully. ''Isn't that *sad?*'' If Rowena didn't find it funny, and she never did—her sympathies always with the latest victim—Claudia took offense. ''You've got no sense of humor, Ro,'' she'd say, and hang up to play the tape to someone more receptive.

Realizing Ian was still awaiting an answer, Rowena said, ''Maybe you could close until the end of next week. I don't want to put anyone out of work, and there are, what, eight employees?''

''Nine, counting me,'' he said with clear relief. ''Times are rough, but the restaurant's been doing well, more than holding its own.''

She knew that. Claudia invariably made a point of telling her how successful Le Rendezvous was. ''Okay,'' Rowena said, operating on automatic pilot as she outlined a schedule. ''We'll probably have the viewing on Monday, set the service for Tuesday. I see no reason to drag this out. Do you?'' He shook his head, and she went on. ''So, you could reopen on Thursday, assuming you have no objection to running things for the time being. Everyone will be paid for the full week. Will that be all right?''

He smiled for the first time. ''I'm sure it will.''

She returned what she hoped approximated a smile. They both knew Claudia wouldn't have paid the staff for days when the restaurant was closed. She'd thought nothing of spending extravagantly on herself but was mean-minded when it came to her employees.

Rowena's instincts were generous; she'd always been willing to share, while Claudia had hoarded everything that came within her grasp. Jeanne had, with peculiar indignation, once declared at the dinner table that Rowena was always attempting to buy her friends.

''Stop giving things away,'' her mother had said, ''and you'll see how quickly your so-called friends stop coming around.''

Crushed, the ten-year-old Rowena had murmured, ''That's not true,'' and wished she knew why her mother was so mean to her, but not to Claudia. It wasn't true, she told herself. But the seed had been planted, and for a time she'd wondered if her friends actually did like her. By twenty-five she knew that the kind of people who could be bought would have no interest in a librarian whose greatest pleasures were quiet dinners with a few companions, and solo annual excursions to Europe or Asia. Still, she never forgot the remark or the cruel look on her mother's face when she made it.

Possibly Ian did have a clear picture of Claudia. After all, he'd managed the restaurant for the nearly twelve years of Claudia's ownership. He had to have seen the facade slip at some point during that time; one night, say, after closing when the last of the customers and staff had gone, and Claudia ranted about breakage, or about the staff helping themselves to after-hours glasses of wine as they cleaned up and readied the place for the next day's luncheon business. She'd heard Claudia curse her employees, just as she'd cursed every friend or lover she'd ever had. Rowena could not, in fact, recall Claudia's ever having had something good to say about anyone, unless she was working to pit people against each other by praising one to the other. God! She had to stop thinking this way. Claudia was dead. The games were at an end. It was sad, her death; sad and pointless and disconcerting. They'd never have the reconciliation Rowena had hoped would one day take place. She'd pictured the two of them in their old age, laughing together over their youthful follies. It was never going to happen now. And Claudia would never tell her why she'd done the terrible things she had.

While they waited for the attendants from the funeral home, Ian called and either spoke to the employees already at the restaurant, or left messages on their machines for those who weren't due in until the evening. Horribly conscious of her sister lying dead upstairs, Rowena ventured to look at the will and was astonished to see she'd been left everything: the house, the restaurant, all Claudia's assets, except for a twenty-five-thousand-dollar bequest to Ian. No one else was mentioned, which confirmed Rowena's impression that Claudia hadn't managed to sustain any lasting friendships. Thinking of friends reminded her she'd have to call Penny and Mark later. They'd help her get through this.

"I should run over to the restaurant, get the reservations book and call round, cancel tonight's bookings," Ian said, holding the coffeepot aloft questioningly.

"No more for me, thanks. You might as well go ahead and do that. I'll wait for the people from the funeral home, then head back to Stamford."

"There's time. I'll wait with you."

"What about Tony Reid?" she asked, suddenly remembering Claudia's psychiatrist lover.

"My impression is they were no longer seeing each other," he said carefully, slightly uncomfortable now.

"But..." She stopped. She'd last spoken to her sister about three weeks earlier, and she seemed to recall Claudia mentioning Reid then. But maybe it had been some other time, some other conversation. Things were very muddled in Rowena's mind; like clothes in a tumble dryer, facts and ideas turning, tangling. She let it drop. "She left you twenty-five thousand dollars. Are you surprised?"

"No." His expression unreadable, he said, "She told me, but I didn't take it seriously. She said a lot of things, mainly for effect."

Perhaps he had known the real Claudia.

They fell silent, and she wondered what she'd do with this house and the restaurant. The thought of coping with the legalities exhausted her. She didn't want any of it, although she did love the house. She looked around the kitchen, then down the hallway at the front door. A car drove past on the road outside. The wall clock ticked loudly—the same clock that had been there when she was a child. The house seemed to be holding its breath. Ian sat smoking, sipping his coffee, his eyes also moving over the kitchen, this perfectly preserved domestic museum of the 1950s.

Half an hour later two sober-suited young men arrived to remove the body. Ian directed them upstairs, and Rowena hovered in the foyer, peering anxiously up the staircase, then backing away as the two men carried the gurney down. Her spine flat against the wall, she watched as they descended with their slim load. Grotesque. Inside that shiny black bag Claudia's body was in the same position it had been in on the bed: head on her right shoulder, thin elbow bent just so. Rigor mortis. Rowena felt a surge of nausea.

As the morticians arrived at the bottom of the stairs and let down the wheels on the contraption, she cried, "Wait a minute!" and approached, indicating they should open the bag. *What was she doing?*

"Rowena." Ian moved to stop her but she shook him off.

Both young men kept their eyes politely lowered as one unzipped the bag. A mistake, she thought, absorbing the full impact of Claudia's face frozen in death: eyes closed, the blue veins visible in the lids; pale perfect complexion; beautiful and dead. A terrible, terrible waste. "I want an autopsy," she said hoarsely.

"Rowena." Ian now put an arm around her shoulders and drew her away. "The medical examiner saw no reason for it. She's dead. It was an accident. Let it go. Be done with it."

She turned to argue, trying to find words for her reasons, but her brain seemed to be swelling dangerously, promising to attain such immense proportions it would shatter her skull. She was startled, then soothed, as Ian turned her around and held her head cradled to his shoulder while the pair of attendants ferried their load out the front door, down the steps to the driveway. They slid Claudia into the back of the hearse, then slowly closed the vehicle's door. The engine growled to life; the ancient black Cadillac rolled from the driveway, turned into the road, and was gone. Too late. But maybe she'd disregard her sister's wishes, not have the body embalmed or cremated. That way Claudia could always be disinterred for a post mortem if Rowena still wasn't satisfied.

As they left the house together a short time later, she said, "Thank you for everything, Ian. I appreciate your help."

"Here's my home number. If you'll ring me later, I'll see to the details of the reception, and so forth."

"Thank you," she said again, pocketing Claudia's keys, having agreed that he should hang on to the spare set for the present. Carrying an Henri Bendel bag containing her sister's handbag, address book and a file from her desk labeled "Important Papers," she got into her car and headed for the funeral parlor. She drove slowly, with exaggerated care, again and again seeing that bottle of Chivas Regal on the bedside table. The medical examiner couldn't have known that that would never have been Claudia's last drink, and that she'd have left a well-thought-out note in her jagged, childish handwriting.

In the late afternoon she arrived home to be confronted by the pile of laundry in the front hall. For some reason the sight of it made her want to weep but she gathered it up, got the detergent, her collection of quarters, and went to the laundry room. Then, back in the apartment, not hungry, but knowing she should eat, she made a peanut butter sandwich, poured a glass of milk and sat in the dining ell to look through Claudia's address book while she ate. Using a red pen she made a tick beside the names of people she thought she should call. There were many names she didn't recognize, and she was surprised to find Penny's and Mark's home numbers as well as their extensions at the library, and those of three other of her friends. Two listings for Anthony Reid, one for the office, one for his home. Tomorrow she'd have to start calling, let people know Claudia was dead. She dreaded it.

Half an hour for the wash to get done. Then an hour for the dryer. By eight o'clock as she folded the laundry she could scarcely stay awake and decided she might as well go to bed. While brushing her teeth she caught sight of herself in the mirror and wished she hadn't looked. Usually she managed to avoid her reflection.

Rowena Graham: thirty-nine, short, and thin, with long brown hair badly in need of a trim—a dreary little troll of a woman. In her favor were good skin, straight teeth, twenty-twenty vision, a good sense of humor, and above-average intelligence. Always unsettled by her mirror image, she turned abruptly and went reeling off to the tiny bedroom to make two quick calls. She left messages for Penny and Mark, relieved not to have to talk to anyone. Then, at last, she let her head sink into the pillow.

It was a terrible night. She slept briefly, having dreadful, anxious dreams not only of Claudia but also of her mother and father and even Cary. But for the most part she hung right below the surface of sleep where she had repeated, infuriating battles with her sister, the two of them bickering the way they had as children—in maddening loops, with Claudia rigidly clinging to her position and using any personal attack, no matter how cruel or ruthless, to win. And she won. She always did. You couldn't defeat Claudia with logic because it had no application. It was on a par with attempting to reason with a force of nature—impossible.

Five, six, seven times in the course of the night she got up and paced the apartment, wishing she had a cigarette. Yawning, eyes watering, she climbed back into bed, desperate to sleep only to find herself wide awake again forty minutes later. Despairing, she thought the night would never end, and, finally, just before six, she gave up and went to the kitchen to make coffee. While it brewed, she tried to make a list of things to be done but ended up simply chewing on the end of the pen and staring into space, wondering why she'd let Ian talk her out of the autopsy. Maybe the truth was she didn't want to believe Claudia had taken her own life, and that the method had been immaterial to her.

Putting the pen down she went to the bedroom to inspect her black dress. She'd neglected to have it cleaned after Tim's funeral, but all it needed was a pressing. Back in the kitchen she poured a cup of coffee and stood at the counter drinking it while she examined the contents of the "Important Papers" file.

Incredibly cavalier, but so like Claudia that the file actually contained documents that should have been kept either in a safe deposit

box or with a lawyer: the title to the Benz, ownership papers for Le
Rendezvous and for the house, insurance policies both business and
personal, and a photograph Rowena hadn't seen in many, many years.
She carried it to the living room, where she could study it more closely
under the desk lamp.

George and Jeanne at the old redwood picnic table in the back garden, Cary seated between them, Rowena on their father's lap, and
Claudia on their mother's; the five of them smiling into the camera.
She remembered how they'd posed for the picture, the heat, and that
it had been taken by a professional photographer, but little else. She'd
been five, Cary eight, and Claudia almost three. It was full summer,
the grass thick, the flowers in bloom, the sun ablaze.

The portrait contrasted jarringly to later images that came rushing
to her mind: of Jeanne in a yellow chiffon cocktail dress, with a mar-
tini glass in one hand and a cigarette in the other, laughing her husky,
breathless laugh while a houseful of guests hung on her every word; of
twenty-three-year-old Claudia being wheeled out of surgery with a
small metal tent protecting her newly narrowed nose, bruises above her
augmented cheekbones, and enlarged breasts beneath the blue hospital gown—in pain but wildly elated, pointedly ignoring Jeanne and
clutching at her sister's hand before sliding back into a Demerol-
induced sleep; of Cary silhouetted against the sun, riding the chop in
his small sailboat, one hand lifted to wave to her.

In the garden it would be forever summer and they would forever
outwardly appear to be a family. Now it was almost thirty-five years
later and miserably cold outside, the sky striated in somber shades of
gray, with a mean rain striking hard against the windows. George
Graham was long gone, possibly to his grave; Cary and Jeanne were no
more; and now Claudia was dead. That chubby-cheeked, impish little
girl with the contagious glissando laugh and the golden ringlets got
carried down the stairs of the old family home zipped up in a black vi-
nyl wrapper. What the hell had *happened* to them? How had things
turned out so badly?

Unless there was a more recent will in a safe deposit box somewhere, Claudia had left everything she'd owned to her sister. She had
also designated Rowena as the beneficiary on a life insurance policy for
a quarter of a million dollars.

Does it mean that you cared about me? Did you also think we'd have
that reconciliation as doddery seniors? Were all your games only a
lengthy, complex diversion you never meant to have such ugly reper-

cussions? Was that what you were trying to say in designating me as your sole heir? Or was I the only one left still willing to talk to you?

More than anything else, she wanted to believe that there had been more to bind them than the accident of their births. Recent evidence, though, had been exceedingly hard to come by, nonexistent in fact. Grown wary with the years, Rowena had learned to protect herself without severing the connection altogether.

Weary, confused, eyes fixed on that long-ago sunlit group, her heart seemed to shrink suddenly, and she erupted into tears.

Three

Somehow, despite nights of constantly interrupted sleep, she got through it. Monday and Tuesday, with her friends Penny and Mark always nearby, she accepted the condolences of many strangers—primarily men—as well as of childhood friends of hers and of Claudia's, and of elderly friends of their mother's, a number of whom moved with slow dignity and the aid of canes or walkers. Their faces fixed and grim, they were the only ones forthright enough to ask how Claudia had died.

Rowena took some liberty with the truth, saying the death resulted from an accidental overdose of sleeping pills and alcohol. The old women shook their heads sadly, spoke with fondness of the Graham family that once was, and settled stiffly into the pews. She was moved by these women and, once the service began, found herself weeping as she grappled with unreasoning sorrow and guilt for having gone against her sister's wishes. Although everyone was under the impression Claudia was being cremated, she was in fact going to be interred in the family plot. Because the circumstances of her sister's death struck her as more and more suspicious, she wanted to have the option of an autopsy at some later date.

It wasn't merely the bottle of Chivas Regal or Claudia's being in bed fully dressed. It had to do with Rowena's strong sense, honed by a lifetime's exposure, of what Claudia would and would not do. And this line of thought led Rowena to recall an unpleasantly typical example of the sort of thing her sister *would* do.

Claudia had phoned one evening near the end of June almost ten years before to ask what plans, if any, Rowena had made for her birthday. Caught off guard, Rowena admitted she hadn't yet made any. Sounding delighted, Claudia had said, "Great! This is an important birthday, you know, your big three-O. Let me take you shopping on Saturday for something you'd like, then somewhere terrific for lunch. We hardly ever see each other anymore, Ro. Come on, say yes."

Finding the invitation appealing because whatever else she was Claudia was never boring, Rowena had agreed.

On the designated Saturday, about forty minutes before they were to meet, Claudia had telephoned to say, "Look, I'm sorry. Something came up and I had to come rushing over to the restaurant. I was wondering if you'd mind meeting me here. It'll save me having to drive all the way back to the house, and we'll be able to leave as soon as you get here."

Again, Rowena had agreed, and drove to New Canaan. It took her a while to find a parking spot, so she was running late as she hurried to Le Rendezvous, wondering if this was going to be another of those occasions when her sister changed everything at the last minute and they wound up not doing any of what they'd planned.

But Claudia was waiting for her in the entry, looking especially glamorous in a white linen dress that showed off her tiny top-heavy body and perfect tan. She wore gold door-knocker earrings and a heavy gold link necklace, white high-heeled sling-backs, and a few rings and bracelets to complete the overall image of health and wealth. Her shoulder-length hair was artfully streaked, her eyes dramatically emphasized with dark shadow and mascara, her collagen-enhanced lips glossed in bright red; but the high color in her cheeks was entirely natural. That telltale flush was the giveaway: Claudia was up to something.

She rushed over, smiling, looked Rowena up and down quickly and said, "You look adorable, Ro! I've always loved you in that dress."

Rowena started to say it was new, but was so intrigued by how at odds with her smile the determined look in Claudia's eyes was that she said only, "Sorry I'm late. I had trouble finding a place to park."

"Forget it! Come sit at the bar and have a drink while I finish up." Claudia took hold of Rowena's arm, all but dragging her inside to where two tables had been pushed together and six of the eight chairs were filled with her friends, who turned, beaming, and cried, "Happy Birthday, Rowena!"

Having always loathed the very idea of surprise parties, Rowena was so dismayed that she began to laugh, holding a hand over her mouth as her knees started to buckle. Her friends, taking this as a positive reaction, all laughed too. Only Claudia knew how profoundly upset she was. And for one unguarded moment, while people were congratulating one another on pulling this off, her sister's contempt for the group showed in an infinitesimal narrowing of her eyes and the slightest curling of the corners of her pouty mouth. Rowena's laughter ready to turn to tears, she obediently took her seat at the head of the table, flanked by Mark and Penny, and tried to make the best of an awful situation.

Throughout the lunch, she couldn't stop thinking about that unguarded moment and what Claudia's features had revealed: her delight in having had control of Rowena's friends, and her scorn at their having allowed it; her pleasure in pulling off something she knew Rowena would find painful in the extreme but about which she could voice no objection without appearing an ingrate and a bad sport. It was the perfect coup. When the waiters came out with a candlelit cake, singing "Happy Birthday," and her friends and the other patrons joined in, Rowena was in an agony of embarrassment, but kept smiling even as her eyes filled.

"Come on," Claudia trilled, standing over her. "Blow out the candles, Ro!"

She couldn't.

Mark saved her, saying, "She's so overwhelmed she can't catch her breath," and blew the candles out for her.

Miffed, Claudia said childishly, "Now she won't get her wish."

"No, but I will, toots," Mark said with a Groucho jiggling of his eyebrows that made everyone laugh.

Claudia busied herself ordering the busboy to hurry with the dessert plates as Mark quickly cut and served the cake. While the others were commenting on the fabulous chocolate cream concoction, he leaned close to Rowena and whispered, "I had a feeling this wasn't such a hot idea, and said so, but she kept insisting you'd be thrilled, so I finally gave in. I was right, wasn't I?"

Aware that Claudia was watching, Rowena took hold of his hand under the table and nodded, more than ever grateful for his intuitive understanding.

"I'm sorry, Ro," he'd murmured. "If it's any consolation, you're doing a great job of faking it." He'd given her hand a squeeze, she'd managed to smile, and the party had gone on.

She blotted her face now with a sodden handful of tissues, thinking if there was any positive aspect to a funeral it was the unique freedom it provided to make a display in public without fearing judgment. A good thing that was, too, because she couldn't seem to get herself under control. Once released, her emotions were charging this way and that like a crowd of unruly children given an unscheduled holiday from school. This was so unlike her, so alarming. She'd spent years perfecting her ability to conceal her feelings, to present a calm exterior regardless of the circumstances. *Take slow, deep breaths. Settle down. You're overboard.*

The service was ending and she regained control, consoling herself with the thought that the assistant medical examiner and the pleasant Officer Kelly couldn't have known how very questionable her sister's death actually was. And so what if she'd denied Claudia's wish to be cremated when Claudia had often, and merrily, violated so many of her wishes? *Breathe slowly, deeply. No more tears.*

During the reception at the house, organized and overseen by Ian and the full-time restaurant staff, Rowena overheard snippets of conversations, some low-toned and angry, others self-mocking. She saw the unmistakable signs of disillusionment on the faces of people who were discovering that their closeness to Claudia had been purely illusory. They were learning about her favorite game of playing their taped messages to others, using out-of-context remarks to show what saps they were.

"She'd make a date, cancel at the last minute, then not return my calls," an attractive brunette was explaining to a riveted quartet. "I'd leave progressively angrier messages, ultimately saying call me back or forget it. Then days later she'd call with some totally plausible story about being run off her feet and wiped out, and she was sorry. So I'd relent, we'd get together, and it would start all over again. In the end, I stopped returning *her* calls. Now I find out she was telling everyone I was pathetic and needy, and she'd play part of one of my messages to prove it."

Another woman said, "She was forever telling me I was the only person she really wanted to see, making it sound as if she didn't even have any other friends. And it turns out she was playing my messages all over town, too. Jesus! I can't believe she did that!"

Unfortunately, Rowena could easily believe it. Claudia had lacked any instinct to share her possessions, and had treated her friends exactly the same way. She kept them to herself and rarely allowed them to meet each other and possibly compare notes. She dealt with people individually, presenting different personae to all—according to what she cleverly surmised was required—and managed to make each person feel a certain prestige in being deemed a friend. It was an impressive juggling act, but inevitably she dropped a ball. Then she found *herself* summarily dropped.

Interestingly enough, what was fairly hazardous in her personal life worked well for the restaurant. Claudia had made the patrons feel privileged, and they came back repeatedly to bask in the glow of her attentions. Word of mouth had, at the outset, quickly built Le Rendezvous into a solid success.

Throughout the late afternoon and early evening Rowena kept on the move, pausing to chat here and there, all the while wondering if the Chivas Regal could have been used for purely expedient purposes. Perhaps, in the final moments of her life, Claudia had abandoned her pretenses and simply grabbed whatever came to hand. It was conceivable. Yet it didn't ring true.

Home at last, Rowena undressed and went directly to bed. As she was falling asleep she realized Tony Reid hadn't responded to her message. And, so far as she knew, he hadn't appeared at the funeral home. She'd have to call again and make an appointment to see him. She very much wanted to talk to her sister's last lover.

She took a month's leave from the library to wrap up Claudia's affairs, and moved temporarily into her childhood bedroom in the Norwalk house.

Once the lawyer and accountant were at work readying the estate for probate, and copies of the death certificate had been sent to the insurance companies, she collected every scrap of paper from her sister's desk and began examining them, searching for any clue as to why Claudia might have killed herself.

She found nothing. A week after the supposed suicide she girded herself mentally and ventured into the master suite to start sorting through her sister's possessions.

Stricken by the sight of the disturbed bedding and the faint but unmistakably ripe odor of death in the room, she flung open the windows to let in the icy air and stripped the bed, shoving everything into two sturdy garbage bags. It was a waste, but using any of these things was out of the question. She carried the bags out to the car and drove directly to the dump.

Later, sitting at the marble table in the kitchen with a piece of toast and a cup of tea, she studied the room with its outmoded appliances and fittings, thinking it was badly in need of renovation. So were the bathrooms. Otherwise the house was sound. Claudia hadn't neglected it; she'd simply kept it much as it had always been. Her only contributions had consisted of a large-screen TV, top-of-the-line stereo components, and new slipcovers for the old Tuxedo sofa and armchairs. The kitchen cupboards still housed Jeanne's china service; the same dull oil paintings hung on the walls; and both the attic and cellar remained repositories of dusty odds and ends no one had looked at in decades.

As she studied the gracious dimensions of the kitchen she thought she should probably hire a contractor, fix up the place, and move in. The idea of having her own washer and dryer, as well as a large dining room in which to entertain friends, was very appealing. She'd lately been considering buying a condo but was reluctant to commit the bulk of her capital. She needed the security of knowing that if she became ill or unable to work there would be money in the bank to live on. Now that was no longer a concern. The unthinkable had happened: Her younger sister had predeceased her and, in so doing, had secured Rowena's future.

Returning to the master suite she spent a long time in the dressing room, admiring Claudia's wardrobe, unable to consign such good-looking, expensive clothes to the trash. Most of the garments had never been worn, and all were designer items, even the jeans. Claudia had inherited their mother's passion for clothes, while Rowena had lost any interest in them as a teenager after Jeanne had declared with what was presumably meant to be sympathy, "You have no feel for fashion, dear. It's a good thing you've inherited your father's academic bent. You'll always be able to find things to occupy yourself."

Crushed, Rowena thereafter carefully disguised herself as a granola grinder, dressing down with a vengeance, not bothering with makeup or jewelry beyond a sturdy men's Timex she wore in preference to the dainty gold watch Jeanne gave her as a high school graduation present. The payoff was in comfort. Nothing she owned was too tight, or likely to become dated. Granola clothes were timeless and all but indestructible; usually they died after hundreds of washings when the cotton, or denim, or corduroy began to disintegrate. Her only indulgence was perfume, and she brought home a different duty-free scent from each of her trips. The fragrances kept the exotic sights and sounds alive for her, until it was time to go traveling again.

Her hands were luxuriating in the feel of a wonderfully sensual silk shirt when the telephone rang. With horror she heard the answering machine click on and Claudia's sultry voice say, "I'd love to talk to you, but I can't at the moment. Leave your number and I'll get back to you very soon."

By the time she got to the desk whoever was calling had hung up. Trembling, she saw that the message light was lit. She hit the playback button and heard Ian Hodges say, "It might be a good idea to change the message. Hearing that gave me rather a nasty jolt." He cleared his throat, then said, "I wondered if you'd be willing to lend a hand here tonight. We're fully booked and there's no one to cover the front. I'll understand if you'd prefer not to but it would be a great help if you could. It's now just gone noon. I'd appreciate hearing from you this afternoon, if possible. Many thanks."

She recorded a new outgoing message and reset the machine before calling him back.

"Good of you to ring," he said.

"I'm sorry about the answering machine. I completely forgot. But I've taken care of it now."

"Not to worry. Look, could you fill in this evening, Rowena? During the week I manage it easily but at the weekends I'm rushing about and simply can't. There's nothing to it really, and it's only for four hours at most. I'd intended to speak with you about hiring a hostess but I'm afraid it got away from me."

"What would I have to do?"

"You say good evening, smile a great deal, show people to their tables, give them menus and wish them *bon appétit.* Stop back once or twice to ask if everything's to their satisfaction. Dead easy. But the patrons here do expect to be coddled, as you know. I have every confidence that you could manage."

"All right, Ian. What time should I come?"

"I'm most grateful, Rowena. Come a bit early, say, sixish. That way I'll have time to go over the seating plan, show you where things are."

"Okay, I'll be there."

She felt a darting excitement at the prospect of entering Claudia's domain. Perhaps she'd gain new insights into her sister by acting as her stand-in at the restaurant. It would also be a challenge to see if she'd make an acceptable substitute. God knew she lacked Claudia's looks, her glamour, her blazing ego, and her style. But she was acquainted with the staff and she did enjoy dealing with the public. Despite her intentionally subdued exterior, she was not without confidence—she had complete faith in her intelligence. What she did not have was anything suitable to wear. So she went back to the dressing room.

From moment to moment she forgot herself, caught in the childish sense of playing dress-up. She settled for a simple but smart black dress with an interesting sculpted neckline and a broad-belted midriff. Then she went to investigate the contents of the dresser.

One entire drawer was filled with Fogal panty hose, and she winced at the fifty-five-dollar sticker on the package of dark gray hose she finally selected. Slippery silk underwear, sleek black suede high heels. She felt decadent, dressed in her sister's clothes, on her way to her sister's restaurant, but her mood was festive, as it was on the eve of a foreign vacation.

The staff was attending to last-minute details when she arrived. Ian greeted her warmly, saying, "You do look nice, Rowena," and she flushed, flattered. He took her coat and handbag to the office while she looked around, seeing the place empty of customers for the first time. It was inviting: indirect lighting; four large abstract impressionist oil paintings on pale gray walls; dark, almost black carpeting that made the room seem to be floating in space; crisp white linens; small vases of fresh flowers and a squat round candle in a polished brass holder on every table; and several oversized glass jugs of cut flowers positioned here and there.

Terry the bartender was organizing the cassettes for the evening, and Stephane Grappelli's violin was emerging from small speakers suspended in the corners of the room. John, Mae and Doug, the three waiters, were wolfing down a quick snack at the end of the bar, and waved hellos. The two busboys, Luke and Mikey, were filling butter dishes and slicing round loaves of crusty white bread.

Rowena pushed open the kitchen door to say hi to Philippe, the chef, and his assistant, Jill, who did the baking, the salads, and the desserts. Then it was time to sit down with Ian while he explained the floor plan and table numbers, and the reservations book.

"It couldn't be simpler. You take the name, cross it off the book, invite the party to leave their coats on the rack, get the menus and a wine list, and escort them to their table. That's all there is to it, and I know you'll do brilliantly." He checked the time, then asked with a smile, "Care for a quick glass of courage?"

Returning his smile, she said, "I'd better not. Sometimes it only takes a teaspoon and I'm completely blotto."

"Well, perhaps later. We usually divvy up a bottle of plonk during the cleanup."

He left to do a walk-through, checking the linens, the table settings, the candles and flowers. She went to the stand in the entry to scan the reservations before having a look at the menu. Regardless of Claudia's charm, the establishment would never have succeeded without Philippe's talent and Jill's imagination. The menu was small, limited to four appetizers, three types of salad, five offerings of pasta, five entrées, and three desserts which changed regularly, depending on Jill's whims. Everything from the bruschetta, to the poached chicken breast with artichoke hearts and sun-dried tomatoes in a champagne sauce, to the lemon syllabub was superb. Le Rendezvous had it all: atmosphere, attentive staff, and excellent cuisine.

The first customers arrived at a quarter to seven, and it was easy to welcome them, crossing their names from the book and reaching for the menus before leading them to table eight. She gave Claudia's spiel, inviting them to enjoy their dinners, and adding a spin of her own. ''Please let me know if there's anything you need.''

Between seven-thirty and eight when the arrivals came all in a rush, filling the narrow entryway, she had to work to stay calm. She was suddenly confused about the configuration of the tables and had to keep people waiting, telling the newcomers she'd be with them in a moment while she referred to the floor plan. By the time she got everything sorted out, she was sweating. But no one seemed to mind waiting, and once everyone was seated, she took a few minutes to look at each table, mentally matching it up to the floor plan, memorizing the numbers. Later, reluctant to turn away a pleasant young couple without a reservation, she asked Ian if she could seat them at the bar and serve them herself.

His expression one of mixed surprise and approval, he said, ''If you think you can handle it, by all means do.''

Aside from very nearly forgetting to pick up their salads from the kitchen, she managed to serve the couple without mishap, and the four hours passed quickly. By ten past eleven the last customers were going out the door and Ian was waiting to lock it behind them. The three waiters were helping Luke and Mikey bus the tables and set up for Sunday brunch. Philippe was wrapping odds and ends and returning them to the refrigerator while Jill finished shaping the bread that would rise overnight and go into the oven in the morning. Julio, the kitchen helper, was putting the final load into the dishwasher.

Ian opened two bottles of red wine and poured glasses for the out-front staff, who finally collected at the large table nearest the kitchen door. John, Mae and Doug tallied up the tips, gave Luke and Mikey their share, then pushed several notes across to Rowena. ''Your tips for tonight,'' Doug explained.

''Oh, no.'' She pushed the money back.

''But you served.'' The money came at her again.

"Did Claudia take tips?" Rowena asked.

"Sure," Mae said, "if she served. The odd few times we let people eat at the bar, she took her cut of the tips."

"Well, I won't," Rowena said lightly. "Okay?"

"We almost never served at the bar," Ian put in quietly.

"Why not?" Rowena asked him.

"Claudia really didn't care to serve." He gave her a meaningful look, and she understood. Her sister would have considered it beneath her to handle food. And she'd have made a production number of it, if and when she did.

"Maybe we'll change that," Rowena said. "Fifteen or twenty additional covers on a weekend would mean more income for everyone." She felt quite foolishly proud of having learned some of the lingo.

"True," Ian conceded. "Certainly none of us would have any objection. The problem is hiring someone for weekends who'll handle the front as well as serve when we're shorthanded."

"Why don't I do it for the time being?" Rowena offered. "If I'm going to be the new owner of the place, I really should get to know how it runs."

"That's your prerogative, naturally." His tone was pleasant enough, but it had acquired a slight edge.

"Would you mind, Ian?"

"Not in the least. As you've pointed out, in short order it will be yours." He busied himself lighting a Silk Cut. Then, as an afterthought, he extended the pack to her. She'd have liked one but thanked him and declined. All at once the atmosphere had become charged.

"You did a great job tonight," pretty, redheaded Mae said.

"Yeah, you did," John and Doug agreed, then quickly downed their wine and began getting ready to leave.

Puzzled by Ian's sudden coolness and the others' hasty withdrawal, Rowena wished she had more of Claudia's assertiveness. She would have liked to know what was bothering the man. But she was reluctant to ask, afraid if she gave him an opening he might respond by pointing out her inadequacies. That was, of course, highly unlikely. But even all these years later she hadn't yet managed to get past her horror of confrontation, or the caution acquired as a result of having either her mother or sister pounce on her for asking some simple question. So, chagrined by her lack of gumption, she went for her coat and bag.

Ian seemed friendly enough as he escorted her to her car. And she thought perhaps what she'd perceived as an abrupt change of attitude had been nothing more than a display of fatigue at the end of a long day. He thanked her again for helping out, and asked if she was quite sure she wanted to come back in the morning. When she said that she was, he told her it would be best if she could get there before ten.

"Drive carefully," he said, and waited until she was safely on her way before heading to his own car.

During the drive home she took stock. Her legs ached from hours spent in high heels, she had learned little new about Claudia, and she wished she'd had the courage to ask Ian what had upset him. But all in all, she'd had a thoroughly enjoyable time.

Four

Rowena and Penny had been friends since the ninth grade. At fourteen Penny had been tall, slim, and very beautiful, with thick ash blond hair, wide-set, large brown eyes, a pert nose, and a generous mouth. They had attended different colleges, and without ever having discussed the matter, each had gone for postgraduate degrees in library sciences. In time, purely by accident, they'd both ended up working at the Magnusson library in Stamford.

Penny had married right after getting her master's degree, giving birth to her son Kip eleven months later. She had trouble shedding the weight gained during her pregnancy and her husband Ken took to making unfunny cracks about her size. By the time Kip was two years old, she'd dieted her way up to a hundred and seventy pounds and Ken's snide remarks had become unbearable, so she filed for divorce. She moved back to her parents' home with Kip, lost thirty-five pounds, then in short order gained back forty-four.

It took more than four years of going without new clothes, of paper-bag lunches, of living on so strict a budget that she even had to ration the mileage she put on the car, before Penny was able to save enough for the down payment on a condo. They were years of maddening parental interference in every area of her life, from the way she was raising her son to the amount of time she spent in the bathroom; years when she had almost no social life and had to bring Kip along on those occasions when Rowena invited her to dinner.

But once she and the boy were finally settled into the condo everything was suddenly much easier. She no longer had to worry that her parents were walloping Kip for minor infractions of their stringent house rules, or walloping him just on general principles—after all they'd raised her that way and it hadn't hurt her any, they claimed. Once free of his grandparents, Kip relaxed, too, becoming considerably less fractious. Penny found several women in the complex who were willing to baby-sit, and she was able to have an occasional evening out. She could have friends in for dinner, and Kip was able to have friends sleep over.

Finally, at the age of thirty, she had begun enjoying her life once again. Except for her excessive weight, she was happy. And to her surprise, men still found her attractive, so she managed to maintain a reasonably philosophical attitude about her screwed-up metabolism and probably permanent bulk.

As for Mark, he and Rowena had clicked from his very first day at the library eleven-odd years earlier. He was five-eight or so, and slight of build, with the face of a film star: fine, chiseled features, clear green eyes, and sandy brown hair he wore short and side-parted. He also dressed like a film star—from the 1930s—in close-fitting pullovers or knitted vests worn over open-necked shirts tucked into belted slacks with a relaxed fit. He liked argyle socks, Bass loafers, Art Deco furnishings, and Canoe after-shave. He adored children, was devoted to his several nieces and nephews, and from their first meeting he and Tim had played paternal roles with Kip.

Rowena was closer to Mark than to Penny, perhaps because he had displayed an almost uncanny insight right from the outset. She'd invited him to lunch that first day at the library and over the soup-and-sandwich special at a restaurant on Broad Street, he'd suddenly grinned at her and said, "So what d'you do, go home after work and slip into a silk peignoir and marabou mules?"

She'd stared at him for a moment, then laughed harder than she had in years, before asking, "Why on earth would you think that?"

"My dear, any woman who'd wear Opium with an L. L. Bean outfit is definitely living a secret life."

Impressed, and finding him enormously likable, she did something she had never done before: She told him about the family, about her father's leaving and Cary's death, and about the strain and uncertainty of growing up with Claudia and Jeanne.

He in turn described his family life which, compared to hers, had been positively idyllic. By the end of his first week at the Magnusson their friendship was solidly established. Through the years they had drawn ever closer, so that by the time Tim developed full-blown AIDS there were few barriers between them.

Since Claudia's funeral, both Penny and Mark had left her several messages. Guilty at having neglected them—particularly Mark who was still actively grieving for Tim—she invited the two of them to come to the house for dinner on the Thursday following her first weekend working at the restaurant.

Sitting in the gloomy living room with drinks before dinner, Penny took in Rowena's dark blue slacks and matching cashmere pullover. "Nice outfit," she commented. "New?"

"No, Claudia's."

Penny's expression turned squeamish, indicating that she'd never have been able to wear a dead person's clothes. "You're not really going to move back into this dump, are you?"

"I've been considering it," Rowena answered, mildly nettled. It may have been run-down but it certainly wasn't a dump.

"It's so *House of Usher,*" Mark said, draped sideways over one of the ancient slipcovered armchairs, a loafer dangling from the toe of his right foot. He shivered for effect. "I keep expecting the elderly hump-backed retainer to appear in the doorway announcing dinner is served."

Rowena laughed.

"Seriously," Penny persisted. "Aren't you scared, staying alone here?"

"I grew up in this house. Why would I be scared?"

"I know, but still." Penny looked into the dark corners of the room and grimaced. "I'd sell it. You'd probably get a bundle for this barn. You could buy something fabulous for the money, and have lots left over."

"I don't know," Mark disagreed. "You could also renovate. Me, I'd donate most of this god-awful furniture to the Sally Ann, have the floors sanded, get the whole place painted, and redo the kitchen and bathrooms. With some new bits and pieces it could be terrific. *And* if you turned the space over the garage into an in-law apartment, I'd be delighted to move in. It would make a *very* nice apartment. Hint, hint."

"I've actually been giving it serious thought."

"Oh, *please!*" Penny said impatiently. "Why bother going through all the hassle? List it as a fixer-upper and get rid of it. And how come you're working at the restaurant?"

"Ian needed someone to fill in temporarily on the weekends. It's fun."

"How temporary is it?" Mark asked. "And do we get comped for meals now that you're the boss?"

"Absolutely you get comped. I'll do it for a couple more weeks, until we hire a new hostess."

"We? You're going to keep the place?" Penny looked doubtful.

"Of course," Rowena said, wondering why Penny was being so negative. "I'd be out of my mind to shut it down. It's thriving."

"I thought you might sell it," Penny clarified.

"Oh, I don't think so."

"Tim and I tried to have dinner there a few years ago," Mark said. "That was interesting. We didn't have a res and Claudia pretended not to know me, came on all fake apologetic and said they were completely booked, even though it was late and there were three or four empty tables. I wasn't about to go through the nonsense of reminding her that we'd met at least half a dozen times at your place. I just hustled Tim out, and we wound up eating Mexican in South Norwalk.

"I'm sorry, Ro, but your sister was one seriously homophobic bitch. She didn't want a pair of gay men in her hoity-toity establishment, and acted as if Tim and I were a couple of raging queens who'd destroy the reputation of the place. It wasn't blatant, but it was pretty obvious she had visions of legions of local gays turning Le Rendezvous into their hangout, with Judy Garland tapes on the stereo and same-sex couples groping each other in the corners. I was livid, to tell the truth."

"You should've told me," Rowena said, appalled.

"Why? So you could've been upset too? It's not as if you didn't know what she was like."

"That's true. But still. I just found out she took a cut of the tips if she had to serve. Isn't that rotten?"

"She was a very mean woman," Penny said. "It always amazed me that the two of you were related."

"Amazed me, too." Rowena smiled. Then, unexpectedly she saw her dead sister's features, waxy and frozen, and felt a terrible sadness. Poor Claudia. She'd lived such a wasteful life; she'd hurt so many people with such reckless disregard, yet it didn't seem right that she should have died so soon. But this wasn't the time to fall into a trough of sentimentality. Her friends were here and she had a meal to finish preparing. "You guys mind eating in the kitchen?" she asked, reaching for her diet Coke.

"Sorry, couldn't possibly," Mark said.

"The kitchen?" Penny made a face of mock horror. "The land that time forgot? You want to *eat* in there?"

"Quit it, both of you." Rowena laughed. "Get in here and keep me company."

Mark brought up the subject of the apartment again as he and Penny were getting ready to go. "If you do decide to renovate, Ro, I'm serious about the garage. It's time for me to move out of the matrimonial home. And Penny has a point. It might not be such a bad idea for you to have someone within shouting distance. Plus, we could drive to work together and do our bit to reduce pollution.''

"If I do go ahead, you've got a deal. I'd love to have you so close by.''

"You're both nuts," Penny declared. "This house is far too big for one person, Ro. But if you insist on living here, I'll feel a lot better about it knowing Mark's here, too, to keep an eye on you.''

"Actually," Mark said, "I was kind of hoping she'd keep an eye on me.''

After they'd gone Rowena went on another tour of the house, picturing it freshly painted, without the heavy drapes and dark, musty carpeting. Maybe she'd call around and get some estimates.

Late Friday afternoon of the following week Anthony Reid called.

"I was sorry to hear about Claudia," he said. "I've been away or I'd have called sooner. May I ask how she died?''

"Apparently it was an accidental overdose of sleeping pills combined with alcohol.''

"Most unfortunate." He paused a moment, then said, "Your message said you were anxious to talk to me.''

"That's right, I am.''

"About Claudia.''

"Yes.''

"I could see you Tuesday afternoon at five. Would that be convenient?''

"Yes. Where?''

He gave her an address in Greenwich she recognized as a medical complex near the hospital. She'd expected her meeting with this man would be more personal, but thanked him and hung up, mildly bothered.

Everything about the brief conversation struck her as odd, from his introducing himself as Anthony, rather than Tony as Claudia had always referred to him, to his comment that Claudia's death was "most unfortunate." He hadn't sounded like a lover, former or otherwise, but like a detached professional being politely sympathetic and accommodating. It was difficult to reconcile Claudia's rhapsodic remarks about the man to the deep, mellow voice that had expressed little upset or surprise at learning of her death. There was no point, though, in being analytical about a single short chat. She tended to be hyper-aware of people's intonation on the telephone, and often garnered an erroneous impression of someone's mood because she'd misinterpreted a tone of voice.

Giving herself a quick once-over in the bathroom before leaving for the restaurant, she thought it was time to do something about her hair. It was far too long, and she'd taken to wearing it gathered in a clip at the back of her neck—a hairstyle at odds with the clothes she now wore. Her unadorned face was also at odds with the clothes, and she reached for one of the unused lipsticks in the box of cosmetics on the bathroom shelf. An awful color she wiped right off. She tried another, and wiped that off too. She was clueless when it came to makeup, hadn't spent her early teenage years, as Claudia had, experimenting with eye shadows and blushers and different shades of mascara. Defeated, she smoothed her hair and left the bathroom.

It gave her a lift just to walk through the door of Le Rendezvous, and she cheerfully greeted everyone on her way to the office. Something had begun to flower inside her, and it grew a little more each time she returned to the restaurant. Partly it was the extraordinary sense of family feeling she had being with the staff; she savored their relative youth and jargon-riddled humor, feeling younger and more alive by association. And partly it was the knowledge that she was playing Claudia's role her own way, and doing it well.

For someone who had been alternately ignored or criticized by her mother, and put down and tormented by her sister, it felt like a significant accomplishment to succeed at something Claudia had done. Her experience at the Magnusson had long since confirmed that she got along well with people. The public tended to think of libraries as esoteric branches of the civil service, and it always came as a surprise to them to encounter friendly staff. She enjoyed their surprise. An upscale restaurant was something else again. Yet she'd discovered that even more than the library, people *really* responded to friendly staff here.

It was amusing to learn that those with the money to pay for an expensive dinner halfway expected to be abused for the privilege. When they were met with warmth they responded initially with cautious disbelief and then with gratitude. And while Claudia had made the patrons feel like cosseted members of an elite group, Rowena strove to make them feel welcome on a personal level. Already she was greeting regulars by name, expressing her pleasure at seeing them again, and the difference this made to the restaurant was obvious. There was more laughter in the course of an evening; the conversations were more energetic; the diners appeared to be having a good time, and the staff interacted with them less formally than before, but with no less efficiency.

"I don't suppose you'd consider working weekends permanently?" Ian asked after the brunch rush on the Sunday of her third week.

"I hadn't thought about it," she lied, having given it a lot of thought.

"You're becoming very popular, with the staff and with the customers."

"That's good to hear. I do enjoy it," she confessed, rather choked up by his approval. "I'm not sure I could handle the library full-time and this, too. I won't know until I start back at the Mag in another week. But to be frank, it feels as if I've been here for years, and I really like working with all of you."

He looked very pleased. "I hope you'll understand when I say that most of the staff were loyal to the income, not to Claudia. I'm sure you're aware how difficult and demanding she could be, inconsiderate to boot."

So he hadn't had any illusions about her sister, she thought, with a gesture indicating that she was, indeed, aware.

"The past few weeks have been a most pleasurable change," he went on. "And the receipts prove that the customers feel the same way. We're getting more weeknight bookings, many of them word-of-mouth referrals. The atmosphere's so much more relaxed, and everyone feels it. Claudia was relentless." His mouth thinning, he looked away for a few seconds. "She pushed hard," he continued. "But to rant at someone like Julio, who earns only minimum wage, is over the top. He's far and away the best kitchen helper we've had, and I was hoping you'd agree to increasing his salary. He's been with us eleven months, three months longer than anyone else has lasted in the job, and he works bloody hard."

"What about his benefits?"

"None of us receives benefits, Rowena."

"No health insurance?"

He shook his head.

Recalling Penny's comment about Claudia's meanness, she was angry and ashamed. "Well, we'd better get someone in here right away to set up a group insurance plan. And maybe you and I should sit down together to review the numbers. Could we do that?"

"Just say when."

"What about Monday around three-thirty? You can show me the figures, and we'll see if we can't make a few changes. For now I'll continue to come in weekends."

"Actually, I have a contact in the insurance area."

"Good. Call your contact and get a proposal put together. We can't have our people going without health insurance. That's criminal! I assume the restaurant has liability and workmen's compensation?"

"We've got the basics, fire, liability, the lot."

"Ian, I realize I'm new to it, but common sense tells me if we treat the staff fairly the business can only grow."

"Quite right." He offered her a Silk Cut.

She took one and leaned toward the flame of his lighter. "Is there anything," she asked, "that you'd like to see changed?"

He thought about that, eyes fixed on some remote point, his expression one of faint, almost indiscernible, disappointment. Then his eyes returned to hers, he smiled suddenly, shook his head and said, "No. But if I think of anything, I'll certainly let you know."

"Please do. And you have to promise to tell me if I'm out of line or messing up. I'd hate to be stepping on toes and not know it."

"Of course," he said. "Anyone would hate that."

Driving home she wondered if Ian had a personal life. He put in long, irregular hours at the restaurant, and the only socializing he seemed to do was in the company of the other employees. After closing, he and some of the staff would go off for a drink or something to eat at one of the many diners on the stretch of Route 1 between Darien and Westport. It appeared to be a pretty narrow existence. But maybe that was his choice. He was a man with a history—the upper-class accent, the fine clothes, that so-British reserve and tendency to understate. It was intriguing to speculate on how someone with his background and breeding had come to be the manager of a restaurant in a small New England town. Perhaps someday he'd tell her.

Five

Monday morning Rowena called her hairdresser.

"Things're quiet," Kate said. "If you want to, you could come right over."

"Perfect. I'll be there in ten minutes."

Although Kate was several years her senior, Rowena had always thought Kate looked the younger of them. A rail-thin, good-natured, energetic woman of about five foot six, she invariably wore skin-tight jeans and bright tops, and gave the impression of being on the move even when she was standing still.

"What're we gonna do with you?" she asked Rowena's reflection in the mirror, holding up handfuls of her just-washed hair. "Aren't you worn out yet with this no-style hairstyle? You've been wearing it this way your entire life, for pity sake."

"It is kind of too long," Rowena allowed sheepishly.

"There's your basic understatement." Kate grinned. "It doesn't do thing one for you, hon. You've got a sweet little face, nice big eyes. But do you show them off? No, you do not. Know what I think?"

"What?"

"I think it's time you took a risk, made a statement."

"What risk? What statement?"

"What're you so nervous about?" Kate came around and leaned against the counter, arms folded over her chest. "You don't trust me after all these years?"

"I trust you. I just don't know if I'm up for taking risks. What d'you have in mind?"

"We cut it way short, and shaggy."

"How short? How shaggy?"

Kate laughed, reached for the cup nearby and took a swig of her coffee. "Real short and a little shaggy." Assessing Rowena's mirror image, she said, "It'll be very flattering, Rowena, bring out your bone structure. It's about time you did something about your looks. I've never understood why you didn't."

Rowena made a face at the mirror.

"Now, that's real constructive. Listen. You want to go with me on this?"

Rowena laughed nervously and said, "What the hell! Let's do it."

"I want you to be sure now. Once it's cut it'll be too late to change your mind."

"I'm sure. Go ahead and cut it."

"You won't be sorry, hon." Kate took a last swig of her coffee, tossed the cup into the trash, and reached for her scissors.

When she'd finished, the two of them gazed silently at Rowena's reflection for a time. Finally, Kate said, "You look adorable, even better than I thought you would. It takes *years* off you. What d'you think?"

"It's...extreme, isn't it?" Rowena scarcely recognized herself. "But I think I like it."

"Trust me. It's fabulous. Now people can finally see your face. You're a very pretty woman. You know that?"

Rowena automatically shook her head.

"Cut that out," Kate said with a smile. "You look great, honestly. Come back to me in six weeks for a trim."

Her head feeling unnaturally light, her bare neck exposed to the sting of the February wind, Rowena stopped at the deli to pick up a turkey on whole wheat with lettuce. She then drove to Stamford to collect her mail and water the plants before her meeting with Ian at the restaurant.

Just bills and flyers in the mail, and no messages on the machine. She made a cup of tea and sat at the kitchen counter to eat her sandwich. Each time she returned she was a bit more dissatisfied with the apartment, and saw less reason for keeping it. She kept putting off making a decision because it hadn't yet been a month since Claudia's death and it didn't seem right to be considering major changes to the house so soon. But just as there was no one to criticize her for cutting off her hair, there was no one to care what she did to the house. The insurance money would cover the cost of the work, so, really, there was no reason not to go ahead.

Feeling as bold and jittery as she had at the hairdresser's, she left messages for the three contractors whose numbers she'd been carrying around for over a week. Then she watered the plants, shoved the bills into her handbag, took a quick, disbelieving look at herself in the bathroom mirror, and set off for the restaurant.

The spritelike Mae was on her way to the kitchen with a trayful of dishes when she saw Rowena, stopped dead, and said, "Hey! Good haircut! You look completely different."

Face on fire, Rowena laughed. "You don't think it's too extreme?"

"I think it's terrific. Really."

"Thank you, Mae."

Ian gazed at her for several seconds, then rather soberly said, "Quite a startling change, Rowena. But most attractive. It suits you."

"It'll take some getting used to," she said, settling with him at the office desk to look over the printouts he'd obtained from the accountant.

The restaurant was solidly in the black, with plenty of cash in the bank. The expenses seemed reasonable, except for the staff salaries. The only one earning decent money was Philippe, the chef. Everyone else was badly underpaid—especially in view of the hefty twice-monthly checks that had gone to Claudia.

"Am I crazy, Ian, or are all of you grossly underpaid?"

"The waiters, busboys, and Terry earn good tips. And they do give Julio a small percentage."

"Even so. Twenty cents an hour above minimum wage? McDonald's probably pays better."

"Probably," Ian agreed. "As I've told you, in the past the staff were loyal to the income, which on a good weekend can add up to a hundred-plus a night each for the waiters, and fifty or sixty for the busboys."

"With no benefits."

"Correct."

"D'you have a calculator I could use for a couple of minutes?"

"Certainly." He got one from the desk drawer, then sat back with a cigarette, watching as she ran through a series of calculations, jotting figures on the side of the printout.

"Okay," she said at last. "Here's what I think. First we double Julio's salary."

"Agreed."

"Then we give everyone out front a dollar an hour raise."

"I wouldn't argue with that."

"Jill gets a seventy-five dollar a week raise."

"Splendid."

"And you should have at least another hundred and fifty a week."

"Oh, now, I don't—"

"Yes," she insisted. "The new totals hardly make a dent in what Claudia was paying herself, and still leave plenty to cover a benefits package. If we continue in the black, I'll start drawing a small amount for working weekends. What's left will stay in the account accruing interest, and cover maybe a staff picnic, say, Labor Day weekend, and a Christmas party, with bonuses."

"It's a very generous proposal, Rowena, but it will cut considerably into the profits."

"I know, but the thing is there will still be profits. We've got a good group, and I want them to be happy. I'd hate to lose them to the competition."

"Small chance of that," he said, "especially once they get wind of your proposal." He was quiet for a few moments, then said, "You're really nothing like your sister, are you?"

"About all we had in common were our shoe and dress sizes."

"Yes, I did notice you've been wearing her clothes."

"A lot of the things hadn't even been worn. It seemed a ridiculous waste to get rid of them," she said in her own defense.

"I quite agree. I intended no criticism," he said quickly.

"Oh, I nearly forgot. Dr. Reid finally contacted me. I have an appointment to see him tomorrow."

Ian couldn't quite conceal his startled—or was it dismayed?—reaction, but he recovered quickly, saying, "I would imagine he was surprised to hear about Claudia."

"He was polite, but didn't seem particularly surprised or upset."

"Hmm. Well. Therein probably lies a tale." He made a show of checking the time, then stubbed out his cigarette. "I don't see any problem with your suggestions. I think the staff will be most grateful. And, of course, so will I. I did speak to my broker friend and he's putting together a proposal for a benefits package. Now, if you'll forgive me, I've got to get over to the bank to make a deposit." He stood, pocketing his cigarettes. "Feel free to take the printout. I won't say anything to the staff until you've had a chance to review the figures."

"No, go ahead and tell them," she said, wondering if it was something about her that kept causing him to run hot and cold. "I'll grab a cup of coffee, then head back to the house. I've got calls in for estimates on renovating the place."

"You're going to take it over then, are you?" he asked with a cordial show of interest.

"I think so." Had he been bothered by her mentioning Tony Reid? Or was it something else she'd said to trigger this latest mood change? Why couldn't she just matter-of-factly ask him what was wrong?

Halfway out the door, he turned back. "See you Friday?"

"I'll be here."

"Good. See you then." He turned and was gone before she had a chance to say anything more.

Bothered by what was becoming a consistent failure on her part to address these instances with Ian, she emerged from the office to find the place deserted except for Julio who was swabbing the kitchen floor. Abandoning the idea of coffee, she pushed out through the rear fire door and made her way to the Honda.

She was early for her appointment and spent twenty minutes in the waiting room, reading a back issue of *psychology today,* and was just finishing an article on Fetal Alcohol Syndrome and Fetal Alcohol Effect when the secretary told her she could go in.

She knocked, opened the door, stepped into the office, and suffered a kind of silent seizure at the sight of the man rising to his feet behind the desk. Wanting to weep, a low-level electric buzzing in her brain, all she could do for a moment was stare. Perhaps six-three, two hundred pounds, with very white skin, thick, side-parted black hair, and startlingly crystalline blue eyes, he was the most beautiful man she'd ever seen. In contrast, she felt smaller and even less attractive than usual. Another moment and she'd recovered, introducing herself and offering her hand across the desk. Her second impression was that as a country, he'd be Finland: large, dark, immaculate, and dour. In a massive and cheerless fashion, he was dauntingly well constructed— like the famous church she'd visited in Helsinki, carved out of and built around a vast rock.

"I appreciate your seeing me," she said, once they were seated on opposite sides of his desk.

He nodded, unsmiling, and she thought he was observing her somewhat guardedly, even fearfully, as if anticipating unpleasantness.

"Claudia spoke so fondly of you," she began. "We weren't in close touch, but she did say the two of you were—"

"I'm going to have to stop you," he said, in that soft deep voice, holding up his enormous left hand. "I wouldn't want either of us embarrassed, and the direction you're headed in tells me your sister said things that simply weren't true."

"She claimed the two of you were having an affair. She'd been talking about it for months."

He smiled for the first time, and was transformed into someone accessible and sympathetic. And lonely? Was that possible? she wondered.

"When I got your message, I thought you and I would probably be having the conversation we're about to have, so I made copies of some articles I hope will help you understand."

"You weren't involved with her," she said quietly, having doubted the truth of Claudia's claims from the moment she'd seen this man.

"No, very definitely not. In fact, I'd stopped seeing her as a patient three or four months ago. I gave her the names of several colleagues, but I don't know if she consulted any of them." He studied his hands, which were folded loosely on the desk blotter. Then again he met her eyes and said, "After giving the matter some thought, I've decided to set aside patient confidentiality in this case. Claudia is dead, and you're here looking for answers. I can't see the harm in my trying to supply them."

"I appreciate that."

"It was my professional opinion that your sister was suffering from de Clérambault's syndrome, more simply known as erotomania. It's quite rare, and to confirm my findings, I discussed the case with two associates who both concurred with my diagnosis. Essentially, it's a delusional belief that a man, often, but not always, considerably older, is very much in love with the subject. This man usually occupies a prominent position in society, or is a public figure. It is the patient's belief—in this case your sister—that this man cannot be happy or complete without her."

"But isn't that transference?"

"Have you been in therapy?"

"No," she replied, "but I'm certainly familiar with some of the terminology."

"Of course. Well it's considerably more complicated than a form of exaggerated dependence on one's analyst. In the majority of case studies, of which, unfortunately, there are not many, the object of the patient's focus is usually a doctor, or a lawyer, or a teacher, someone whose attentions are interpreted as being amorous. Claudia was convinced I was deeply in love with her. She began calling the office several times a day. When she couldn't get through to me, she started calling my home. Ultimately, I was left with no choice but to act. On her next office visit, I explained that I could no longer continue with her as a patient. As I've told you, I recommended several colleagues, and that was the last I saw of her."

"Let's back up a bit," Rowena said, unable to imagine Claudia simply giving up and going away—from anything or anyone—without a fight. "Why did she consult you in the first place, and when?"

"She came to me a year or so ago, for depression."

That sounded valid. Claudia had undergone bouts of depression since adolescence, and had seen a number of psychiatrists over the years. "What, may I ask, was your diagnosis?"

"I'd have to refer to my notes for specifics, but generally I found her to be suffering from mild anxiety and depression. I also suspected she had an eating disorder. But that was a subject she refused to discuss. I ordered a blood workup to eliminate the possibility of any chemical imbalance. She had none. I placed her on an antidepressant and for a time she seemed to be doing well. Then she developed the syndrome and it soon became obvious that I couldn't keep on as her doctor."

"How long had she been your patient when this, uhm, syndrome developed?"

"Five, possibly six, months."

"And how many more times did you see her before you referred her elsewhere?"

"I think perhaps she had a dozen or so more sessions. Initially," he explained, "I saw her twice a week, then weekly. Without checking my records, I'd guess it was roughly two months before I had to terminate her as a patient."

Terminate, Rowena repeated to herself, skeptical. On the one hand what he was saying sounded like so much bullshit. On the other, knowing Claudia, she could easily imagine her deciding to pursue this man. He was magnificent, and there was nothing Claudia liked better than going after someone who was off-limits. That didn't, however, mean she had that fancy syndrome.

"I realize it sounds bizarre." He gave her an apologetic smile. "I personally had never encountered erotomania before. I'd read a paper on it in the *American Journal of Psychiatry,* and it was mentioned in a book on uncommon syndromes written by a British team back in the sixties. But until your sister, I had no direct experience of it. Few of us have had. In the end I consulted with one of my former professors, and he provided me with some case notes, and copies of the articles I've Xeroxed for you. I was sorry to hear of Claudia's death. I didn't believe her to be suicidal."

Rowena started. She hadn't mentioned suicide. In their telephone conversation she'd told him it had been an accidental overdose. "I don't think she was," she said carefully.

"Sometimes an 'accidental' ingestion of drugs and alcohol is a subliminal form of suicide."

"Really? That sounds awfully facile, sort of like retroactive diagnosing."

Those crystalline blue eyes regarded her steadily, as if he were reevaluating his initial assessment of her. "Claudia did say you were highly intelligent."

"I very much doubt she meant that as a compliment. She placed a far greater value on other things."

"Such as?" He folded his arms on the desk and leaned closer, interested.

"Physical beauty, conquests, even aggression. Intelligence was valuable only in helping her get what she wanted. Everything was a game to her, and she played to win. She was clever, cunning, and ruthless. She thought people with scruples were idiots. She thought just about everyone was an idiot, and she was prepared to go to almost any length to prove that. Look, Dr. Reid. Claudia was a lot of things, but what she definitely *wasn't* was delusional or suicidal. I simply can't buy what you're telling me."

"I know it's difficult. But you admit the two of you weren't close. And even with the most apparently confiding people, it's often not easy to know them well."

"I'll concede that point. I still have a big problem picturing Claudia *imagining* someone was in love with her. Usually she was fighting men off with a stick."

"It's only one doctor's diagnosis. Based on her behavior, and on consults with associates, I drew the only conclusions that seemed to fit her symptoms. I'm the first to admit psychiatry's a less than perfect science, but we haven't yet come up with anything to replace it. Let me give you the data." He removed a large envelope from the desk drawer and handed it across to her. "I hope it helps. I'm sorry I can't give you more definitive answers."

"Aside from the telephone calls, what exactly was her 'behavior'?"

"Primarily, she made dozens of calls. A few times she actually showed up at my home. She *believed,* Ms. Graham, that I was in love with her, and she behaved accordingly. The sessions became, frankly, disconcerting. She was reading things into what tie I might happen to wear, or the way a file might be positioned on the desk. She interpreted everything and anything as an encoded message. If I didn't respond to her in the office it was because my secretary would be jealous if she discovered that Claudia and I were romantically involved. My secretary, as you may have noticed, is a happily married grandmother with a tendency to treat me like an overdeveloped twelve-year-old." He smiled, and Rowena smiled back, amused. "If I didn't respond when Claudia arrived unannounced at my front door, it was because the neighbors might find out and report back to my former wife. Which was nonsense. But people with emotional problems commonly can and do create their own version of what's real or viable. In any case, it went on and on."

"How did she know your home address and telephone number?"

"Come on now," he chided, smiling again. He seemed to be enjoying sparring with her. "You're a librarian, aren't you? Surely you're aware of the wide variety of directories available. It's not that hard to find out where someone lives, if you're determined."

"That's true."

"I had to threaten to take legal action to get her to stop."

"And she did?" That really didn't sound at all like Claudia.

"Once we sat down here together and I explained my reasons for discontinuing the therapy, she seemed to accept that if she didn't voluntarily desist, she'd be confronting a restraining order. I took pains to be as nonthreatening as possible, pointing out that finding herself involved in legalities might have negative repercussions on her business. I tried, in the kindest way I know how, to discourage her. It wasn't easy, but ultimately I succeeded. It was not a pleasant experience, Ms. Graham. Anything but."

"No, I'm sure it wasn't."

"Please read the articles. Then give me a call and we'll talk further." He got up and walked out from behind the desk. "I am very sorry about your sister's death."

"Thank you."

They shook hands, exchanged smiles, and for a second time she experienced what felt like a seizure. Walking carefully, an aching in her midriff, she left his office. The cold air revived her as she crossed the parking lot, and she climbed into the Honda uncertain whether she'd just been fed the biggest load of crap ever, or if she'd heard the truth.

Six

"What hat makes the situation notable is the fact that the fantasies are not contained within the mind by an intact ego; instead, they are dramatized in real life, casting an unsuspecting and usually unwilling man of some importance in the role of the lover...."*

"The focus is not on what the woman feels for her would-be lover but on the feelings she imputes to him; not on how she loves him but on how he loves her...."

"Delusional thinking, which may lead to bizarre behavior results from some change in or defect of the ego. The specific content of the delusions, however, is largely shaped by life experiences that probably result in a feeling of being unloved, or perhaps even worse, unlovable...."

Sitting at the kitchen table surrounded by the half-dozen documents Anthony Reid had given her, Rowena suddenly, vividly, remembered a preteen Claudia shrieking at Jeanne. Her fists clenched, face red and twisted with rage and misery, Claudia was crying, *"If you loved me, you wouldn't make me do this!"* And Jeanne, looking upset yet determined, stood solid as a stone column, refusing to be moved.

Rowena concentrated on remembering, and gradually it came back to her. Jeanne had taken Claudia out of the local junior high and enrolled her midyear in a prep school in Stamford. Claudia had begged not to go. But Jeanne for once had been adamant. She believed Claudia would fare better in a private all-girls school with no boys to distract her, and with the very best teachers who'd pay more attention to her.

Claudia was miserable. She hated the uniforms, hated the rigidity of the teaching methods, hated the other girls. She found it impossible to keep up with the homework, and cried almost constantly throughout her first month at the school. Night after night Rowena heard her sobbing in the next room, and felt progressively sorrier for her. When moved to try to comfort her, Claudia cried even harder.

"Why is she doing this to me?" she'd lamented, collapsing into Rowena's embrace.

"It's not really that bad, is it?" Rowena had asked, finding it strange to be holding her younger sister for the first time since Claudia was a toddler.

"I *hate* it! And I hate *her* for sending me there! I wish I was dead. Or that *she* was!"

"It'll be okay." Rowena was awkward in the role of comforter. But the very fact that Claudia permitted this unprecedented degree of closeness convinced Rowena of her sister's despair. This time Claudia wasn't acting.

"No, it won't! It'll *never* be okay. I want to *die!*"

Frightened, Rowena had said, "Maybe I could talk to her."

"Oh, *please,* Ro! She'll listen to you. Tell her I can't stay there! I'll die if I have to stay there."

"I'll try," Rowena promised, and had gone downstairs to talk to Jeanne.

Her mother was on the telephone and impatiently waved Rowena away as if she were as bothersome as a housefly. Rowena retreated to the far side of the living room to wait. After a minute or two, aware Rowena was still there, Jeanne said, "Hold on a minute, darling, would you?" and covered the mouthpiece with her hand. "What are you doing?" she asked, annoyed.

"I'm waiting to talk to you."

"Wait somewhere else, please. I'm trying to have a conversation. Can't you see that?"

"It's important," Rowena said quietly.

"I'll deal with you *after* I get off the phone."

Jeanne waited to go back to the telephone until Rowena tiredly got up and started out of the room. Then Jeanne said into the receiver, "Sorry, darling. Now, where were we?"

Rowena returned to her room to get some homework done, wondering, as she often had before, why Jeanne's social life was so much more important than her children. The only time she'd paid any sustained attention to her daughters had been for several months after Cary's death. Then it seemed as if her wounds had healed over completely, and she took up again with her friends and their endless plans for lunches and dinners and trips into the city.

It was more than an hour before Jeanne appeared in the doorway of Rowena's room, saying, "You wanted to talk?"

Reluctant to have her sister overhear, Rowena closed the door and said, "It's about Claudia."

"Oh, dear. What now?" With a sigh, Jeanne walked over and sat on the side of the bed. "Can't you do something with your hair, Rowena?"

"What's wrong with it?"

"It's so *unbecoming,* parted in the middle and just *hanging* like curtains. I wish you'd make an effort to look your best."

"We have to talk about Claudia," she reminded her mother. "She's miserable, and keeps saying she wants to die. I don't think you should force her to stay at Brandon."

"But it's such a good school. She was so distracted, and her grades were very poor...I thought this would be much better for her." Frowning, she gazed down at her Ferragamo pumps.

"It isn't, though. She can't keep up and it's making her feel stupid. She thinks the other girls are all laughing at her because she's so dumb."

"She's not dumb!" Jeanne said peevishly. "I grant she has problems with mathematics, and her handwriting's atrocious, but she's certainly not dumb."

"No, I don't think she is either. But she hates Brandon. So why force her to stay there?"

"It's very disappointing, but naturally I don't want her to be miserable. She will have to finish the semester, though. What if that's not enough?" she asked, as if Rowena were another adult whose opinion carried weight.

"I think if she knows she won't have to go back there in September she'll be okay."

"Why did she tell you and not me? And why are you speaking up for her?" Jeanne asked. "This isn't like either one of you."

"She *is* my sister, you know, and I've never seen her so unhappy."

"You're such a kind-hearted girl," her mother observed, seemingly bewildered by this fact. "In years to come you'll want to be careful it doesn't get the better of you."

Not knowing how to respond, Rowena kept silent.

Jeanne sighed, and said, "I really had hoped this change of schools would be the making of her. Obviously, I was mistaken."

"You tried," Rowena told her.

"Yes, I did," Jeanne said, surprisingly grateful for this recognition of her efforts. "I thought long and hard before moving your sister to another school, but I suppose I'll have to give in and let her leave. It's a great pity."

It was and it wasn't, Rowena thought. She'd have loved the opportunity to go to Brandon, a school with the very highest academic standards, and a 99.9 percent college acceptance rate. But when midway during her eighth-grade year she'd raised the subject, Jeanne had flatly said no. "You're bright enough to do well at whatever school you attend. You'll go to Brien McMahon. End of discussion."

As Rowena had predicted, once Claudia learned she only had to finish out the semester, her misery ended and she actually enjoyed the remainder of her time there. She made a few friends, one or two of whom she saw from time to time for years after. And she even managed to pull off halfway decent grades.

The following September Claudia returned to the nearby junior high, but ever afterward there existed a deep and all-but-unbridgeable rift between her and Jeanne. Like some trap set in the forest, the surface was cleverly camouflaged, yet a single false step could send Jeanne plummeting into its depths where Claudia lay waiting to attack. Among many other things, she never forgave her mother for those awful months at Brandon.

"The possibility remains, nevertheless, that narcissistic blows still serve to shape the erotomania. As is well known, even an attractive woman may struggle with a poor body image and self-concept...when she feels rejected, the old picture may come into sharp focus...."

Rowena closed her eyes and thought back to telephone conversations she'd had with her sister the previous autumn, hearing again Claudia gloat, "Tony's crazy about me, thinks I'm the best thing that ever happened to him. He can't get enough of me."

"The patients may bring chaos to the lives of their victims, who usually give them no encouragement whatsoever...."

"Recurrent-group women are all fairly aggressive in everyday life.... They are all ambitious, competitive women who may well initially feel a combination of rivalry, resentment, and anger directed at the powerful men in their lives. If these feelings are unacceptable, they may get transformed into admiration and a conviction of mutual attraction...."

"The second group (erotomania proper) is healthier and is composed of sexually active, aggressive, impulsive women." Rowena sat up straighter. This sounded like Claudia. *"They select prominent, powerful men, imagine they are loved for several months, finally re-*

*nounce the man, and start again with another ... it may be an attempt
to incorporate power and success into one's own self-image."*

*"...patients lacked early meaningful relationships with their
mothers ... the symptom has served the purpose of warding off depression and loneliness by filling up these women's inner worlds with
controlling, nurturing, yet persecuting men ... patients felt their
therapist-lovers were in complete control of their feelings, actions, and
future ..."*

Her head filling with recollected images, Rowena turned finally to
the notes of a case conference dated September 1985, from a hospital
of which she'd never heard. This was obviously the documentation
Reid had been given by his former professor.

*"All of our patients sought out the object of their delusion and
confronted him with the situation as they saw it.... In time, however,
usually after several denials on the part of the man, they accepted the
impossibility of anything coming of this love and went on to repeat the
cycle with another man...."*

She had to concede that much of what she read could have applied
to her sister, and by the time she'd gone over the material again she was
partly convinced that Reid's diagnosis might well have been accurate.

Perhaps the roots of Claudia's disorder were tangled around their
childhood, which had been, to say the least, unusual. No one would
ever have mistaken Jeanne for a nurturing mother. Her primary interest had always been her social life. The running of the house and over-
seeing of the children had been left to a series of housekeepers. None
had stayed long and the majority had been decidedly peculiar.

Two were particularly memorable: The first had been a very young
woman perhaps nineteen or twenty, washed-out and pale, with long,
stringy hair, and an attitude of angry helplessness. She hadn't known
how to cook and the three children had lived on peanut butter sand-
wiches and Kraft Dinner for close to three months before Cary finally
got fed up with being constantly hungry and complained to their father, who promptly dismissed her. The second had been in her mid- to
late fifties—round, red-faced and grim—and a religious fanatic. She'd
had the three terrorized children praying at random moments
throughout each day. Her tennis game rained out, Jeanne had arrived
home ahead of schedule one afternoon to find the housekeeper and the
children on their knees in the kitchen.

"What in *hell* is going on here?" she'd demanded, to the relief and
gratitude of the children who'd quickly jumped to their feet.

"We're praying to the Lord to save your sinning soul," the house-keeper had declared righteously, still on her knees.

"I want you out of here in one hour!" Jeanne had shouted, herding the children up to their rooms. "Goddamned lunatic!" she'd muttered, pouring herself a drink in the living room while she watched through the window for the arrival of the taxi she'd called to take the woman away. "Save my sinning soul. That's rich." Back and forth she paced in front of the living room window, drink in one hand, cigarette in the other, muttering under her breath until the housekeeper was gone.

And that had been the end of that one. But there had been at least a half dozen others, the majority characterized by their strangeness.

The Graham children had had a careless upbringing, short on mothering and long on things. To his credit, their father had tried to demonstrate his affection for them with occasional outings. But George had been too busy with his law practice to have much time for more. He'd been putting in as many billable hours as possible in an effort to maintain the family in the style Jeanne deemed appropriate.

Rowena remembered him as a handsome, soft-spoken, tired-looking man with a lost look to his gray-blue eyes. She also remembered that he'd have a drink upon arriving home each weeknight, and he'd sigh as he sank into one of the living room chairs, loosening his tie. She recalled few of their outings but had an enduring impression of his patience and gentleness in dealing with the three of them.

Jeanne, though, had always been too busy to be patient or gentle. She spent even less time at home than did her husband. But she was generous, perennially willing to underwrite Claudia's passion for clothes, and Cary's for sports and sailing. And although she'd wrinkled her elegant nose, dismayed by her older daughter's introspective nature, she had never refused Rowena's requests for books. Mystified by the emotional needs of her family, she had found it simpler to deal in tangibles. But as a child, Rowena had believed her mother disliked her and only bought the books to get rid of her.

Her doubts about Jeanne's love for her children were temporarily wiped out following Cary's death. Her mother's grief had been like a barricade that kept everyone but her two surviving children at a respectful distance. After the coffin had slowly descended into the earth, Jeanne had turned her back on the grave and enclosed her daughters tightly in her arms, weeping in noiseless gusts, her narrow body rigid. Even Claudia was awed by this show of emotion into a state of mute immobility. And Rowena, guiltily luxuriating in the fierce embrace while simultaneously wanting with all her heart to have her brother back, could only think, She really does love us.

Her father came to Cary's funeral. He remained in the background, and Rowena didn't spot him until they were about to leave the cemetery. Then, ignoring her mother's command to, "Stay right here!" she ran to catch up to him as he was heading for his car. She was so out of breath and stricken that she could only tug on his jacket to get his attention. He turned, saw her, and dropped down to hold her.

Clinging to him, she'd whispered, "I miss you so much, Daddy. When are you coming back?"

"I miss you too, sweetheart," he said, holding her away to look at her. "But I won't be coming back. I can't."

His eyes were damp, and the evidence of his unhappiness had made her sad and lonely and afraid.

"Why not? Don't you love us anymore?"

"Of course I do. But your mother and I don't care for each other the way we used to. That happens sometimes, honey. People change and find they can't live together anymore. But I'll always be your father and I'll always love you. Will you remember that?"

"Unh-hunh."

"If there's ever anything you need, you'll let me know, won't you?"

"Okay."

"And, Rowena?"

"Yes, Daddy?"

"Don't ever believe you're not as pretty as your sister, because you are; you're even prettier than she is."

"But Mommy says—"

"Never mind what she says. *I'm* saying you are! Okay?"

"Okay."

He straightened, ran a hand over her hair and said, "I love you, sweetheart, and I'll see you again soon."

"Promise?"

"I promise."

He started to walk away. She watched him for several moments then cried, "I love you, too, Daddy!" He looked back over his shoulder and blew her a kiss.

Her mother was calling her to come but she stayed where she was until his car was out of sight. In the following months, every time the telephone rang she expected it to be her father. But he didn't call and he didn't come to visit. She never saw him again.

With time Rowena came to think of her mother as someone who had never been schooled in the ways of the heart. As a result she was a woman highly conscious of surfaces but with little inclination to delve beneath them. She meant well but lacked the insight to recognize when her generous gestures went amiss. Eventually, Rowena came to respect and even to love her to a degree, but she never liked her.

Nearing the end of her life, Jeanne had capitulated to Claudia's persistent and blatant engineering, and amended her will, leaving her the bulk of the estate.

Only hours before she died, Jeanne had said to Rowena, "You'll always be able to manage. But Claudia can't. Please don't hate me, dear. She needs the money more than you do. You can understand that, can't you?"

"I understand," Rowena told her, hurt nonetheless.

"You're a good woman, Rowena," Jeanne said. "I've always been very proud of you."

It was the only overt approval her mother had ever given her, and Rowena couldn't help wishing it had come sooner. They might have been close. But it was too late. The era when Jeanne's carping comments were like sudden stinging sandstorms and Rowena lived like a mushroom in Claudia's shadow had long since ended. Rowena had acquired a thickened skin and an independent life.

Claudia had never become independent. In Rowena's opinion that was because she lacked the ability to turn her attention to mundane tasks like cooking and cleaning. She wasn't lazy. It was more as if she couldn't comprehend the need to prepare meals for herself when she could go out to restaurants, or the point of cleaning when there were people she could hire to do it for her. Jeanne may not have been outwardly loving but she wasn't stupid. She had probably seen her younger daughter more clearly than anyone else ever had. Certainly she spent more time with her, because Claudia never did leave home. She merely moved from one bedroom to another, finally ending up in the master suite less than a week after Jeanne's death.

So shattered and bereft was Claudia following the death of their mother that for only the second time since babyhood she sought comfort in her older sister's embrace. And Rowena was surprised to find herself willing to provide it. Blood was blood, after all, and the two of them were bound by ties neither fully understood. As well, Rowena wanted to believe that Claudia would one day explain her actions, and they would reminisce and laugh at what a devil Claudia had been, at the awful games she'd once played.

So Rowena moved back to the house to be close to her sister, and sat with her late into the nights as Claudia tried to put her feelings into words.

Without her makeup and looking far younger than twenty-five, her eyes red rimmed, she said, "I know it must've looked as if me and Mummy fought all the time, but we didn't, Ro. We went to the club for lunch or dinner. And shopping. We had a good time together."

"I'm sure you did."

"We *did,*" Claudia insisted, picking at the lace trim on her silk nightgown. "What am I going to do without her?" she asked, gazing fearfully into the dark corners of the room. "I'll be all alone."

"No, you won't. You've got tons of friends."

"When I come home," Claudia said, her eyes haunted, "I'll be alone."

"We'll see each other more often," Rowena told her, softened and sympathetic.

"That'd be great, Ro. We could go into the city to see shows, and have dinner sometimes. That'd be really great."

Rowena told herself she could do those things, if it helped Claudia. And maybe their mother's death would pull them close. But at the end of their week together, Claudia couldn't find a dinner ring of Jeanne's she wanted to wear on a date and marched into the kitchen to accuse Rowena of taking it.

Astounded by the ludicrousness of the accusation, Rowena had said, "I don't even wear jewelry, and you know it. So why on earth would you think I took her ring?"

"Nothing you've ever done makes any sense to me," Claudia had countered. "But that ring's not here and you're the only one who *could* have taken it. Now give it to me, please." She'd stood tap-tapping her expensively shod foot, arms folded over her chest, her expression aggrieved.

Rowena suddenly knew exactly what her sister was doing: Claudia hated herself for having let down her guard. She'd exposed her weakness, and since she had boundless contempt for weakness in others, she had to remedy this lapse by putting Rowena firmly in the wrong, thereby putting herself back in a position of strength. It was a transparent and pathetic ploy, but realizing that didn't make the situation any less infuriating.

So outraged at having yet again been taken in that she could hear the blood pounding in her eardrums, Rowena said, "I'll tell you what.

When you find that ring—and I don't doubt for one minute that you will—do me a favor, Claudia, and shove it right up your ass!'' Then she'd run upstairs to grab her things, and stormed out of the house. Claudia followed her and stood in the driveway, watching as Rowena tossed her bag into the trunk and then unlocked the car door.

"I don't know why you're making such a fuss, Rowena. You always overreact. If you're not careful, one of these days you'll have a stroke. You really should do something about your terrible temper, you know."

Quaking with indignation, her foot bouncing up and down on the accelerator, Rowena had managed to drive home. She wept noisily and slammed things around for an hour or so, feeling like a complete fool. After downing a shot of neat vodka she began to calm down, and vowed that this was the very last time she would let Claudia take advantage of her.

Now, Rowena roamed through the old house, mulling over what she'd read and what Reid had told her, trying to match things up with the memories residing in every room. At the top of the house, where dust danced in the thin light of the naked overhead bulb, she recalled with a smile how she and Cary had played up here on inclement afternoons—lengthy games of cowboys and Indians, or board games, or taking turns reading each other stories. He'd been such a decent boy, with his mother's generous instincts and his father's warmth; he'd been sturdy and fun-loving, adventurous and kind. Even more than thirty years later, she still missed his laughter, his unflagging energy, and his sweet nature. Cary's death had been like the amputation of an invisible limb whose phantom pain she continued to feel.

Descending from the attic, she paused in the doorway of her sister's first bedroom. Narrowing her eyes, she could see Claudia—at eight, at eleven, at fourteen—jumping in surprise as she was caught in yet another furtive enterprise. The room had been a small-scale treasure trove, the repository for everything she'd either cajoled Jeanne into buying for her, or that she'd taken from Rowena's or Cary's rooms. She had been a sneak thief as a child, and as an adult she'd engaged in a sport that had as its object the acquisition and manipulation of the emotions of others.

Claudia had lived her whole life according to what she so accurately sensed others wanted or needed. She'd had an unerring ability to pinpoint a person's weak spots, and no compunctions about probing them. Any sensitivity she displayed was superficial, and she completely lacked a sense of humor about herself. Claudia had never grown up; she'd been an eight-year-old with money, and charm, and well-honed performance skills. And that profile *did* coincide with Reid's diagnosis. So perhaps Claudia had been running on sheer nerve since Jeanne's death; and maybe, finally, she'd hit the wall. While it left a number of questions still unanswered, it seemed to fit. Rowena was now fairly satisfied that Claudia had indeed taken her own life.

Relieved at having settled the matter, Rowena sat down to an early dinner of diet Coke and a cheese and cucumber sandwich at the kitchen table. Eager to put the subject of Claudia's death out of her mind, she decided to relax and watch a movie on the VCR.

In the living room she scanned the titles of her sister's sizable movie collection, marveling at the number of tapes and their variety—everything from *The Wizard of Oz* to *Casablanca.* Settling on *The Maltese Falcon,* she curled up on the sagging sofa with the remote control. After fast-forwarding past several minutes of blank leader tape, images appeared on the screen, and for a moment she couldn't quite believe what she was seeing. An involuntary, embarrassed laugh escaped her at the sight of a naked woman on her knees fellating an equally naked man. The laugh turning to a gasp of shock, she realized the woman was Claudia. The man was no one she knew.

Feeling voyeuristic, she gazed at the screen, trying to make sense of this. Neither Claudia nor her partner displayed any awareness of the camera and, judging from the sidelong angle, Rowena had to conclude that it had been positioned inside the dressing room of the master suite. Had someone hidden in there with a camcorder? If so, why? And how could Claudia have done such a thing: allowing a third person to witness and record her lovemaking? Or had she known it was happening? Since the tape ended up on her shelf, she *had* to have known.

The couple in the silent film had moved to the bed. Face afire and an odd agitation tightening her chest, Rowena stared at the screen, deciding that the camera must have been mounted on a tripod. Which meant that in all likelihood Claudia herself had made the tape.

"Why am I watching this?" Rowena exclaimed aloud suddenly, mortified, and used the remote to stop the tape. Ejecting it from the machine she examined it front and back. The label had come from a genuine copy of *The Maltese Falcon* and had been glued onto this cassette which bore the Sony imprint on its spine. Turning, she looked at the other tapes on the shelves, wondering if the commercial packaging concealed more disturbing home movies.

She took down *Easter Parade* and fed it into the VCR. The usual warning appeared on the screen, followed by the MGM logo, then the credits. She fast-forwarded through the first few minutes, then stopped, satisfied, and rewound it. The only way she would learn which tapes were genuine and which were home-made was by checking each of them individually. Since it seemed a terrible waste to throw away good movies, she was going to have to look at all of them.

What she'd do, she decided, was view as many as she could before the contractor began work on the house. Then she'd store the tapes in the cellar until the renovations were completed.

She pulled half a dozen boxes at random from the shelves, sat on the floor in front of the TV, and began viewing snippets of each tape. By midnight she had found no more of her sister's pornography, and put to one side the films she'd already checked. Then, not sure why, she pushed Claudia's tape back into the machine.

Claudia and her partner engaged in some highly acrobatic sexual activity, but throughout she seemed uninvolved, gazing expression-lessly at the ceiling. Rowena was fascinated by her sister's lack of emotion. The tape was proof somehow of Claudia's incompleteness as a person, and seemed to confirm Rowena's long-held belief that something had been fundamentally wrong with Claudia. She'd always had to simulate emotional responses to others, because only her own feelings had been real or significant to her.

Rowena was unable to stop studying the sordid evidence of her sis-ter's sexual secrets. Some previously unknown, prurient aspect of her-self kept her going; and the longer she watched, the greater were her shame and guilt.

Compared to Claudia, her own lovemaking experiences had been abbreviated and uninspired. Viewing this tape made her see herself a failure as a woman. Which was utterly ridiculous. One's sexual trans-actions had no bearing on one's worthiness—male or female. Logi-cally, rationally, she knew herself to be a better person than Claudia could ever have pretended to be. Yet the longer the tape ran the more unattractive and undesirable she felt. From beyond the grave Claudia was still overshadowing her, robbing her of her small, precious store of confidence.

On the screen Claudia's partner shuddered his way to a climax and collapsed heavily on top of her. After a minute or so, he pulled away, got off the bed and moved out of range. Then—Rowena gasped, star-tled—Claudia turned and smiled into the camera. A few seconds passed and the film dissolved into snow.

While the tape was rewinding Rowena sat with a pounding heart, trying to believe that the smile had never been intended for her eyes. But, God! It felt as if it had, as if her sister was saying, "So there!" one more time.

Rattled, she went to the kitchen, poured an inch of vodka into a glass and gulped it down. She grimaced, feeling the burn, then marched to the living room, snatched up the cassette and carried it back to the kitchen. Opening the business end, she hooked a finger under the tape and began unspooling it. With a pair of scissors, she cut it to shreds, then shoved everything into a small trash bag, and took it outside to the garbage bin. Inside again, still very shaken, she drank another half inch of vodka and went upstairs to get ready for bed, not sure anymore of Reid's diagnosis, or of Claudia's suicide. The tape had changed everything.

Seven

Instead of that last image of Claudia in death, Rowena now repeatedly saw her sister turning to smile at her—a gloating, self-congratulatory smirk—at random moments throughout each day. Her sleep was again disturbed, and she dreamed either of Claudia naked with an entire series of men, or of one unknown man carefully staging her death to look like a suicide. Reid's diagnosis no longer fit—it didn't seem to apply to a woman capable of filming her sexual exploits—and Rowena reviewed again and again the deathbed scene, more than ever bothered by the Chivas Regal. But the one thing on which she did agree with Reid was his observation that even the most apparently confiding people weren't easy to know well. It appeared there was quite a lot about Claudia she hadn't known.

She searched the house and found the empty packaging for a video camera, but not the camera itself. As a byproduct of her search, she unearthed a great deal of rubbish, which she took to the dump in several trips—thereby accomplishing something. But the camera wasn't in the trunk of the Mercedes, or anywhere in the office at the restaurant, which she checked at the first possible opportunity.

In her limited free time she went through her sister's video collection, and discovered two more of Claudia's performances. Swallowing her disgust, both for herself and her sister, and wondering each time what she thought she was accomplishing, she watched both tapes through to Claudia's signature closing smile. Then she destroyed what she now thought of as the visual diary of her sister's conquests. Some people had engraved silver cups. Claudia had tapes. It was a struggle not to be repelled by the cool, uncaring creature who had filmed her lovers without their knowledge or consent.

In a decidedly harried state of mind, Rowena approved one of the contractor's estimates, arranged for the bulk of the old furniture to be picked up by the Salvation Army, and moved back to the Stamford apartment as the renovations got underway. Most evenings after leaving the library, and on the weekends before going to the restaurant, she stopped by the house to see what progress had been made and to return two or three cassettes that she'd checked and remove a few more from the cellar.

Repeatedly she asked herself why she didn't take the entire collection to the dump. It would have spared her a lot of time and anxiety, but she needed, for some reason, to ferret out all the trophy tapes. She wouldn't be comfortable in the house, wouldn't feel it was actually hers until she'd found and destroyed every last one of them. It was illogical; it even lacked common sense, but she couldn't abandon her seek-and-destroy mission.

The renovations seemed to go very slowly. However, once the kitchen had been gutted, with the walls stripped back to the studs in order to replace the old wiring, and the floor pulled up to give access to the lead piping that had to be removed, her enthusiasm returned. With the few remaining pieces of furniture collected beneath a drop cloth at the far end of the dining room, she could see the living room's potential. Daily she had affirmation that her decision had been a good one, particularly concerning the garage apartment.

That space had been the living quarters for the various housekeepers. But for at least twenty years it had remained empty, and in its present state it was doubtful many people would have seen its potential, as Mark had with one quick look. The steeply pitched roof was unfinished, its rafters exposed. The floor was no more than crudely laid sheets of raw plywood, warped and wavy from decades of leaks. The walls had been packed with Fiberglas insulation, with drywall nailed over top. In places the Sheetrock had belled and buckled. The only partitioning had been around the rudimentary bathroom consisting of toilet, sink, and rusted tin shower stall at the near right-hand end of the large space. Three narrow casement windows overlooked the driveway at the front and three on the rear wall had a view of the neglected garden. The twenty-five by sixty-five-foot area was bleak and cheerless, and Rowena wondered how her parents could have allowed that peculiar series of housekeepers to live there.

Now, with the old fixtures torn out and framing in place for an expanded new bathroom, and bright copper waste and water pipes installed in what would be the kitchen, and with the old windows gone and wide new ones fitted, it was possible to see what had attracted Mark.

He had insisted on paying for the extras he wanted: a large, north-facing skylight in the roof; hand-painted Italian tiles for the bathroom; a butcher-block counter in the kitchen; built-in bookcases in the living area; and a freestanding Scandinavian fireplace for the living room, to be vented through the rear wall.

"I'm starting to get very excited about moving in," Mark said over dinner at Le Rendezvous toward the end of the third week of renovations.

"Me, too." Rowena smiled, wishing she had the courage to tell him about Claudia's tapes. She loved and trusted Mark, but not only would she find such an admission mortifying, she also feared losing his respect.

"The thing is," he said soberly, "I keep getting very up, then I come down with the guilts, and have to tell myself Tim would've wanted me to move on. I can just hear him saying, 'You're only thirty-six. You can't stop living because I croaked.' It would've bothered the hell out of him to think my life ground to a halt because nothing feels right without him."

"He would've said that, Mark. It's the truth."

"Sure, but it's still rough. I think about him constantly. I dream of him every night. There's this massive hole in my life, on top of which I keep thinking any day now I'll test positive and that'll be the end of me. So what's the point of doing anything? Of course that's survivor's angst, and maybe someday I'll get over it."

"You can't think that way," she told him. "You have to keep going. We all have to do the best we can with the time we've got." How could she be saying this to him when she was wasting her own precious time watching her late sister fornicate? Bad enough Claudia had made the tapes, but what did it say about her that she couldn't quit watching them? For a moment she was drowning in shame, and told herself she had to get rid of the damned things, and soon.

"Easy to say," Mark said. "Not so easy to do. But seeing the apartment taking shape ... It means a lot to me. I want you to know how much I appreciate that."

"I do know." She reached over to lay her hand on his arm.

Making an effort to lighten the mood, he said, "So what d'you think? Should I get one of those cunning little signs made to hang out front? Bide-a-wee, or The Nook. Something the teeniest bit camp."

"Great." She chuckled, giving his arm a squeeze before withdrawing her hand. "Why not just call it Radclyffe Hall?"

"Oooo, *very* good! You're such a sharp little cookie."

"How's everything?" Ian asked, stopping by the table.

"Hey, join us!" Mark invited. "Pull up a chair, sit a minute."

Ian looked questioningly at Rowena, saying, "Perhaps for coffee."

His look told her Claudia would never have countenanced his sitting with the patrons, and she felt a quick rush of anger. With warmth, she said, "Please do, Ian."

"Thank you, Rowena. I'd like that very much. Enjoying your meal, Mark?"

"It's phenomenal. Kiss the chef for me."

Ian laughed. Until that moment Rowena hadn't realized she'd never heard him laugh. It was a good, hearty sound, and she was glad it was Mark who'd elicited this response from him.

"How is the work on the house coming on?" he asked, looking from Mark to Rowena then back to Mark.

"It's looking very good."

"Very good," she echoed. "You must drop by and see."

"Yes. Well." He shot his cuffs, said to Mark, "I'll convey your compliments to Philippe," nodded at Rowena and went off to continue his rounds.

"Did he just undergo a quick mood change, or am I imagining things?" Rowena asked Mark in an undertone.

"You're imagining things. He takes his job seriously—which is undoubtedly why this place has survived. So is he gay or what?"

"I don't know. I'd have thought you would. Don't gays have secret signals or something?"

Eyebrows raised, he said, "You can't be that naive. Tell me you don't really believe that."

"Not really. But how *do* you know if a man's gay or straight?"

Mark ate some more of his pasta before saying, "Eye contact, primarily. But that's no guarantee. Pheromones probably, something that gets into our nostrils." Breaking into a grin, he said, "Did you honestly think it was like a secret Dick Tracy signal or something, that we have decoder rings or whatever?"

Her face hot, she said, "In a way, I guess I did."

"You're so ingenuous," he accused fondly.

"I am not. Just because I don't know how gay people identify one another doesn't make me simple-minded. For God's sake." She laughed. "You said you don't know either. And what makes you think he might be gay, anyway?"

"The clothes. I'll bet big bucks that's a Savile Row suit he's wearing. And the Gucci loafers. He's got great taste."

"That's true," she agreed. "He does."

"And some money he didn't get from working here."

"He does give the impression of being upper class, doesn't he?"

"Definitely." Mark took a slow look around, then said, "Okay, so you're not ingenuous. But naive, yes."

"Probably."

"And unpretentious," he continued.

"Because I have nothing to be pretentious about."

"You only *think* you don't."

"No," she insisted. "I *know.*"

Mark picked up his wine and gazed at her assessingly. "This makes me sad, and a little angry, Rowena. You are good-looking, especially with the new haircut." She made a face. "You *are!* But I know how pointless it is trying to convince you of that."

"Correct."

"If you plan to keep your mind closed, we'll change the subject."

"Yes, let's. You don't have to scrounge around for ways to compliment me. I know you love me. And I love you, too."

"I don't have to 'scrounge around,' Rowena. I'm telling the truth. From the day we met, you've talked about how beautiful Jeanne was, how beautiful Claudia was. I never met your mother, so I'll have to take your word on that. But I sure as hell met your late sister. She was eye-catching, definitely. But beautiful? No way. She was too hard, too contrived, too fake, to be really beautiful. The first time I got a look at Claudia after hearing you talk about her, I thought maybe you'd been joking. But I looked at you, and you weren't kidding. And that blew my brain. I mean, it was like some Grimm's fairy tale or something, the way those two women had you convinced you were ugly." .

Discomfited, Rowena laughed.

"It's not one bit funny. I think you always laugh automatically, as a defensive measure, whenever the subject of your family and how they treated you comes up. Why do you do that, Ro?" he asked earnestly.

"I have to laugh about it. If I thought for one minute my mother had been intentionally cruel and not just a basically shallow woman, I'd have to rewrite my entire personal history. She grew up with that kind of input. I can remember hearing my grandmother talk to her the way Jeanne talked to me."

"That might be reasonable were it not for the fact that Mommy dearest didn't treat Claudia that way."

"No, but that's because Claudia was more like her, interested in the same things. And I wasn't. I tried to be, but I couldn't get into it—

hours spent deliberating over a pair of shoes or a handbag. It bored me silly, but Claudia lived for that stuff. Also, there was a huge guilt factor involved that had Jeanne overcompensating, because Claudia was an accident, a child she hadn't wanted.''

"I suppose I can buy that." Mark drank some of his wine, then said, "Not to change the subject or anything, but how long d'you figure you'll be able to keep juggling two jobs? The past week or so it's been like working with Sybil."

Rowena laughed so hard her eyes watered.

"Seriously," he persisted. "How long? Or do you think you can keep on the way you're going indefinitely?"

"I don't know, Mark. Every time I walk in here I have to ask myself if I'm playing at being Claudia—a thought that's enough to make me go cold. I have to stop and think before deciding no, I'm only being me, but doing something I enjoy a lot. The thing of it is, it'd be easier being me if I hadn't had Claudia for a sister."

"I can imagine."

"You don't know the half of it," she said, dangerously close to telling him about the tapes.

"Anyway, it's obvious you'd rather be here."

"I think maybe I would," she confessed apologetically.

"Listen to you!" He slapped the flat of his hand against his forehead. "Will you come *on,* please? You said that as if you were confessing to granny bashing. There's nothing wrong with wanting to change careers, with wanting to change, period. This gig's a hell of a lot more glamorous and interesting than the library. Why shouldn't you prefer it? I definitely would. Of course, the first thing I'd get rid of would be the Grappelli and Feinstein tapes." He mimed gagging.

"Do I take it you don't care for the music?" she asked with a smile.

"Your basic yawn, cupcake. A notch up from elevator music."

"Maybe I'll talk to Terry about it."

"Who's that, the barkeep?"

"Right."

"A seriously great-looking guy," he observed, leaning to the side to look past her. "An interesting group here altogether. I thought that at the funeral. Very tight-knit. Good people."

"Ian said in so many words that they banded together for protection against Claudia."

"I'd have joined that band in a New York minute. They sure seem happy enough with you, though. I saw all the smiles when you walked in."

"Really?"

"Why wouldn't they like you, Rowena? You're a dear little enchilada. What's not to like?"

She shrugged and busied herself eating the last of her chicken.

"Another month, six weeks at the outside," he said, "and I see you as the star of a farewell party at the Mag. If I wasn't going to be living mere yards away, I'd be getting very maudlin. If you're not going to finish that salad, I'll have it. The vinaigrette's fantastic."

Ian came to join them for coffee, and he and Mark chatted effortlessly while Rowena excused herself to have a word with Terry about the music. Now that Mark had pointed it out, she had to agree that Terry really was very attractive, with dark curly hair, a squarish face with deep brown eyes, and a wide mouth that smiled readily.

"I could bring in some of my dubs," he said eagerly. "Stuff that'd be perfect—cool jazz, mellow but with an edge."

"Let's try it."

"All *right!*" he said happily. "I'll bring in a few tapes tomorrow. And listen, Rowena." He dropped his voice. "I want to thank you again for the raise. It means a lot—to everybody. It sounds kiss-ass, but since you've been here, it's a whole other place. Way better."

"I want everyone to be happy."

"We are." He gave her a thumbs-up, then turned to fill a drinks order for Mae.

Before they left, Mark insisted on leaving a twenty-dollar tip for John, who'd served them.

"I love your sense of fairness," Rowena told him. "I really do."

"What about my ineffable charm, my extraordinary sense of style, my perception, sensitivity, and wit?"

"Oh, those too. Terry's going to bring in some dubs tomorrow."

"What kind of dubs?" he asked suspiciously.

"Jazz."

"Okay. For one awful moment I imagined him showing up with stuff like Jane's Addiction or the Dead Kennedys. But I guess he's a bit too old."

"Dead Kennedys?" She stared at him, then said, "Never mind. Don't tell me."

"Think it'd be all right if I ducked out to the kitchen to thank Philippe?"

"Of course."

She took a look at the reservations book while he went to the kitchen, and smiled at the laughter that erupted back there. When they were walking to the car, she asked, "What did you say that had them in such fits?"

"State secret. I did ask Philippe if he'd give me his vinaigrette recipe, but in his delectable Gallic way he said he couldn't. But he's going to send you home Friday night with a bottle for me. Forget to give it to me, Rowena, and you die."

"Oh, I'm so scared! Dennis the Menace is threatening me. Oh, help!" With a laugh, she slipped her arm through his.

She began sorting and packing the contents of the apartment and, via a notice she tacked up on the bulletin board in the laundry room, managed to sell most of her furniture.

On two successive Saturday afternoons she and Mark went shopping. She ordered a sleek new sofa, several deep armchairs, some lamps, four new chairs to go with the old marble-topped kitchen table, and an antique silk-on-silk Persian carpet for the living room. After much deliberation Mark placed an order for slate gray broadloom to be fitted through the apartment, a new bed, and a pair of handsome Italian lacquered night tables.

Once the kitchen appliances had been installed and the master bathroom was finished, Rowena moved back into the house even though the work wasn't scheduled to be completed for another month or so. She wouldn't be able to move her things in until then, but she wanted to be there to see the daily changes, and to deal immediately with any problems that might arise.

She actually enjoyed getting up at six-fifteen in order to be out of the bathroom and dressed, ready for the crew of four to arrive at seven-thirty. With a cup of coffee, she'd stand by the rear kitchen window, noting the snow's creeping retreat from the back garden, while she entertained random memories: of the playhouse that had once stood at the foot of the lawn; of the elderly, soft-spoken Italian gardener who long ago had come twice a week to weed the flower beds and cut the grass; of herself and Cary building a snowman with fresh, powdery snow while Claudia, forced to remain inside because of a cold, watched them through the dining room window.

When Frank Reilly, the contractor, came, she'd have a second cup of coffee with him while they reviewed his team's progress, before she set off to the library.

As the weeks passed it became clear she was merely marking time, getting through the hours at the library until she could go to the restaurant. Mark had joked about it, but she really *was* beginning to feel like Sybil, with two distinct personalities: one who wore the shapeless granola clothes and worked at the Mag, and the other who put on silk underwear and fifty-five-dollar panty hose under designer dresses to work at Le Rendezvous. She was going to have to leave the Magnusson, because the restaurant offered her an opportunity to shine as she never had.

By early April the work on the house was far behind schedule. The wrong kitchen cabinets had been delivered and had to be sent back, which meant a delay until the right cabinets came. The linoleum she'd selected was no longer available, so she had to return to the store to choose another pattern. Her second choice, naturally, was more expensive and not quite what she'd wanted.

Then there was the dirt and debris. Every surface was thickly coated with a combination of construction dust and sawdust kicked up by the floor sander. Each evening, before she could even consider eating, she had to wipe down the counters, clean the sink, and sweep up the crumbled fragments of drywall, snippets of wire, bent nails, wood curls, and even empty take-out food containers the crew left here and there. The Dumpster parked conspicuously at the top of the driveway had yet to be removed, even though Frank Reilly had been promising for two weeks to see to it.

The cumulative effect of all this was a low-grade depression. Telling herself to be patient didn't help because returning home every night to see how little had been done that day was starting to get her down, making her wonder if she hadn't perhaps made the biggest mistake of her life. She was spending her savings on a job that was costing a fortune and seemed interminable. There was no sign yet of the insurance money, and the lawyer had told her it would be at least seven or eight more months before Claudia's estate cleared probate.

As she'd always done in the past, she confided her misgivings to Penny in the course of a phone call near the end of the second week in April.

"I *told* you I didn't think it was such a good idea," Penny said. "But I guess all you can do now is tough it out. It can't take that much longer. And they're probably making more progress than you realize."

"Probably," Rowena said, disappointed by Penny's lack of support—something she'd always been able to count on in the past. "I'd better go. It's late and I'm wiped."

"You're doing too much," Penny warned in the admonishing tones of a disappointed parent. "You'll burn out at the rate you're going."

"I doubt it'll come to that. But I'm considering my options."

"Meaning what? You're going to quit the library?"

"I'm giving it serious thought."

"Don't do anything you'll regret later. I mean, the renovation's one example of just how wrong things can go."

"It hasn't gone wrong, Penny. It's taking the better part of my adult life, but it hasn't gone wrong. It's just kind of hard on the nerves being so unsettled. And as far as work goes, to be honest, aside from you and Mark, I wouldn't miss the Mag. The restaurant's great. Every night's kind of like a party. I get to dress up and meet new people. It's been a long time since I actually looked forward to going to work."

"Has it occurred to you that maybe you're trying to become Claudia?"

Rowena had to laugh. "Pen, that's so absurd I can't believe you actually said it."

"It's not absurd."

"The truth is you don't want me to quit the library."

"You're right," Penny admitted. "I don't. And you really should be aware of what you're doing."

"I'm *very* aware of what I'm doing."

"Don't be offended. I'm your friend and I care about you. Try to see it from my viewpoint. First you started out staying over at the house temporarily to get things organized for the probate. Now you're having major work done on the place and moving back for good. First you were filling in on the weekends to help out at the restaurant, now you're thinking of making it your *career,* and talking about giving up an important job. You're wearing her clothes and her shoes. You even cut off all your hair."

"Wait a minute!" Trying not to get angry, Rowena interrupted what sounded like a grievance list. "In case you're forgetting, Claudia had shoulder-length hair. That one won't fly."

"Okay," Penny cut back in. "But think about how hard you worked to get to be head librarian, and now you're talking about throwing it aside, as if it wasn't an important accomplishment. Don't you think that's a bit rash?"

"No, actually, I don't. You're making it sound as if I'm betraying you, or the library, or something. And not only is that not the case, it's not even relevant. It's my *right* to make decisions, to make changes, even to make mistakes. God knows, I've made them before and I'll make them again. What I can't believe is your attitude. I thought you, of all people, would understand and be supportive.''

''Let's not fight.'' Penny backed down. ''I was only trying to say I'm worried, that I think you're moving too fast. That's all.''

''There's no need for you to be worried. Everything's under control, and I'm moving at a comfortable speed. I have to go now,'' she said coldly. ''I'll see you tomorrow.'' Without giving Penny a chance to say another word, she put the receiver down.

Penny's so-called concern was overblown and insulting. As if resigning from the library was the end of the world! She'd made it sound as if Rowena was suffering from diminished capacities and lacked the ability to make rational decisions. Which was definitely not the case, and by God she'd prove it!

In a fury she grabbed a trash bag from the box on the counter, marched down to the cellar and began filling the bag with the remainder of Claudia's cassettes. *We'll see who's rational!* Maybe she had been off-track for a while, thrown by discovering her sister's unique trophy collection and obsessively watching the tapes at the expense of her self-confidence. But she was perfectly rational now! Back up the stairs and out to the trash bin, and that was the end of that!

While she washed the dust from her hands she told herself to calm down. Penny was an old and valued friend who'd spoken from a depth of genuine concern. She hadn't meant to be insulting. Bullshit! Penny was being a classic curmudgeon, painting every scenario in shades of gray and black. So why should Rowena bend over backward to be fair to her when the truth was that Penny was upset by the prospect of Rowena's casting aside a job Penny had wanted badly. They'd both gone after it, but Rowena had been chosen. Well, maybe Penny would get the job now. And she was welcome to it.

First thing the next morning, Rowena submitted her resignation.

Eight

"You did this because you're mad at me," Penny said in a voice husky with upset that day at lunch.

"I did it sooner than I planned because you made me angry," Rowena acknowledged. Then, hearing how childish they sounded, she relented. "I'd already decided to leave. And I'm not mad at you. Listen to us." She smiled. "We sound like a pair of eight-year-olds."

"I was hoping to change your mind." Penny smiled too, but with obvious effort. "I'm used to being able to walk through the building if I want to see you." She groped for words. "It won't be the same . . . I'll miss you."

"Come on, Pen. It's not as if I'm leaving the state. We'll see each other."

"But it won't be the same," Penny insisted.

Rowena had a number of responses to this statement but chose not to give any of them. The fact was that her relationship with Penny—or with Mark, or any of her other friends—hadn't figured into her decision to quit, and she was surprised and bothered to discover that Penny was so dependent upon her. She'd assumed that her present friendships would continue but, of necessity, on slightly different terms. And there really was no reason why they shouldn't.

"The primary difference is that we won't be working in the same building. And let's be realistic. We don't see each other every day as it is."

"It won't be the same," Penny repeated doggedly.

Suddenly Rowena could see that her friend's life had fallen into a groove so comfortable that she now viewed change as bad, and unlike the rest of the staff who had been unanimously congratulatory, Penny wasn't happy for her. Perhaps she'd been counting on Rowena's presence at the library until retirement, having viewed Rowena as something as fixed and immutable as the decorative stonework on the face of the building. Or perhaps she felt slighted by Rowena's failure to consult her. Whatever her reason, Rowena felt oppressed by Penny's negative attitude, by the selfishness she was attempting to pass off as concern. It reminded her of countless occasions growing up, when Claudia had decided Rowena had something that by rights should have been hers. She'd been relentless in her determination to have it, and until she left home to go to college, Rowena was obliged to take great care to ensure that whatever or whoever she brought into the house didn't catch her sister's eye.

Claudia had taught her that few people, especially men, were able to resist attractive surfaces. Like fish, they went after the shiny lure every time. And Claudia did shine. She had, after all, spent better than half her waking hours working on it.

Claudia, and Jeanne too, had taught her a lot, not the least of which was to rely solely on herself. And ultimately she came to have more faith in her friends than in her family, particularly Penny who'd been unflaggingly supportive and loyal. Now, for what appeared to be ego-centric reasons, Penny was attempting to cast a pall over Rowena's decision to move on. It was a let-down, but she wasn't going to allow it to throw her off course. She was almost forty, and wanted to relish pursuing a new direction while there was still time to enjoy it.

"We'd better start getting back." She looked pointedly at her watch—actually Claudia's, a vermeil Cartier tank watch with a pale gold face and black Roman numerals. "We'll be late if we don't get a move on."

"You think I'm being selfish," Penny guessed correctly, her lovely face creased sadly. "Maybe I am. But I really do care about you, Ro, and I'm scared you're turning obsessive, that the real you is being sublimated as you take over Claudia's life."

"Penny," Rowena said quietly, loathing this conversation, "drop it, please!" For a moment, she saw her old friend as pre-World War II Germany—large, beautiful, but fanatically fixated. She felt a surge of dislike for this woman with her rigid views. But no, no. This was her beloved long-time friend. She couldn't let the situation evolve into a verbal shoving match. Dredging up a smile, she opened her bag, left two dollars for the waitress, and got up to go, saying, "Come on, Pen. Time to get back."

Penny started to say something, then obviously changed her mind.

The silence between them held all the way back to the library.

Once the renovations on the house were finally completed some two and a half weeks behind schedule, and the crew was working flat-out to put the finishing touches to the garage apartment, Rowena's mood improved. Each morning as she descended the stairs she had to pause in the foyer to look with pleasure at the gleaming refinished wood floors and the pale yellow living room walls, the sleekly simple new furniture. Then she moved into the kitchen, to delight in the glass-fronted white cabinets set off by the hunter green walls; the ultra-modern appliances and spotless countertops; the glossy white-on-white linoleum; and the old marble-topped table now cleaned and polished and possessed of an old-world charm that was complemented by the fluid lines of the four new white-enameled tubular steel chairs.

After starting the coffee, she'd open the white miniblinds and admire the way the light entered and reflected off the interior surfaces, forming irregularly shaped splashes of warmth on the walls. In gutting the room old memories had been uprooted and carted off along with the outdated appliances, so that this area had no unpleasant resonance. It was completely hers, completely welcoming. She liked the way her cookbooks and her mother's dinner service looked through the glass cabinet doors. She even enjoyed the geometry of the sundry cans and boxes on the shelves. The house had become hers, had become, finally, home.

As the garage apartment neared completion, Mark, too, expressed his satisfaction. "I can't wait to move in. I feel like a bride," he said with a laugh at lunch on Rowena's second to last day at the Magnusson. "I go breathless just thinking about having my very own washer and dryer."

"Hey, me too. No more hoarding quarters, or saving up laundry until it's a mountain in the front hall."

"How well I remember those mountains," he intoned, as if reciting poetry.

"Once. You saw one mountain once."

"Okay. But I remember it. So what's up with you and Penny? Is this a forever rift, or are you guys going to patch it up?"

"I don't know, Mark. She's been such a spoilsport. Having her tell me, every chance she gets, that I'm turning into Claudia was wearing me out. So for the time being I've backed off."

"Maybe she's jealous."

"Of what? Why would anyone in her right mind be jealous of an almost-forty, lapsed granola grinder who happened to inherit some property that rightfully should have been hers years ago?"

"A lapsed granola grinder," he repeated, with a sad shake of his head. "Such an interesting bent you have for self-deprecation. I've never known anyone more skilled at it. In the beginning, I used to think you were just fishing for compliments. But then I saw you actually meant it. You haven't got a clue how you appear to others."

"Of course I do."

"Rowena, I love you dearly, but you don't. You. Do. Not. But okay. Let's look at this objectively. Number one, Claudia croaked and now you've got some bucks, the house, the restaurant, and the Benz, which, for some unknown reason, you're letting gather dust in the garage. Number two, you're *thin*. That alone would've been enough to drive Penny bananas from day one except for the fact that you cleverly concealed your lack of bulk under a wardrobe that might have been selected by a blind person from a Braille catalogue." She had to smile at this. Encouraged, he went on. "So, you're thin and looking very soignée these days, *and* if that isn't bad enough, you're getting to hang out where the upper crust wine and dine. Suddenly, there's moolah and glamour. Put this package of goodies in the face of a woman whose entire adult life has been a diet, and your verdict has to be—ladies and gentlemen of the jury—jealousy in the first degree."

"I don't know, Mark."

"Hey! For the first time since I've known you, you've started displaying outward signs of confidence. Wearing those designer duds has been good for you, my tiny tortilla. Now, even in your Beaners you've got a certain panache. People notice these things, and the majority think what's happening with you is great. Most of us wish we were quitting the Mag, too. Penny, unfortunately, doesn't see it the way the rest of us do. From her POV you're abandoning us in general, and her in particular."

"It's ridiculous. I mean, my God. We've been friends for twenty-five years. She should know me better than that."

"Ah, but cupcake, maybe she doesn't know *herself* better."

Rowena sat back. "I hadn't thought of that."

"She probably hasn't either. She's overreacting like crazy right now. I think you should give things time to settle down. None of this is worth busting up the friendship for."

"I agree."

"So, fine. Chill out and be friendly. Give her time to come around. And do me a favor and explain why you won't use that gorgeous hunk of expensive machinery mildewing in the garage."

"It's silly, I know, but every time I picture myself driving the car, I'm horrified by the thought of ever, in any way, being remotely like Claudia."

"Oh, please! It has not escaped my notice that you've been decked out in some of her subtler jewelry. You're living in the house and wearing clothes she bought; you're shifting over work-wise to the restaurant. Why not go whole hog and drive the car, too?"

"I'll think about it," she hedged, dissatisfied with the way she'd tried to explain her feelings.

"What's going on, Ro? Is this about Penny, or is there something else?"

"Let me ask you something. Why aren't *you* jealous of my supposed good fortune?"

"Well, for one thing, I don't do drag, so the clothes would be completely wasted on me. For another, I like getting comped to meals at an upscale eatery. And, kidding aside, here's why. Because after the past two years, watching someone I loved with all my heart and soul dying by agonizing inches, I wouldn't begrudge anyone anything. If it makes you happy, dear heart, have it, do it, eat it, wear it. Because, contrary to those nice fairy tales we were spoon-fed with our mashed bananas, you can die way ahead of time, way before anybody should. So if you want to eat your dessert first, do it. If you want to change your life at the halfway mark, I'm for you. As long as you're not knowingly hurting anybody else, do whatever the hell feels good. I'll lead the parade for your right to do it. And do it today because tomorrow could be too late."

She reached over and took hold of his hand and said softly, "Thank you."

"And start driving that goddamned car or I will!"

"We'll see." She smiled.

By the end of April she and Ian had worked out a schedule. Since the restaurant was closed Monday nights, he covered the front Tuesday through Thursday evenings, and she took over on the weekends. Monday through Sunday she worked the lunch shift from eleven-thirty till two-thirty. It added up to a work week of thirty-one hours—a very relaxed schedule by her standards. They also hired an additional part-time waiter to work lunches on the weekends, and to fill in, if and when needed, for the regulars.

In early May, on the Saturday after her things were finally transported to the house, she got Scott, the new part-timer, to cover for her on the lunch shift so she could be there when Mark moved into the garage apartment.

Half a dozen of their mutual friends, including Penny and her son Kip, loaded Mark's possessions into a rented truck, then piled into several cars to follow the truck to the house where Rowena was waiting with a large ice chest full of beer and soft drinks and a lunch she'd spent the early-morning hours preparing.

Everyone was impressed by the apartment and obediently wiped their feet before walking on the new carpeting. They admired the cathedral ceiling with its skylight, and the open-plan kitchen with its indirect lighting and stacked washer/dryer. A beaming Mark, clad in pristine white painter's overalls, a yellow T-shirt, and Day-Glo orange high-tops, showed off the spacious new bathroom with the hand-painted tiles, the customized closets with mirrored doors, and the elevated rear bedroom area which could be closed off from the rest of the apartment by folding louvered panels that flattened back to the outer walls.

In just under two hours, the truck had been emptied and the furniture was in place. Penny, who continued to be somewhat distant in the aftermath of their minor confrontation, gave Rowena a hand arranging the food on the counter but when Rowena tried to talk to her, she responded only with yeses and nos, and seemed to have trouble making eye contact. Rowena was hurt, but pretended not to notice and busied herself filling the extra-large percolator she'd brought from the house. By the time she got it plugged in and the first inner groans began, Penny had taken a plateful of food and gone to sit with Marcia, one of their co-workers from the Mag.

Rowena opted to take her own food and sit near Mark who was searching through a carton of cassettes and CDs, looking for something suitable to play.

A beer in one hand, an overflowing plate in the other, Kip approached them to say, "This is most cool, Uncle Mark. Really. An excellent place."

"I'm glad you like it."

"Yeah, oh very," Kip said earnestly.

Mark grinned, put a cassette into the player, and said, "Let's do this food."

"Definitely," Kip agreed, settling on the floor as "Sergeant Pepper's Lonely Hearts Club Band" emerged from the speakers and everyone—except Penny, Rowena noticed—automatically smiled and nodded approvingly. "I'm way up for your deviled eggs, Auntie Ro."

"I can see that." She laughed as Kip popped half of one into his mouth. He was a big, sixteen-year-old golden-haired, blue-eyed, perfectly beautiful physical specimen of young manhood with an equally beautiful nature—openhearted and generous—who had no idea of his attributes. He simply considered himself lucky because he very much liked young women, and they very much liked him. Unlike most of his peers who fell into serial monogamy as if they were jumping from the upper stories of skyscrapers, Kip dated quite a few girls, and was unfailingly attentive to whomever he was with. He was also comfortable with any group, regardless of age, and he worked hard to be deserving of the friendships that came his way. Rowena couldn't have loved him more if he'd been her own child, and she'd have been even more generous with the birthday and Christmas gifts she'd given him every year of his life if she hadn't felt that Penny would have been bothered by it. Which, now that she thought of it, was unreasonable. Rowena had to wonder if she hadn't been making allowances for Penny for a very long time, tiptoeing around Penny's sensitivities at a certain real expense to her own.

Glancing over, she saw that Penny was glowering at Kip from across the room, as if angry that Kip had chosen to sit with Mark and Rowena instead of with her. Hoping to put a stop to this, Rowena signaled her to come join them, but Penny gave her a bright, synthetic smile and shook her head.

"Oh, to hell with it," Rowena muttered under her breath, and went on eating. She wasn't about to let Penny spoil the occasion.

Before they left, the crew wanted to see the house. So Rowena gave them a tour. Everyone had something nice to say, except for Penny who said nothing. Rowena wondered why she'd bothered to come when she so plainly disapproved of everything.

Yet when she was leaving, she stopped to give Rowena an emphatic, somewhat sorrowing embrace very like the one she'd given her at Claudia's funeral, and said solemnly, "The house is fabulous. I hope you'll be happy here." Then she turned and marched briskly to her car, calling to Kip to hurry up, they were going.

Kip shrugged, his fair brows drawing together, hugged Rowena, then Mark, handed Mark his unfinished beer and got in the car. He rolled down the window to say, "Invite me to dinner soon, Uncle Mark, Auntie Ro. Okay?" He was still talking as his mother drove off and their last view was of Kip turning angrily to say something to Penny who was staring rigidly straight ahead.

"That was weird," Rowena observed to Mark after everyone had gone. "Penny could hardly bring herself to talk to me, and acted as if the place was haunted."

"I noticed," Mark said wryly, collecting paper plates and dumping them into a garbage bag. "That parting shot was a little too much like the wicked queen as she gave Snow White the poisoned apple. She's playing the role of the injured party to the hilt. It's starting to get on *my* nerves, so I can imagine what it's doing to yours. Hey! Do you *believe* the size of Kip? I swear he's grown six inches in six months. I'll bet he hits six-six by the time he's finished. And did you see how much he ate?"

"Did you see how much Penny ate?" she countered.

"I saw." Mark rolled his eyes. "She'd be bulimic if she could get it right and remember to upchuck after the binge."

"That's awful!" Rowena laughed.

"Yeah, but true. Did you hear the way Kip talks? It's hilarious."

" 'The apartment is most cool,' " she quoted, smiling.

"God, I love that kid. He's such a sweetheart. It's the one thing I really miss—not having kids of my own. I always thought it'd be so great to be somebody's dad. Tim and I talked about adopting. But it would've meant his coming out publicly, which would've cost him his job. Anyway, it's academic now."

"You'd have made wonderful parents, the two of you."

"I think so, too. What about you?" He dumped the plastic cutlery in the sink to be washed for future reuse. "Did you want kids, Ro?"

She paused in wiping the countertop and said, "A hundred or so years ago, I thought I'd grow up, get married, and have three or four kids. Then Claudia took away my first boyfriend, Davey O'Connell, and laughed when he followed her like a puppy. She took away the next two, and then I got wise and starting meeting my dates up the road. But part of me had lost interest. It was too much like a contest, and over the years men took a progressively lower position in my priorities. I mean, you remember Gil."

"I remember Gil." He made a face.

"Right. Well, one morning not so long ago I woke up and it was too late. For about a month I walked around, almost in mourning. But then, when I considered the difficulties, not to mention the expense, of being a single mother, I decided I was only regretting a fantasy. Besides, I probably wouldn't have made a very good mother. You need to have had some bona fide nurturing somewhere along the line in order to be able to pass it along to a child, and Jeanne, as I've told you, had no skills."

"But from the sound of him your father did. You got what you needed one way and another. And as usual, you're wrong. You'd have been a terrific mother. We both would've made good parents, but it's not likely we'll get a shot. Life's harsh, huh?''

''Very, sometimes.''

''This is no good,'' he said suddenly. ''We're both getting bummed. Let's get out the Benz and go for a drive.''

She was about to protest, then reconsidered. ''Why not?'' she said. ''I'll go get the keys.''

She ran into the house and as she went to open the kitchen drawer for Claudia's keys, she noticed the message indicator on the answering machine was lit. She hit the play button.

''Hello, Ms. Graham. It's Tony Reid. I was expecting you to get back to me after you read the data on de Clérambault's syndrome. So I was calling on the off-chance you might be free to talk today over lunch. But I guess not. I'm heading off to San Francisco this evening to attend a conference and I'll try you again when I get back. Bye.''

The sound of his voice had given her another seizure. And conjuring up his image, recalling the show of dimples when he'd smiled, made her midriff ache again.

''What's up?'' Mark asked, reading her expression when she returned with her handbag and the keys.

''Tony Reid called. He wanted to talk to me over lunch. Don't you think that's kind of strange?''

''Maybe he likes you, cupcake.''

''No, he's after something.''

''Your fine little body perhaps?''

She laughed and punched him on the arm. ''Get real please!''

''You get real,'' he countered, as Rowena unlocked the garage door. ''And try being a little more open-minded. Anything can happen.''

First Ian having unpredictable mood changes, then Penny acting all bent out of shape, now Claudia's former shrink calling to ask her to lunch. Everything was out of whack. She pressed the button to raise the overhead door, suddenly wishing, the way she had as a child, to be left alone.

Nine

Late in May Ian asked Rowena into the office to discuss creating a dining patio in the unused area at the rear of the building.

"I've been wanting to take advantage of that space for quite some time, but Claudia wouldn't consider it. I'm sure you're aware how strongly she resisted change."

"Yes," she said, mildly jolted by the truth of the statement. It had never crystallized into an actual fact for her until he said that, but to Claudia change had been something to be avoided whenever possible. It was probably why she'd never left home, and had never made any improvements to the house.

"For a minimal outlay," he went on, "we would accomplish several things. May I tell you my ideas?"

"Please. I'd like to hear them."

Encouraged, he said, "Well, first off there would be the expense of buying outdoor furniture, flowering plants, and so forth, for atmosphere. Also, we'd have to enclose the area. I think stockade fencing would be the least offensive, and it would allow us to have a gate for access to the alley. What we lose is rather an ugly parking area, which is no great loss, given there's a large public lot not fifty yards away. I've worked up some numbers and I think you'll see the overall cost is reasonable. There would be room for four tables of four and four tables of two, twenty-four diners at maximum capacity. And we could take on students for the summer—a waiter, a busboy, and a sous-chef. Scott has said he'd be interested in working full-time during the summer. So," he wound down, "I've gone over the projections with the accountant, and he's for it. But of course the final decision rests with you."

After a quick look at his calculations, she said, "We should probably get an estimate for an awning. That way, if it rains, we don't lose out altogether on the space."

"Oh, very good!" He beamed at her. "I hadn't thought of that."

"You've certainly thought of everything else. I think we should get going on this right away. And I know someone who'd jump at the busboy's position. I'll call him and get back to you on that. In the meantime, why don't you start looking for the waiter and sous-chef.''

"Happy to. I am so glad you agree with me on this.''

"It's a damned good idea, Ian. I'd be crazy not to agree with you.''

She spoke to Kip later that same afternoon.

"That'd be way cool, Auntie Ro. I've been applying everywhere for more than a month and there are no jobs. Zip, *nada*. I was starting to get nervous in the extreme. I definitely want the job. When would I start?''

"About the time school lets out, say three weeks. You'll need black pants, a white shirt, and comfortable black shoes because you're going to be on your feet a lot, Kip. We'll supply the bow tie and apron.''

"I'm so psyched! Thank you, really. I'll be the best busboy you ever had.''

"I know that, sweetheart.''

"You're good people, Auntie Ro.''

"So are you, Kip. Take care now, and I'll see you soon.''

At ten past six that evening Rowena was sitting at the kitchen table about to take a closer look at the cost projections, when the telephone rang.

Without preamble, her tone enraged, Penny said, "What d'you think you're doing, calling my son?''

Bewildered, Rowena said, "Pen, I offered Kip a summer job. We're opening a patio, and we'll need extra staff.''

"You're trying to win him over, get him on your side.''

"What are you *talking* about? I don't need to win Kip over, and there are no *sides*. This is a simple case of supply and demand. We need staff, he needs a job.''

"No, you're trying to prove points, showing him how glamorous your life is now.''

"Penny, that's preposterous. I am not now, nor have I ever been glamorous. And what points would I be trying to prove to Kip? This is a job offer, plain and simple.''

"Well, he's not taking it.''

"Please don't do this to him.''

"Do *what* to him? *I'm* not doing anything to him. *You're* the one!''

"Penny, you're depriving him of a job he wants and needs because you're mad at me for some reason. That's really not fair to him. And what *are* you so mad about anyway? Let's clear this up, please. If I've upset or offended you, I'd like very much to know how.''

"You know perfectly well what you've done, and I'm not in the mood to rehash old business. My son is *not* going to work for you, and that's that!"

"First of all, I have no idea what 'old business' you mean. But whatever it is, I'm sorry. Second, please don't take your anger with me out on Kip. He doesn't deserve to be put in the middle, between us."

"Don't you tell *me* how to deal with *my* child! You're the last person to be telling *anyone* how to deal with people! He is *not* taking the job, and don't you *dare* go behind my back and call him again!" With that, she slammed down the receiver.

Shocked, Rowena sat for a few moments, trembling. She felt guilty, as if she'd been caught watching the trophy tapes, or worse, and couldn't understand why she should feel that way when she'd done nothing wrong. Jumping up, she grabbed her keys, and drove to the nearest liquor store to buy a pack of cigarettes. Home again, she got an ashtray, sat back down at the kitchen table and lit up.

At once dizzy, with a sudden buzzing in her hands and feet, she concentrated on remaining upright in the chair. After a minute or so, the dizziness passed and she took another drag. Then she bent her head into her hand and wept. Here she was, trying so hard to get on with her life and be happy; trying to do something helpful for a young man she loved very much, and her oldest friend started making crazy accusations and hanging up in her ear.

What was happening, and why? It seemed as if every time she took one small step forward, something set her three steps back. Ironically, despite her accusation, it was Penny who was behaving like Claudia. And Claudia at her worst—engaging in a pointless diatribe thinly disguised as disagreement. But while Claudia had had innate charm she could turn off and on at will, Penny had always been a solid, consistent presence. Now, for reasons only she understood, Penny had turned against her. It was one of those hateful situations where Rowena couldn't defend herself and couldn't win.

The cigarette finished, she got up and poured a shot of vodka. While she drank it, she had two more cigarettes. The alcohol and nicotine blurred the edges, dulled the pain, and revived her appetite. She scrambled two eggs, grated some sharp cheddar over top, and ate the concoction right from the pan. At last feeling a bit better, she went upstairs to change into more comfortable clothes.

Sitting on the floor of the dressing room, she pulled on a pair of socks, thinking how Penny's rage would have washed right over Claudia. Then she would have said either, "So, okay. Now that that's out of the way, you want to get together tomorrow night?" or, "Hey! What makes you think I give a shit?" Claudia had had an enviable ability to remain unruffled. And right then Rowena missed her acutely. There had been times when Claudia had been infectiously effervescent and genuinely lovable, in particular the occasion when, soon after Le Rendezvous opened, Rowena had taken Marcia there for dinner.

Breaking into a wide smile, Claudia had come hurrying to hug her, exclaiming, "Ro, this is great. I've been meaning to call and get you over, but it's been wild around here." Her elated smile holding, she'd extended her hand to Marcia. "Hi, I'm Claudia. I'm so glad you could come. Let's get you guys a really good table." After seating them, she summoned their waitress over, and said, "Mae, this is my sister, Rowena, and her friend Marcia. Take special care of them. Okay?"

Claudia then leaned close, one hand on Rowena's shoulder, and said, "Try the chicken, you guys. It's divine. Okay. Enjoy yourselves. I'll be back."

They ordered, and Mae brought them a complimentary bottle of wine. While they each had a glass, Marcia watched an animated Claudia chatting with a couple across the way, saying, "Your sister's gorgeous, Ro. And so cordial."

Rowena had agreed. Claudia had looked like a healthy, seductive teenager in a scoop-necked, long-sleeved, full-skirted black crepe dress that showed off her ample breasts and tiny waist. Cheeks ripe with color, her excitement palpable, she had moved through the restaurant, pausing to talk to her customers, sending complimentary liqueurs to a distinguished-looking middle-aged couple, then laughing with a pair of businessmen at the bar. She was having a wonderful time, and Rowena felt a gush of pride. Claudia was in her element, the star of her own little show and handling it well. Constantly moving, constantly smiling, yet missing nothing, she was impressive.

When Rowena and Marcia were finishing their coffee, she returned to the table, bringing with her a fragrant warmth. "How was it? Did you love the chicken? Isn't it great? Aren't you going to have dessert? Jill's made a fabulous raspberry Pavlova in a meringue shell with lemon cream. Don't you want to try it?"

"It sounds wonderful but I couldn't eat another bite," Rowena had told her.

"What about you?" Claudia asked Marcia.

"Sorry," she said. "I'm stuffed."

"Too bad. It's *so* good. I had some instead of dinner," she confessed with a giggle.

"That sounds like you." Rowena smiled. "Dinner was terrific, but we really should get the check."

"Hey! You're my sister, remember? When you come to my restaurant, it's on the house. Take your time, you guys. I've got to circulate some more, but I'll see you before you leave."

Rowena and Marcia each left five dollars for Mae, then got their coats. Claudia came to shake hands again with Marcia, saying, "It was so nice to meet you. Come back soon. Okay?"

"I will," Marcia said, completely won over.

"Ro." Claudia hugged her again, her cheek hot against Rowena's. "I'm so glad you came," she whispered. "Will you call me?" She let go and stepped back, saying, "Call me. We'll get together and have lunch, or go shopping or something."

"I'll be in touch," Rowena promised. "And thank you for the dinner. Everything was wonderful."

"Good, good. Don't forget to call me, Ro. I mean it. Okay?" She blew a kiss, pivoted on one stiletto heel, and went back to her rounds.

"Your sister's adorable!" Marcia had said as they walked to the car. "And so attractive."

Rowena wept some more, there on the floor of the dressing room, surrounded by Claudia's possessions. She'd loved her sister unreservedly that night. But as time passed, that particular Claudia had showed herself less and less often. Where had she gone? Or had she ever been real? How had she come to be someone who took pleasure in filming her sexual performances? What had caused her to change steadily and irredeemably until that lovable Claudia ceased to exist?

A CD of David Oistrakh performing the Tchaikovsky violin concerto was on the stereo, and she had settled on the sofa to try for a second time that evening to review the cost projections for the patio when the telephone rang.

Hoping to God it wasn't Penny, she picked up the receiver.

It was Kip, calling from a pay phone. He was every bit as angry as his mother, but infinitely more rational.

"I don't *care* what she says, Auntie Ro. I'm taking the job. I *need* it."

"I know you do, Kip. And I'd like you to have it. But your mother doesn't want you working for me, and there's nothing I can do about that.'' She felt actual physical pain at saying this to him. ''I feel terrible about it, but I don't see any way around this.''

''I'm taking the job!'' he insisted.

''Sweetheart, please calm down, and let's talk sensibly. Do you really want to go to war with your mother over this? Because I think that's what it's going to be.''

''If I have to, yes. No way am I gonna sit around on my butt all summer when I could be working, putting money away for school. Come on, Aunt Rowena! I'm gonna be seventeen in September. I'll be a senior next fall. I'm not some clueless twelve-year-old, that my mother has to tell me what I can do. It's insulting, for chrissake. Like I have no brain and can't think for myself. I want the job!'' He hesitated, then said, ''Course, if you've changed your mind, I'm fucked for sure.''

''Let me ask you something, Kip. Just out of curiosity, how d'you think you could swing it?''

''Oh, easy,'' he said, his anger waning quickly. ''I'd make out like I'm still applying at places for the next week or two. Then I'd say I landed a gig at Caldor's or the Grand Union. I've got my own bank account, and Mom would never see my paychecks. I'd deposit them in the ATM machine as soon as I got paid. Easy,'' he repeated. ''Really. Please let me have the job? *Please,* Auntie Ro?''

''I do want to,'' she said, torn. ''But what happens if your mother finds out somehow? She's going to accuse you of being disloyal, and me of going behind her back and employing you for nefarious reasons.''

There was another pause, and he asked, ''Nefarious? Is that like sexual?''

Rowena laughed. ''No, sweetheart. It's like evil.''

''Cool word. Nefarious. Listen, Auntie Ro. I'll deal with Mom if I have to. Okay? I have no clue why she's so griped. When I ask her what's going down, all I get is never mind, it's nothing I'd understand. Like I'm this major chowderhead who doesn't know dick. You didn't have a fight, did you?''

''Kip, I honestly don't know why your mother's so upset. She won't tell me what's bothering her.''

''Well, she's down on Uncle Mark now. She's been raging about him big time the last couple of days.''

''Oh, no. What's Mark supposed to have done?''

''Who knows? It's not like anybody can *talk* to her or anything. I think she's losing it big time. Anyway, can I still have the job?''

An anxious roiling in her chest, she thought for a moment. "I'm probably going to get both of us in even worse trouble, but okay, sweetheart, yes, you can."

"All *right!* Thank you. I knew you'd be fair with me. And don't worry. It'll be okay. You'll see."

"I hope so, for your sake."

They ended the call, and she lit a cigarette, thinking nervously that there was bound to be trouble over this.

As in the immediate aftermath of Claudia's death, Rowena slept poorly that night. Hovering in the shallowest level of sleep, where her conscious self looked on and provided an annoyed running commentary, she repeatedly confronted Penny in an attempt to settle their differences. But Penny remained implacable. The circular, repetitious nature of the argument was maddening, and she told herself either she could lie there, neither truly awake nor asleep, or she could wake up. With a mental heave, she dragged herself awake.

In the dark she started down the stairs and paused, picturing one of the men from the trophy tapes holding a pillow over Claudia's face until she stopped breathing. Then, using a handkerchief to prevent his fingerprints from transferring to anything he touched, he emptied a container of her pills into his pocket, and left it empty on the bedside table. Grabbing the first bottle that came to hand, he swilled some Chivas around in a glass, then carefully poured it back. Upstairs, he wrapped Claudia's lifeless hand around both the glass and the bottle. Then, as a final touch, he held the rim of the glass to her mouth before putting it on the table.

It could have happened that way. Of course an autopsy would have shown an absence of pills and alcohol in her sister's system, which was why Rowena had kept the body intact. Even years after the fact, it could be exhumed and examined.

Yawning, eyes watering, she went to the kitchen, poured a glass of spring water, and sat down at the table to drink it, telling herself she was indulging in grotesque fantasies. Or was she? She might never know how or why Claudia's life came to so premature an end, but that wasn't going to stop her from trying to come to terms with it.

The next morning, badly in need of a boost, she made a trip to the Stamford Town Center where an enthusiastic young woman in the cosmetics department at Macy's gave her a half-hour impromptu lesson in applying makeup. The sight of her altered face in the cosmetician's mirror took her by surprise. If this new image was anything to go by, perhaps she was not as ugly as she'd always believed.

"You look good," the young woman declared judiciously. "And it's not like you need a whole ton of stuff." She began putting boxes on the counter. "Eye shadow, mascara, some blusher and lipstick, and you're a whole other person."

A whole other person, Rowena thought, getting out her credit card. Maybe that wouldn't be such a bad thing. She definitely felt a new self-assurance as she carried her small bag of cosmetics out of the store and she understood, to some extent, why Claudia had so enjoyed her teen-age experimentation. Using makeup was like donning a subtle disguise, a thin mask behind which one could hide in full view.

By late Saturday night, driving home from New Canaan, snug in the luxurious interior of the Mercedes, she had managed for the most part to put Penny behind her and was compiling a mental list of things to be done. She really had to book an appointment to get appraisals of the old oil paintings that she'd stored in the cellar prior to the renovation. And something had to be done about the neglected garden that had once been her father's primary source of comfort and pleasure. She knew little about gardening, but decided that would be her next project.

Early Tuesday morning, she set to work. She redefined the borders of the old flower beds and spent hours weeding the first of them. Then she drove to the nursery and bought flats of flowers and ground cover. As she sat on her heels painstakingly pulling weeds, she remembered her father in worn cotton pants and rolled-up shirtsleeves tenderly placing seedlings in the earth, carefully packing soil around their fragile roots. She saw herself squatting next to him on a mild autumn day, listening closely as he explained how the bulbs he was planting would sleep through the winter and then begin to grow in the warmth of spring. Those bulbs had continued to flower year after year, pushing through the encroaching weeds, and in tearing out the weeds now, she was, after a fashion, paying homage to a man who had left behind an impression of decency and kindness that, like the perennials, refused to die.

She had derived an unparalleled pleasure in that time spent so many years ago with her father, and thought Mark had made a significant point: Her father *had* been a nurturing man. Both she and Cary had benefited from their hushed conversations in his long-ago garden. Claudia, though, had been too young to be influenced by him. By the time she was four years old, he was gone.

Rowena had had seven years of George Graham's affectionate attention, of his patient explanations about how things would flourish if they were well tended and properly nourished. His words now gave direction to her hands as they plucked and planted, gradually returning the shape and color to her father's garden. And her father became clearer, too, as she trimmed the bushes and cleared the earth beneath them, watching earthworms writhe in the upturned soil and beetles scurry for cover. She hoped he was still alive somewhere, perhaps with a second family, with children he'd taught the simple metaphors of the garden. If he was alive, perhaps she could find him.

Ten

Since it was her least favorite way to dine, Rowena was amazed at the number of people who actually wanted to eat outdoors. They were even willing to wait at the bar until a table was free, with the result that the bar receipts rose along with the revenue in general. After two weeks they had to begin taking reservations for the patio. Ian's idea was a huge success.

As well, everyone was taken with Kip. He worked nonstop, refilling the bread baskets, whisking away dirty dishes almost the instant the last knife and fork at a table had been set down, topping off cups of coffee, fetching extra cream, or a spoon, or anything else a customer might request. He was helpful without being obsequious, and willingly pitched in wherever needed. If he noticed the coffee level was getting low he started a fresh pot brewing; if he saw that the wait-staff were busy and a table had been sitting with a tab for several minutes, he scooted over to collect it and take it to Terry who either ran the credit card or rang in the cash. Nothing was too much trouble. Kip even brought in a bottle of Miracle-Gro because he thought the outdoor hanging plants needed extra nutrients.

"He's a honey," Mae told Rowena. "I could eat him up with a spoon."

Rowena couldn't have been happier with Kip, but nevertheless was conscience-stricken for having given him the job in defiance of his mother's wishes. She knew in her bones that Penny was going to find out somehow, and when she did, there was going to be trouble.

When she finally discussed her concerns with Mark over a pasta dinner he cooked for her on the Monday evening after Kip's third week at Le Rendezvous, he heard her out, then said sadly, "It stinks, Ro. Here you do something decent for a very deserving kid, and you have to worry it's going to blow up in your face. Which, I'm sorry to say, could well happen. You'll be interested to know that I'm now on Penny's shit list, too. I wouldn't care particularly, if she wasn't actively campaigning to enlist charter members for the Let's Hate Mark and Rowena Club."

"Don't tell me she's airing her grievances at the Mag." She was horrified. It was her long-held rule that you didn't bring personal problems to work, and she'd believed Penny felt that way too.

"What's awful," he went on, "is it seems to be backfiring. People are more pissed off with her for whatever she's been saying, than with you or me. My chums are still my chums, and yours are still yours, but Penny's been lunching alone a lot lately. I'd feel sorry for her if I didn't think she was behaving like such an absolute wiener."

Rowena sighed. "I wish I knew what was bothering her."

"When are you going to accept this for what it is, Ro? For the hundredth time—it's jealousy. I have two older sisters, remember. Believe me, I know the signs intimately."

"I believe you. I just can't comprehend why. It's so pointless."

"Tell that to the Israelis and the Palestinians."

"That's religious," she said. "It's different."

"Most of the world's turmoil has a religious base, supposedly. But what it's really about is jealous individuals battling for ascendancy."

"I don't know that I subscribe to it, but that's an interesting theory." She used a piece of French bread to mop the last of the sauce from the plate, then popped it into her mouth. "Delicious, my darling."

"Thank you. In my humble opinion, the majority of people operate from the lofty notion, however deluded, that what they've got is better than what you've got, be it race, religion, or whatever. On top of that, you don't deserve what you've got, so to drive my point home, I'll take it away from you. Check out the synonyms, cupcake—resentment, ill will, distrust, rivalry. It fits Penny's behavior lately to a T. Think of her as a Serb and yourself as a Muslim."

"God, Mark! What a horrible analogy!"

"Maybe, but accurate. Kip and I have talked on the phone a fair bit since he started working at the restaurant, and his level of anxiety's pretty high. He thinks his mother's wrong, but she *is* his mother after all, and he's a loyal kid. He wants everybody to kiss and make up, so things can go back to the way they were. I've tried to explain, without dumping on Penny, why that's unlikely to happen. But, like you, he doesn't really get it."

"He hasn't said a word to me," she said, feeling even worse now.

"You've gone out on a limb for him, Ro. He's very aware of that, and doesn't want to come whining to you about his home life."

"But he knows he can always talk to me."

"This time it's different. It's an adult situation and he wants to deal in an adult fashion. And that means not running to Auntie Ro to tell her how rocky things are at home."

"I guess you've got a point," she said.

"Yes, I do. So, not to change the subject or anything, but I'd like to bring a friend to dinner Friday night. Are you full up, or could you pencil me in?"

"Sure. Which friend?"

"Someone I met at the support group," he said, with a self-conscious smile. "It could be something, but it's probably nothing. He's decent, and we've gone for coffee a couple of times. Last week he asked if I wanted to get together, so I suggested we do dinner at your place. That way you can check him out and tell me what you think."

"Bringing him home to mother, huh?" She smiled.

"Well, sort of."

"What time do you want to come?" she asked, thinking he was probably anxious about seeing someone new after so many years with Tim.

"Eightish?"

"No problem. Consider yourself booked. So, are you going to tell me anything about him?"

"Nope. I want you completely open-minded."

"Fair enough. How do you feel about it?"

He grimaced. "Nervous, and kind of guilty. But basically okay, I guess. It's time for me to start reconnecting, and I know it. And speaking of connecting, did the shrink ever call you again?"

"He left a message about a week ago, but I didn't phone him back."

"Why not?"

"The truth?"

"Definitely. I want to know what's going on with you, Ro. Dessert now or later?"

"Later, please, but I'd love some coffee."

"Coming right up."

She moved to help him clear the table but he said, "Go sit on the sofa and let me do this. You could throw on another CD if you want."

She put on an old remastered Frank Sinatra album, then curled up on the sofa and watched as with quick efficiency Mark loaded the dishwasher before plugging in the kettle.

"You were about to tell me why you didn't return the shrink's call," he reminded her, getting mugs from the cupboard.

"If you recall, according to Claudia the two of them were a hot item."

"And you're not interested in your sister's leftovers, imagined or real." He leaned against the counter.

"That's right. And if he's not after something, then he's only trying to be kind, and I don't need that."

"What, like he thinks you're a charity case?"

"Maybe."

"Rowena, why would he think that?"

She shrugged.

"You're short and ugly, so he couldn't possibly have any genuine interest in you. Right?"

She shrugged again.

"You break my heart. You know that? *When* are you going to get *over* this? How do you know he didn't take one look and decide you were his favorite flavor?"

She barked out a laugh. "That's highly doubtful, my darling."

"I hate it when you do this," he said quietly. "I really do. You're more attractive than Claudia ever could've hoped to be. There's not one single synthetic thing about you. And if you lived someplace like Manhattan instead of in your basic commuter town full of yuppie schmucks and their perfect families, you'd have guys climbing all over you. But okay." He threw up his arms in a gesture of surrender. "I can see you want to argue, so I'll drop it."

"If he calls again, maybe I'll meet him for lunch. Okay?"

"Hey! Don't go doing it to prove something to me, Ro. Why not meet the man and at least find out what he wants?"

"He probably won't call again."

"What an attitude." He shook his head and reached for the coffee canister.

Mark's friend Richard was in his early forties, about six feet tall, solidly built and very well dressed, in a slate gray suit, crisp white shirt with a hairline burgundy stripe, and a dark gray silk tie. His nose was slightly too long, and his deep-set brown eyes had a mournful cast behind gold wire-framed glasses, but he was appealing, with a shy smile and a direct gaze. Rowena liked him at once.

Leading them to the best table for two by the front window, she said, "I'm so glad to meet you, Richard."

"Me, too, you. Mark speaks of you often."

"Don't make it sound as if all I do is talk about her," Mark complained. "She'll go all vain on us." His color was high and he looked happier than he had in a long time, especially when Kip came hurrying over.

"Hey, hi, Uncle Mark. I didn't know you were coming. This is way cool."

Mark introduced Richard, and the two shook hands.

"I gotta bus a table," Kip said, "but I'll swing back. Okay? Nice meeting you, Richard."

After he'd gone, Rowena set down menus and a wine list, then glanced over to the entry where a couple was waiting. "Have whatever you want, please, and take your time. I'll stop back when I get a chance."

Every so often she looked over to see how they were getting on. At one point, the two men burst out laughing, and she smiled automatically. Richard obviously had a good sense of humor—something Mark considered a must in any friend. It had to be difficult for both of them, hampered as they both were by memories of the love they'd had, and lost, but she hoped this worked out. Mark wasn't meant to live alone. Evidently, Richard wasn't either.

When Doug delivered the complimentary bottle of wine, both men looked over and raised their glasses to her. She smiled, then turned as the front door opened, and Tony Reid walked in with another, older, man.

For a few seconds she was immobilized by shock. What on earth was he doing there? And why had he chosen to come to the restaurant on the night Mark was there too? That dull pain gripped her midriff again and she was suddenly sweating as she summoned back her smile.

Reid approached with a smile of his own and his hand out, saying, "Ms. Graham, how are you? This is Colin Innes, a colleague visiting from London. We don't have a reservation, but I was hoping you might be able to squeeze us in."

"Rowena, please," she said. Flummoxed, she shook hands with both men, then scanned the restaurant, aware there were no available tables but using the time to try to collect herself. "We're full, but if you don't mind sitting at the bar, I could serve you there."

"That would do nicely for me," Innes said in a plummy upper class accent, giving her a toothy smile.

"It's very good of you, Rowena," Reid said gratefully.

"Not at all."

She got them seated, then asked Ian to keep an eye on things for a few minutes while she went downstairs to the women's room. She held her wrists under the cold water, then dabbed some on her throat and the back of her neck, trying to cool down. Finally, she examined her reflection in the mirror and for a moment didn't recognize the woman with the closely cropped hair and cosmetically enlarged eyes gazing back at her. For a few seconds she admired the mirror image. Then familiarity clicked in and what she saw was the same troll's face that looked out at her from every mirror.

Why had Reid come? And what was he after? Stop fussing, she told herself. She had nothing he could possibly want, and therefore no cause to fear him. Reid would have dinner and go. And that would be the end of it.

Returning upstairs, she stopped to tell Mark in an undertone about Reid's unscheduled arrival.

"Oh, this is *very* interesting," he said gleefully. "This I've got to see. Which one is he?"

"The very tall dark one at the bar."

Mark leaned forward slightly, took a quick look, then sat back with raised eyebrows. "Well, now I know why Claudia was busy fantasizing. That is one glorious man. And look at you, my little cupcake," he teased. "You've gone all dazed and dewy. I want a full and detailed report tomorrow."

"You're impossible. And you're mistaking panic for interest."

"Oh, right."

"Would you give me a break, please?" Her face was burning, the ache inside had intensified.

"Don't let him get to you," Richard said. "That is one very handsome man, though, Rowena."

"I will kill the two of you in my first free minute. Count on death for dessert."

"Oh, I'm so scared, Richard," Mark said in an undertone, his green eyes bright with merriment. "Thumbelina's going to hurt us. Oh, help, *help.*"

Overheated, she laughed and turned away.

Reid couldn't have been more genial. He broke off conversation with his friend to smile when she came to take their order, and listened attentively to her recitation of the evening's specials.

"Everything sounds delectable," he said. "What would you recommend?"

Skewered by his eyes, she said, "The red snapper is very good. My personal favorite is the angel hair pasta with smoked chicken, sun-dried tomatoes, black olives, and artichoke hearts, in a white wine sauce."

With a hint of innuendo in his deep voice, he said, "I'll have your personal favorite," and she felt her face burning but kept her eyes on the ticket as she wrote out the order.

"Since your personal favorite's been taken," Innes said, "I shall try the red snapper."

"I'm sure you'll like it," she told him, and headed for the kitchen, asking Ian en route to bring them complimentary glasses of wine.

Upon emerging from the kitchen she circulated among the tables, acutely aware of Reid's massive presence. He was far too large to ignore, and despite the air-conditioning she was perspiring as she paused to talk to the patrons. Claudia would have taken this in stride, but Rowena had never been pursued, and if that was indeed what was happening she didn't think she cared for it. It was debilitating and made her want to hide somewhere and weep.

By ten o'clock the remaining diners—three tables on the patio and four inside—were lingering over coffee and liqueurs. She went to sit with Mark and Richard, asking, "How was your dinner?"

"Everything was wonderful," Richard said. "I have to ask you. Is he *really* a psychiatrist? He definitely doesn't look the part."

"He really is," she confirmed. "I've been to his office."

"Which, of course, is very large," Richard quipped.

Rowena stared at him for a second or two then began laughing almost uncontrollably.

"Oh, no," Mark said sotto voce, "you're not interested. What a liar! And he's been watching you practically nonstop. I do not think charity comes into this, cupcake."

"Stop it," she pleaded.

"You stop it," he countered. "Why can't you just enjoy it?"

"I can't, so stop. Okay?"

"The music's a big improvement. Tell the barkeep I approve."

"I'll do that."

"So? Anything to report?"

"Mark!"

"Such a disappointment. I was hoping for a little drama."

"Leave her alone now," Richard interjected. "Rowena doesn't think this is funny."

"Thank you, Richard," she said gratefully.

"You're welcome. Anyway, you talk a good game, Mark. I bet you'd have a coronary if anything did happen."

"You're right. I probably would," he admitted. "Ro and I bonded my first day at the Mag when this woman came in and tried to return some books she'd had out for over a year. She started shrieking when she found out how much the fines were. Ro and I looked at each other and promptly took off for lunch together."

"God!" She laughed. "I knew we had lunch that day but I'd forgotten why. It was awful."

"What happened to the woman in the end?" Richard asked.

"I think they settled on half what was due," Rowena told him.

Mark glanced at his watch, then said, "We should get going. Richard has to work in the morning."

"Oh? What do you do, Richard?" Rowena asked, getting up to walk with them to the door.

"Nothing very exciting. I have a menswear store in Southport."

"A very upscale store," Mark put in. "I dropped a bundle just stopping in to say hi. From now on, we say hi by phone." He grinned at Richard, then turned back to Rowena. "Seriously, Ro. The dinner was superb."

"And thank you for the wine," Richard added. "That was very generous of you, Rowena."

"My pleasure. I hope to see you again very soon." She shook Richard's hand before giving Mark a hug, saying, "You, I will see tomorrow."

"Believe it. I'll want a full report."

"Go home!" She laughed and held open the door, wishing she could leave with them. The stomach-ache was getting worse.

Mark leaned close to whisper, "Try to enjoy it, cupcake."

"I don't think I'm capable of it," she whispered back truthfully.

"Yes, you are. Just be open-minded."

She remained in the doorway for a minute, watching them walk off up the street. Then, she closed the door, took a deep breath, and went to the bar to invite Reid and his companion to shift to one of the free tables where they'd be more comfortable.

"Please join us for a drink," Innes invited. "I'd like the opportunity to compliment you on your restaurant."

"That's very kind," she began, "but—"

"Join us, Rowena," Reid urged, his eyes boring into hers. "Please."

"All right," she relented, unable to see any way out. "Give me five minutes."

She sent Kip to take their dessert order while she did a quick check of the patio and the kitchen. Everything was under control. Nothing required her immediate attention. Too bad. She was going to have to sit down with Reid and attempt to make conversation. She paused at the bar for some fortification in the form of Cointreau over ice before at last joining Reid and his friend.

Both men got to their feet upon her arrival, and she found this courteous display charmingly quaint. Innes, who appeared to be in his early sixties, and had the slightly disheveled appearance of a long-time bachelor, launched into a detailed, most complimentary commentary on everything he'd eaten.

Painfully aware of Reid, she steadily sipped the Cointreau and listened. When she looked over and met Reid's crystalline gaze, she was taken aback by the seriousness of his expression. What was wrong? A second or two and his features relaxed, and again he smiled.

"Colin is a foodie," he explained. "There's nothing he likes better than trying new restaurants, unusual things to eat."

"I'd prefer an epithet a tad politer. Gourmet, perhaps." Innes made a face. "'Foodie' is so—argotic."

Rowena decided he was the perfect match of person to country. Innes was England: formal but genial, compact and mature. She laughed, and he was visibly puzzled. "Argotic is very good," she congratulated him.

"Is it?" Innes looked even more puzzled.

"In a previous life," Reid clarified, "Rowena was a librarian."

"Ah, well," said the older man. "That would of course explain her appreciation of linguistic distinctions."

Rowena laughed again and repeated, "Of course." She loved his rounded vowels and carefully articulated consonants. He had a splendid speaking voice.

"Might one ask how you and this outsized fellow came to meet?" he asked her.

Just then, Kip arrived with the desserts and coffee. Aware that this was one of those occasions when the smallest amount of alcohol would turn her tipsy, Rowena asked him to bring her some coffee.

"Coming right up," Kip said brightly, and hustled off to get another cup.

"Is it Dr. Innes? Are you also a psychiatrist?" she asked him.

"I am, although I'm no longer in private practice. I've been teaching the past few years."

"I've always wondered. Do your analytical faculties operate full-time, or do you turn them on for office hours?"

"An interesting question," Innes said.

"Very," Reid concurred, as Kip slid a cup of coffee in front of Rowena and she whispered a thank-you.

"I think," Innes answered between bites of a summer pudding oozing fresh berries, "one does or does not have an analytical bent. If one does, regardless of one's profession, I think it tends to operate full-time, but at different levels. Awareness, after all, is always there. It's a matter really of the degree of attention one pays. And that would be the determining factor. So, in answer to your question, I'd have to offer the analogy of the three-way light bulb. It can be turned on to varying degrees of brightness, and I would suggest that one's skills operate similarly."

"In other words," Rowena said, "the answer is yes, to a degree."

"Nicely put, Rowena. And that's what you get, Colin, for being a pompous old curmudgeon. Whatever happened," Reid asked, "to a simple yes or no?"

To Rowena's delight, Innes burst into a red-faced fit of laughter that stripped away the years, making it possible to see the clever and playful little boy he'd once been. As well, she found herself warming to Tony Reid, and had to wonder why she'd been so suspicious of him.

"It's true," Innes told Rowena. "The older I grow, the more pompous I become. It seems exponential."

"It seems," Reid disagreed, "fatuous. He tends to get this way in the company of pretty women. Underneath the professorial crust, he's a marshmallow with an eye for the ladies."

"You'll ruin the good impression I've made," Innes complained. "Has he ruined it?"

"Not at all," Rowena said, trying to relax her abdominal muscles, which had contracted abruptly at Reid's referring to her as a pretty woman. She was going to have to revise her concept of him. Finland was no longer apt. Denmark seemed more appropriate. The Danes had humor, unlike their lugubrious Finnish neighbors who enjoyed gloom—in the same way Jeanne used to say that Rowena's grandmother had enjoyed ill health. Recalling this set her laughing.

"You appear to be in very high spirits," Innes observed.

"It's the liqueur," she explained. "I have an unpredictable capacity for alcohol. Sometimes I can drink a glass or two of wine and I'm fine. Other times, half a teaspoon turns me silly. Tonight happens to be one of the latter occasions."

"Oh, lovely! My late mother-in-law was very like that," Innes said, "which is why we only allowed her a thimbleful of sweet sherry at Christmas. Anything more and she tended to recite naughty limericks while doing unseemly bits of business with lamp shades."

"Is that true?" Rowena asked.

"Not a word of it." He erupted into more red-faced laughter, in which Rowena joined merrily. Mark had been right. She was capable of enjoying the situation.

"If you're not already spoken for," Innes said upon regaining his breath, "perhaps you'd consider the offer of my hand in marriage. It's rather an aged, unattractive hand, but it could be yours."

Impulsively she put her hand in his and said, "That's the nicest offer I've had today and I'll give it serious consideration."

"Don't you dare!" Reid warned. "He has all sorts of offensive habits. You'd be very unhappy. Besides, it's not fair. I haven't had a chance to state my case, or even take you to lunch."

"Oh, dear," Innes said. "The lad's got his blood up. I expect we'll have to duel at dawn."

"You're both crazy as bedbugs," Rowena said happily. "I hate to break up the party, but I've got to make the rounds again."

"Please consider my proposal while you do, dear lady," Innes said.

"Don't you dare!" Reid warned a second time, grinning.

A short time later, Reid beckoned her back to the table to say, "There seems to be some mistake, Rowena. We haven't been charged for the wine."

"No mistake. It's on the house." Extending her hand to him, she said, "Thank you for coming. It's been good to see you again." To Innes, she said, "It was wonderful meeting you. Please come see me next time you're over."

"Indeed I will," he promised, holding her hand warmly in both his own.

The patio had been swept, and Mikey and Kip were stacking the chairs under the awning while Luke carried the candles to the service area. Everything still under control; nothing needed her attention.

Reid and Innes were almost to the front door when she came back through the restaurant. Reid left his friend and approached her to say, "Have lunch with me one day next week."

Her lungs heaved and she wanted to say, It was just a lark. We were only playing. Don't make it real. I don't know how to protect myself from someone like you. I'd fall in love and make a fool of myself. "I work lunches every day," she said with what she hoped was outward calm.

"All right, then. Dinner."

"Why?" she asked, daring to look directly into his very clear eyes.

"Why not?"

She didn't have a ready answer. "Call me," she said, "and we'll see."

"Are you this hard to pin down with everyone?"

"Unh-hunh."

He laughed, kissed her on the cheek, and said, "It was fun. Cointreau brings out the best in you. So I'll call you, and we'll see."

Stunned, she watched as he went back to Innes who waved and blew a kiss before going out the door.

"Who *was* that?" Mae asked, a trayful of dishes held aloft, her eyes on Reid.

"Claudia's shrink," Rowena answered, her eyes on him too.

"No way!"

"Yes way."

"No way!" Mae insisted. "Shrinks are terminally ugly, squadgy dudes with dandruff, thousand-year-old suits, and critically flawed personalities. That guy's *gorgeous.*"

Rowena made an offhanded gesture.

"You don't think he is?" Mae asked, staggered.

"He's all right, I suppose."

"All right? You cannot be serious. He kissed *my* cheek, I'd follow him home. But okay. Never mind."

Mae carried the tray out to the kitchen, and Rowena shook herself into action, relieved the evening was finally over. She was exhausted, as if she'd spent four hours running nonstop. She decided that if Reid did call, she'd go out with him. But she knew he wouldn't call, because he'd only been being kind.

Eleven

On arriving home that night it occurred to her that there was a way to verify at least part of what Tony Reid had told her about Claudia's behavior.

She went down to the cellar to look through a large collection of cartons containing both her mother's and sister's personal papers. While she was incapable of simply consigning these to the trash, she'd put off going through the boxes, reluctant to begin what was bound to be a tedious chore.

Starting with the newer-looking cartons, she managed to locate the right one fairly quickly. She lugged it up to the kitchen and left it on the table. After a quick shower, she sat down in her pajamas with a cup of tea and Claudia's address book to examine her sister's telephone bills.

According to Reid, Claudia had started calling him approximately three or four months prior to her death—which would have been in the late summer or early autumn of the previous year. Rowena found the Southern New England Telephone bills, put them in order by month, then started going through them.

Greenwich was outside the local calling area so those charges were listed separately. Between January and August there were only a few calls to Reid's office number, most likely when Claudia had phoned to make appointments. In August there had been four calls to his office, and two to his home; in September four more to the office, and four to his home; in October nine to the office, and eleven to his home. Not the "dozens" Reid had spoken of, but a fair number.

Lighting a cigarette, she thought back. Claudia had started talking about her affair with Reid sometime in August when she'd mentioned him in passing during one of their infrequent conversations. Then she had, most unusually, begun phoning once or twice a week and Rowena had been of two minds about this: On one level she suspected her sister had turned gloating into an art form; on the other she found Claudia's energetic monologues so entertaining that she hoped perhaps they'd arrived at a new plateau where communication between them might be ongoing. But then the calls came less often, so that by the time of her death it had been several weeks since the telephone rang and Rowena had picked it up to hear her sister say, "Ro, Ro, Ro, *when* are you going to come see your little sister? You *never* want to come out to play anymore." She'd laughed her silvery laugh, and sailed on. "I went completely crazy at Bergdorf's yesterday, spent a *fortune*. There was this darling dress that would've looked so good on you. The most marvelous heliotrope color. Which, of course, you'd *never* wear, but you should. You should get *out* of those nun's habits and into some- thing *pretty*. I almost bought it for you. But I knew you'd only go red in the face and make me take it back, so I didn't buy it. But I would have, if I'd thought there was any chance you'd wear it. You wouldn't wear something like that, would you?"

A heliotrope dress. Rowena knuckled away tears, took another drag on her cigarette, and went back to the bills, noting that her Stamford number was listed eight times in September and fourteen in October. It was true. They had spoken more often then than they had in years. Had those calls been Claudia's clumsy attempts to reach out for help? *You never want to come out to play anymore.* Also true. But it wasn't safe, Claudia. People got hurt playing with you.

She sighed, put out the cigarette, and drank the last of the now-cold tea. Going by the bills, Reid had exaggerated the extent of Claudia's telephone harassment. But perhaps twenty calls in a month had been enough to prompt him to end their doctor-patient relationship—a fact borne out by there having been only one further call to his office in November, and none thereafter.

Reasonably satisfied, Rowena tossed everything back into the box. It was almost two in the morning and she was too tired to ponder the matter of how many unwanted telephone calls might constitute ha- rassment. It was like one of those awful questions on a math exam in- volving two trains, each traveling at so many miles per hour, and how long it would take to arrive at their destinations. Leaving the box parked by the back door, she went up to bed.

She couldn't get to sleep and lay, eyes closed, listening to the hum of the air conditioner in the window, feeling again the Cointreau-inspired giddiness, the commingled panic and stimulation Reid had inspired: all the symptoms of attraction, which she intended to ignore, unwilling to put whatever peace of mind she had on the line for any man. Affairs always brought varying degrees of anxiety, and after the three years of on-again, off-again involvement with Gil Prasker, she'd vowed never again to compromise herself, in any way, for the sake of romance. In the two years since they'd split up, she'd been sailing along on calm waters—until Claudia died. Now her life had been redirected and she found herself grappling with leftovers of her sister's that came in many forms, remembering things long forgotten, and wishing she could have back her previously placid existence.

She did retrieve it again during her hours in the garden, and in the afternoons spent reading and listening to music. But the life she lived was no longer safe and sheltered, as it had been at the library. People, men, had access to her now. They could simply walk into the restaurant, as Reid had, placing themselves in her sight-line and insisting she pay attention. Smiles and laughter, compliments and kisses on the cheek. She'd have to be careful. No matter what happened she would *not* get involved.

It was late in the evening and she was curled up on the sofa in her pajamas, watching television, when the doorbell rang. She went barefoot through the hall and opened the door expecting to see Mark but there stood Tony Reid, in chinos and an open-necked navy blue shirt. Speechless, she stepped back and allowed him to enter.

"You can't keep avoiding me forever," he said, looking troubled as he closed the door.

"I'm not avoiding you," she lied. "I just don't know you."

"Of course you do. Think about it."

It was true, she thought, looking at his exotic eyes made deeper and darker by the blue of his shirt, then at his mouth. She did know him. And, even more extraordinary, he knew her, too. So what was her reason for avoiding him? She couldn't answer. She was very aware of being naked under the cotton pajamas, and crossed her arms over her chest.

He smiled rather sadly at this and said, "That wasn't necessary, Rowena. No one's going to attack you."

"It's late and I'm tired. What do you want, Dr. Reid?"

"What we both want," he answered unaffectedly.

God! Now she was in trouble. He'd effortlessly taken control of the situation, and she had no idea how to retrieve it.

He moved closer and ran a hand over her hair, across her cheek, down around her neck. Her mouth suddenly dry, her arms fell to her sides as she waited to see what he'd do next. Anticipation caused her abdominal muscles to clench, made it difficult to catch her breath.

She'd fought so hard not to succumb to her intense attraction to him, and her efforts were suddenly inconsequential.

His hand was heavy and warm on her neck. She relished the feel of it, wanting more. Her heartbeat accelerating, she had to tilt her head back in order to see his face, to absorb the contrast of his black hair and milky skin. A flurry of fear shivered down her spine as she waited for his hand to move again. She willed it to move. The initiative had to be his.

He smiled and bent to kiss her cheek as his hand boldly slid under the pajama top to cover her breast. Her control evaporated. She looped an arm around his neck, keeping him bent toward her so she could press her lips to his cheek, breathing in his scent.

"You're very sweet," he murmured.

Now she smiled, but couldn't speak. Her fingertips played over the smooth nape of his neck, sending encoded messages, revealing what Mark had guessed about her the very first time they met: that she'd long been hiding her instincts under layers of calculated clothing, concealing an appetite that, alarmingly, grew greater with every passing year.

His free hand lifted her chin, then closed around her throat, holding her captive. It frightened her. Heat turned so quickly to cold that her fingertips felt numb. "Let me go," she said softly, wondering if it was he who had killed Claudia, and if he was capable of killing her now, too. All he had to do was tighten that huge hand around her neck, and she'd strangle. It wouldn't take unusual strength to snuff out the life of one small unattractive woman. "Claudia may have been beautiful," she explained in a whisper, "but, you see, I was the one with a heart."

"Poor Rowena, you keep getting everything wrong." He smiled in that same sad fashion and released her.

The heat flooded back into her body, fusing her mental circuitry so that the instincts for once had dominion. Without taking her eyes from his, she shed the pajamas, then wound herself around him as he lifted her.

Shutting her mind to images of her sister on the trophy tapes, they made love on the sofa. She climbed onto his lap and, with breath held, impaled herself in a slow descent. She had to remain very still for a time—her heart rapping in a crazed tattoo—until her body softened, accepting. The television set cast multicolored shadows over them, flickering bursts of light. She was frantic with excitement and kept

losing the rhythm, floundering. His hands on her hips held her an-
chored outside while her skeleton seemed to collide with the fleshed
parts of her body and her brain finally short-circuited and disconnected altogether. She had to close her eyes and trust him not to let her
fall.

This was the sexual encounter she'd been anticipating her entire adult
life. She had never been so frighteningly aroused, and wondered, in a
last rational moment, if it was possible to die from such an utter loss
of control. She didn't care if she did die. Her prior experiences had
been only faintly stimulating, mere suggestions of what might be possible. She'd kept her senses alive with exotic sights and fragrances. Now
she was discovering the full extent of her appetite, and it was enormous.

The ride culminated in a seizure so violent that it sent her briefly to
the surface of sleep, and she opened her eyes, appalled to discover she
was on her back with her hand between her splayed legs, her body
quivering in the aftermath of orgasm. Withdrawing her hand, she
clamped her knees together, turned onto her side and plunged, exhausted, back into sleep.

In the shower the next morning it returned to her, and she leaned
against the wall with the water beating down on her and wept in angry
humiliation at the realization that she had, with so little provocation,
revealed herself thoroughly in the dream. Pathetic creature, she
thought miserably. All that crap about giving up men but throwing
yourself open like a vault in your sleep.

After a time, her perennial common sense prevailing, she straightened and reached for the shampoo. Nothing so terrible had happened,
really. It wasn't as if she'd never touched herself before. There had been
too many occasions after Gil had climbed from her bed and gone
home, when she'd been left dangling and had quickly finished for herself what he had started. She alone knew what she did in the privacy of
her bedroom, in the sanctity of her dreams.

"So what did you think of Richard?" Mark asked. "The truth. And
what's that?" He pointed to the carton by the back door.

"Some of Claudia's bills I was going through last night. What did
you think of Richard?" she countered, taking the French toast from
the griddle.

He drank some coffee before asking, "Why were you going through
her bills in the middle of the night?"

She smiled over at him. "I feel like the mother of a five-year-old. I was looking for something, okay? And it was not the middle of the night."

"Oooo, grouchy. Not enough sleep, or the wrong side of the bed?"

"You're supposed to be telling me about Richard," she prompted, bringing the food to the table.

"I think he's incredibly decent. Shy, but truthful. That was what impressed me when he joined the support group. He made such a monumental effort to be open about his feelings, even though it was difficult, because he knew he needed help. I admired that, because he's a very private person."

"Oh, please, Mark. That 'private person' business is such garbage. We're *all* very private people. Could we just agree that the man is shy?"

"We are *way* beyond merely grouchy this morning." He held his hands up palms outward, as if to ward off blows. "Something happen last night?"

"I'm sorry. I'm just tired. For the record, I liked Richard. He's unpretentious. He's got a good sense of humor. And he dresses beautifully."

"All true. I like him, too. The thing is I don't know how much. My feelings are out of whack. Tim and I were together thirteen years. It's forever. Most of the men I know would give anything to have something half as good as what Tim and I had, that would last even half as long. It's a whole other world out there now and I'm not sure I know how it operates."

"You seemed to be managing well. Both of you did. I think you're a good match."

"Really?"

"Really."

"You're not just being kind?"

"Mark, he's very likable. And the two of you seemed to be enjoying each other. Did you have a good time?"

"Yeah, as a matter of fact, I did."

"But the past keeps getting in the way."

He looked over at her. "Yeah, it does. Big time."

"Don't you think it's the same for Richard?"

"It probably is. I hadn't considered that."

"It takes time. There's no big rush, is there?"

"No, not really." He gazed at her for a long moment, then said, "You're a smart little cookie, aren't you?"

"I have my moments."

"So, how did it go with the shrink?"

She thought of the previous night's dream activities and drank some coffee to ease the sudden constriction in her throat.

"What happened?" he asked cannily. "You've got telltale color in your cheeks."

She laughed and shook her head. "*Nothing happened!* He makes me very nervous. Okay?"

"That's because you find him attractive."

For a moment she was on the verge of tears. Then it passed and she was able to say, "You'll be interested to know I managed to get bombed on one Cointreau, so I found everything hilarious."

"Gee, am I ever sorry I missed that. I know how entertaining you can be on half a glass of the hard stuff. No wonder you're so miserable this morning. You've got a teeny-tiny hangover."

She laughed again.

He ate some of his French toast before saying, "So, did he ask you out?"

"As a matter of fact, he did." Heat once more rushed into her face, and she paid close attention to her food.

"Why does this embarrass you, Ro? Seriously. I want to know. And what did you tell him?"

"Seriously? I hate the whole game—being on display, hoping someone will come along and legitimize you. It's that dreary hogwash about being popular that Jeanne thought was so important—doing anything to make yourself attractive to men, so you'll be rescued from the horrors of life as a single woman. I gave all that up after Gil."

"If I'd dated a dork like that, I'd give up on men, too. I never understood what you were doing with that guy."

"Nobody else wanted me," she said quietly. "It's not as if I was in a position to be choosy."

For several moments he chewed his food and sat staring at her. "So," he spoke at last, "you told the shrink no go."

"Basically, yes."

"Let me be sure I've got this right. The man comes all the way up to New Canaan from Greenwich, with a friend in tow, to have dinner in your restaurant. He spends most of his time while he's there following you around with his eyes, and you think he's got a hidden agenda. He'd have to, because he couldn't possibly be attracted to someone as ugly as you, with so little going for her. Have I got it right?"

"More or less."

"Okay. Tell me. What's the worst thing that could happen, Rowena?"

I'll make a fool of myself and he'll walk away laughing. "I'm not interested in getting involved."

"You see having a meal with the man as an involvement?"

"Come on, Mark. It's no different for me than it is for you. You were just agonizing over a dinner with Richard, were you not?"

"Yeah. But at least I *went*. You won't even risk that much."

"When are you seeing Richard again?"

"Next Sunday. We're going to have lunch, see a movie. The thing is, neither of us knows how we feel. So for now we're friends, with the added benefit of knowing where we've been. I think part of your problem is the shrink makes you nervous because you don't know where *he's* been. Am I right?"

She thought about that, and answered, "Yes."

"Here's how I see it: He's so good-looking you feel like a hag by comparison. Have I got that right?"

"Yes."

"Has it occurred to you that maybe he finds *you* so good-looking it makes *him* feel like Rumpelstiltskin?"

She laughed and said, "Nice try."

"I think it's the truth, but never mind. If he calls up and asks, will you go?"

"I might."

"Well," he said with a shrug, "I guess that's progress. So what's with going through your sister's stuff in the middle of the night?"

"I wanted to verify what Reid told me about her harassing him with dozens of phone calls. There weren't dozens, but one month she did get up to twenty."

"Hey, if you don't want even one call from somebody, twenty would be way too many."

"This is true."

They ate in silence for a few minutes.

"Very good chow," he said, helping himself to more coffee.

"Speaking of food, I was wondering if you'd like to come for dinner on Wednesday."

"Absolutely. But don't think you're fooling me. I know it's your birthday, cupcake. I was going to invite you out, but if you'd prefer not to celebrate, I understand. How d'you feel about turning forty?"

"Mostly relieved, glad I'm not young anymore. Come as soon as you get home. You can keep me company while I cook. And don't you *dare* buy me a present! Don't even *think* about it! I mean it, Mark."

"You're acting very strange today, my crazy little cabbage. What aren't you telling me?"

"What would you say if I told you that Claudia filmed herself in bed with her boyfriends?" she asked with a dismayingly obvious throb in her voice.

He studied her eyes, asking, "You found tapes, is that it?"

She nodded.

"A few or a lot?"

"Quite a few. I didn't bother going through all of them."

"Different guys on each tape?"

Another nod.

"Was the shrink on tape?"

"God, no!"

He drank more coffee, his eyes still on hers. "You watched them and now you feel like a perv. Right?"

"Something like that."

A slow smile took shape on his mouth and he reached over to stroke her cheek. "Don't be offended, but you are so adorably naive." He withdrew his hand, saying, "People keep souvenirs. Obviously, Claudia was into visuals. It's not the first time I've heard of it. Unfortunately, it's clear it's the first time *you* have."

"You actually know people who tape themselves making love?"

"Some, sure. It's about on a par with mirrors on the ceiling—narcissism, basically. Some people get off on seeing themselves in action. Not my kind of thing, but there you are. What'd you do with the tapes, toss 'em?"

"I cut them into small pieces and *then* I tossed them."

He laughed gently at her vehemence. "So they're gone. That's the end of it."

"But they were *obscene,* Mark."

"Oh, I sincerely doubt that. Any bondage?"

She shook her head.

"Whips and chains? Embellishments?"

Another shake of her head.

"Torture, blood, pain?"

"Mark!"

"Hey, I'm not kidding. People get into *very* weird stuff."

"I'd prefer not to know, thank you."

"So it was your fundamentally straight, hetero humping, then?"

"I guess."

"If that's the reason for your mood, you're overreacting. Trust me. I've seen and heard way worse."

"Honestly?"

"Believe it. There are a *lot* of people in this world who think they deserve to be punished for their preferences—whatever they are—and they've devised unbelievable means of accomplishing that."

"That's sad."

"Yes, it is," he agreed.

"It has been worrying me," she confessed.

"My advice is forget it and stop worrying. So you watched your sister being naughty, and maybe you got a little turned on. That doesn't make you a perv, Ro. It just means you're human."

She bent her face into her hands to hide her embarrassment, then straightened, saying, "I wish I'd told you sooner. I'd have saved myself a lot of anxiety."

"You really shouldn't keep things bottled up. It's not healthy. This was eating at you, but if I hadn't kept pushing you wouldn't have said anything. Didn't I come whining to you about Richard?"

"You didn't whine. And, besides, you've had a very rough time."

"So have you, but you don't seem to see it that way."

"I haven't at all," she argued.

"You have, but never mind. Next time something comes up and you're having trouble, tell me. It's what friends are for, Rowena. I'm not purely decorative, you know."

"Sure you are. Living art with a functional brain."

"I think I'm insulted."

"Don't be. I love you dearly."

"I love you, too, Ro. And I mean what I said. Don't sit around driving yourself nuts. *Tell* me!"

"Okay, I will. Thank you."

"And one last thing. The shrink thinks you're anything *but* ugly. Trust me on this. I was *there* and he couldn't stop looking at you. And not because you're the ugliest woman he ever saw but because he's got a case on you."

"Please, let's drop it," she begged, eyes brimming.

"Okay, dear heart. I'm sorry. It's dropped."

Twelve

When she got to the restaurant on Tuesday morning Ian explained that Amanda, their patio waitress for the summer, had called in sick.

"We're going to be shorthanded, so I was hoping you wouldn't mind filling in this evening, Rowena."

"No problem."

"We've a fair number of bookings, otherwise I wouldn't dream of asking."

"Ian, it's fine. I don't mind."

"That's very good of you," he said with relief, and went off to the kitchen to speak to Philippe. She watched him go, touched by his diffidence.

After the lunch rush she went home to relax for a couple of hours, settling with a book on the chaise in the back garden in the shade of the old oak. The air was hot and thick with humidity but a steady light breeze kept the temperature bearable. Within half an hour the print on the page began to blur. Her eyelids drooping, she turned the book face down in her lap and almost at once fell asleep.

For a second time she had a heated, graphically sexual dream about Tony Reid, and was grateful when the ringing of the telephone separated her from it. Struggling up from the chaise, she ran to the kitchen but by the time she got there the caller had hung up without bothering to leave a message. The answering machine was in the process of resetting itself, and for a minute she stood staring at it, logy from the heat. She got a Barq's diet French vanilla from the refrigerator and went back outside.

According to her watch she'd slept for less than an hour, but in that time clouds had begun collecting and the temperature had fallen by at least ten degrees so that she now felt slightly chilled. As she drank the soda more clouds gathered, gradually blocking out the sun. The breeze was becoming a wind; a storm was brewing. Eyes on the sky, she thought of Mark's comment on her naiveté, and had to concede it was true.

Having refused to listen whenever her mother attempted to impart the rules—as she understood them—of the male-female game, Rowena had never discovered how to play. She didn't understand the laws of attraction, what drew men to certain women—like Penny, for example. Try as she might, Rowena couldn't determine what it was. Certainly Penny was lovely looking, and her bulk seemed to enhance rather than detract from her beauty. She was big and round, with great pillowy breasts, and like an overstuffed armchair, offered the promise of comfort. Maybe that was the basis of her appeal. What, then, had Claudia's been?

As a teenager Rowena had seen her younger sister in action, and it had been tantamount to viewing a foreign film without benefit of subtitles. Perhaps, in the way of all teenage boys, they had been attracted to Claudia's dangerous aura, to the impression she gave of volatile unpredictability. Maybe they saw her as the living equivalent to a souped-up car that could take them on the ride of their lives—at excessive speeds that would put their very beings at risk. Or maybe they knew intuitively that Claudia would, if approached properly, open her legs and facilitate their longed-for introduction into the wonderful world of sex. Who knew? The whole subject was a mystery. And it was one of the reasons why Rowena was so very wary of Reid—he represented another journey she was reluctant to make into that vast psychological ballroom where men and women joined in ancient dances she had never learned. They performed modern minuets and quirky regional rigadoons while she stood on the sidelines, impressed by their talent but not tempted to find a partner and venture out onto the floor because she hated the idea of being doubly disadvantaged—both in experience and in comprehension. She'd danced, as it were, a time or two and had felt only self-conscious and clumsy. Her real interest in men manifested itself now and then in dreams that were safe and satisfying.

As the first drops of rain fell she got up and went inside. In the dressing room, trying to decide what to wear for the evening, she thought about turning forty the next day, and for a moment the bottom of her stomach seemed to drop—as if she had, like a single-engine plane, hit an air pocket. God, forty! Where had the years gone? She was starting along the downhill side of her life, and the effects were already showing. She was, indisputably, growing old.

And all at once, she again found herself missing her sister. Claudia had been like an intriguing, ongoing theatrical production that played day in, day out. Self-absorbed and vain, sometimes hurtful and sometimes astonishingly playful, she had been mean and calculating one minute and wholeheartedly generous the next, but never, ever, had she been boring.

Rowena turned and looked over at the bed—once Jeanne's, then Claudia's, and now hers—in which her sister had died. She saw Claudia as she'd been at the last; rigid and still, the abandoned husk of what had been a puzzling, ultimately unknowable, woman.

Then, like one of the flick books she'd so loved as a child, she saw scenes from Claudia's trophies: herky-jerky movements, and a final triumphant smile. And for the first time since her discovery of the tapes, rather than shame or anger she felt pity for the woman who'd required tangible proof of her potency and desirability.

Poor Claudia, she thought, missing her even more in the absence of anger. Or was it the intermittent drama, the astonishing highs and lows Claudia had managed to attain, sometimes within the framework of a single conversation, that she missed? Rowena had not liked or trusted her sister but she had, often in impossible circumstances and for no discernible reason, loved her. It was a pale, blind emotion like an earthworm forever burrowing underground, and it had survived countless attacks as a result of a tenacious life force all its own.

She remembered arriving home from school late one afternoon and opening her bedroom door to find Claudia sitting at her desk, reading her diary. Caught in the act, Claudia had automatically taken the offensive. "Why're you always sneaking up on people?" she'd asked crossly, tossing the diary back into the drawer and slamming it shut. "I really hate the way you do that, Ro."

Too flabbergasted to speak, Rowena could only stand there with her mouth open as her twelve-year-old sister pushed past her, saying, "There's not one single interesting thing in that whole diary. Even your dreams are boring. I've got way more interesting stuff in my diary. Maybe sometime I'll show it to you." Then, as if nothing out of the ordinary had occurred, she said, "Mommy phoned and said she's staying at the club for dinner. It's Irma's day off, and she left us this pukoid-looking casserole I absolutely refuse to eat. Someday Mommy's going to hire a housekeeper who can cook and I'll probably drop dead from the shock. So what d'you think, Ro? While you're doing your homework I could ride over on my bike and get us a pizza. Then we could watch TV together. Okay?"

It was so outrageous that all Rowena could do was laugh. And in so doing she discovered a very valuable tool in dealing with her sister because as she laughed, most of the starch went out of Claudia. Her eyes lost their defiant spark and a bewildered and lonely child gazed out at Rowena.

"Come on, Ro," she'd pleaded. "It's boring sitting all by myself down there, and when you see that casserole you won't want to eat it either."

"Okay." Rowena gave in, prompted by something she saw in her sister but couldn't name at the time, which in retrospect she could identify as desperation. "But, I'm warning you, from now on, stay out of my room."

"Okay," Claudia had agreed happily. "Sure."

Desperation, Rowena thought, looking again at the bed. If Claudia wasn't rooting through her mother's and sister's closets and dresser drawers, if she wasn't experimenting in the bathroom with makeup or different hairstyles, if she wasn't on the phone with someone, she couldn't bear being alone. It was a torment for her to have to find ways to occupy herself. She liked books with photographs, or glossy fashion magazines, but she never sat down simply to read. She couldn't concentrate, and reading bored her. She hated every class at school, particularly phys. ed. because she lacked coordination and thought team sports stupid. Homework was something to be ignored if possible, and the concept of studying eluded her altogether.

"What for?" she'd asked every semester before exams. "It's crap I'm never going to have to use in my life, so what does it matter if I pass exams?"

Her spelling was atrocious, her handwriting labored and jagged. Rather than important points from classes, the pages of her notebooks were filled with doodles and notes back and forth between her and her friends.

"Claudia, want to go to the movies Sat. nite with me? You know who."

"Dear you know who, I dont know yet. Meet me in the paking lot noon and well talk about it. OK?"

"Claudia, Caroline said she heard Jed by the lockers telling Nick he shouldn't ask you out. I thout you shd know. Love, Me."

"Dear Me, Carolines full of it and evrybody knows it!!! Screw her anyway. Call me tonite. xoxoxo, Claudia."

Her social life had always been prodigious, which was hugely gratifying to Jeanne. Being *popular* was what it was all about. And Claudia was invariably the most popular girl in her class—except for the semester she'd spent at Brandon. She was also a physical coward, unable to bear pain. The one aspect of her supposed suicide that rang true was the manner in which it had been accomplished. The only time Claudia had ever subjected herself voluntarily to anything that would hurt was the occasion of her cosmetic surgery. She'd had everything done in one go, and lived on large doses of Valium for two solid weeks afterward, while complaining to anyone who'd listen about how much pain she was in.

She'd actually opened her pajamas to show Rowena and Jeanne the incisions beneath her newly enlarged breasts. "See!" she'd cried, her voice and demeanor swollen with childish pique, as Jeanne had grimaced and turned away, busying herself lighting a cigarette, and Rowena had gazed, fascinated, at the too-taut mounds of inflated flesh her sister gingerly lifted with both hands in order to reveal the angry stitched-up slits beneath. "See?"

As a child, even a trip to the dentist had filled Claudia with dread. Rowena vividly recalled one occasion when she'd looked across the waiting room in time to see the color drain from Claudia's face as her nine-year-old sister fainted and slid bonelessly to the floor. Jeanne had sent Rowena in for her checkup, and when she emerged, the three of them had gone directly home. Claudia escaped having to see the dentist for another month.

Now she'd escaped for good, and there was no more pain, nothing to fear. But why had she taken her life? Or had someone taken it from her? If only she'd left a note, a few scribbled words. In the absence of any explanation, Rowena felt she had no choice but to keep seeking one.

The evening threatened to go sour from the moment she got back to the restaurant. Not only was Amanda out sick for the day but Ian had gone off on some errand just prior to Rowena's arrival, which meant that she had to ask Mae to keep an eye on the front while she ran downstairs to fill the first wine orders. Being unfamiliar with how the wine cellar was organized, it took her anxious minutes to locate the bottles. Then she had to go to each table to verify the selections before enlisting Kip's help to do the opening, sampling and pouring which he handled with aplomb, as if he'd done it dozens of times before. Pleased by his ability to rise to any occasion, but feeling harried, she rushed to seat the most recent arrivals.

It was a relief when a very wet Ian finally arrived.

"So sorry, Rowena. I got a flat and had to stop in the middle of nowhere in the pouring bloody rain to put on the spare. Everything all right?" he asked, peering around worriedly.

"Fine, Ian. Why don't you go have a coffee or something and relax for a few minutes?"

"You're sure? I could do with some coffee, actually."

"Go ahead. Kip's playing sommelier, and doing a good job of it."

"Clever lad." He ran a hand over his rain-damp hair. "I'll be five minutes," he said, and went off to the kitchen.

Even with the awnings the rain was so heavy that the few intrepid couples who ventured out to the patio were forced to admit defeat and move indoors. Fortunately, the restaurant wasn't fully booked for the evening, so everyone was accommodated inside. By ten-thirty the last of the customers was gone, and the cleanup was underway. The kitchen staff were preparing a light staff meal—an idea Ian and Rowena had agreed on the previous week and that had been well received by the employees; the three busboys were setting up for the next day's lunch, and Ian and Terry were at the bar totting up the night's receipts, while Mae and Doug divided the tips.

They'd just finished eating when the lights went out. The kitchen door opened and a perfectly healthy Amanda came in carrying a large birthday cake festooned with candles. Everyone began to sing "Happy Birthday" and for a few seconds all Rowena could think of was the upsetting surprise party Claudia had thrown here years before. But this was quite different. Touched by the elaborate planning they'd engaged in in order to carry this off, she smiled and obediently blew out the candles before accepting the gift they'd chipped in to buy: a small, exquisitely crafted Lalique bowl. Tearful, she thanked them. Ian produced two bottles of champagne, Terry popped a tape into the cassette player, and the party was on.

By midnight Ian was well on his way to being drunk. He'd lost his usual stiffness, becoming quite loose-limbed, and after an energetic dance with Mae he sank into the chair next to Rowena's, raised his drink and said, "To the bitch goddess Claudia, wherever she may be." He drained the glass, then turned to Rowena with one long hand covering his mouth. "Oops." He gave her a hangdog smile and said, "Sorry. Frightfully bad taste, that. Sorry, really. *In vino* rather too much *veritas.*"

"It's okay, Ian."

"No." He shook his head, eyes half closing for a moment. "All that love-hate rubbish. Know she was your sister, but such an appalling to-do, really. Taking dreadful advantage of people. Utterly remorseless woman, no heart whatever. Oh, dear. S'unforgivably rude of me. Your sister, after all. Blood thicker than water. Should know better. In my cups, you see."

"I know she gave people a bad time. I have no illusions about her, Ian."

His eyes filling with tears, he patted her on the arm. "Damned good sort, Rowena. No harm intended. Things got rather out of hand. Never should've happened, but there you are. Best laid plans of mice and so forth."

She was about to ask what plans he meant when Jill and Mae appeared with his raincoat. "Come on, Ian," Mae said. "Time to go. Me'n Jill will take you home."

Lurching to his feet, he allowed himself to be put into his coat.

"Happy birthday, Rowena," the two women chorused as they directed him out the door.

"Damned good sport!" Ian called over his shoulder. "You're a star, Rowena. You really are."

Within twenty minutes, the party was over and the staff were leaving. Kip walked Rowena to the Mercedes, asking, "Did you have fun, Auntie Ro? Were you really surprised, or did you guess?"

"I was really surprised, and I did have fun."

"Cool! And you like the present, for true?"

"It's beautiful, sweetheart."

"I knew you'd like it," he said happily, his handsome features aglow. "Way good party. See you tomorrow, Auntie Ro." He kissed her cheek, then stood by until she was driving out of the lot. In her rearview mirror she saw him jogging toward his car.

The instant she stepped through the front door, she knew something was wrong. The internal climate of the house had been disarranged; it didn't feel right. Flipping on the foyer light and leaving the front door open, she moved into the living room doorway, feeling along the wall for the light switch. She gaped at the mess. Everything had been pulled from the bookshelves and pitched to the floor. The wall unit stood angled away from the wall, its drawers and doors hanging open.

Trembling, eyes straining to see into the darkened dining room, she snatched up the telephone, punched 911, then, dry-mouthed, told the woman who answered, "My house has been broken into." She gave the relevant information, then flew outside to wait in the car until the police arrived.

Frightened, she locked the car doors and lit a cigarette. It was unlikely the burglars were still in the house but she wasn't about to go back in until the police told her it was safe. God! To think that strangers had been inside her home, rummaging through her belongings, leaving their foul imprint on everything they'd touched, taking whatever they fancied. She felt transparent, as if her body had turned to glass, and sat shivering, swallowing down an almost overwhelming desire to scream, while silently urging the police to hurry.

The minutes ticked off on the dashboard clock and she wondered if one of Claudia's former lovers had broken in looking for the tapes. But had anyone known of their existence? One of those men could somehow have found out and come intent on destroying the tapes. But why now, when she'd been dead for months? And then there was Ian. Maybe he hadn't been delayed by a flat tire but by his search of the house. Maybe he, too, had made a guest appearance on one of the tapes. But, again, why wait so long? She was too distraught to think clearly but she couldn't help believing this was no ordinary break-in.

Ten minutes after her call a cruiser pulled up. She climbed out of the car on rickety legs to talk to the officers, then they all entered the house. While she stood in the untouched kitchen with one officer, the other did a quick tour from attic to cellar.

"It's clear," he said, returning. "Looks like they concentrated on the master bedroom and the living room. Why don't you take a look, let us know if anything's missing."

Her drastically weakened legs threatening to buckle at every step, she climbed the stairs and went along the hallway to the master suite to see that every drawer had been turned out and the dressing room was in chaos. A brief look around, then she made her way back downstairs, clinging to the banister for fear her spindly legs might give out.

A second look at the living room, and she turned to the policemen to say, "The stereo, VCR and TV are still here. None of the jewelry seems to be missing, but it's hard to tell." She found no comfort whatsoever in everything that only hours before had been so familiar. "I just don't know," she said inadequately.

The three of them sat down at the kitchen table to fill out the incident report. "For the insurance," the older officer explained, "in case it turns out things're missing after all."

That done, they advised her to have an alarm system installed. "A child could've broken into that back door," the younger officer said, showing her where one of the glass panels had been smashed, allowing ready access to the lock. "We'll keep an eye on the place the next couple of days," he said as they were leaving. "But you wanna see about getting a security system soon as can be. Anybody watching could figure out your schedule, and with the house sitting empty three or four nights a week, it's an open invitation."

On that daunting note, they left. Rowena locked the front door then walked stiffly through to the kitchen to stand gazing at the back door and the glinting glass shards on the floor. There was nothing she could do to secure the rear of the house beyond locking the screen door. Even more frightened now, she got a pot of coffee started before going upstairs to change clothes. Feeling alien to herself in the electric blue silk dress that Claudia had purchased, she wanted her unpretentious old clothes, the garments a librarian had once worn.

Weeping, she picked through the pile of things on the dressing room floor, finding a pair of baggy cotton drawstring pants, a T-shirt, and her old moccasins. Dressed, she went back to the kitchen, swept up the broken glass then studied the door. All she could think to do was to move the marble table over in front of it. That, at least, would offer some resistance should anyone attempt to get in before she had an opportunity to arrange for the installation of an alarm system.

Quaking from exertion and residual fear after shoving the heavy table across the room a few inches at a time, she got a cup of coffee and a cigarette, and went to the living room to stand in the doorway for a time, smoking, drinking the coffee, surveying the mess and asking herself what possible reason Ian could have for breaking into the house. None. She couldn't picture him doing it. That flat tire story sounded hokey, but he could have been out buying the champagne, or collecting the birthday cake.

With a burst of angry energy, it didn't take long to return the room to order. And nothing appeared to be missing. All the tapes seemed to be there. Of course they were there! she chided herself. The trophy tapes no longer existed. Who'd break in to steal a bunch of old movies?

Her cup refilled, she went upstairs to work on the bedroom, pausing every few minutes to drink some of the coffee. By the time she'd finished, her arms and shoulders ached from putting clothes back on hangers, folding items and returning them to the shelves and drawers. By a quarter to five she was utterly done in.

Leaving every light in the house burning she went down the hall to her childhood bedroom, lay down on the unmade bed, pulled the comforter close, and curled tightly into herself.

She awakened with a start, not knowing where she was. A moment, then she remembered, and the fear rushed back. Pushing off the heavy comforter, she sat up, looked at her watch, saw that it was almost eleven and ran to the telephone to call the restaurant. Ian answered and again she wondered if he'd been responsible for the break-in.

"There's a problem," she told him. "I'm afraid I won't be able to come in today."

"Nothing serious, I hope."

"No, no. Just something that came up unexpectedly."

"I see."

"Will you manage all right without me?"

"Oh, certainly." A pause, then he said, "Ahmn, Rowena?"

"Yes?"

"I, ahmn, wanted to apologize for last night. I had rather too much to drink."

"Ian, there's nothing to apologize for. Don't give it another thought."

"It was a bit over the top," he said.

"Forget it," she said, deciding it was absurd to have suspected him. "It was a lovely party, and I had a very good time. I'll see you tomorrow. Okay?"

"Of course."

After a quick, nervous shower during which she kept glancing over at the bathroom door, halfway convinced someone would materialize there and come leaping at her, she dressed again in her old clothes and went downstairs. While the coffee was brewing she got the telephone directory, called the company with the biggest ad in the Burglar Alarm listings in the Yellow Pages, and was promised that a representative would call on her before two o'clock that day. Next she managed to reach Frank Reilly, the contractor, who said he would stop by within the hour. "I can hear how upset you are, Rowena, so I'll make sure that door gets hung today." Her breathing at last began to slow and her shaking subsided.

In daylight she made her own tour of the house, and still was unable to determine what, if anything, was missing. Perhaps the burglar had heard Mark's car pulling in, assumed she was returning home unexpectedly, and had fled empty-handed. She made a mental note to ask Mark what time he'd come home.

Frank left his car running while he measured the door. "I'll be back in a couple of hours with one of my men to hang it," he said, sliding into the station wagon.

By two-thirty she was signing a contract for the best security system the company had to offer, having been assured installation would begin first thing the following morning. She handed over a sizable check to the salesman who, in parting, confessed, "It's the easiest sale I've ever made. But I guarantee you it's a first-rate system. It'll give you peace of mind."

"Would that it were so simple," she said wryly.

He didn't get it, his face blank.

She thanked him and saw him out.

While Frank and one of his crew trimmed the new solid wood door out on the back lawn, she began preparing a steak and mushroom casserole for dinner. As she washed and trimmed the mushrooms, then sliced the steak and onions, she thought if someone was after the trophy tapes, he might return to try again. If only there were some way to let the world know the damned things were gone. She imagined posting a notice on the front door: NO MORE TAPES. DON'T BOTHER LOOKING. She emitted a grim laugh. Someone had broken in and shattered her sense of privacy. As she rinsed her hands she wished she'd never given up the apartment in Stamford. It may have been cramped, but she'd always felt safe there. It was going to take a lot more than an expensive security system to make her feel safe again in this house.

Thirteen

"Why didn't you come *get* me?" a distraught Mark asked. "And why did you bother *cooking* under the circumstances?"

"It was late and I didn't see the point of both of us being upset. And I cooked because I needed distraction."

"But, Ro, it's your *birthday,*" he said, as if this fact should have influenced her behavior.

She tried for a laugh that didn't come off. "This is one birthday I'm not likely to forget, that's for damned sure."

"I can't believe you didn't even call me." He looked around. "They didn't take *anything?*"

"As far as I can tell, no." She too looked around the living room, angry and afraid. Her gaze settling on the yellow roses Mark had brought, she wanted to do damage, break things, put her foot through a wall, her fist through a window. She also felt a desperate desire to run, to throw her old clothes into a bag, climb into the Honda and drive until she got to the top of the Yukon where the air was so cold it would solidify her thoughts. One hard shake and the frozen notions would come spilling out of her head, leaving her ready to start anew, clear-minded, with the entire continent spread before her.

She'd always been a secret runner, contemplating escape whenever people were unkind. At the worst moments, her mind would take flight while her body remained rooted in the disagreeable reality of the present. When months and then years passed and her father didn't telephone or come to see her, she ran far away in her thoughts, traveling to a place where her father stood in perpetuity with open arms, ready to catch her in his embrace. There had to be some reason why he hadn't been in touch, *had to be.* He would never have abandoned her, never. But Jeanne had emphatically repeated that he had. "He only cares about himself," her mother had declared. Each time she said it Rowena began to hum, shutting out her mother's voice as she revved the engines of her escape mechanism.

"Everything seemed okay when I got home at about six-fifteen," Mark was saying. "I would've heard the glass being smashed if it had happened after that because I had my windows open. Which leaves a pretty narrow time frame of opportunity—roughly forty minutes between when you left and I got back.''

"And that," she picked up, "would mean the police were right. Someone was tracking my comings and goings.'' She took a hard drag on her cigarette. "God, that's frightening.''

"It doesn't make sense. With the houses set so far apart, we'd notice somebody loitering. This smells funny to me, Ro.''

"To me, too. Ian has the spare set of keys," she said, thinking of the morning he'd let himself in and discovered Claudia's body.

"If it was Ian, and he has a set of keys, why smash a pane in the door?''

"To make it look like a break-in?''

"Why go to the trouble, if nothing was taken?''

"Frankly, I can't think of any reason why he'd do it," she said, as the oven timer went off. "But somebody did, and they were definitely after something other than the usual booty like VCRs and jewelry.'' She put out her cigarette and got up. "Come keep me company while I make the salad.'' Saying this, she saw her sister again as a young girl, begging Rowena to come keep her company. "I hate being all alone,'' she'd said so many times.

Who *were* you? she wondered, an odd pain in the center of her chest. Why did you have such swings high and low, such a roster of fears and phobias? What kept you in this house from cradle to grave? And why do I have the feeling the break-in was about you, not about the doubtful contents of this house?

"Hello?" Mark waved a hand in front of her eyes. "Planet Earth to the little cupcake.''

"Sorry.'' She took hold of his hand as they started for the kitchen. "I didn't get much sleep last night, so I've been kind of zoned-out all day.''

He gave her hand a quick squeeze, then moved to examine the new back door. "It's not as bright in here now, which is a pity. But on the positive side it'd take a battering ram to break this baby in.''

"That's the whole point. Sit down, Mark, relax," she said, lighting another cigarette.

"Relax? With you practically vibrating? I'm really sorry this happened, Ro. Are you smoking full-time again?''

"Today I am. Tomorrow, who knows?'' Propping the cigarette in an ashtray, she positioned a green pepper on the cutting board and reached for a knife.

"Want me to open that bottle of wine?"

"Yes, please. Oh, and before you go, remind me to give you a key for that door."

"Listen, Ro, you can't let what happened spoil your feelings for the house. I know how much you love this place."

She put down the knife, retrieved her cigarette, and turned toward him. "When we were kids the TV set was downstairs in the rec room. Claudia loved television. She'd have watched from first thing in the morning until the test pattern at night, but she was scared to be down there alone. She was forever begging me to watch with her. Yet in the end she wound up living here alone."

Puzzled, he asked, "What's your point?"

"Last night I hated this house and I couldn't help thinking it must've been how Claudia felt as a child, frightened of things in the dark, and angry with the house for making her afraid." She took a drag on the cigarette then stubbed it out.

"Maybe I'm dense, but I still don't get your point."

"I'm not sure I have one, except that I don't believe Claudia committed suicide, and my gut feeling is the break-in is connected somehow to her death."

"Rowena, honey, you are not making sense." His handsome chiseled features pulled downward in worried lines.

"Maybe not, but that's my feeling."

"You were frightened. Now you're trying to rationalize it." He crossed the room to put his arms around her. "There's no shame to having been scared."

"I still am," she admitted, holding on to him.

"It's okay to be scared," he repeated, automatically smoothing the back of her neck the way she imagined he'd stroke a small nervous house pet. "But," he went on, "it is *not* okay to be obsessing about Claudia. I thought you'd come to terms with it. Now I see that you haven't, and it bothers me. She's dead, Rowena. You have to let it go."

"I want to, but it's hard. There's a lot about Claudia I may never understand, things about her personality that didn't make sense. But the one thing I do know with absolute certainty is that my sister would *never* have killed herself."

"The medical examiner concluded it was an accidental death. Why isn't that good enough for you?"

"I'm sorry, but it isn't." She backed out of the embrace, saying, "Weren't you going to open the wine?"

He stared at her for several seconds more, then shrugged as if to say, Okay, I tried, and opened the drawer to get the corkscrew.

They scarcely spoke until she had served them both and they were settled at the table. Then, in an effort to lighten the mood, she said, "The staff threw me a surprise party last night."

"Uh-oh! Your least favorite thing. How was it?"

"Fun, actually. They gave me a lovely little Lalique bowl."

"The one in the living room? I was wondering where that came from."

"You don't miss a thing, do you?"

"Not things like Lalique bowls, I don't. That's a swell present, cupcake. Maybe now you'll start believing those people actually do like you."

She looked away for a moment, then looked back at him and smiled brightly. "I managed to drink a glass of wine and one of champagne and stayed completely sober. Ian, however, got pissed as a newt."

"Get outta here! That bastion of British correctness tied one on?"

"Big time. He danced like crazy for about twenty minutes—he's a very good dancer, which surprised me because I always think of him as being so stiff—then he came to sit next to me, and got all teary. He started mumbling a lot of incomprehensible stuff about Claudia, which set me right on edge. I kept hoping he wasn't going to make a heavy-handed pass, or say something that'd destroy my respect for him. You know that feeling when you start praying you didn't just hear something racist or bigoted, because if you did, the friendship's over? And worse, you might have to tell this person you liked five minutes ago he's the biggest asshole you've ever met?"

"Only too well," he said. "I've been dealing with that crap my whole life."

"Okay, right. So just when I was beginning to get antsy, Mae and Jill appeared with his coat and hustled him out. They were so—caring and protective of him. I can't imagine someone who inspires that kind of fondness in people faking a break-in."

"We're back to that again," he said impatiently. "This is delicious, by the way. Why don't you eat some?"

"I'm not very hungry." She took another sip of wine.

"Humor me, and eat some of your goddamned dinner, Rowena!" he snapped, startlingly. "Your body needs more than wine and nicotine. And my idea of a good time is not sitting here eating like Stanley while you do Blanche Dubois, recalling faded memories of Claudia as a lonely little girl, and romanticizing a tight-assed Brit who got drunk and probably acted human for the first time in years."

Stung, she said softly, "That was uncalled for."

"It was very definitely called for. You're starting to go weird on me, Rowena, and it's no fun. You need to eat."

She thought of the lengths to which he'd gone to provide Tim with nourishment in the final months of his life—cooking his favorite foods, driving all over Fairfield County to find fresh papaya, or ripe mangoes—and the anguish he'd tried to hide when Tim had been unable to swallow more than two or three mouthfuls before losing what he'd managed to ingest. She thought of the last weeks when he'd cradled the wasted man in his arms, holding a can of Ensure steady while Tim drank through a straw, and of Tim apologizing between wrenching spasms, while Mark kept saying, "It's okay, honey, it's okay. Don't worry about it. It's okay."

"I'm sorry," she said, picking up her knife and fork.

He watched her eat for a minute or so, then made peace, saying, "Good, huh?"

She smiled and they ate for a time without speaking. At last she said, "I've been feeling kind of a fraud lately."

"Which is why you've gone back to your Granny Yokum duds, right? Trying to locate yourself."

"I'm recognizably me to myself in these 'duds.' "

"You know, my charming chinchilla, once you stop thinking of yourself as the outsider at the restaurant, you'll stop being one."

Surprised, she said, "How did you know that's how I feel?"

"Come on, dear heart. I've known you a long time now. You've stepped into your sister's stilettos and you're feeling kind of wobbly after so many years of sensible shoes."

"You're a very wise man, Mark Daley."

"Not really. I'm just experienced. The thing is, when you realize at an early age that your instincts run counter to what's acceptable—not only in your home but in general—and you see that if you follow those instincts you're going to find yourself in a world of trouble, you get frightened and sad and, ultimately, philosophical. It doesn't stop you wishing to the bottom of your soul you could be like everybody else, because life would be *so* much easier, but you can't change what you are. You can try to hide it, but it's not going to go away. And it doesn't stop you from feeling guilty, because you're *not* like everybody else— can't be, never will.

"What makes it a little less painful is having people to open up with and talk to. I know that doesn't come easily to you. It's as if you think you don't deserve to be heard. Sometimes, like tonight, I walk in and I can see how you're struggling, and I think, Come on. Just tell me, and I'll help in whatever way I can. But you never volunteer without serious prompting."

She thought of her father climbing into his car at the cemetery and driving out of her life forever; of her twelve-year-old sister flouncing past her, declaring, "Even your dreams are boring," and knew why she was perennially reluctant to confide in others. She also knew she had to make an effort. So she told him about that day when she'd come home to find Claudia reading her diary.

"I'd have *killed* her," he said indignantly.

"I stopped keeping a diary, because it wasn't safe. What I'm trying to say is I know you're right. But my initial reaction to any situation is—I'm alone in this, so I'll have to handle it somehow. I didn't call you last night because it never occurred to me to come knocking at your door." He was shaking his head, and she said, "I will try to be more forthcoming, I promise."

"That's all anyone could ask, Ro. You know I'll meet you better than halfway."

"I know."

"Could you also try, please, to forget about your sister, and get on with your life?"

"I'll try." But even as she said it she was again analyzing the deathbed scene, still—perhaps forever—bothered by that bottle of Chivas Regal. Someday, somehow, she was going to find out what really happened.

She couldn't shake her jitters, and scanned the area around the house when coming and going, looking for anyone suspicious. The security system was a nuisance—one more set of numbers to remember, along with two PINs for her checking and savings accounts, sundry telephone numbers, Social Security, even her driver's license number—but it and several timers to turn the lights off and on automatically in various rooms of the house did make her feel marginally less exposed. And her doubts about Ian were wiped out when, after hearing of the break-in, he insisted on seeing her to the car on those nights she worked.

She kept expecting to find items missing but weeks passed and she had to conclude that nothing had been taken. In her free hours she worked in the garden and kept reminding herself to start going through the boxes of papers in the cellar but never seemed to get around to it.

Meanwhile, at the point when she'd begun to believe she wouldn't hear from him again, Tony Reid left messages two days in a row. She was gratified but didn't bother to call him back, determined not to get involved. He was too attractive; she was too susceptible.

He finally caught up with her in the afternoon of the last Sunday in July. Hearing her voice he said, "I can't believe I'm not getting the machine. I was prepared to give it one last shot before folding my tent and skulking away."

"I meant to call you," she lied, wishing she'd stayed outside and let the machine pick up. "Frankly, I've been in no mood for socializing." Considering her dreams of him, she felt acutely self-conscious just talking to him on the telephone. Yet there was something so seductive in the rich depth of his voice, the hints of humor in his tone.

"Why not?"

"Aside from being very busy at the restaurant, there was a break-in here a few weeks ago."

"That's too bad. Was much taken?"

"Oddly enough, no, nothing."

"That *is* odd. But it's an upsetting experience, I know. My car's been broken into a time or two. You could probably use a distraction. Why don't you let me buy you dinner tonight?"

"Thanks, but I don't think so. Restaurants don't have the appeal for me they once did." She laughed, wishing he'd say okay, never mind, forget it.

"Fair enough. How about a ride on my boat?"

"You have one?"

"I do, a cabin cruiser I keep at Norwalk Cove marina."

"Why so far from home?"

"It's cheaper. If you know anything about boats, you'll know they've become a major luxury the past few years. Mooring charges and the rest of it are astronomical. But I've had the *Jiminy Cricket* a long time, and I won't give it up. So for the past few years I've kept it in Norwalk. Does a boat ride interest you?"

She looked out the window, thinking how pleasant it would be on the Sound. And how bad could a man be who named his boat *Jiminy Cricket?* "It kind of does," she said in spite of the inner voice telling her to say no. "When did you have in mind?"

"How about right now? I'm at the marina. I could come pick you up."

"I've got a refrigerator full of food. Why don't I bring some along and we can have dinner on your boat?"

"Terrific. What's the address?"

She told him, and he said, "See you in twenty minutes," and hung up.

She'd have liked more time to get ready, change into something more attractive than a faded blue cotton sundress and sandals, but by the time she'd unearthed the cooler and filled it, he was ringing the doorbell. On edge, sure this was a mistake, she hurried to open the door, and there he was, grinning at her.

In baggy khaki slacks and a white long-sleeved shirt, bare feet in Top-Siders, he seemed even bigger than she'd remembered, but every bit as beautiful. Like a silent mantra, she kept repeating, I'm not ugly, not ugly, not. She didn't believe it but at least it served as a distraction.

"This'll be fun," he said, depositing the cooler on the back seat of his Chevy Blazer. "I'm glad you decided to come."

"How do you manage to sail and not get a tan?" she asked, fastening her seat belt as they started off. "You must use a sun block of about two hundred."

He laughed and looked over. "You're very funny."

"For someone who's vertically challenged, I'm not bad," she quipped, and he laughed some more. How was it that she could behave in an apparently relaxed manner when he made her more agitated than anyone ever had? The mantra changed to Let me just be myself, let me just be me.

"SPF thirty," he said. "And I always wear a hat. I don't tan, and red's not one of my better colors."

"Me, neither. My brother Cary loved to sail."

"I seem to remember Claudia mentioning that. He had his own boat at a very young age, didn't he?"

"That's right. We belonged to a beach club back then, and Cary went sailing almost every day." She paused and gazed out the window as they went down Washington Street. "I often went out on the boat with him. It amazes me to think our mother let two young kids go out on the Sound alone. But Cary was a born sailor, and very careful. He always made me wear my Mae West."

"But *he* never did."

"Is that what my sister told you?"

He nodded.

Astounded, she said, "That's simply not true. He *never* went out without his vest. Why would she have lied about that? The fact is, if he hadn't been wearing one, his body might never have been found. I can't *believe* she told you such a bizarre lie."

"What happened?" he asked quietly.

"He was pretty far out when a storm suddenly came up. He lost his sail, and the boat overturned. He suffered a head injury—evidently he was very bruised. The Coast Guard found him the next morning, floating facedown. I overheard them telling my mother that it looked as if he'd lost consciousness and drowned. *God!* How could Claudia have misrepresented something she was too young to remember?"

"I'm sorry. It was insensitive of me to mention it."

"No, it's okay. I'm the one who raised the subject." Her mood was collapsing like a punctured balloon. Her brother was gone. How had she lived for so long without him? As a child she'd coped by running away from it in her mind, just as she'd run from thoughts of her father. Safer and wiser to flee from pain.

She was returned to the present by Reid's hand descending over hers, and she tuned back in to see they were parked at the edge of the marina. The hand withdrew and she shifted to look at him. For a moment she was caught in what seemed to be a dream, finding the sight of him wonderful and terrible. Her hand could still feel the weight of his.

"Let's agree not to talk about Claudia today," he said.

"Yes," she said with relief, able to smile again. "Let's not."

The twenty-eight-foot cabin cruiser was more than twenty years old but impeccably maintained, and he handled it effortlessly, with manifest pleasure. Once they were well out on the Sound with the Long Island shoreline clearly visible on the distant horizon, he cut the engine and sat down opposite her under the canopy, asking, "How're we doing?"

"It's great," she answered, lulled by the gentle rise and fall of the boat on the slight swell. A steady salt-breeze kept the edges of the canopy flapping, and the reflected late-afternoon sun had a soporific effect. "I could curl up here and go to sleep."

"I've been known to take a nap out here now and then." He looked over his shoulder at the expanse of water between them and the Connecticut shore. "Sometimes I even do some fishing."

"Catch anything?"

"The occasional bluefish, which I throw back. I'd be afraid to eat a fish that came out of this water."

"Me, too. A shame, isn't it?"

"It's cleaner than it was ten years ago, but that's not saying much. So." He swiveled to face her, his hands on the bench either side of him, his long legs stretched out and crossed at the ankles. "We know I've got the boat. What kind of toys d'you have?"

"Nothing this big." She smiled at him. "Mostly books. This summer I've been working on the garden, something I haven't done since I was a child. My father loved the garden. I remember him spending all his free time out there. He used to let Cary and me help him. It's funny." Her eyes were caught by pinpoints of sunlight reflecting off the water. "I never realized how addictive it can be. I'll be at the restaurant and I'll start thinking about making a quick trip to the nursery to pick up a bush or shrub to go in a particular spot. I'm beginning to understand the British passion for gardens. And I saw some incredible ones in China. My favorite was the Humble Fisherman's Garden in Suzhou."

"I've always wanted to go to China," he said. "As a boy, I traveled every summer with my parents. I was crazy for ocean liners, and for years my greatest regret was that I was born too late to sail on the *Normandie*—the most beautiful ship ever built. I did get to go on the *Ile de France* and a couple of others. Ever traveled by ship?"

She shook her head.

"It's the only civilized way left to go. I intensely dislike flying, the crowds in the terminals, the crush of passengers at the carousels. When I retire I'd like to spend a solid year cruising the world—do the fjords, the Mediterranean, the west coast up to Alaska."

"In other words, what you secretly want is a *really* big toy."

He threw back his head and let out a great burst of laughter.

She wished she felt less like a spectator and more like a participant. Alone with a man she involuntarily fell into a performance mode, working to be clever and appealing even though she was repelled by the realization that, despite her best efforts to resist it, her mother's influence had taken a firm grip on her subconscious.

Mopping his eyes on his shirtsleeve, he asked, "What is it you secretly want, Rowena?"

The question undid her—*You, I want you*—and she had to pause to be sure she was in control before answering, "What I've always wanted, to be left alone."

"You feel beset upon?"

Tilting her head to one side, she asked, "Are you playing shrink with me?"

"Nope. Just curious."

"I'm not all that interesting." She shrugged and risked meeting his eyes that in the reflected sea light seemed even clearer and bluer.

"Of course you are," he disagreed. "For someone vertically challenged." He let loose another burst of laughter and again wiped his eyes on his sleeve. "I enjoy you, Rowena. Not a lot of people make me laugh."

"Me, neither. Every time somebody says I have to read this hilarious book that had them in fits, I wind up wondering if there's something wrong with me or if they're just easily amused."

He nodded, concurring. "You're a woman of intriguing contrasts. Not too many people are outspoken *and* shy."

"You are," she ventured.

"True. I am. You're perceptive." He delivered this in a complimentary tone, his eyes filling with approval and what appeared to be affection.

"You just ran aground. I'm only good at seeing other people's problems. When it comes to my own I'm hopeless."

"That doesn't mean you're not perceptive. Anyway, what say we investigate the contents of that cooler?"

"Sure. I'm kind of hungry myself." She began to unwrap the food while he set up a table and two captain's chairs.

"This is wonderful," he said of the spread. "Way better than the sandwich I usually make for myself."

"What're you going to do with the one you brought today?"

"Eat it for breakfast," he replied without hesitation.

She smiled and shook her head.

"What? You think I was so confident of getting hold of you I didn't bother fixing myself something to eat?"

"I believe you."

"Baked ham on whole wheat with mayo and mustard. You want to see it?"

"No. I believe you," she repeated. He had the ability to charm and disarm her, and it gave her a torturous pleasure to look at him. If only life were simpler and it was safe to follow one's instincts. But it wasn't, and it would be madness to let herself care for this man. She was only there because she was Claudia's sister, and it was just a matter of time before he got around to letting her know what it was he wanted.

Fourteen

Throughout the drive back from the marina she debated whether or not to invite Reid in for coffee, hating the idea that she might appear overly eager. Finally, irked with herself for her lack of spontaneity, she said, "Would you like to come in for coffee? I've got some divinely decadent cake I brought home from the restaurant last night."

"Coffee and leftover cake." He smiled, showing his dimples. "How could I refuse?"

He waited in the foyer, holding the cooler, while she punched in the code to disarm the security system, then followed her lead to the kitchen.

"Have a seat," she invited, relieving him of the cooler and setting it down on the far end of the counter. "I'll just get the coffee started."

"This is a wonderful house. Mind if I take a look around?"

"Go ahead. Put some music on if you like."

He pushed through into the dining room, then she heard him go on to the living room. "Good big rooms," he called. "Nice high ceilings, and honest-to-god plaster instead of drywall. I don't suppose you'd be interested in selling it to me?"

Amused, she shook her head. After a minute or so the opening notes of Bruch's "Scottish Fantasy" sounded. He'd chosen one of her favorite CDs. She shook her head again, confounded.

The coffee started, she removed the slab of chocolate mousse cake from the refrigerator and put it on the table with a knife, plates, and forks. It took only a minute or two to empty the cooler, wipe down the interior with a damp cloth, and place it by the cellar door. Then she went to find Reid.

He was by the wall unit, bent close to study the video cassettes, and jumped when she spoke from the doorway. "You like movies? Sorry, didn't mean to startle you." He was a remarkable study of contrasts, of form and color, and she thought women likely threw themselves at him regularly.

"I like old movies," he confirmed. "You move very quietly. I didn't hear you coming."

"Like the fog, on little cat feet."

He chuckled, and turned again to look at the rows of video cassettes.

"Most of those were my sister's. Evidently she liked old movies, too." Claudia was crazy about them, she thought, especially the packaging.

"You don't?"

"Oh, I do. I've just never been into buying them. I'm a renter." She leaned against the wall with her arms folded, watching as he picked up the Lalique bowl.

"This is very nice." He turned it into the light to admire the design.

"A birthday present from the restaurant staff."

"Rats! Did I miss your birthday?"

"By several weeks."

"Too bad. I'd've sent you a good Gary Larson card if I'd known. Obviously the staff think well of you. My former wife collected early Lalique. An expensive hobby."

"Were you married long?"

"Nine years."

"D'you collect anything?" she asked. "Big toys notwithstanding, of course."

"Like you, mostly books and CDs. I've never had much interest in owning a lot of any one thing. Have you been married?"

"Nope." She unfolded her arms and pushed away from the wall. "Come on. The coffee's ready, and I'll give you some of this fabulous cake."

For a second time he followed her to the kitchen. The house felt smaller with him in it. Or perhaps, being overly aware of him, it was the space in her head that was diminished by his presence.

"This is one of the few houses I've been in that doesn't give me claustrophobia," he said, settling at the table while she poured the coffee. "You had the kitchen renovated recently, didn't you?"

"How do you know that?" At once her suspicion was aroused.

"It still has a new smell to it."

She paused and sniffed the air. "Can't smell a thing but the coffee."

"The cabinets and counters are obviously new," he added. "Nice job. Did you want to be married?"

"When I was about twelve, and didn't know any better."

As on the boat, he threw back his head and roared with laughter. "When did you start to know better?"

She shrugged. "Sometime between then and now."

"Brave of you to resist the social pressures."

"You're assuming I was asked."

Looking skeptical, he said, "You mean you weren't?"

Faintly ashamed, she said, "Nope," and found herself blushing as she added, "but I wasn't out there, actively campaigning to get myself asked."

"Why not?"

"Perhaps because I wasn't especially impressed with the example set by my own family."

"Care to elaborate?" he asked, digging into the cake with gusto. He was a man who very much enjoyed good food. She liked watching him eat.

"Why?" Surely Claudia had told him about the family.

"I'm interested." His expression was open, attentive.

"My father married a woman who, I believe, for the most part merely tolerated him. I think she saw him as a live-in escort, someone to take her to the country club dances on Saturday nights, and to pay for whatever fell beyond the means of her trust fund. He worked fifty and sixty hours a week to give her what she wanted, but, from as far back as I remember, he wasn't happy. When I think of him—and lately that's been often—the image I have is of a sensitive, lonely man who had a gentle way with his children.

"The last time I saw him was at Cary's funeral. He stayed in the background and he was going to leave without speaking to us. I think he was afraid Jeanne would create a scene. And she would have, too. I had to run to catch him before he left. We talked for a few minutes, and he said he'd be in touch, but I never saw or heard from him again."

"That's a sad story," Reid said soberly.

"We were a sad excuse for a family. What about you, Reid?"

"No family drama," he said apologetically. "My parents were both academics. Father was a history professor, Mother taught English. I'm an only child and had an obscenely happy childhood. We traveled a lot, and I was—indulged, I suppose. They catered to my curiosity, encouraging me with chemistry sets, creative toys, and books by the carload. I loved the company of my parents, still do. We talk on the phone a couple of times a week, and I go up to Maine to visit about once a month. Father got into fly-fishing after he retired, and Mother began painting water-colors. They live half an hour from Portland, right on the coast. They're very happy being away from the passive/aggressive politics of academia."

"You're very lucky," she told him, and at last took a bite of the cake. He had, with only a few strokes, painted a vivid portrait of a close, loving unit, and she envied him his cloudless memories.

"Yes, I was," he agreed. "It must have been very difficult for you, losing your brother and your father."

She couldn't respond to this and got up, went for the coffeepot and brought it back to the table to refill their cups.

"I upset you," he said. "I'm sorry."

"Please don't play shrink with me," she said quietly. "I'm trying to have an ordinary conversation."

"An ordinary conversation doesn't include responses?" he asked mildly.

"I'm at a disadvantage here, Reid. I can't possibly know how much you've already been told about the family. After all, my sister *was* your patient."

"True. But you're not. It's not how I think of you."

It was the perfect opportunity for her to ask how he *did* think of her, but she couldn't, and the moment passed. He looked at his watch and said with seeming reluctance, "I guess I should be on my way. Monday morning the world begins again."

"Is that how you see it? You drop out of the world on weekends?"

"I see patients Saturday mornings. But from Saturday afternoon until Sunday evening, that's pretty much how I do see it. Would you like to come out on the boat again next Sunday?"

"I don't know. Call me and we'll see."

"Is it me, Rowena, or are you generally reluctant to commit?"

"Is a date to go boating a commitment?"

"Neat trick." He grinned at her. "Deflection by answering a question with a question; a well-known trick of the analytic trade. It's a *small* commitment, nothing that'll stand up in court in a breach-of-oral-contract case."

"A point to the big guy." She returned his smile. "Why did you get divorced?"

"It turned out I wasn't the man of Susan's dreams after all."

"Was she the woman of yours?"

"For a time. People change. We always think we're different, that we'll be immune to the loss of enchantment. But we're all fallible, and not so different as we'd like to believe."

"True," she said. "Children?"

A spasm of pain contorted his features for a moment, then he blinked it away. "We had a daughter. She died at four and a half months of SIDS. The marriage didn't survive Annie's death. Both of us tried very hard, but somehow we lost more than the baby. We staggered along together for another year and a half before we agreed to call it quits.''

"I'm so sorry," she said, her throat suddenly constricted.

"These things happen," he said, reminding her for a moment of Mark's hard-won philosophical stance. Did wisdom only come as a result of pain?

"I think I would like to go next Sunday," she told him. "So why don't you call me during the week and we'll see."

"I'll do that."

They walked together to the front of the house. She opened the door, glanced out, then turned back to him.

"Are you nervous being here alone?" he asked with what appeared to be concern.

"It's a little scary the way you pick up on things. But no, I don't mind being alone here. I grew up in this house. I know every inch of it, from the attic to the furnace room. What does make me nervous is that, according to the police, my comings and goings have been watched. It'll be a while, if ever, before I'm my old devil-may-care self again."

"You should try being a little kinder to yourself, Rowena."

"What does that mean?"

"You have an oblique way of taking potshots at yourself, as if you want to get them in before anyone else has a chance to do it."

"Maybe I do," she allowed, considering the observation. "It's a long-term habit."

"Habits are for breaking. What prompted you to give up the library and take over the restaurant?"

"It wasn't a difficult choice. As head librarian I was an administrator, handling endless paperwork. I wasn't cut out to be a paper pusher. I missed dealing with the public and jumped at the opportunity to get back to it."

"You're good with people. They respond to you. I noticed that the night Colin and I came to dinner."

"Why did you come that night?"

"I wanted to see you again."

"Why?"

He looked a bit lost. "Why?"

"Yes, why?"

"Because I liked you. Colin, as you noticed, also liked you."

"I noticed. He proposed to me, remember?"

"And I warned you off, remember?"

"I do. And I'm not sure I've forgiven you for that. I don't get pro-posals every day, you know."

He laughed, kissed her cheek, gave her arm a light squeeze, said, "I'll call you," and went off.

She waited until, with a toot of the Blazer's horn, he drove away. As she coded the alarm system, she was reviewing their day together. By the time she set aside her book and reached to turn off the bedside light, she was already looking forward to seeing him again. And when she again dreamed of making love with him, she simply abandoned herself to it.

When by Friday of the following week he hadn't called, she was dis-appointed but told herself it was probably because she hadn't been particularly encouraging and undoubtedly his pride—that enormous organ that occupied so much of the space in the male skull—had been wounded. Or perhaps he felt, as she so often did, that he'd revealed too much of himself. Who knew? Whatever his reason for failing to call, she wished he hadn't said he would. The silence hurt, and she felt foolish. One of these days she was going to have to learn not to take people so literally.

Friday evening, Le Rendezvous was fully booked, inside and out. Within minutes of arriving she fell into the agreeable rhythm of the evening. Each night had a different mood, played itself out to a dif-ferent tempo, depending upon the patrons. On this night the volume of conversation was high, with much laughter, emanating primarily from a table of eight who were celebrating the fifth anniversary of a lively and attractive couple visiting from Brazil. Terry had put on a Getz-Gilberto tape that drew approving applause from the table, and in due course he followed it with one of sambas played by Laurindo Almeida. The high spirits of the group were contagious, elevating ev-eryone. The staff all but danced as they moved between the tables, back and forth to the bar, in and out of the kitchen.

Rowena offered the party a round of complimentary liqueurs with their coffee and in turn they were effusive in their appreciation of the food, the service, the ambiance of the restaurant. She had just re-turned to the front to scan the reservations book—nine-thirty and two late bookings due at any moment—when the door opened. She smiled automatically as she raised her head, expecting to see one or both of the parties.

But there, looking like an overinflated cherub in a hot pink track-suit, sweat socks and Reeboks, hair skinned back in a ponytail, stood Penny, poised on the threshold, positively exuding rage.

Adrenaline flooding her system, Rowena knew there was going to be a scene. She wanted help, some way to avoid a confrontation, but knew with an inner sinking there was no escape. All hell was about to break loose.

Her features set in a contorted mask, Penny advanced on her.

"I told you my son was *not* to work here! I *told* you that! And you *countermanded* my wishes!" Ranting, she closed in until she had Rowena backed up against the wall. "Who the *hell* do you think you *are?* Where do you get *off* interfering in our lives?"

"Penny—"

"Shut the hell up!" Penny lifted one clenched fist and held it inches from Rowena's face. "I'd like to punch you silly. Don't tempt me!"

"Penny, will you please *listen?* This is not the time or place—"

"I told you to shut up!" Penny's voice grew louder. "I've come to get my son. I'm taking him home, and I don't want to hear *one word* out of you! Understand? Not one goddamned word! Now where is he?" She took a quick, unseeing look around, oblivious to all the people watching.

"We can't discuss that here—" Rowena began.

"You *just* don't *listen,* do you?" She slapped Rowena's face, then jabbed her fist hard into the fleshy part of Rowena's upper arm. "I am not interested in anything"—another quick, hard jab—"you have to say." Jab, jab. "Just get Kip out here *now!*" One more jab, as if for emphasis.

"Stop that!" Rowena whispered, wondering where Ian was, and why no one was coming to help her. How could this be happening? Anxious to put some distance between them, she held out her hands, trying to get Penny to move back and give her some room.

Interpreting this as an aggressive gesture, Penny punched Rowena's other arm, and Rowena instinctively crossed her arms to protect herself. Under her palms, she could feel heat radiating from the blows she'd received. Tears sprang to her eyes.

"I could *kill* you!" Penny waved her fist in Rowena's face. "Acting so goddamned *superior,* so *smug.* Get my son out here *now,* or I swear I'll beat the living shit out of you."

At that moment, returning from the patio and pushing in through the kitchen door, Kip cried, *"Mom!"* and came running over at the same instant Ian emerged from the office. "Are you *nuts?* What're you *doing?* Stop that!" Kip grabbed hold of his mother's arm only to be shaken off as if he were no more substantial than a toddler. He grabbed her again with both hands. "I said stop it!"

Penny turned her fury on him. "You're in big trouble, mister. Get your stuff. You're leaving right now!"

"What's going on here?" Ian demanded, his crisply delivered words falling into the awful silence that had descended upon the restaurant.

"Mind your own business!" Penny barked at him.

"Mom, chill out!" Kip begged in low tones.

"Don't you *dare* tell me what to do!"

"Let's move along, shall we?" Ian said smoothly, taking a firm grip on Penny's other arm.

The voice inside Rowena's head kept repeating, *I don't believe this, I don't believe this!* while Kip and Ian maneuvered Penny out of sight of the diners. It seemed as if the altercation had lasted forever but in the dreadful, continuing silence, Rowena realized the same song was still playing on the stereo. Only a minute or two had passed. Chest heaving, she gazed over at her longtime friend whose face was set in irate lines as though carved from a block of marble. Penny actually looked ugly.

"Please take her to the office," Rowena said in an undertone. "I'll be there shortly and we'll discuss this matter in private."

Penny was ready to go on battling but Kip and Ian forcibly propelled her down the hall between them.

Rowena watched the trio disappear into the office. Then, dredging up a smile, she straightened—she'd actually been *cowering,* and felt sick with humiliation at having had so many people witness that insane scene—then pushed herself away from the wall, and said to the patrons in a voice that scarcely sounded like her own, "Please excuse this. It was a misunderstanding. My apologies."

Dazed, she turned and started toward the office, walking with difficulty. Her hip and leg joints seemed to have fused, and with each step her torso protested painfully. Her cheek and upper arms pulsed with the same rhythmic throbbing as a toothache. Behind her she heard the buzz of a dozen different speculative conversations starting simultaneously. God, the shame of it! Mortified, she held back tears, longing to hide someplace dark, where she could curl up around the pain and cry. But that wasn't an option.

She opened the office door to find herself facing an intense three-way argument.

"Are you *crazy?*" Kip was asking his mother. "How could you *do* that?"

"You do *not* go against my wishes!" she insisted, but with less energy than she'd displayed moments earlier.

"*You* have no right to create scenes whenever and wherever the fancy takes you!" Ian declared with cold disdain.

"Mind your own damned business!" Penny shot at him. "This has nothing to do with you. Kip, you're coming home now!"

"No way! I'm not even sure I want to live in the same *house* with you."

"Kip," Rowena said softly from the doorway, "go back to work, please. We'll talk later. I have a few things to discuss with your mother."

"Oh, man," he said wretchedly. "This is so fucked."

"I *told* you to keep away from my son!" Fist raised, Penny started toward Rowena.

"I'd sit down if I were you." Ian stepped in front of her. "If you don't, regardless of Rowena's wishes, I'll summon the police to remove you. And I *will* press charges."

Penny seemed prepared to challenge him but evidently saw something in his eyes that changed her mind. Her arm fell to her side and she moved toward the chair but didn't sit down.

"Go on, Kip. We're very busy," Rowena reminded him.

Kip looked first at her, then at his mother.

"Carry on, there's a good chap," Ian said briskly, reinforcing Rowena's authority.

Reluctantly, Kip opened the door and left.

Her eyes on Penny, Rowena said, "Ian, would you please bring us some brandy?"

His eyes also on Penny, he said, "Certainly," and went off to do her bidding.

Frazzled, faintly ill, and in the grip of an arctic anger, Rowena sank into the chair behind the desk and said sharply, "Sit down, Penny!" Surprisingly, Penny obeyed. "What, pray tell, was that assault supposed to accomplish?" Rowena asked hoarsely. "Did it make you feel better? Has it solved all your problems? Do you have a new sense of power now, because you've managed to attack someone considerably smaller than you?" She waited for an answer. None came. "Well?"

Rowena pushed, but Penny sat like a large, stubborn child, glowering at her with hate-filled eyes.

The anger turning her body cold, Rowena yanked open the bottom desk drawer, found her bag and, hands shaking, got out a cigarette. She lit up, took a long, hard drag, then sat staring back at her former friend until Ian returned with two snifters.

"Will you be able to manage this person, Rowena, or shall I stay?" he asked, regarding Penny with unconcealed contempt.

"I'll be fine, thank you, Ian."

"Madam," he addressed Penny, "you have an appalling lack of self-control."

"I'm not interested in your opinion," Penny said dismissively.

"I'd wager you're not interested in anyone's opinion on anything. You really should be locked up somewhere," he said coldly.

"Thank you, Ian," Rowena said again, finding his support most welcome.

"I'll be close by, should you need me, Rowena," he told her on his way out.

Rowena picked up one of the snifters and drank half the brandy in a single gulp. It took her breath away, and she shuddered as the alcohol melted a narrow channel through the internal ice. She took another drag on the cigarette then said, "Drink some of that, Penny, and stop all this melodramatic crap. Say whatever you have to say, then get the hell out of my restaurant."

Thunderstruck, Penny stared at her. "Even the way you *talk* has changed," she accused. "You don't even sound like yourself anymore."

"You just attacked me in front of a restaurant full of people and you're complaining about the way I *sound?* You've lost your marbles. You really have." Rowena had to laugh. The sound that emerged was more like a croaking cough than a laugh, and she felt all at once a thousand years old and too enervated to deal with this insanity.

"It's not fair, any of it," Penny said petulantly. "You have no right to try to turn Kip against me."

"*Please!* You're talking nonsense, and I'm in no mood for it." Rowena took a final drag on the cigarette then stubbed it out and sat back holding the snifter in both hands as if it might warm her.

"It isn't fair," Penny persisted, picking up the second snifter and downing its contents in one noisy swallow. Setting the empty glass on the desk, she said, "Claudia dies and suddenly you've got everything—her clothes, her money, the house, this restaurant. Haven't you got *enough?* Why d'you have to have Kip, too?''

Mark had been right again. This was about jealousy. And it was ridiculous. No one, ever, had been even remotely envious of her. There had never been any reason to be, and still wasn't. "I don't *have* Kip, for God's sake. He has a *job* here. He's an employee, a very good, well-liked one, too. I can't *imagine* why you're so determined to read more into it. And it's none of your business, but as a point of interest, I don't actually have anything of my sister's yet. The estate's still in probate. I'm running the restaurant on an interim basis as co-executor, with the lawyer and the bank. The renovations here and on the house were paid for by a life insurance policy she'd had for so long that—*another* point of interest—the suicide clause didn't apply. I did get her clothes. That's true. And I am driving her car. *So what?* When the estate clears probate, I'll come out ahead, but not by the millions you seem to think. These supposedly *unfair* things are all in your mind.''

"No, you've changed...." Penny started along another track.

"That's my *prerogative!*" Rowena brought her fist down hard on the desk, the shakiness getting worse as the anger gelled. "You come barreling in here and humiliate me in front of a few dozen people because things, from your dismally distorted point of view, aren't *fair?* When was life ever *fair?* And who the *hell* are *you,* to be judging me? Have you lost your mind completely?''

"*Me?* What about *you?*" Penny's face again suffused with color as she leaned closer to the desk.

"What *about* me?" Rowena countered, wondering if she'd ever actually known this woman.

"You've changed beyond all recognition. You don't have time anymore for the people from your old life.''

"You couldn't be more wrong," Rowena said tiredly. "I'm the same person I've always been. Right now you're the one who seems to have changed—so much so that I've been sitting here wondering if I've *ever* known you. You've been giving me a hard time since Claudia died, and I've tried every way I know how to make peace, but that's not what you wanted. I don't know *what* you want. But it no longer matters, because I no longer care. You've gone too far, and it's too late. For old times' sake, though, I'll give you some advice. Leave Kip alone or you'll lose him, if your performance tonight hasn't already achieved that. He's not a child, and you can't control his every move.''

"I've watched you turning into Claudia," Penny said in dire tones, lumbering to her feet. "I tried to warn you, but you wouldn't listen.

You're *still* not listening. So no one can blame me for what happens. She was the biggest bitch who ever lived, and you've become just like her.''

"Oh, fuck off!" Rowena said, completely exasperated.

In a strangled voice, Penny said, "Kip won't be coming back here, and from now on you keep away from him! You can't buy my son the way you've bought Mark and the others!" With that, she stormed out, leaving the door open.

"Jesus H. Christ," Rowena said under her breath and drank the rest of the brandy, hearing Penny's heavy footsteps recede. "The woman's out of her goddamned head." The emotions she'd held in check took control. Too tired to move, she sat gazing at the chair Penny had vacated while tears ran down her cheeks.

After a time, knowing it was vital for the restaurant's reputation that she reappear looking unscathed, she blotted her face with a tissue, applied some blusher and fresh lipstick, then got up and with a determined smile went out to circulate. She paused at each table to reassure the customers that what they'd witnessed was nothing more than a misunderstanding. Aware of both Kip and Ian keeping an eye on her, she smiled at them, too, and kept going. And, at long last, the evening came to an end.

During the cleanup, she asked Kip into the office, to talk.

"No way am I going home tonight!" he stated. "And no *way* am I giving up this job! I don't care *what* she says!"

"Sweetheart, you have to go home. If you decide in a week or a month to make other arrangements, you should probably consult a lawyer and find out exactly what your legal rights are. You're under eighteen," she pointed out, wishing she could take him home, install him in one of the empty bedrooms, and be done with it. "You can't simply leave because you want to, regardless of how justified your reasons might be."

Deflated, he sagged in the chair. "She's been a fruit loop since last Christmas, getting nuttier every single day."

"Why? What happened?" she asked, anxious for some insight into his mother's behavior.

"Dad gave me the car."

"*What?*" This was quite a revelation. As far as she knew, Kip had been a toddler the last time he'd seen his father.

"Mom told me not to," he continued, "but I went ahead anyway. Phoned up and asked him to help me out buying some wheels. He actually sounded like really glad I called. He said they'd been planning to trade his wife's car in on a new one. Instead, he signed it over to me. I went to his place, and we were both pretty nervous. You know? He said he felt majorly bad he'd never done that much for me, but he had these two other kids and it'd been pretty tough just coming up with the support money every month."

"But he never paid any support." Rowena was very confused.

"Yeah, that's what she *said*. But he did. He showed me the canceled checks, a whole box of 'em. Four hundred a month for thirteen years. A hundred and fifty-six checks, all endorsed and cashed. Sixty-two thousand, four hundred bucks. I did the math." He chewed on his lip for a moment, then said, "When I had a showdown with her over it, she said, no way, the son of a bitch never paid penny one. Then, when I said, *excuse me,* I've *seen* the checks, it turned into this thing about how he was only trying to impress me, win me over—the same bizarro weirdness she's been saying about you, Auntie Ro. She *screamed* at me. How the hell did I think she'd bought us the condo and paid for my clothes and the rest of it, like everything was my fault. It was getting big-time weird, so I said okay, never mind, forget it. Sorry I spoke, sorry I *breathed,* sorry I got in your face.

"After that it was cool again for a while. Then your sister died and right away Mom got on your case, so I started staying out a lot because I did not want to hear that bogus shit, 'specially when she started on Uncle Mark, too. It's like everybody's evil and she's the one who decides who's to live or die. I don't know. But tonight. That was *heinous,* man. Truly *sick.* You know what, Auntie Ro?" he asked tearfully, looking very young, his nose red and lower lip quivering.

"What, honey?"

"My dad said he'd asked her maybe a thousand times if he could see me, and she said, in your dreams, and hung up in his ear every time." A tear slid down his cheek. "It would've been so cool. You know? I've got these two half brothers, cute little dudes, and I didn't even know their *names.* She always told me he didn't want to know about me, and it hurt a lot. I mean, I loved Uncle Tim and Uncle Mark. I still really miss Uncle Tim a lot. But this is my *dad.* You know?"

"I know." She wondered suddenly if Jeanne had done the same thing to her father, and there'd been no abandonment; maybe he hadn't been allowed to get near her. "I'm sorry, Kip," she said thickly. "I had no idea."

"Yeah, well. Who did?" He knuckled the tears off his face and looked at the door, saying, "I should be out there, helping."

"Don't worry about it. The question this minute is, what're we going to do about your situation?"

"I don't know," he said sadly. "Am I fired?"

"No you are not! You're a valued employee. I have no intention of letting you go."

"Thanks, Auntie Ro." He managed a watery smile for her.

"For the time being," she counseled, "hang in at home. We'll work something out, I promise."

Before leaving the office, Kip gave her a hug. For a very large young man, he was exceedingly gentle, as if aware of how easily he could hurt people who were smaller. "I'm sorry about the whole wicked thing, Auntie Ro."

"None of this is your fault, sweetheart. None of it!"

"But I feel like it is."

"I know you do, and that's why I'm telling you it isn't. Remember that. Okay?"

"I'll try. I just wish I knew how things got to be so totally *weird*."

"Believe me," she said fervently, "so do I."

Fifteen

Distracted and depleted, she had to keep pulling her attention back to the car and the road ahead all the way home as the scenes with Penny replayed in her mind. She'd been completely justified in the way she'd handled matters, yet she felt guilty—which was ludicrous in view of Penny's barbaric behavior. Nevertheless, she kept trying to see ways in which she might have dealt differently with the situation. The effort made the twenty-minute trip seem far longer. Bruised and sad, she wanted only to get home and into bed. But the sadness was like some feral creature that had escaped from a cage within her, and was holding her trapped in its hot, heavy grip, slowly squeezing the air from her lungs. It was an old, old emotion she'd managed to keep contained for many years. Now freed, it threatened to overwhelm her.

Long-forgotten childhood scenes flashed on an internal screen, random images that were spotlit for a moment before being replaced by others in a lengthy sound-and-light show. She couldn't fix on any single one long enough to examine it. As soon as she began reining in her focus, the image shifted and changed. Tears near again and her throat aching, she worked to come to terms with the loss of Penny's friendship and tried to get a grasp on why things had gone so wrong.

The sadness was like a liquid key that flowed into an inner lock and opened it, releasing a flood of recollected losses. She missed Tim, his kindness and humor and grace; she missed her brother and father, even her mother. Thinking of Jeanne reminded her of the boxes in the cellar which, in turn, made her even wearier. She put her foot down harder on the accelerator, anxious to be home.

Coming through the front door, she reached automatically to disarm the security system and saw with a stab of fright that it was already off. Instead of the flashing red light indicating the system was activated, the green "off" light glowed steadily. Immobilized, mouth gone dry, heart drumming, she looked around, hearing the sound of running water. Then it stopped and a dark figure appeared at the end of the hall, lit from behind by the kitchen light. Her heart seemed to seize and stop as she opened her mouth to cry out but couldn't make a sound. For a second time someone had broken in, and she would be harmed, perhaps killed. This *couldn't* be the way her life was meant to end. She was only forty. Too soon. She told herself to move, run, scream. But as in a nightmare she was mute, paralyzed. And the sadness held her in its smothering embrace as she mourned in advance the loss of her life. She had no wish to die, and railed silently against the monstrous unfairness of this. Why, *why* couldn't she move?

"Are you okay?" Mark hurried over to put his hands on her shoulders, searching her eyes. "Kip called and told me what happened. I came right over to wait for you."

Delayed shock and relief came simultaneously, and she was on the verge of wetting herself as her useless mouth continued to hang open. Then control kicked back in and, trembling, she cried, "Mark, I was so *scared!*" Falling against him, she blurted out her upset in incoherent fragments punctuated by sobs.

He held her, saying, "Dear heart, you're not making a shred of sense. I want you to go up and get into your jammies while I make us something to eat."

"I'm not hungry." She sniffed, fishing in her pocket for a tissue.

"Please, do *not* argue over this. I won't stand for it. I know you haven't eaten, and I don't like the way this is starting to become a habit. We'll have a snack and a cup of tea, and we'll talk. Then you'll take a hot bath and go to bed."

"Okay." She gave in, calmed by his taking charge.

By the time she got back downstairs, he'd put bread, cheese, fruit, and half of one of Jill's peach pies on the table. He frowned when she sat down and at once lit a cigarette.

"I'm not happy about your smoking. But for tonight, I won't nag." He brought two mugs of tea over to the table. Setting one in front of her, he said, "Now, I want to hear all of it."

In the course of her narrative she managed to eat some cheese and a narrow slice of pie. Telling him about Kip's revelations regarding his father, she found the sadness had receded, although she could still feel its menace as it loitered nearby, waiting for her to come into its range.

"No wonder you were babbling when you got home," Mark commiserated. "What is *wrong* with that woman?"

"When I first met him at his office, Tony Reid made the point that it's often difficult to know even the most apparently confiding people, and since then I've been wondering if I ever really *knew* Penny. I think maybe I didn't, and it's an ugly way to feel, Mark—angry and helpless and stupid. If Kip hadn't told me what he did about his father, I'd have thought this breakdown or whatever it is was very sudden. But to have lied to her son for most of his life! To tell him his father wanted no part of him! And to tell everyone else that Ken never paid a cent in child support! Why, for God's sake? Why didn't she just tell the truth?''

''A lot less wear and tear on all concerned if she had,'' Mark said. ''Maybe she needed the sympathy vote.''

''I keep thinking I shouldn't have sent Kip home. But I didn't want to exacerbate the situation.''

''No. You did the right thing.''

''Mark, do we ever really know anyone? Do I know you? Do we know each other?''

''This mess has got you seriously rattled.'' He placed a comforting hand on her arm. ''You know me, Ro. Next to Tim, I'm closer to you than I've ever been to anyone. I *know* you.''

''But didn't you think you knew Penny, too?''

''The truth? Maybe forty percent. I accepted her because she was your friend. My connection, though, was always with you. And with Kip, because I've loved that kid from day one. But my impression from the outset was that Penny had a whole load of emotional baggage she was keeping out of sight.''

''How come you never said anything?''

''Ro,'' he said patiently, ''you've had an upsetting night and you're not thinking straight. Would you have criticized Tim to me? No way, unless I'd given you an opening. You wouldn't have wanted to risk saying anything potentially hurtful, or that might have reflected negatively on my judgment. The same goes for you and Penny. If you'd offered an opening, I'd have said what I'm saying now.''

''Would you tell me if you thought I was getting peculiar, or going out of control? Would you wait for an opening?''

''No, I certainly would not wait. I'd tell you straight out.''

''So you don't think I'm turning into Claudia?''

''Ah, babe.'' He looked cut up. ''Is that what she said?''

''It's what she's been saying all along.''

''That silly bitch! Listen to me, my love. If I got even the slightest whiff of Claudia, I'd be all over you like a Bedouin's tent. Trust me on this, okay? Your sister was one of the most seriously fucked-up people I've ever encountered. She had this phenomenal lack of *affect*. And she would hit on absolutely anyone. I mean, she even tried to hit on *me,* way back when."

"Are you *serious?*"

"Believe it! She called up one night, all breathy and eager, to invite me over for a drink."

"My God! When was this?"

"Way back, when you and I first met. She thought the two of us were an item and she wanted to blow it sky-high. It was such a transparent ploy it was almost funny, but it gave me a very clear picture of how she operated, and that *wasn't* funny. I turned her down. She was not pleased, but covered nicely. A couple of years later when I turned up at the restaurant with Tim she twigged I was gay and made out like she didn't know me."

"I'm stunned! I can't believe she did that."

"*I* could never believe the two of you were related. But the longer I know you, the more all kinds of things make sense."

"What things?"

"Let's go into it another time, Ro. It's late and you're wiped out."

"No, tell me."

"It's the same old stuff, Rowena—the dichotomy between how you actually look and the way your mother and sister convinced you to *think* you look. Claudia wasn't the beautiful one, cupcake. *You were.* See! You don't believe me and I'm not about to debate this with you. But answer me this. Who are you going to believe—someone who just auditioned for the title role in *Lizzie Borden, The Musical*—or me?" She laughed, and he said, "I mean it! Haven't I been telling you for months that Penny was eaten up with jealousy?"

She nodded, the laughter having somehow taken the last of her energy.

"You need to go to bed, cupcake. I brought you a Valium, just in case." He deposited a small blue tablet on the table. "Will you be okay? Or would you like me to camp out in one of the guest rooms?"

"I'll be all right." Her voice thinning, she whispered, "Thank you, for everything."

"Go have a good soak, then straight to bed." He kissed her forehead, and headed for the back door. "Don't forget to set the alarm."

"I won't."

"I love you, Rowena. Everything's gonna be okay."

Too choked to speak, she could only offer him a wobbly smile as he blew her a kiss before letting himself out.

She sat for a while, finishing her cigarette, thinking about Claudia making a pass at Mark, too readily able to picture her sister doing it. What had gone on in Claudia's mind when she'd done these things? What had she been trying to prove, and to whom? The sadness threatening to swamp her again, she went to arm the security system before trudging leadenly up the stairs.

While the tub was filling she undressed, stricken by the livid bruises on her upper arms. Running her fingers gingerly over them, she replayed the confrontation once more.

For the duration of the attack, she had found herself in an arena where intelligence and the ability to reason were utterly insignificant. Only physical strength had mattered, and she'd had none. She hated her weakness, and hated Penny for stripping her of her small, precious store of self-esteem.

She took the Valium and soaked in the tub until she caught herself nodding off. Climbing out, she toweled dry, crawled into bed, and plummeted into a dense, mercifully dreamless sleep.

She arose in the morning with a headache and sore arms, and got a pot of strong coffee started before checking the answering machine. The only message was from Tony Reid, whose mellifluous voice said, "As an excuse for not calling sooner, this has to rank way at the bottom, but I didn't have a minute to myself all week. I hope we're still on for Sunday. Call when you get a chance and let me know. Okay? Talk to you later."

She was pleased that he'd called after all, but she lacked the energy to deal with him. Recalling that he worked Saturday mornings, she rang his home number, got the answering machine and said, "Hi, it's Rowena. I'm not sure about Sunday. Let's play it by ear and see how it goes. I'll be back from the restaurant by about three tomorrow, so we'll talk then."

She took two extra-strength Tylenol caplets and spent forty minutes drinking coffee and smoking, trying to think what, if anything, she could do for Kip. With his mother in her current frame of mind, he was going to have a rough time getting through the remainder of the summer, let alone the coming school year. Yet the lamentable fact of the matter seemed to be that there wasn't anything she could do that wouldn't make things worse. She had no right to interfere. And in all fairness—her recent conduct aside—Penny had always been a devoted mother. It wasn't by accident that Kip had turned out to be such a decent young man. Rowena could only pledge her continuing support, and hope like hell that his mother had enough sense to leave him alone.

The headache gone, she went down to the cellar to confront the boxes stacked haphazardly against the far wall of what had once been the rec room—an area that took up a full three-quarters of the space beneath the house. The remainder had been partitioned into two rooms—one housing the furnace, the circuit breaker box, and hot water tank; the other the sinks and laundry equipment. With a sigh, she began separating the cartons, placing those that a cursory inspection showed contained Claudia's papers on one side, and those of Jeanne's to the other. An hour or so later her hands were filthy, she'd worked up a sweat, but she had two separate lots of boxes. She set up the bridge table and a folding chair, brought down a lamp from her old bedroom along with a package of large garbage bags, and began sorting through the first batch of her mother's papers.

It was a jumbled mess, and she could tell that Claudia had simply tossed things in after Jeanne died. There were paid bills, long outdated credit cards, bank statements, and a considerable number of get-well greetings as well as cards that had accompanied floral arrangements. Jeanne had been in and out of hospital for the better part of a year before she died, and she'd received many flowers from her friends during every stay.

Rowena checked each item before discarding it, a time-consuming chore but not an uninteresting one. Jeanne's spending had always been prodigious and remained so until a few months before her death. There were, however, sales slips from stores in Manhattan she couldn't possibly have visited in her very frail state, which meant that Claudia had used Jeanne's credit cards to buy a Louis Vuitton handbag, half a dozen dresses at an average of eight hundred dollars each, and an equal number of shoes, the cheapest pair costing one fifty and the most expensive an astounding five hundred and fifty dollars. She'd bought several cashmere sweaters, a lot of silk underwear and several nightgowns. At a rough estimate, she'd spent close to fifteen thousand dollars just prior to their mother's death. Rowena wondered if Jeanne had known, or cared. Probably not. It certainly didn't matter now. She tossed the sales slips into a garbage bag, along with sundry utility bills, receipts for property taxes, a plumber's statement for work on one of the bathrooms, invoices from a heating and air-conditioning firm for servicing the furnace and on and on. There were even several magazines and an old *TV Guide*. Getting to the end, Rowena flattened the carton and set it aside to go into the blue box for recycling.

Halfway through the second box she came upon two family albums and her parents' wedding portrait, items she'd made a fruitless search for soon after moving into the house and which she'd come to believe Claudia had discarded. Elated at this find, she carried the framed portrait and large leather-bound volumes up to the kitchen where, with another cup of coffee and a cigarette, she sat down to look at photographs she hadn't seen in more than twenty years.

George Graham had diligently kept a visual record of his family that began with the honeymoon and ended the year before Cary's death. There at the beginning of the first album, in black and white prints with deckle edges, were her newly wed parents having cocktails on the patio of a Nassau hotel, looking impossibly young and attractive: a laughing Jeanne in a full-skirted cocktail dress, her blond hair in a French twist, drink in one hand, cigarette in the other; and a tuxedoed George gazing adoringly at his slightly older, infinitely more sophisticated wife. George and Jeanne were further captured playing tennis, sunbathing on a deserted stretch of beach, and astride bicycles.

Then came the baby pictures, first of Cary: his gentle nature evident in toothless smiles; then of Rowena: a fat, happy infant cradled in her father's arms; and finally, her face crumpled, six-month-old Claudia held on her grandmother's lap, arms reaching out to her unseeing mother, who was seated nearby with a cigarette, her gaze distant.

Rowena stared at this photograph for quite some time, finding the shot meaningful—something about the way Jeanne was turned slightly away from her mother and small daughter; something about the baby's obvious misery. It reminded her of—what? She closed her eyes for a moment, trying to make the connection, but it wouldn't come clear. She eased the picture from its four gold corners and set it aside to study again later.

She went on, slowly turning the album pages to smile automatically at the sight of her brother taking his first uncertain steps; then as a cheerful overalled toddler in a playpen surrounded by toys; and the next year as a three-year-old in a rain hat and slicker, holding his father's hand on the deck of a good-size sailboat, both of them offering near identical grins to the camera's eye. A tightness in her chest, she longed to have them back—the patient, loving father and sweet-natured brother. She had to close the album and go stand by the kitchen window, letting the sun warm her as she looked out at her father's recreated garden, imagining Jeanne doing to her what Penny had done to Kip. And she thought it was a good thing her mother was dead, because she felt a murderous rage merely considering the possibility that Jeanne might intentionally have kept her and her father apart.

When she arrived at Le Rendezvous near six o'clock that evening, Kip was already there. He looked somewhat the worse for wear, and she took him aside to ask how he was.

"I'm fine, Auntie Ro."

"You don't look fine, sweetheart. You look as if you slept in your clothes."

"Does it show?" he asked apprehensively. "I was hoping it didn't. I, uhm, slept in the car. I didn't want to go home, so I phoned and told Mom I was staying over at Luke's place. Before she could start in, I told her there was no way I was giving up my job and if she didn't like it, I'd find somewhere else to stay for good. I was set for a major fight, but she said okay, whatever.

"The car was kind of stuffy and cramped, but okay. I parked way in the corner of the lot and sacked out in the back seat, hit the drugstore when it opened this morning, got a few things, then went'n cleaned up at the gas station, grabbed some chow at the McDonald's drive-thru before I came to work the lunch shift. I know I'm kind of wrinkled"—he tried with both hands to smooth the front of his shirt— "but it's okay. Isn't it?"

He was so young, so earnest and innocent that she felt a pang of loving sympathy for him, wishing she had the right to give him a room in her home and the freedom and space to grow that he deserved. But Penny had made it graphically clear how she viewed Rowena's desire to be helpful. There really was little she could do for him.

"You can't sleep in the car indefinitely, Kip. What about your dad? Could you stay at his place?"

"It's way small, Auntie Ro. He'd say yes, for sure. But there's no room."

"This is ridiculous!" she said impatiently. "Here I am with a big house and four empty bedrooms. It should be a simple matter of your coming to stay, but nothing's simple right now. The thing is, you can't live in your car, sweetheart. You're not homeless. There are any number of people who love you and want you, including your mother. She's behaving strangely right now, but she does love you. And you know that."

"I know. And she'd go totally apeshit if I stayed with you." Lowering his voice, looking bewildered, he said, "It's like all of a sudden she *hates* you. And Uncle Mark, too. It's scary, and I don't get it. It's not as if you guys did anything to her."

"She seems to think I did. Evidently, from her point of view, the thought is as good as the deed."

"It's nuts. But I will go home tonight, see how it is. Maybe she'll be chilled out by then." He looked doubtful.

"If you feel you really can't stay there, call me, or Mark, or your dad. Call one of us. But, please, honey, no more sleeping in the car."

"Okay."

"Promise?"

With a forlorn smile, he said, "I promise." Doubt still clouding his eyes, he went off to fill the bread baskets.

She watched him go, praying Penny would back off and leave him alone.

Sunday she awakened to the sound of rain pinging on the outside of the air conditioner and was relieved. There was no question of her going out on Tony Reid's boat. She'd be free to spend the late afternoon and evening sorting through more of the cartons in the cellar.

Removing her pajamas, she discovered that her arms were sorer than the day before, and looked much worse. The bruises were ripening in an array of colors from a purple-red to deep blue. She stepped into the shower but the impact of the spray was so painful she quickly turned it off and sat shivering on the tub floor, waiting for it to fill.

She kept expecting Reid to call but he didn't, so before setting off for the restaurant she rang and left a message on his answering machine suggesting they try to get together some other Sunday.

Immediately after stowing her handbag in the office desk she went in search of Kip who looked more rested but only slightly less care-worn than the previous morning. He told her that his mother had been asleep when he returned home the night before.

"By the time I got up this morning she was gone. I have no clue where she went, but at least there were no hassles."

She put an encouraging hand on his shoulder. "Just remember, sweetheart. If you need help, you've got plenty of friends to call."

"I'll remember. And I won't go sleeping in the car. Thanks, Auntie Ro."

Because of the weather a few people called to cancel their reservations but the majority showed up. Since there was only room at the bar to seat six, the others were offered tables under the canopy on the patio. Three groups of four said that would be fine, and two couples said thanks but they'd try someplace else and come back another time. Which worked out perfectly, because the restaurant itself was full to capacity.

Just past noon, at the height of the brunch rush, Mae came over to Rowena to say, "We're gonna have trouble with table six."

Glancing past her to take a quick look at the quartet seated there, Rowena asked why.

Mae wrinkled her freckled nose. "See the fat one? Guy's a gripe artist, the kind who doesn't like anything, no matter what. Jerk combs his hair sideways from over his ear, shellacs it with a blast of hair spray, and thinks nobody notices he's covering a bald spot the size of a dinner plate."

A hand over her mouth, Rowena laughed, then asked, "Has he complained yet?"

"Nope. But he's gonna. I can spot these people at a hundred paces."

"Let's see how it goes. Okay?"

"You bet."

Rowena kept an eye on the table and, sure enough, when their meals were served, the man imperiously summoned Mae back to the table. At once Rowena went over, asking, "Is there a problem?"

"The eggs are *runny,*" he complained belligerently. "I distinctly *told* her I wanted them firm."

"Of course," Rowena said soothingly, signaling Mae to remove his plate. "We'll take care of it."

She accompanied Mae to the kitchen, where the waitress predicted, "This is only the beginning. He's gonna bitch about every last thing 'cause he wants his meal comped. He wants something for nothing. I *hate* guys like him. Makes me want to spit in his goddamned eggs Benedict."

"No need for that." Rowena took the plate, popped it into the microwave, set the timer for ninety seconds on high, saying, "Now they'll be nice and firm. Just yessir and nosir him, and comp the table for their coffee, nothing else."

Tickled, Mae said, "Way to go, boss!"

Observing from the bar, Rowena watched the man poke with dismay at the rock-hard yolks of his eggs. Then with a shrug, as if conceding he'd lost that round, he plowed diligently through the plateful of food, pausing only to order Mikey to refill their bread basket. "And bring more butter, while you're at it. What is it, rationed?"

Mikey looked at him askance but said nothing, and at a nod from Rowena, added bread and a fresh crock of butter to the basket.

The party of four ordered desserts and coffee. When, finally, they received the bill, Rowena's presence was demanded.

"I had to send my food back and you're *charging* me for it?"

"But, sir, you ate it. And you'll see we didn't charge the table for coffee," Rowena said sweetly, noticing that the woman with him seemed to be in an agony of discomfort, while the other couple held a heads-down murmured conversation.

"Last time I come *here,*" the man grumbled, slapping down a Platinum American Express card.

"I'm afraid we don't accept American Express," Rowena told him. "We do accept MasterCard or Visa."

"Oh, for *chrissake!*" He snatched up the card and exchanged it for a MasterCard, saying, "What the hell kind of chintzy place is this, you don't take a *Platinum* card?"

"Sorry, sir," Rowena said pleasantly, handing the bill and credit card to Mae before continuing on her rounds.

The party left and Mae muttered, "The prick stiffed me. Didn't I *tell* you?"

As Rowena was about to reply, the door opened and the woman in the foursome who'd been so obviously embarrassed came back in, spotted Mae with Rowena, and came over.

Pressing a ten-dollar bill into Mae's hand, she said, "I want to apologize. He's a client, otherwise I'd have walked out on him." To Rowena she said, "Would you mind calling a cab for me? I need a ride home."

"Sure. Please have a seat at the bar while you wait."

The woman went toward the bar and Rowena told Mae, "Have Terry give her whatever she wants to drink on the house."

"Decent of her to make good, huh?"

"Unh-hunh," Rowena agreed, putting in the call for a taxi as the door opened again and Tony Reid came in with the Sunday *Times* tucked under his arm.

Experiencing a sudden lift, she smiled and held up a finger, indicating he should wait, while she spoke to the dispatcher at the cab company. Mark would undoubtedly say she was cynical, but she couldn't help believing some ulterior motive was fueling Reid's persistence.

Sixteen

Tony Reid was happy to settle with his newspaper at one of the vacant tables under the canopy outside. Rowena promised she'd stop back when the rush was over, and returned to the front of the restaurant just as the taxi driver appeared.

"She'll be right out," Rowena told him, and went to the bar to inform the woman waiting there with a cup of coffee that her cab had arrived.

"The bartender was telling me you're Claudia's sister. I thought there was a resemblance."

"Did you know Claudia?" Rowena asked the sharp-faced, fortyish blonde whose expression was perhaps intended to be friendly but which, in fact, bordered on the supercilious. She was dressed for business in very high heels, a power suit with one of those uncomfortable-looking ruffled high-necked blouses, and too much makeup.

"I'm a lawyer." She handed Rowena a card she'd had at the ready. "I used to bring clients here for lunch now and then, but I had to stop. You may or may not know it, but your sister treated this place like a privately stocked fish pond. There actually used to be a bowl next to the reservations book where customers were encouraged to deposit their business cards. I was relieved to see it's no longer there."

Why the hell are you telling me this? Rowena wondered, looking over to where she now remembered the bowl had once sat. She'd never known its purpose, and hadn't noted its absence. "Your taxi's here," she said with a polite smile.

"Oh, good. I found out after the fact," the woman continued in a muted, confiding tone, "that Claudia called up two of my clients. Both were married men, and were rattled by her—let's call it interest. I considered having a quiet word with her but decided instead to take my clients elsewhere. I wouldn't have come today, but that fool had already made a reservation." At last getting to her feet, she said, "I realize Claudia died not too long ago. I hope I haven't offended you, but you strike me as a sensible woman. You must've known what your sister was like."

Rowena glanced belatedly at the card, irked by this woman's lack of sensitivity in raising an issue that no longer had relevance—if it ever did. "The driver's waiting, Ms. Brewer," she said evenly, anxious to have her gone.

"Right. Well, if you ever need legal representation, my office is right here in town."

"Actually," Rowena said pleasantly, "I couldn't possibly trust my legal work to someone who doesn't test the waters before she dives in. But thanks all the same. Have a nice day." She turned and walked briskly toward the kitchen, feeling the woman's eyes, then heard her move off. The front door opened and closed, and she was gone.

"Frightful bitch, isn't she?" Ian observed sotto voce as she entered the kitchen where he was drinking a glass of mineral water.

"I'll say!" Rowena agreed, lifted by the comment.

"She's the sort who'd happily do you in with her 'honesty.' "

"Exactly."

They smiled at each other, a moment of complete accord. Then he finished the water and headed back inside, and she went to pick up the salads for one of the couples she was serving at the bar.

By two-fifteen when the rush had died down, she went out to the patio carrying a cup of coffee and her cigarettes. The only remaining customer outdoors, Reid was lingering over his own coffee as he worked the acrostic puzzle in the magazine section. He gave the impression of being perfectly content.

"I thought I'd take a break, if my smoking won't bother you," she said, sliding into the chair opposite his.

"Be my guest," he said expansively, putting down his pen and positioning the ashtray closer to her. An empty glass with the dregs of a drink sat waiting to be removed by one of the busboys.

"How was your lunch?" she asked from habit, lighting a cigarette and listening to the rain pattering on the canopy as she studied him: wide-set eyes of the purest blue, well-defined arching eyebrows as black as his hair, enviably thick eyelashes enhancing the luminosity of his eyes, a strong, prominent nose and squared jaw. She supposed people had been hitting on him all his life because of his looks. It was so easy to be drawn to beautiful people; she'd seen it time and again with her sister. There was an instinctive tendency to assume that the personality of someone physically appealing had to match the exterior, which was not only a foolish assumption, it was also a potentially dangerous one. So many people had pursued Claudia because of her looks. She had spent most of her adult life working to perfect her appearance, and what had it brought her? A shelf of homemade video tapes with partners some of whom she'd culled from business cards casually deposited in a large glass bowl. She must have been desperate to do such a thing.

"I've yet to be disappointed by the food here," Reid was saying, "or the service."

"Good. That's good." She couldn't take her eyes off him, noticing the faintly blue shadow of his incipient beard and the tidy shape of his ears, the precision of his side-parted haircut. He was like an exhibit in a gallery, as captivating as a work of art executed by someone at the peak of his creative power. Something low in her belly stirred, like an awakening serpent slowly uncoiling.

"Because of you," he went on, "coming here isn't like going out to eat alone. You know those deadly occasions when you take along reading matter in self-defense—at conventions, or traveling; those times when you feel too visible."

She nodded, watching his lips as he spoke, hints of his tongue lifting in the interior of his mouth, shaping the words. "When I'm traveling," she said, feeling drugged, "I never mind eating alone. Although I do always take something to read."

"Kind of a pity about the weather." He turned to gaze at the rain, then turned back. "I was looking forward to our going out on the boat. I don't suppose you're free for dinner?"

"Not tonight, no." She refused as a matter of course, even though she had no plans for the evening. She saw herself climbing naked across his lap, and a tremor started up in her hands; internally a subtle expansion was taking place. She wanted to touch him, to shut her eyes, press herself up against his body and absorb him through her skin.

"Short notice, I know. Maybe one evening this week?"

"Maybe."

He started to smile. "I should call you, right? And we'll see."

"Right." She smiled back. Did he know the effect he had on her? Probably not. She was highly skilled at concealing her feelings; she'd had years of practice when the only defense against her mother and sister had been an impassive expression, maintained no matter what the provocation might be.

"Fair enough. We'll leave it at that."

"Are you always so obliging, Reid, or is it strictly for my benefit?"

"Well, now." He sat back, folding his arms across his chest. "Were you to talk to my former wife, she'd undoubtedly tell you what a miserable son of a bitch I am. 'Gloomy' was one of her favorite adjectives. 'Unsociable' was another. The truth is that, like most people, I tend to respond to whomever I'm with. So the answer is—yes and no."

"Meaning it's strictly for my benefit." She inhaled deeply and held the smoke in her lungs.

"And partly for mine."

"Why?" she asked through the cloud of her exhalation.

"Because I like you, Rowena. It's not terribly complicated."

"I think it is."

"No, it really isn't. We all behave well toward people we like."

"The lyrics go we always hurt the ones we love. And I've given you no reason whatsoever to like me."

His eyebrows lifted as if she'd accused him of something illicit. "Emotions are rarely logical. They usually have a life of their own."

"Emotions?" Her eyes at long last left his to find the ashtray. She stubbed out the cigarette, aware of the intensified rhythm of her heartbeat, the looseness at the apex of her thighs, the growing heat there. If this were another dream, she'd get up, walk around the table, hoist her skirt, and straddle his lap. "What emotions?" She lifted her coffee cup and regarded him over top of it, the rich French roast pleasing to her tongue.

"I told you. I like you. And," he said almost slyly, "I enjoy looking at you, too."

She flushed, abashed.

He tilted back in his chair, one hand anchoring him to the table. "It appears to be a mutually agreeable pastime."

"You're crazy," she said softly. "People have been known to run screaming at the sight of me."

His eyes widened. "Oh, I doubt that. You're lovely." He paused, head canted to one side. "You have haunting eyes, penetrating eyes that change color. Last weekend on the boat they were blue. Today they're green." Again he paused. She was aware of the pulse beating strongly in her throat and hoped he couldn't see it. "A sweet mouth, with an almost childlike innocence. No one's *ever* run screaming at the sight of you." Coming forward, he propped an arm on the table and rested his chin in his upturned hand, looking squarely at her with a smile.

She remained perfectly still while inside her the serpent seemed to increase in girth, acquiring a definite rhythm as it slithered through the bottom of her belly. It was surpassingly odd to hear herself described in this fashion, and impossible to believe. She felt as if she were listening to a piece of fiction, intrigued more by his intent than his words.

"I know you don't believe me, because you have no idea how you actually look. I find that truly lamentable. But on the other hand, people who *know* they're good-looking are intimidating. Don't you think?"

"I haven't given it any thought," she lied.

"Oh, come on," he teased. "Sure you have."

It was her turn to pause, using the time to scramble through her mental archives, searching for precedents, all the while knowing she had none. Nothing in her life could have prepared her for this man.

Kip appeared in the doorway with the coffeepot. She gave an almost imperceptible shake of her head. He made a Boy Scout salute, did an about-face, and went back inside. "This is verbal lovemaking," she declared, eyes again on Reid, her body's heat so high she thought it must be rising in waves into the damp air, like a shimmering mirage. "You're quite the con artist."

"It's not a con," he said, as if injured by the allegation. "It's the truth. And as for verbal lovemaking"—his smile ripened—"that's a particularly intriguing concept. Is that how you perceive my observations?"

"You're doing more than making observations." She lit another cigarette, trying to conceal the now full-fledged tremor in her hands. The serpent's scales were gently abrading her tissues, its forked, flickering tongue creating tiny spasms each time it touched her. It was an effort to sit still. She was strongly tempted to put her hands on him. For a moment she wondered why she couldn't go around to his side of the table, take his head in her hands and kiss him. Her entire life had been built upon constraints—both social and self-imposed. She was the antithesis of her sister who hadn't understood the meaning of the word, and had always reached out with both hands to take what she wanted while Rowena had felt obliged to earn every last thing. Just once she wished she had the temerity to act upon her instincts. But of course she didn't. All she could do was engage in artful badinage.

"That's true," he admitted, looking at her mouth. "But if it's upsetting you, I'll stop."

She laughed hoarsely. "You won't stop, Reid. You're enjoying yourself too much."

"So are you, Rowena."

"It's a game, and you've played it before. Maybe too many times."
She heard the austere, censuring edge her voice whittled into the words
and knew she'd managed to snap the tenuous mood. She wasn't sorry.
In the ensuing silence she became aware again of the rain pattering on
the canopy, of the breeze lifting the edges of the newspaper and cooling her skin.

He let his hand drop to the table, the merriment leaving his eyes.
"No, I haven't. I loathe games. I *was* enjoying myself. It was something different, new—a psychosexual jousting match. It was novel, and
exciting. And we were both playing. But no matter. I've never been
able to derive satisfaction—from anything—at someone else's expense. I'm sorry you're upset."

He was telling the truth, and it floored her. "How old are you,
Reid?"

"Forty-four. How old are you?"

"Forty. Are you trying to tell me you've lived forty-four years and
never indulged in the games your looks entitle you to play?"

"My *looks*," he said with disgust. "I hate that superficial drivel.
What makes you assume I'm different from you? I live in here"—he
tapped his left index finger to his temple—"the same way you do. I'm
not on the outside, admiring the facade. Neither are you. Which is why
you view compliments as a form of manipulation. Because the immediate and obvious assumption is that someone's paying undue attention to an aspect of yourself you consider has minimal, if any,
relevance to your identity."

"Please don't analyze me."

"I'm always analytical, Rowena. But I'm sorry." He smiled again,
with less wattage.

She said, "So am I," and meant it, wishing yet again that life were
as simple and direct as dreams, with no need for apprehension or explanations. But people were never simple and rarely direct. Too often
they said and did things for reasons others would find incomprehensible; they were driven by forces it would take years to track back to
their origins. And psychological backtracking was what this man did
daily. He was an archeologist of the psyche, cautiously whisking aside
the dust of decades with a delicate brush, looking to unearth fragments of truth. "I am sorry," she repeated. "I had an ugly encounter
with a former friend Friday night. I took a pounding, so I'm feeling
kind of fragile at the moment."

Immediately responsive, he asked, "A pounding? Literally?"

"Literally. Although, to be fair, I don't think she entirely knew what she was doing."

"That's awful! What happened?"

"A misunderstanding, the end of a long friendship." She shrugged, reluctant to go into it.

"Are you all right?"

"I've got some spectacular bruises, but otherwise I'm okay." She sighed, disappointed with the direction in which she'd taken the conversation. "I should get back inside."

"Have dinner with me," he urged. "Let's talk more. It's important."

"I don't want to like you, Reid," she confessed abruptly, wearied of fencing. "I don't want to care about you. Being around you turns me skeptical. I have trouble believing the things you say, the reasons why you say them. I don't know you."

"Of course you do. Your instincts are very solid. I recognized that at our first meeting."

She was so overwhelmed by a sense of déjà vu that she lost track of what they'd been saying. Chilled since her body was no longer generating intense sexual heat, she shivered and extinguished her cigarette. "My instincts are not to be trusted right now. And the truth is, you scare me. You're so far beyond my limited experience that I'm not even sure who I am when I'm with you. I begin wobbling, falling off my axis, every time you leave another message or show up here unannounced. I'm more attracted to you than I've ever been to anyone." *What are you doing? Don't admit that! He'll use it against you.* "I don't like feeling that way. I don't want to care about you." She moved to get up, convinced she'd committed a form of suicide.

"Wait a minute! How do you know this isn't about friendship?"

She laughed. "Please, Reid, don't insult my intelligence."

"You're right. That was a trite, self-defensive comeback inspired by *my* misgivings. But why do you assume this is one-sided, that you're the only one out there on the high wire?" He spoke quietly, without animosity. "It's tiring, pursuing someone—even on the least aggressive level—with little or no encouragement. Frankly, it's kind of demeaning. I'm more attracted to *you* than I've ever been to anyone. And admitting that scares me just as much as it does you. It's risky, exposing one's self. My experience is probably only marginally less limited than yours. But never mind that. Do you want me to back off, Rowena?"

The question and his clear anticipation of pain—an infinitesimal drawing together of the arching brows, the flattening at the corners of his mouth—made her want to comfort him. "I don't want to hurt anyone," she answered. "I don't want to be hurt."

"Nobody does," he said reasonably. "But if we allow ourselves to be dictated to by fear, we wind up with half-lived lives. And I don't want that. Maybe it's too soon for you. There's no prescribed time limit to the grieving process."

"It's odd," she said, taking advantage of the offered opening. "I miss her at times, sort of in the way you notice that the pills have finally worked and the headache's gone. Other times, I miss the drama. It's like having one of your favorite TV shows canceled. And sometimes I simply miss her, and can't believe she's gone for good. I loved my sister, Reid. Maybe it was an ingrained habit, or a conditioned response. Who knows? She engendered affection in me, in spite of everything. I really did love her, and I don't know why she died. So you could be right. Maybe it is too soon. Or maybe I'm a congenital coward who's going to live a half-life. I really must get back inside now."

"Hold on one more minute. Okay?" His hand on her wrist stopped her.

She remained seated, thinking how sticklike her arm looked in his grasp. His hand was huge but gentle, and she was reminded of the caution of Kip's embraces.

"You didn't answer my question. Do you want me to back off? It's your call. Say yes, and I will. It's that simple."

"I don't *know!*" She felt horribly pressured. Avoiding his eyes, she slipped away, escaping inside. Halfway through the restaurant the old sadness assaulted her. She stopped by the bar, vexed at having handled things so ineptly. *Could* she be content with what he'd termed a half-life? Or was he baiting her? A man who admitted to insecurity was a rare man indeed. Or was he exceptionally clever? She closed her eyes for a moment, experiencing again that inordinate desire to put her hands on him and prove to herself he was real and not some outsized figment of her febrile imagination. After a minute she opened her eyes and went back.

He was sitting staring off into space, and she thought he was right. She did have a strong sense of him, but only at random moments and usually from a distance. She knew that at that moment he was hurt, and lonely. And she was, in large measure, responsible. Again like Kip, he demonstrated an alarming and surprising vulnerability. She wanted to move up behind him and take her hands lightly over his face, the way someone sightless might, learning him through her fingertips. *Oh, be careful,* her inner voice warned. *You're awfully close to falling here. One little push and you'll be saying and doing things you'll wish later on you hadn't said and done.*

"It scares me silly, but I don't want you to back off," she said from the doorway. "The thing is, I can't promise anything. I'm very afraid of making a fool of myself." She groped for other words but failed to find any. "That's all I can say."

He shifted to look at her, one arm resting on the chair back. "No one could reasonably ask for more." He looked relieved and boyishly pleased. "I'm not fond of the idea of making a fool of myself, either. Isn't it a pity we can't get guarantees on people the way we do with new cars and appliances?"

"A great pity," she concurred. "I really do have to go in now."

"Of course."

Quaking inside, she let his eyes hold hers. Strangely, the visual contact was more intimate than the verbal one. She felt it like an electrical current traveling through her veins. Giving in one more time to impulse, she crossed the patio, put her hands on either side of his face, and kissed him on the mouth. Then, breathless, she hurried inside, leaving him sitting there dumbfounded.

"I'm going home now," she told Ian, emerging from the office with her handbag.

"Did you want to comp any portion of your friend's meal, Rowena?"

"The coffee," she said, the car keys already in her hand. As long as she didn't have to encounter Reid again just then she'd be all right. She could, if she wanted, pretend nothing had happened. "See you in the morning."

"Cheers. Have a good one," Ian said pleasantly.

Kip waved as she rushed through the restaurant, on her way to the front door. Giddy, she waved back and made good her getaway, a frantic, euphoric rapping in her chest.

She arrived home with no recollection of the drive; she'd made the trip on automatic pilot. That was risky. She was going to have to be more careful. But, God, she was positively flying, way up there on an adrenaline high. Humming to herself, she ran upstairs to get the laundry and carried it down to the cellar. With the first load of whites going, she started back upstairs again to change clothes, but her eye was caught by the cartons sitting in the middle of the old rec room. She'd have a quick look, she thought, and settled at the bridge table to go through a box of Jeanne's, which turned out to hold nothing but monthly bank statements—a good ten years' worth. They went directly into a trash bag. She opened another carton. The topmost item was a bulging brown envelope that upon inspection proved to contain every report card she, Claudia, and Cary had ever brought home from school. It threw her. She would never have believed her mother cared enough to keep things like this.

Further envelopes contained artwork all three of them had done as well as Christmas, birthday, Valentine's, and Mother's Day cards, along with notes in Cary's printing, in Claudia's sprawling scrawl, in Rowena's tidy handwriting. Apparently Jeanne had kept every last piece of paper ever produced by her children—from kindergarten crayon drawings and finger paintings to quite good fashion sketches Claudia had done in high school.

Rowena looked at everything, particularly Cary's drawings, wondering what kind of woman treated her children with such casual disregard, yet squirreled away anything they created. It was a kind of caring not readily comprehensible, but it was something positive nonetheless. She lingered over the drawings, the colors as fresh as if they'd been applied to the paper only hours or days before. They took her back to an image of herself and her brother propped on their elbows on the living room floor, both of them with large newsprint pads, a brand-new box of sixty-four Crayolas within easy reach. She must have been about seven, and Cary ten. They chatted away as they drew their pictures. Hers was of a square house with a chimney from which a curl of smoke rose into the sky. There was a big yellow sun, puffs of cloud in the sky, and V-shaped birds. Flowers grew around the base of the house, and a winding path led to the front door. On the grass just off the path stood the family that lived in the house—a father and his two children.

Cary's drawing was of an expanse of wavy blue water upon which sat a small boat with a triangular white sail. He too showed a big yellow sun and puffy clouds in the sky. And on the boat, a hand on the tiller, was a small, smiling stick figure wearing blue pants and a yellow Mae West.

Carefully returning everything to the envelopes, she put them back in the box and got up to shift the whites to the dryer. The second load in the washer, she switched off the lamp on the bridge table and went upstairs to change her clothes. Humming again, she stepped out of the moss green linen Valentino dress and placed it on a padded hanger. She felt wonderfully well as she removed the silk underwear and dropped it into the hamper. Stepping into a pair of old cotton underpants, she looked on the shelves for the oversize yellow T-shirt she'd bought ages ago at a South Norwalk street fair. She distinctly remembered replacing it on the shelf after the break-in. She thought of the softness of Reid's mouth and felt a spasm of response in her belly. *Stop this!* She got the desk chair from the bedroom, climbing up to get a better look at the shelf.

The next time he phoned asking to see her they'd very likely end up in bed together. She could hardly go on discouraging him after their exchange on the patio—after she'd made the single boldest gesture of her life. God! She'd actually taken his face in her hands and kissed him. She could feel the impression of his lips on hers, the aftertaste of coffee and alcohol. *Stop! You're out of control.*

The T-shirt was at the rear of the left-hand shelf and she reached for it, then stopped. Turning, she looked down at the right-hand side of the dressing room, then again at the left. Was it an optical illusion, or was the left-hand shelf deeper? Picking up the T-shirt, she climbed down from the chair to examine the undersides of each shelf. Both halves of the dressing room seemed the same, but somehow they weren't. She pulled on the shirt and a pair of baggy shorts, trying to figure out the visual discrepancy.

Determined to solve this, she went down to the kitchen for the tape measure, and took the stairs back up two at a time. The underside of the right-hand shelf was sixteen inches deep. The left-hand one measured twenty-four inches. The upper surface of each shelf was twenty-four inches. How could there be an eight inch difference underneath?

Pushing the clothes aside, she examined the wall closely. If she hadn't been looking for it, she'd never have noticed the seam, or the fact that this wall, unlike the one opposite, was painted wood and not plaster. Upon closer inspection, she discovered that the seam was in fact a junction, where the wood met the plaster. Able to get her fingernails into the join, she pulled, and the wood slid smoothly aside, revealing a hidden compartment roughly three feet wide and a hand span deep. Inside, leaning against the wall, was a folded tripod. Resting on the floor next to it was the video camera that belonged to the packaging she'd found in the attic, along with a small timing device. And beside that was a Fuji VHS cassette.

Seventeen

The camera was surprisingly light and compact, and as alien to her as a laser gun or a book in Sanskrit. While she examined it, her eyes traveled to the cassette, and her brain said, *Don't even think about it! Take it right out to the garbage. You don't want to know what's on it.*

The problem was she *did* want to know. The tape drew her, even as the warnings sounded in her head, telling her this was nothing more than another opportunity to see Claudia performing like a contortionist, being penetrated in yet another impossible position. It seemed there had been little her sister wouldn't do, and with an absence of emotion that was far more troubling than the use she'd allowed so many men to make of her body. The strongest reaction she'd displayed on any of the tapes had been a grimace of unadulterated pain as one of her partners had sodomized her with such angry vigor that he'd had to keep a firm grip on her narrow hips to prevent her from collapsing. Watching this act had been deeply disturbing, yet Rowena had been unable to look away. She needed to try to comprehend why Claudia had so willingly, and so often, submitted to these indignities, these monstrous assaults upon her fragile, undernourished body. But all Rowena had so far discovered was that people could be astonishingly inventive and cruel about the ways in which they sought sexual gratification.

Putting aside the camera, she picked up the cassette and headed downstairs, on her way to the trash bin outside. When this last one was disposed of, the trophy tapes would all be gone. Halfway along the hall she found herself slowing, coming to a halt. She could pop it into the VCR, take a quick look, fast-forwarding through the paired acrobatics, and be done with it. It was unlikely she'd see anything she hadn't seen before.

Don't kid yourself! Whatever she saw would upset her. She was already agitated, her good mood squashed. She took a step toward the kitchen and stopped. In the grip of intense ambivalence, she stood for quite some time, unable to throw the tape out or to bring herself to view it. At last she put it on the floor and inched away into the kitchen where she sat at the table and lit a cigarette, turning periodically to look down the hallway to see that, yes, the tape was still there. It was not magically going to self-destruct.

After a second cigarette, she got up and went to peer out at the garden in the downpour. As a result of her labors the flower beds now had a tidy definition, their edges rimmed by healthy, close-clipped grass. If she narrowed her eyes she could see her father out there on his knees, his head shielded from the hot summer sun by a battered old Panama hat as he pulled weeds, then leaned back to admire the hydrangea's lush green-white flower clusters. From where she and Cary sat on the swing set she could see him raise his head as Claudia came spinning across the grass like a small human top, arms outflung, whirling around and around, mouth open, laughing. George Graham regarded his youngest child with an expression of disheartened affection as, carried by her own giddy momentum, Claudia went spinning into the nearest bed, trampling the flowers underfoot before tumbling sidelong to the ground, her fall cushioned by bluebells and lady's slipper and primrose. Immobile, he observed as his mercurial five-year-old compounded the damage with her thrashing limbs. Then, tiredly, as if aged suddenly, he plucked her from the bed and set her down on the grass, quietly telling her to run along. Harum-scarum, off she went, leaving her father sorrowfully surveying the wreckage she'd left behind. Not long after this incident he had telephoned to say he wouldn't be coming home again.

Coincidental probably, the destruction of the garden and the timing of his departure. But all her life Claudia had left wreckage in some form or other in her wake. Oblivious, she'd moved on to whatever next caught her eye. She seemed to have no sense of cause and effect, didn't feel what others felt, and was baffled by their upset and accusations. She just didn't get what all the fuss was about. How many times, Rowena wondered, had she seen that expression of unfeigned mystification on her sister's face? Dozens, hundreds, of times. It was in large measure why Rowena had, for a lifetime, maintained a safe distance but kept on forgiving her: because she believed that Claudia suffered from some fatal flaw. There was only empty space where her reactive emotions should have been. She could not empathize, could not conceive of any joys or woes other than her own. By definition, that made her sociopathic. Rowena had used the available resources at the library to do an in-depth study of her sister's personality and had arrived at this conclusion. What she'd never been able to determine was why her sister had come into the world damaged. There appeared to be no answer for this, just as there was no apparent reason why her life had ended so abruptly.

The thing of it was, the general population was prepared to make all sorts of concessions for those visibly disabled, or in some way impaired. That same population was not, nor could it have been, prepared to make any allowance for someone who seemed, in the most obvious ways, entirely normal. But so-called normal people did not do the things Claudia had done. Which brought Rowena full circle back to that damned tape sitting on the hall floor.

"This is bullshit!" she said aloud, turning from the window. She was hungry. She'd skipped lunch, too distracted by Tony Reid even to consider food. She tried to concentrate on him now, eager for the distraction. Perhaps he'd call this evening. Then again he probably wouldn't. Men never did what women would if their positions were reversed. They had totally different priorities. She wanted him to be atypical, to act on those feelings he claimed to have, and call her. But it didn't matter whether or not he did. She couldn't allow her life to be directed by anyone's whims. So she'd fix something to eat, watch a couple of hours of TV, then have a long soak in the tub before bed.

Opening the refrigerator door, she stared at the contents, faintly put off by every last thing on the shelves. Next she looked in the freezer, but found nothing appetizing there. And nothing in the cupboards appealed to her either. She lit another cigarette and began pacing, one arm wrapped around her midriff, detouring now and then to tip the ashes into the sink or the ashtray, her thoughts sliding into turmoil. The minutes ticked by as her eyes went first to the telephone, then to the cassette on the hallway floor, and back to the telephone, until the cigarette burned down to the filter and she dropped it into the ashtray.

Why should Reid phone just because she wanted to be rescued from temptation? He wasn't time-sharing her brain or her impulses. *I like you. It's not that complicated.* It was probably only a line with a hook on the end of it to reel her in. He'd offered to back off. She should've said, Do that. Then she wouldn't have been fretting about whether he'd call and save her from temptation.

Claudia, why did you have to make a visual record of your conquests? Why did you have to leave it behind to torment me? All my life, every time I've come close to being happy, something you did destroyed it. My head's like an old warehouse, piled high with tainted memories and unvoiced recriminations.

She hated this! Getting herself tied in knots when what she really wanted was to be left alone. No tapes, no men. Yet she'd been so moved by Reid's aura of loneliness, and his compliments had felt like gifts. But being Claudia's sister had taught her that it was better to live a half-life of quiet predictability than to become embroiled in the bewildering needs of men; better to savor each day's small pleasures than to lose precious time in anticipation of an intimacy that was too fleeting and never complete.

What am I doing? she wondered, light-headed from too many cigarettes, too much coffee, and too little nourishment. Determined not to let her sister ruin her fragile connection with Reid, she marched down the hall, snatched up the cassette, and took it out to the garbage. Back inside, satisfied, she washed her hands, then pulled out the crisper drawer and a can of V-8 from the refrigerator. She'd have the juice and a salad while she watched *60 Minutes*.

All evening she had the disconcerting sensation of being outside her body, observing. Hovering up in a corner of the room near the ceiling, she looked down and saw herself sitting on the sofa watching television. She saw herself get up during a commercial break to go to the bathroom; saw herself acting out a parody of normalcy, pretending she was unaware of the tape outside in the trash.

She was so agitated she scarcely knew what she was watching. The shows began and ended and she hadn't the least idea what they'd been about. When the telephone rang at a quarter to nine she jumped, then smiled. Reid was calling after all. Her buoyant mood restored, she reached over to pick up the receiver.

"You've got a very sexy telephone voice. Did you know that?"

"No, but I'm glad you think so."

"I think so. And how are you this evening, dear heart?"

"I'm fine," she said, making an effort to keep the disappointment out of her tone. She'd gone from high to low so fast she actually felt dizzy. "How are you?"

"Good. Want some company?"

"Thanks, but I think I'm going to make it an early night." She didn't dare let Mark see her. He'd pick up at once that something was wrong, and she lacked the energy to explain. "How was your afternoon with Richard?"

"Pretty good. We had lunch in Westport, then took in a flick. It's funny, you know, Ro. In another lifetime, I wouldn't have thought he was my type. But I guess my type's changed. He's no ball of fire, but he's easy to be with and right now that's what I need. I couldn't deal with someone young and gung ho and all hot to trot. I don't have the energy. Isn't that a kick in the ass?''

"Poor you. It's no fun getting old, is it?''

"Beats the hell out of the alternative," he said, chortling. "Anyway, if you're okay and really don't want company, I think I'll grab a sandwich and watch *Masterpiece Theater.*''

"Me, too.''

"Any word from the shrink?''

"Actually, he showed up at the restaurant for lunch.''

"Didn't I tell you he's interested? So, come on. I want the juicy details.''

"There aren't any. Don't go betting the ranch on this one, my darling.''

"Could that be the jaded warble of the disenchanted cockatiel I hear?''

"No. It's the self-sufficient trill of the ruffled grouse. Go have your sandwich and we'll talk later.''

Chuckling, he said, "Take good care, Miz Grouse.''

She put down the receiver and got up to put on the kettle for tea, lighting a cigarette while she waited for the water to boil. Eyes on the telephone, she thought about how, during her ninth-grade year, she'd spent hours after school going through the directories at the telephone company office, trying to find a listing for her father. She'd called a fair number of G. Grahams in towns all over the state and had even spoken to two George Grahams, but neither was *her* George Graham. When she'd gone to work at the Mag she'd spent time on a second, more intensive search that proved no more productive than the first. She could only conclude that her father had moved out of state, and she gave up trying to find him.

Always in her mind she could hear Jeanne insisting that he'd wanted nothing to do with his children. And Rowena had reasoned that he'd had years to get in touch, but he hadn't, so perhaps there was some truth to what her mother had said.

Returning to the living room sofa with her cigarettes and tea, she settled in and stared fixedly at the TV screen, thinking she should've asked Mark to come over. But she didn't want to sound stupid, confessing she was worked up about having found another tape, so she'd just have to pull herself together.

At ten she switched off the set, activated the alarm system and went to soak in a hot bath laced with Epsom salts. Immersed in the steaming water, she studied the evolution of the bruises on her arms, the overlapping areas of blue and red and purple, and thought of how Penny had been keeping secrets for years. Claudia had kept her fair share, too. It wasn't difficult to withhold information, permitting others to know only certain edited facts. Much of Penny's appeal as a friend had been her openness, but it had been an illusion. And it was galling to realize she'd been taken in, duped by someone to whom she'd given her unqualified trust.

Maybe she was also being taken in by Reid. A not-quite-buried core of need had started her dreaming about the man, had her subconscious buying into fantasy scenarios, and she didn't know how to stifle the need, kill it for good.

Three years of Gil Prasker had shown her she was best off alone. Years of last-minute cancellations of plans that had been vague to begin with, of increasingly arid evenings when they could find nothing to talk about, and of feeling that she'd made a commitment to a set of rules rather than to a person. Since then she had enjoyed the freedom to offer spontaneous dinner invitations to friends without having to check first with the man in her life who automatically assumed his plans took precedence over hers. And she preferred to do without lovemaking rather than go through the onerous process of playing tour guide to her own body. These were the things she probably should've told Reid, but it wouldn't have mattered because she had crossed the line when she'd taken the initiative and kissed him. It was too late now.

Once in bed with a book, she tried to pay attention but when she found herself reading the same paragraph over and over she set the book aside and switched off the light, glad this long day had come to an end. Early in the morning the garbage truck would come along and the tape would be gone.

God! She sat up in a sudden sweat. She'd left it right on top. It'd be the first thing the garbagemen would see when they lifted the lid. She could just hear their comments: "Hey! Willya look at this! Imagine throwing away a perfectly good cassette!"

"Go figure, huh."

One of them would shove it into the pocket of his coveralls, shaking his head in amazement at the things people on the route decided were fit only for the trash. He'd take the cassette home and after dinner pop it into the VCR to check it out....

Leaping from the bed, she tore downstairs, paused long enough to punch in the security code, then raced along the hall, and out the back door. Five seconds and she'd retrieved the tape and was inside again. Heart drumming, she coded the alarm, telling herself she'd get the scissors in a minute, as soon as she caught her breath.

The illuminated numerals on the stove panel showed 11:12 p.m. She turned on the light and sat at the table. Her hands were damp. She put the cassette down and wiped first one palm, then the other on her pajama leg, feeling as if she were inside that flimsy house in *The Wizard of Oz,* sent spiraling aloft by forces beyond her control. She noticed that this cassette, unlike the others, had no film label. Maybe it was blank and had been sitting, waiting for Claudia's next session.

Only one way to find out. She went to the living room, turned on the TV, pushed the tape into the VCR, and sat down on the floor, remote in hand.

There was a minute or so of fuzz before, with a suddenness that startled her every time, she was watching her naked sister holding her breasts from underneath with both hands, as if offering a pair of impeccably firm melons to a potential purchaser. It was one of her stock gestures but this time it generated no response in her fully dressed partner whose back was to the camera. Undaunted, Claudia proceeded to wind herself around the man. Still no response. His hands went to her shoulders, holding her off. She stood listening with a smile as he said something. Then, disregarding whatever he'd said, she turned up the wattage, using all her seductive skills. Pushing like a persistent terrier, she finally got him turned so that his profile was presented to the camera.

Sudden pain drove the air from Rowena's lungs. She bent into it as she heard the eerie-sounding moan of some wounded animal, and thought abstractedly someone must have run over one of the neighborhood pets. It escalated into a primitive keening and several seconds passed before she realized the sound was emerging from her own throat as the pain spread to encompass her totally. It didn't feel possible to survive such an affliction, such monumental anguish. Arms folded tightly over her chest, rocking back and forth, she wept in noisy gusts as, on the screen, Claudia launched her entire arsenal of sexual weapons at Tony Reid.

Time passed. She fumbled for the remote control, found the Stop button, and some nature program took over the screen—wildebeests or springboks, exotic creatures of some sort, sprinting with effortless grace across a grassy plain, their haunches sleek and powerful. The burst of noise after the silence of the tape was so assaultive that she clapped her hands over her ears. Then, grabbing the remote for the TV, she muted the sound, let the device fall to the carpet, and held her head with both hands. Her body didn't feel big enough to contain the expanding sense of betrayal, and of shame.

Her joints seemed to have lost their natural lubrication. Rising to go to the kitchen, she creaked, hurting, still bent almost double over the injury to her solar plexus. Everything ached. Seizing the first bottle that came to hand, she unscrewed the cap and choked down a mouthful of vodka. It took her breath away. She had to hang on to the counter, shuddering, until the liquor pooled in her stomach, radiating fiery heat. Then she took another swig.

Reaching for her cigarettes, she slumped heavily into a chair as she got one lit with palsied hands. She studied those hands for a few moments, fascinated by the tremors that shook them. Then her head dropped onto her arm. *Why?* Why did he have to do that? Her heart had gone sluggish, grown so weighty it seemed to be pulling her down. *Why, why, why?* He'd played a monstrous game with her. But why? Why had he worked so hard to make her care? She'd been doing well for a time. *I was almost happy.* God, why hadn't she left the damned tape in the trash? No matter. It was all over now—another misshapen package of shopworn dreams to be stored away in the old warehouse.

She sat up and blotted her face on her sleeve, then took a slow, hard drag on the cigarette, noticing distantly how the TV sent flares of color spilling into the hallway. Quite pretty, those intermittent bursts of color. She watched them for a time, finishing the cigarette. Then, moving unsteadily, she went back to the living room. Folding to the floor, she got hold of the remote and pressed the Play button.

Drawing her knees to her chest, she wound both arms around them, letting her chin rest on her knees as she stared blearily at the screen where Claudia had managed to get Reid's trousers down. She reached for something on the bedside table and popped it into her mouth, then slithered down his body. Reid remained half-turned away from the camera, thereby blocking off full view of the action. But it was obvious what Claudia was doing—head bobbing, hands moving beneath Reid's shirt.

He pulled free, took hold of Claudia under the arms and threw her backward onto the bed. Then, his movements angry, he pushed off his shoes, stepped out of his puddled boxers and slacks.

As if determined to offer the camera the best possible view, Claudia shifted so that her head rested on the pillows. Reid was now in profile as he knelt on the bed. His expression grim—Why did he look so incensed?—he lifted her from underneath, dragging her lower body forward into his lap. Opening her like some alien, overripe fruit, he pushed into her without preamble. Claudia smiled and arched her back, hips lifting, legs spreading wider.

Rowena watched fixedly, aware that Claudia wasn't in control. Reid was. Insistently he directed the timing, holding her at a downward angle, watching her face while he thrust into her, as if to gauge his accuracy. And for the first time ever, Claudia's face was as naked as her body. Eyes squeezed shut, teeth sunk into her lower lip, she clutched fistfuls of the bedclothes, her head whipping from side to side. Suddenly she went rigid, the tendons standing out prominently in her neck. Her mouth opened and in a dumb show she cried out as her body leaped, in spasm.

"That's real," Rowena murmured, blinking. No one could have created at will the paroxysm that shook her sister or the deep flush that made her upper chest and face appear scorched.

Reid stopped moving, and sat with Claudia spread, twitching, across his lap. When she grew quiescent he withdrew, and pushed her not ungently away. Scooping up his clothes, he pulled them on, jammed his feet into his shoes, and walked out as Claudia sat up saying something. He ignored her and kept going. The tape went fuzzy. No signature smile for the camera, only an abrupt end.

Rowena stopped the tape, turned everything off and sat staring at the dead screen, feeling gutted. Her chest had become a rickety shelter of brittle sticks that housed an impaired, faltering heart. She had the identical, excruciating sense of aloneness that she'd had after Cary died. But it was worse now because at least back then there had been the future to anticipate, the happily-ever-after part promised in every fairy tale she'd ever read. Now there was nothing.

She'd trusted, and it had been a mistake—not once, but twice. "Takes a lot to convince you," she berated herself. "Got to learn the hard way." First Penny, now Reid. Penny was history. She'd have to think about how to handle Reid. But first things first. Staggering, she climbed the stairs, got the video camera from its hiding place, and carried it down to the cellar. Kneeling on the cold cement floor of the laundry room, she smashed the camera to bits with a hammer. Panting, she scooped the pieces back into a pile and pounded away until she couldn't raise her arm one more time. Leaving everything on the floor, she dragged herself up to the kitchen to gulp another mouthful of vodka. Then, mopping her face on her soggy sleeve, she went reeling off to bed.

Eighteen

Shrill mechanical beeping pierced her skull like quick stabs of a needle. With a groan she silenced the alarm and sat up, the movement creating what felt like an avalanche of stones inside her head and a pulsing throb at her temples. Her mouth and tongue were so dehydrated she couldn't swallow. She had to remain hunched over on the side of the bed for several minutes, unable to move farther. She seemed to have flu symptoms—the overall ache, the headache, the fever. Whatever the ailment was, it felt terminal.

Then, bit by bit, she remembered—the tape, the many cigarettes, the vodka—and understood that she was experiencing a hangover. It was horrendous. Her stomach roiled, her hands shook, and her head felt as if it had turned to glass, tripled in size, and was on the verge of shattering from the tremendous internal pressure.

Stooped over in pain it seemed for a time as if she were contained in a vast empty place, and she wished she were dead. No games, no conflicts, no pain whatsoever. Just wonderful white nothingness. But why should she surrender her life because people had treated her badly? Shouldn't they be the ones wanting to die? People she'd cared for who did harm as if it were second nature. They might hurt her but she wouldn't die, couldn't.

Going very, very slowly, she managed to get to her feet and shuffle into the bathroom. She turned on the light, felt the bulb's sizzling radiance sear her pupils, and quickly turned it off. That small hasty motion heightened the nausea. She gagged down three extra strength Tylenol caplets with some water, got the Alka-Seltzer from the medicine cabinet, and painstakingly made her way down to the kitchen—a trip that seemed to take at least an hour and threatened to dislocate both her hips.

Cigarette ash was all over the floor. The open vodka bottle stood on the countertop. A burned-out cigarette floated in an inch or so of brown-tinted, reeking water in the sink. Trying to keep her head upright while moving with maximum caution, she deposited the butt in the trash, drained and rinsed the sink, got the coffee maker started, then dropped two Alka-Seltzer tablets into a glass of water—wincing at the explosive fizzing—and drank it down.

Food was out of the question, yet she knew she had to eat. Dry toast would, she hoped, soak up some of the poison in her system. God! She groaned again. The pounding was so ferocious it felt as if two giant hands were attempting to crush her eggshell-thin skull. She wanted to sweep the floor but didn't dare. Instead, she crept to the table, lowered herself into a chair and began an inventory of her physical woes, deciding only her toes were free of pain. The aroma of the dripping coffee wafted across the room, causing her stomach to clench and begin rising. She hobbled into the downstairs bathroom, arriving just in time to throw up in the basin. Eyes tearing, she rinsed the sink, then drank some more water.

The headache worse now, she returned to the kitchen and stood, eyes closed, while she waited for the toast, one hand fastened to the counter, the other clutching a mug half-filled with black coffee. After chewing the hot dry bread, washing it down with coffee, she began to think she might live after all. The Tylenol was taking effect, reducing the throbbing in her temples. She eased back into the chair at the table with a fresh mug of coffee.

Forty minutes later she felt sufficiently recovered to go along the hall to open the front door. The *Times* was waiting in its blue plastic sleeve. Underneath it was an envelope, her name printed on its face in block letters. Gritting her teeth, she retrieved both items from the mat. Head pounding again, she tottered back to the kitchen.

With dread she examined the envelope, hoping it wasn't from Reid. But she knew who'd left it as soon as she saw the corny artwork on the card. It was so typical of Penny: a watercolor dove and the word "Peace" written in rainbow brush strokes. The message inside read, "I never meant to hurt you, and I'm <u>deeply</u> sorry. Please forgive me. We can't let such a good, long friendship end this way. Call me? Love always, Penny."

It was tempting. One phone call would put things back in order and she'd have Penny's support again. She longed for the comfort and understanding her friend had always been ready to offer; she could almost feel the cushioning warmth of Penny's pillowy embrace. Then she thought of how Penny had behaved toward her since Claudia's death, of the ignominious scene at the restaurant the previous Friday night, and knew she wouldn't call. How could she possibly go back to confiding in someone who'd been deceiving her for years? The trust had been broken. It was too late for apologies; too much damage had been done. You couldn't shame someone publicly and then ask to be forgiven. It wasn't reasonable even to ask. She ripped the card in two and regretfully dropped the pieces in the garbage.

The telephone rang and her head jerked toward the sound. Dreading the possibility that it might be Reid, she let the ringing continue, hands over her ears to lessen its drilling into her brain. God! This was agony. What she needed was Caller ID. Then she'd know instantly who was calling and wouldn't have to go through this torment. The answering machine clicked on after the fourth ring, and the outgoing message played. The tone sounded, then a hesitant Penny said, "I hope you got my card. I drove by early this morning to make sure you'd find it first thing. I never meant any of it to happen, Ro. Things just got so out of hand...about Kip, and the restaurant, about everything. Please call me. We really have to talk. There are things I should've told you a long time ago. I don't honestly know why I didn't. I kind of got locked into my story. And about what happened the other night, I realize I went way overboard. I'm just sick about it. Please believe that I'm sorry. We've *got* to talk, so call me. Okay? Please? Okay. Hope to hear from you later. Bye." She hung up, the machine sounded another tone, then began resetting itself.

Her sadness and dismay renewed, Rowena sat, weighted down. She longed to run away, but of course she wouldn't—never had, never would. It was her nature to see every last thing through to the bitter, bloody end. What she could do, though, was stop by the SNET office in the afternoon and arrange for Caller ID on both this line and the one at the restaurant. She'd get Ian or Terry to field any calls there that came in from Penny or Reid. If Reid showed up at the restaurant, she had no idea what she'd do, but she'd deal with that when it happened. She could scarcely function let alone sit and plan a strategy for dealing with people she no longer wanted to see.

It was nine-twenty and she was due at Le Rendezvous in less than two hours. She'd never make it unless she did something about her head. In the upstairs bathroom she examined Claudia's numerous prescription vials. She hadn't bothered to discard any on the remote chance she might someday need one of them. Her sister had suffered from interrupted sleep, migraines, anxiety, depression, and a whole host of maladies. Medications had been prescribed to deal with all of them.

There was a nearly full container of Fiorinal-C capsules marked "For migraine." She washed one down with another cup of water, and tucked the rest into her handbag.

A very hot shower with the shower head adjusted to the gentlest possible spray helped unlock her joints, and by the time she was dressed, the Fiorinal had begun to relieve the headache. Her hands were far too unsteady to apply more than some under-eye concealer, blush, and lipstick. She decided she looked nowhere near as awful as she felt, which was nothing short of remarkable. A little luck and she'd make it through the lunch rush without incident.

In the parking lot across the alley from the rear of the restaurant, she sat with the engine running and the air conditioner on full blast, trying to remember something that was tucked away in a corner of her mind. The ache lingering at the base of her skull made it difficult to think. Three hours and she'd be free to sit quietly and sort through the several theories taking shape in her mind, but there simply wasn't time now to consider the very real possibility that Tony Reid was involved in Claudia's death.

She turned off the ignition and climbed out into the baking heat of the morning, blinded by the glare of sunlight reflected off the parked cars. Donning her sunglasses, she locked the car, then walked through the lot, aware of each step reverberating through her skeleton. Her bones seemed to be holding together by sheer good fortune. Any misstep might cause them to collapse in a disconnected heap. She had little confidence in her hipbones in particular, and felt bowlegged, as if she'd just spent hours on horseback.

Kip was wiping the tabletops on the patio. He looked over as she came through the gate, and she was touched by the brightness of his smile at the sight of her. It made her feel less alone and, at the same time, even more of a fool.

"How's it going, Auntie Ro? Cool dress. You okay?" A crease of concern formed between his eyebrows.

She looked down at herself, unable to remember what she'd put on. Right. Another of Claudia's dresses, in navy linen. It felt a bit baggy at the waist and hips. Was she losing weight? She really had to start paying more attention to meals. "Can you keep a secret, sweetheart?"

"Course I can," he answered, dropping his voice.

"I've got a hangover," she whispered. "I'm close to death."

"Oh, bad," he sympathized. "I've had a couple. Total annihilation. Want me to get you aspirins or coffee or like that?"

"No, thank you." She gave him an intentionally grim smile, and he responded with a sad little shake of his head. "Everything all right at home?" she asked, wondering if it was unfair to deny his mother an opportunity to state her case. But how many opportunities did the woman need? She'd been given several already, and only when it was too late did she begin begging for yet one more chance.

"Seems to be. Mom's like nothing happened, so I'm going with it. Since that scene Friday night she hasn't said word one about me working here, so maybe she's over it, whatever had her so griped."

"Maybe. Hot out here." The heat seemed to be sucking the marrow from her bones. Even moving her eyes required too much of an effort.

"Yeah, way," he agreed. "You better get inside into the cool."

"You're right, I'd better. The plants are doing wonderfully well."

"Yeah." He looked around proudly. "They're good."

She started toward the door then turned back, remembering what it was that had been eluding her. "Sweetheart, did you happen to notice what Dr. Reid was drinking yesterday?"

"Your friend, big guy sat out here doing the *Times* puzzle in ink?"

"That's the one."

"I bussed the table, so I should remember. Hang on a sec. Let me think." He looked off into space for a few moments. "He had the eggs Florentine, and coffee. But he had a drink. What was it?"

"Scotch?" she prompted.

"Right!" He smiled at her. "Chivas rocks." The smile fading, he asked, "Why? Did I mess up or something?"

"No, no, honey. I just couldn't recall what brand he drinks, that's all. Thank you."

"Okay, cool. Hope you feel better soon."

"Me, too." She made it inside, at once revived by the wall of cool air that met her beyond the door. Removing the sunglasses, she headed for the office, saying hi to the staff as she went, and to Ian who was at the bar, going over an invoice with Terry.

She sat down behind the desk, stowed her bag in the bottom drawer, and lit her first cigarette of the day. Big mistake. It tasted terrible and brought back her nausea. She was putting it out when Ian came in.

"I was thinking we should get Caller ID installed," she told him. "Would you have any objection?"

"It might be handy in terms of reservations, having a number to jot down. So no, I'd have no objection. Quite a good idea, actually."

"That's what I thought. Oh, and I've been meaning to ask but keep forgetting. Where are the restaurant's SNET bills kept, Ian?"

"In the basement storeroom, with all the other bills. Why?"

"There's something I want to check." She tried to sound offhand.

"Anything I could help with?"

Wishing she were better able to read him, she watched him slide gracefully into the chair on the far side of the desk and light a Silk Cut. "Possibly," she replied. "According to Tony Reid, there was a period of time last fall when Claudia was calling him dozens of times a day. I checked, and her bills showed some calls but not the dozens he claimed. So I thought—"

"She rang him from here," he said flatly, with an expression either of distaste or annoyance. She couldn't tell which. "He wasn't exaggerating. Every few minutes she'd leave the front and dash in here to the telephone. If anything, I expect he understated the case. Frankly, I don't know how he could tolerate it. Or rather, how his secretary could. I overheard Claudia leaving messages with her any number of times."

It was distaste and annoyance both, she decided. He stated the facts with thinned lips, as if he'd bit into something rancid and was too well-mannered to spit it out.

"So she really was hounding him."

"Oh yes. The monthly charges suddenly shot sky-high. The accountant was disconcerted, to say the least."

"How long did it go on?"

Ian focused on the ash he was carefully pushing off the tip of his cigarette. "Two months perhaps. I can't recall precisely." He raised his eyes, asking, "Is it important?"

"I'm not honestly sure. I just found it a little hard to believe."

"Yes, well." He took a long drag on the cigarette, then exhaled a plume of smoke toward the ceiling. "Didn't we all?" he observed derisively. "It was a frightful disruption. One couldn't count on her to cover the front, and she was decidedly less than her best in dealing with the staff and customers." He shrugged, and took another thoughtful drag on his cigarette. "You'll find the bills easily enough, if you don't mind getting a bit grubby. Look, Rowena. I realize it's none of my business, but why go into any of that now? What's the point, if you don't mind my asking."

"The point," she said guardedly, "is that I still have a number of questions that don't have answers."

"About what?"

"About how and why my sister died."

"Ah!" He nodded and sat back with his hands steepled under his nose, the cigarette sending smoke directly into his eyes. "May I speak candidly?"

"Please."

Letting his hands settle on the arms of the chair, he said, "In the past year or two, Claudia's behavior upset a fair number of people. She even cost the restaurant income. All that is most unfortunate, but the fact is she's dead, and it's finished. You've done a super job, and business has never been better. Couldn't you set aside your questions? I mean to say, I know she was your sister, and I'm well aware that family attachments are never easily broken, but I do think it would be in your best interest to remember the happy times."

She couldn't help herself and gave a short, sardonic laugh. "Sorry, but our family did not deal in happy times, Ian. I thought you'd already guessed that."

He shrugged and said, "Fair enough. Then perhaps you could think of her as being of the past. Which is only the truth, after all."

"That's easier said than done."

"Why upset yourself further, Rowena, mucking about in what's done and can't be changed?"

"I have to know," she said inadequately.

He seemed ready to say more, but glanced at the time instead, and stubbed the cigarette. "Duty calls." He stood with an apologetic smile and brushed imaginary lint from his immaculate dark gray sharkskin jacket.

"I'll be right there."

"No rush." Still smiling, he shot his cuffs as he left the office.

She was intrigued by the responses he'd displayed when describing Claudia's calls to Reid from the office. It wasn't unreasonable that he would have distressed, given that he'd borne the full responsibility for running the restaurant. Claudia had been primarily window dressing. Or rather *un*dressing, she thought, feeling a wave of sadness and pain at the image of her sister spread, naked and quivering, across Reid's lap. She blinked it away to review the things she now knew for a certainty: Reid drank Chivas Regal, for one. Which very possibly meant that he had either been at the house the night Claudia died, or that she'd been expecting him. For another, he hadn't lied about the phone calls. But what difference did that make, when he'd lied about so much else? And he *had* lied. The tape was proof of that.

She got up, started toward the door, then stopped. Could it have been Reid who'd broken into the house to search for the tape? He was familiar with her work schedule and with the house as well, having been in it at least once before. But would he have known of the tape's existence? Had Claudia told him of it, with some form of blackmail in mind? Trying to sort this out was bringing her headache back. It would have to wait.

On her way out of the office she collided with Ian coming back in.

"There was one more thing I wished to say, Rowena, if I may."

"Yes, of course."

"It's to do with Claudia and that wretched business with Dr. Reid. She was completely obsessed with the man for a time. Fortunately it didn't last long, and things returned to what used to pass for normal around here. What I mean is, of course you're free to examine the telephone bills and anything else you might care to see. It is your business now, after all, and we've been doing wonderfully well in recent months. You've been a tonic and everyone's grown very fond of you. But I simply cannot think what possible satisfaction you might derive from delving into old news that's no more than today's bin liner." He placed a cool hand on her bare arm. "Best to let it go, my dear," he suggested. "Why mess about digging into the past? It can't do you any good. I'm sure Dr. Reid didn't intentionally mislead you. I expect he was simply trying to be kind by understating the case."

"Perhaps. I'll give some thought to what you've said."

"Good. I do apologize if I've stepped out of line."

"No, no. I appreciate it."

"Good." He gave her arm a slight squeeze before turning away.

She studied his elegantly lanky figure as he retreated, trying to decide if there had been a message beneath the message. If only it were easier to decipher his meanings. So often he managed to be both direct and oblique, with smiles and gestures further at variance with what he seemed to be saying. What was clear was his dislike for Claudia, hence the cautionary advice. She did appreciate it, but she couldn't possibly stop now, not when she was beginning to get some answers. They might not make her happy but they would at least give her the satisfaction of knowing what had happened.

Nineteen

She ejected the tape from the VCR, then stood holding it, trying to think what to do. Her thoughts were muddied, sluggish as a result of the second Fiorinal she'd taken at the height of the midday rush when the headache had returned.

She was so sleepy all she could think of was a nap. Tape in hand she went to check the answering machine, jolted to hear Reid's voice, deep and seductive, saying, "I want you to know I was thinking about you all last evening. Why don't you let me take you to dinner tomorrow night or Wednesday? I'll be at the office today until roughly six-thirty. So call and let me know which night's better for you. I look forward to talking to you later."

This is what happens to ugly little women who have the audacity to dream. You end up mired in hopelessness, a victim of wishful thinking and unscrupulous men. The tone sounded and the recording stopped. She stared at the flashing message light, frightened and depressed, that pain in her midriff back. Since finding the last tape she'd begun thinking of Reid in the past tense. He couldn't know of her discovery, so he was still actively in pursuit, sounding convincingly eager and sincere. Resetting the machine, she wondered nervously how to handle this. He wanted something from her. If he didn't get it, would she be at risk? Might she, too, wind up dead? She didn't want to believe he meant to harm her, but that was only because, in spite of everything, she was so strongly drawn to him. Hearing his voice had given her gooseflesh, bringing back vividly the taste and feel of his mouth. God! It was the stuff of an aging spinster's dreams in some Gothic novel.

Yawning, unable to marshal her thoughts into any cohesive order, she went upstairs. The sight of the unmade bed and still-drawn curtains struck her as emblematic of her chaotic emotional state. She had admitted to her interest in Reid the day before, and she was going to be made to pay for that blunder.

She slipped the cassette into the drawer of the bedside table, set the alarm to rouse her in an hour's time, then undressed and lay down in her slip. But tired as she was she couldn't fall asleep. Her thoughts kept returning to Reid, and how credulous she'd been, how readily he'd persuaded her to capitulate. Her defenses were far flimsier than she'd believed. After a lifetime's exposure to her sister, she had thought herself adept at recognizing practitioners skilled in the subtle art of manipulation. But she'd been wrong. Reid was a virtuoso, and she'd been hoodwinked. Trying hard not to despise herself, she closed her eyes.

The alarm startled her awake and she lay for a time in the cocoon of bedclothes, thinking of reasons why she shouldn't stay there and sleep right through until the next day. But her hand, of its own accord, was reaching to open the bedside table drawer, closing around the cassette. And then she was up, headed into the dressing room to put on a T-shirt, one of her faded cotton jumpers, and the shabby white moccasins with the unraveling beadwork.

While the kettle was boiling for tea, she wet-mopped the kitchen floor and wiped down the counters, erasing every trace of the previous night's debauchery. Then she sat and read the *Times* while she drank a cup of strong tea with milk and sugar and smoked several cigarettes.

The phone rang and she stiffened, listening to the ringing and then the outgoing message. Tomorrow, when the Caller ID went into effect, she wouldn't have to suffer any more of this anxiety.

"Come on, Ro," Mark said. "I know you're there. The Benz is in the driveway. Pick up, there's a good little tike."

Relieved, she lifted the receiver.

"How come you're playing possum, my tiny treasure?"

"I'm wiped out and not in the mood to talk to anyone."

"I hope that doesn't include *moi.*"

"No, never *toi,* my darling."

"That's very good for my poor, battered ego. So, want to go out for Chinese, maybe catch a flick?"

"Not tonight. If the smoke alarm went off right now I'd have to think for a while about whether or not to move."

"O-kay. Alternate plan number one. How about I go pick up some Chinese and we eat in? I'd like to bring you up to date on a few things."

"I haven't had Chinese in ages. I'd love some moo shu pork. And maybe there's something decent on the tube we could watch."

"Nope, already checked. It's all dreck. Got any of that jasmine tea left?"

"Sure do. Up to date on what? And what's alternate plan number two?"

"I go pick up a pizza. We eat in and I bring you up to date on a few things."

"Oh. No, I want plan number one. What things?"

"I'll see you in a while and fill you in then," he said, and hung up.

She hurried to hide the tape in the dressing room, then ran back down to make sure nothing was out of order in the living room. The telephone rang again as she was setting the table. Clamping her jaws shut, she held her hands over her ears and hummed, for the first time in years revving the engine of her escape mechanism. When she saw the message light go on she stopped and lowered the volume so she wouldn't have to hear future incoming messages.

"You're looking a tad ragged, Miz Grouse. What've you been up to?" Mark asked, rolling himself another pancake.

"I stayed up too late last night, and then I couldn't get to sleep. You know how that happens, when your brain goes into overdrive?"

"I certainly do. Only too well."

"So what's new with you?" She spooned more fried rice onto her plate before he had a chance to comment on how little she was eating. Her stomach was not yet back to normal.

"Well," he drawled, "Miz Penelope and I went out for lunch together today."

"Are you *serious?*"

"Absolutely. She invited me, and I was curious, so I said yes. She was very subdued, pensive. Strange, you know. For the first time ever, I had the feeling I was seeing the real Penny. And she's diffident, defensive, but quite dear. She told me about the card she left for you this morning. Did you call her?"

Rowena shook her head.

"Up to you of course, but maybe you should."

"Why?"

"Please don't be deliberately obtuse, Ro. You should because she's trying every way she knows how to make amends for what she did; because she cares about you, and you care about her. You said yourself people don't throw away twenty-five years of friendship just like that."

"Maybe she should've thought of that before she went on a public rampage."

He frowned and said, "I know. It was bad. But things got out of hand."

"Now there's an understatement, if I ever heard one."

"Everyone agrees she went too far. Okay? Could you please bend a little? Nothing's etched in stone here."

Testily, she said, "I'm the one who got shat upon from a great height, Mark. Let's not play that down to the level of a prank. She's been on my case for months, and you know it. Friday night was the *coup de grâce.*"

"I guess from your POV that's true."

"Who else's POV could there be? Never mind. Tell me what she said."

He looked as if he wanted to argue but after a moment said, "She apologized to me for the way she's been acting at work, said she'd been so sure I'd automatically side with you that she got defensive without ever talking to me. She admitted she'd made remarks about both of us and, naturally, the Mag being the colossal rumor mill it is, everything got blown way out of shape. She swore the remarks were relatively innocent, and I tend to believe her. She was also quick to agree when I pointed out that she shouldn't have said anything at all. But she claims she was frightened, and wanted some support. Unfortunately, she went looking for it in the wrong place and definitely in the wrong way. So instead, she got the pariah treatment specially reserved for those of us who will insist on speaking out when nobody else wants to know or hear."

Rowena took a bite of her pancake and washed it down with some of the fragrant tea.

"No comment?" he asked.

"Not yet. I want to hear it all first."

"Okay. Well, I accepted her apology. I think it took guts for her to approach me. She put herself on the line, and I respect her for that. She also didn't try to justify her behavior. She just laid out the causes and effects as she saw them."

"I'm sure she was the essence of quiet civility. What about Ken and the child support?"

He popped the last morsel of food into his mouth and drank a mouthful of tea before answering. "She says she was so demoralized by the breakup and the divorce that she wasn't willing to give Ken any points whatsoever. So she lied, and made him out to be a complete villain. Later on, when Kip was old enough to start asking about his father, she got scared that if she allowed Kip to see him the truth was bound to come out and she'd be the one who wound up looking bad. So she kept them apart, meanwhile feeling guiltier and guiltier.

"Finally, as we now know, the truth came out at Christmas, and she couldn't deal with it. She resigned herself to losing Kip to his father. The whole thing was ludicrously one-sided, but she was convinced no one would ever believe it all started way back when she tried to make herself feel better about being ridiculed and dumped by verbally painting Ken in unrelenting shades of black."

"She never gave Kip a chance to decide for himself."

"She was hurt and scared, Ro. She'd lost her perspective. She thought Kip would see his father as the injured party, and her as the bad guy. With a less intelligent, less sensitive kid, you know, that wouldn't have been beyond the realm of possibility."

"Kip's no fool. He'd have been able to figure it out for himself."

"She realizes that now. She left work early to meet him this afternoon, to talk it all out."

"About time, wouldn't you say? It's only thirteen or fourteen years later."

"Why are you being so hostile, Ro? This really isn't like you."

"Maybe it is, Mark," she said, reaching for her cigarettes. "Maybe this is *exactly* like me. I've never been in quite this position before, so how do we know I'm not reacting entirely in character?"

"We don't. Listen, I know you need a fix, but if I ask very nicely, could you please wait till I finish eating before you light up?"

"Oh sure. Sorry." She was about to refill their teacups when the telephone rang. She ignored it, applying herself to keeping a steady hand as she poured.

"How can you stand it? Letting the phone ring and ring would drive me completely berserk."

"I meant it when I told you I'm not in the mood to talk to anyone." It impressed her how calm she sounded. In the ensuing silence they heard the outgoing message play. Then a woman's voice could barely be heard, but they both knew who it was.

"You should talk to her. She's making sense."

"For God's sake, Mark! She accused me of trying to steal her son, among other things. It's only been a few days since my last, very nasty encounter with her, and I'm not over that yet—if I ever will be. I know you're sympathetic to her, but try keeping some perspective on this, please. *I'm* the injured party here, not her!"

"She told a lie. It grew up to be Godzilla and destroyed everything in its path."

"Nice imagery."

"Maybe this isn't a good time to talk about it," he said soberly. "You're definitely not receptive."

"No, I'm not. I'm too tired even to take this in properly." Then she couldn't resist saying, "I suppose she started in again with that arrant asininity about how I'm turning into Claudia."

"You're right. You *are* too tired to take this in. Let's read our fortune cookies and then I'll go home."

"I'm sorry to snap at you. But don't you think it's my *right* to be upset? Why should I pass it off and forgive her just because she's asking politely?"

"You have a valid point. I guess I thought things could be patched up more easily than this."

"I'm a little confused at your playing devil's advocate. I thought you didn't even particularly like Penny."

"When did I say that? I *never* said that. What I said was I didn't feel as if I really knew her, that I thought she was carrying a lot of emotional baggage. Which, it turns out, happened to be right on the money. But I never said I didn't *like* her, because that's not the truth. I *do* like her."

"Obviously I misinterpreted your remarks."

"What's going on, Rowena?" he asked for a second time. "Is this really about Penny, or is there something you're not telling me?"

He was giving her a chance to unburden herself and for a few seconds the thought of his consolation was most tempting. He'd tell her the tape was no big deal, that she was making too much of it, and that a few unwise choices on Reid's part didn't make him a murderer. But she couldn't bring herself to admit that she had, however briefly, cared very much for a man who'd been involved with her sister, lied about it, and began wooing her. It was such a sordid tale, with decidedly macabre overtones.

She thought of *Heart of Darkness,* and Marlow saying, " . . . it was written I should be loyal to the nightmare of my choice." It was precisely how she felt: that there was a script somewhere, and she was obliged to play out her role as written. And the script dictated that she should keep the tape's existence and her own pitiful gullibility a secret.

"It'll be a while before I'm ready to discuss this. Penny may have managed to get it out of her system in one fell swoop, but it's going to take me a bit longer than a couple of days to deal with everything she said and did. I *trusted* her, Mark. And she betrayed that trust. If this was about you, I don't think you'd appreciate my suggesting you just forgive and forget. It's simply not realistic.''

"Okay. You're right. I didn't think it through. I'm sorry. Fortune cookies, and then I'm out of here.'' He took one and handed her the other.

She sat gazing at the brittle confection cupped in the palm of her hand, too weary to assimilate facts and attempt to deal with them.

"Faith can move mountains," Mark read, "but only when she's in the mood. The lever is disputably man's greatest tool. Never park your water buffalo in a loading zone. One man's yak is another man's dromedary.''

She tuned back in to see him holding the slim strip of paper lengthwise, squinting as he pretended to read from microscopic print. "I'll take you home again, Kathleen, if you'll wait till the sun shines, Nelly.''

Laughter erupted out of her. He glanced across, scowling, said, "Kindly do not interrupt!'' turned the paper over, and went on. "There'll be bluebirds over the white cliffs of Dover, but only if Cliff's into a little kinky shit today.'' Breaking into a grin, he asked, "So what does yours say?''

"You are certifiable!'' She couldn't stop laughing, and felt herself sliding toward the edge where the laughter would turn to weeping. Drying her eyes with a paper napkin, she worked to get herself back in control.

"Oh, and you're not. Miss Reptile World of '95. What does it say, please?''

" 'Pride goeth before a fall.' '' She frowned and picked up her cigarettes.

"What kind of crummy fortune is that? That's a proverb, not a fortune. We should ask for our money back!''

"One man's yak is another man's dromedary?''

"Yeah, well. Extemporizing ain't exactly easy, you know. It takes years of practice. So.'' He began pushing the empty containers into the take-out bag. "I'll dump this stuff in the bin on my way home.''

"Thanks for the dinner.'' She hesitated, framing her words. "Please try to see this from my viewpoint, Mark. I'm sure Penny had lots of reasons that made sense to her. But she gave me a very hard time for close to five *months*. It isn't fair to expect me to get over it in five *minutes*.''

"Seeing you both so miserable, I thought I'd try playing intermediary. I guess I pushed too hard.''

"You can't force people to be reasonable, my darling. You, better than most people, know that."

"Yeah, I do."

"The fact is, it's over, Mark. How could I be friends with someone I no longer trust? Someone who punched me black and blue in front of an entire restaurant full of people. Have you any *idea* what that was like?"

He grimaced and said, "My poor poppet. And here I come on full of missionary zeal. I won't say another word on the subject. Now you finish that cigarette and go to bed."

She walked him to the back door where he set the bag of garbage on the counter and put his arms around her, saying, "You smell great. What's this one? I don't recognize it."

"Tocade," she murmured, resting her head against his chest. "Nice, isn't it?"

"Delicious, kind of like a vanilla ice-cream cone with rose petals."

She laughed and gave him a gentle push.

"Sleep well, cupcake."

"I love you very much, Mark. I don't know what I'd do without you."

"Ditto very much. Take it easy, and get some sleep. We'll talk tomorrow." He kissed the tip of her nose, grabbed the garbage and went on his way.

She cleaned the kitchen, loaded the dishwasher, then headed directly upstairs to bed, falling off almost instantly. Waking four hours later to go to the bathroom, she couldn't get back to sleep. For close to an hour she turned restlessly from one side to the other. Finally, she sat up, got the tape from its hidden compartment, and went downstairs.

Leaving the room dark, she settled on the floor with her cigarettes and an ashtray before pushing the cassette into the maw of the VCR. Then, remote in one hand, cigarette in the other, she sat and watched the tape, loathing herself and wanting to loathe Reid too. But she couldn't. All her negative emotions were directed back at herself. She'd been stupid, deluded. She had no idea what he'd been. While the tape was rewinding, she went to the downstairs bathroom to blow her nose and wash her face, bothered by something about the video recording—something wrong, off-kilter.

She shifted to the sofa to run it again. And while it was rewinding a second time, she fell asleep and dreamed she was in the dressing room watching Reid and her sister in the bedroom. At moments, it was she, not Claudia, spread naked across Reid's lap; she whose thighs were held wide by his large hands; she who felt that first fierce thrust. Then she'd be back in the dressing room again, watching. Back and forth she traveled, playing both witness and participant, seeing each move from outside, yet feeling every sensation too. After he'd angrily driven her to a convulsive climax, he pulled out of her so abruptly that it hurt, and her sense of loss was like a form of death. *Don't leave me! Please don't go!* she cried, too cold in the sudden withdrawal of his warmth. *It's a mistake! A mistake!* But he didn't hesitate, didn't look back.

A muffled thump outside the front door awakened her. Instantly she was on her feet, peering through a crack in the vertical blinds to see an automobile slowly accelerating away down the road. Spooked, she tiptoed to the front door and opened it to find the *Times* on the mat. Exhaling tremulously, she picked up the paper and relocked the door, soundlessly laughing at herself.

It was 5:37 a.m. She'd been on the sofa for nearly three hours, which meant that altogether she'd managed to get seven hours' sleep. Tossing the newspaper onto the table, she set about making herself breakfast, enjoying being up so early. It reminded her of those weeks when Reilly and his crew had been working on the renovations. She liked seeing the garden attain color as the sun rose and she breathed in the rich, damp, loamy fragrance that wafted through the window on a cool breeze.

There was ample time, before heading off to the restaurant later that morning, to view the tape two more times. Like an itch she couldn't reach to scratch, whatever was wrong about it continued to nag her. She simply couldn't get a fix on it; it refused to come clear. She'd have to keep studying the tape until it did. A problem to be solved; something to keep her occupied. And what else did she have to do, really?

Twenty

Kip had obviously been waiting for her and hurried over, all smiles, as she came through the gate.

"Hi, Auntie Ro. Feeling better?"

"Much, thank you."

"I thought you'd want to know Mom and I had a really good session yesterday. *Really* good. Got a bunch of stuff cleared up."

"That's wonderful, sweetheart."

"Yeah. For once, she leveled with me, told me how things got so messed up with Dad, and how she got like locked into her story, then it was too late to go changing it. You know?"

"Mark filled me in on some of it last night."

"Right. They had lunch. So you know she apologized and they cleared up a bunch of stuff, too. It's good, because I hated her being so down on you guys."

"She was afraid of losing you, Kip. When people get scared they sometimes act irrationally."

"No doubt!" he agreed emphatically. "We discussed that, too, and it was way weird—like I was the parent and she was the kid, assuring her nobody was gonna go losing anybody, that I could see my dad without comparing the two of them, so she came off the loser. That's not the way it is with me'n him. Anyhow, now things're finally making some sense."

"That's great news, sweetheart. I'm happy for you."

Some of the light dimming from his expression, he said, "She'd be majorly bummed if she knew I said anything, but Mom *really* wants to talk to you, Auntie Ro. I mean, you and Uncle Mark, you're family, you know. And Mom's beating herself up big time over what happened. No question, she definitely lost it there for a while. But you know her. You know it's not her style to go whaling on people. She'd never hurt you on purpose. I mean, she *loves* you. We both do."

"Kip, let's sit down for a minute."

"Okay, sure."

Opting for a table in the shade of the canopy, she slid into a chair
and opened her bag for a cigarette, aware of Kip's tracking her every
move. "It's very important to me that you understand, sweetheart,
because *I* love *you.* You're very special to me. The thing is, I can't talk
to your mother right now. I'm having trouble dealing with what she
did—and in front of a restaurant full of people. I was *mortified,* Kip,
utterly humiliated. And I think you'll admit you were embarrassed,
too."

"It's true, I was, big time," he admitted openly, as if he'd been
seeking an opportunity to say this. "I could not *believe* my *mother* was
acting like some total crazoid. Since she and I talked yesterday, in my
mind it was like that whole thing happened a way long time ago. But it
was only last weekend."

"That's right, it was. And it's still very fresh in *my* mind. But there's
also the fact that she lied to me for a lot of years. That bothers me almost more than anything else. What I'm trying to say is, I might be
able to talk to your mother in time, but I can't ever be friends with her
again, not the way we were. I know that isn't what you were hoping to
hear, but it's the truth."

"I wasn't being very realistic, was I, thinking you guys could get
back together?" he asked dispiritedly.

"You're a lucky person, honey. You've got an open, easygoing nature. Things happen, you get upset, and an hour later, you're over it.
I'm not like you. I'm someone who broods. I go over things again and
again, until I can make sense of them. Once all the pieces fit, I can put
the matter aside. So even though I'll probably forgive your mother
eventually, I'll never be able to trust her again. Because she was dishonest. Can you understand that?"

"Yeah, I can. She blew it totally." He grabbed an ashtray off another table and placed it in front of her. She thanked him and put out
her cigarette. "I'd feel the same way," he said. "A part of me's never
going to trust her again a hundred percent, 'cause she lied to me, too.
But she's my mother. You know?"

"Of course I do."

"Thanks for not trying to dick me around with a lot of crap about
how I'm too young to understand. I appreciate that."

"I have too much respect for your intelligence ever to do that to you,
sweetheart."

"Me too, you. As far back as I can remember, you've always been
way cool with me, made me feel like a person and not just some dorky

little kid. You never asked me dumb shit about school, or dished up bogus platitudes. I guess I wanted you two to patch it up so I wouldn't go losing you.''

She put her hand on his cheek, looking into the depths of his eyes, and love for him was like a clamp suddenly tightening around her chest. "You're never going to lose me, Kip. I'll always be here for you. Always. If there's anything you need, you can come to me. You know that, don't you?''

"I know," he said quietly.

Withdrawing her hand, she said, "One more thing, sweetheart. You're not responsible—for your mom, or for me. What does or doesn't happen between her and me has nothing to do with you. Each of us is going to go on caring for you, regardless of whether or not we're still friends. Okay?''

"Okay."

"You're sure?"

"I'm sure."

"Good." She smiled at him. "I'd better go in now. Unless there's anything else you wanted to talk about."

"No. I guess we've covered it all."

"Remember, honey. There's nothing you could ever say or do that would change my feelings for you."

"Me, too," he said staunchly.

They sat looking into each other's eyes. After a few moments, she went inside and directly down to the women's room. Closing herself into one of the stalls, she held a hand over her mouth and wept.

Having the Caller ID was reassuring. It was purely illusory but that didn't matter. Each time the phone rang and the incoming number was displayed on the screen, she felt that much less at the mercy of the capricious, sometimes barbarous whims of others. And when, near two that afternoon, an incoming call registered a familiar Greenwich number, she asked Ian to take the call. "Would you please tell Dr. Reid I'm not available?''

Coolly, he said, "Of course," and picked up the receiver.

She made a tour of the half dozen tables still occupied and by the time she got to the bar, Ian was there to hand her a folded slip. She thanked him. He nodded curtly, and continued on his way to the kitchen. Patently, he was not pleased at fielding her personal calls. She hoped there wouldn't be many; she really had no desire to alienate him.

The note read, "Pls. ring Dr. Reid." Only four words, but they made her fearful and melancholy. Reid wasn't going to vanish just because she wished he would. She dropped the message in the trash and went to check the patio. Sitting outdoors in oppressive heat was her idea of torture but it was clearly not an idea widely shared. Half the tables were still occupied.

The heat brought *Heart of Darkness* back to mind. Telling Ian she had to run a quick errand, she got her bag from the office and walked up the street to buy a copy. It had been at least twenty years since she'd read Conrad's work and she very much wanted to read it again.

As she was entering the store she bumped into a man on his way out. Each took a step back, apologizing. In his thirties, well dressed and handsome, he looked very familiar. Assuming he was one of the restaurant customers, she smiled and said, "Hello. How are you?"

He too smiled, but the blankness of his eyes was a dead giveaway. "I'm great," he said. "Sorry. I can't seem to remember your name."

Her face afire, she realized he seemed familiar because she'd seen him before—on one of the trophy tapes. His had been one of the few that hadn't made her squirm. Because of the heated delight he'd taken in making love, and because of his dark good looks, she'd dubbed him Spain—hot-blooded, passionate, tropical in temperament, and very unlike Claudia's other partners in that he appeared to enjoy and respect women. Now he was patiently waiting for her to tell him her name, and she wished she could dematerialize.

"My mistake. You look like someone I know." She offered him a sickly smile.

"*You* look like someone *I* know, but I can't think who." His smile was glorious, revealing very white teeth. He also had on a wonderfully aromatic after-shave.

She apologized again, and attempted to go past him into the store, not quite able to take her eyes off him.

"Give me one more second and I'll have it," he said, holding up the forefinger of his right hand. "Her name's on the tip of my tongue."

"I'm in kind of a hurry." She wanted to be well away when the name came back to him. But he was thinking so hard he didn't realize he was blocking her path. "If you'll excuse me." She indicated the door, feeling a trickle of perspiration travel slowly between her breasts.

"Oh, sorry." He stepped aside just as he made the connection. His expression becoming one of confusion, he began, "Aren't you...?"

She didn't give him a chance to finish, pushing past him into the store.

Going directly to the literature section at the very back, she stood for several minutes pretending to scan titles while her breathing slowed. When at last she risked a look around he was nowhere in sight. She quickly found the book she wanted, paid for it, and went to the door. After checking that the street was clear, she hurried back to the restaurant.

Ian was sitting behind the desk in the office, having a cigarette. He moved to offer her his seat but she gestured to him to remain where he was. Fumbling a cigarette out of her bag, she got it lit, then stood with one arm tight around her waist as she took the first drag.

"You've gone very pale, Rowena. Has something happened?"

"I just came this close to making the most disastrous gaffe." Eyes on the wall, she shook her head. "Going into the bookshop I bumped into a man I recognized, so I said hello and how are you, and he said fine, and what was my name again. And suddenly I realized I had no idea who he was. I'd recognized him from one of Claudia's tapes." *What the hell was she doing?* Confounded, she looked at the man behind the desk. It wasn't *Ian* with whom she'd discussed the tapes, but Mark. *Not Ian!* Was she losing her mind, blurting that out without thinking?

"Ah, yes," he said with a wry smile. "The famous tapes."

"Famous?"

"No, of course not. I heard about the bloody things so often, and for so long, I took to thinking of them that way. Must have given you quite a turn, running into one of her unwitting victims."

"I'll say."

"Too bad." He studied the lit tip of his cigarette for a few seconds before directing his eyes to hers. "Claudia had an unfortunate habit of trolling rather too close to the shore."

It was almost exactly what that lawyer had said. What was her name? She couldn't remember. It didn't matter.

"And everyone here knew about the tapes?"

"Only I knew, actually. Certainly her star performers didn't. She was all sorts of things, was our Claudia, but never stupid. Half the fun was in possessing potentially damaging evidence of infidelity. She tended to favor married men."

"But you saw the tapes?"

"No, I merely heard about them, ad nauseam. What a pity you had the misfortune to come across them. I had hoped you wouldn't. My understanding was they were hidden, and if one didn't know precisely where, one would never find them."

She nodded and took another drag on the cigarette. "She cleverly hid them in plain sight. I came upon them by accident, and once I saw what they were, I got rid of them. Why did she tell you?" she asked, already knowing the answer. Claudia would have needed someone to show off to, and Ian was the perfect confidant. Telling him a secret would be tantamount to storing it at Fort Knox.

"As I expect you're well aware, your sister liked to brag about her exploits. Nothing was really quote fun unquote unless she could talk about it—at length and in great detail. She mistook my lack of response or comment for interest."

Rowena nodded again, able to see Claudia making that mistake. Ian's inscrutability could be very misleading.

"She liked to regale me with tales of her skulduggery, using me as a sounding board. Or more accurately, her captive audience. It must have been frightful for you," he sympathized.

"It was not my all-time favorite experience."

"I can well imagine. It's rather interesting, but for someone who was positively phobic about things technological—I mean to say, the new computerized cash register defeated her to the extent that she refused to use it—Claudia was like a child with a splendid new toy when she got the first camcorder. That was, oh, six or seven years ago. After several false starts she got the hang of it. Then she became quite the technician, upgrading her equipment every time something new and better came on the market. As I recall, Philippe got the first camera. And Jill got the second. Well, we can only hope you won't run into any more of Claudia's playmates, and you've disposed of the tapes, so that's the end of it. Relax now and finish your cigarette," he suggested, putting out his own and getting to his feet. "I'll have a look round, see if the last of the lunchtime crowd's gone on their way."

"I'd like to continue this conversation sometime."

"Why, Rowena? To what end? I daresay you know the worst there is to know about her by now."

"As it turns out, I don't. But the two of you were friends."

"Oh, my dear." He seemed highly amused. "Claudia was no one's *friend.* Surely you, of all people, know that."

"How can you speak of her almost fondly in one breath, and so angrily in the next? I find that very confusing."

"I do apologize," he said, reverting to the stiff formality she'd come to understand he adopted when upset or angry. "It was never easy maintaining my equanimity where your sister was concerned. In the early days she had a certain youthful enthusiasm and charm that was quite irresistible. I liked her. But that was before I got to know her better. Now I'm doing my damnedest to forget she ever existed. And in my cack-handed fashion, I've been trying to encourage you to do the same." Voice and features softening, he said, "For your own good, my dear, I do wish you'd follow my advice and leave it be."

"Why do you keep telling me that?"

He sighed and asked, "What possible good can it do you to dig up Claudia's nasty secrets? Look how upset you are with what you've already learned."

"I'll be a lot less upset when I have answers to all my questions."

"Life is seldom that tidy or obliging, Rowena. We're lucky if we get answers to *some* of our questions. And often those answers can be most unpleasant."

"True. But I still need to know why she did certain things."

"Oh, I think you already do know."

Do I? An image flashed in her mind: her mother and sister in the kitchen, Claudia on a rampage, Jeanne cowering. An instant, then it was gone. "You're wrong," she said. "I don't."

Speaking slowly, as if to someone with impaired cognitive skills, he said, "You are a singularly intelligent and sensitive woman. If you think about it, you'll see that you do indeed know. Now, if you'll excuse me, I'll go have my look round." With that, he left, quietly closing the door behind him.

On her way home, she reviewed the conversation. Ian claimed never to have seen the tapes, and she had no reason to disbelieve him. Which meant that while he'd known of Claudia's obsession with Reid, it didn't necessarily follow that he was aware of their sexual involvement. Perhaps Claudia hadn't come crowing to him about that particular conquest.

Knowing what he did, Ian was probably wondering why Reid was now pursuing her, and why she'd taken to avoiding the man's calls. It was impossible to guess what Ian was thinking. For all she knew, he could be one of those rare people bereft of curiosity who hadn't given the matter a moment's thought. But what had he meant by saying she already knew Claudia's reasons? Again that scene of her mother and sister flashed in her mind—like a light turned on, then instantly off, so that she was left with nothing more than a phantom impression that caused an anxious inner quaking. She tried to force the memory back in its entirety, but it refused to come.

*   *   *

Leaving the day's mail at the foot of the stairs, Rowena went up to shower and change clothes. Then she got the tape and collected the mail on her way to the kitchen. While the incoming message cassette on the answering machine was rewinding, she leaned against the counter and lit a cigarette. After the several messages left by Penny the previous day came one from the dental office reminding her she was due for a cleaning. Next was Reid, sounding tired and mildly irked. "I realize you have a busy schedule, Rowena, but please take a couple of minutes to call me back. Dinner tonight's obviously not going to happen, but what about tomorrow? Or have things changed for some reason since Sunday? Either way, I'd appreciate a call. It's now three-ten and I'll be here at the office until six-fifteen, give or take. Talk to you later. Bye."

"Please leave me alone," she whispered, as the tone sounded. Each successive message he left made her feel a little more vulnerable, a little more in doubt—of too many things.

"Hi, Ro. It's Marcia. We haven't talked in ages, and I'm dying to see you. The Mag isn't the same without you. But I'm sure leaving here's the best thing you ever did. Call me and let's make a date to have dinner, maybe get together with some of the gang. Everyone misses you and sends their love. Bye for now."

The next three messages were from Penny, begging Rowena to call back and talk to her. These repeated pleas made her feel as if she were the one in the wrong, and she thought she should write a note, asking Penny please to back off for the time being.

Finished with the cigarette, she went to look out the window. The garden seemed to mirror her mood—everything slightly wilted and motionless. There wasn't even a hint of a breeze; the sky was cloudless, bleached to a watery blue-white. The heat seemed to lean against the house, seeking cracks and crevices where it might gain entry. She went out to turn on the sprinkler, returned inside and resumed her position at the window, shadows from the past moving all around her: her father mowing the lawn, her mother in the kitchen talking to one of the housekeepers; Cary wheeling his bike out of the garage; and Claudia on the back steps, jumping down them one at a time, then turning to jump back up—up and down, over and over and over. She looked fine in memory—a pretty child with a wonderfully contagious laugh—but there was something subtly wrong with that little girl.

Wishing she could get a firm grasp on the scene that kept flashing at random moments in her mind, she got a Barq's diet French vanilla from the refrigerator and went down into the damp cool of the cellar to sort through the last of Jeanne's boxes.

Twenty-One

It was at once obvious that Jeanne herself had packed the contents of this box. There were quite a few small envelopes containing brittle, yellowed death notices clipped from newspapers. Rowena recognized some of the names as friends of her mother's but the majority she didn't. Nevertheless she read each with interest, including one for her grandfather who had died in 1948. He was a man about whom she knew little except that he'd come from Paris before the turn of the century, married late in life, and did very well in real estate, leaving a sizable estate to his wife and two daughters. Jeanne's older sister, Genevieve, had died—"after a short illness" another clipping read— the following year, in 1949. Jeanne's mother died, following a massive stroke, in 1966. What Rowena remembered of that was how very long the service had seemed, the biting cold at the graveside, and her mother's dry-eyed, stony silence throughout. More than anything else, Jeanne had seemed very angry.

Another, larger, envelope was filled with a variety of legal documents: her grandparents' marriage and death certificates; her mother's diplomas from primary and secondary school, semester grade notices and her B.A. from Vassar; a Photostat of her birth certificate; several more obituaries, a dozen or so unrelated newspaper clippings on human interest stories; issues of *Life* and *Look* from the forties and fifties, which Rowena set aside to look at later; a couple of dozen postcards, most with indecipherable signatures, from as far away as Singapore and as near as Boston; and the original offer to purchase the house. There was a handful of recipes torn from magazines—which was odd because Jeanne had never cooked, so far as Rowena knew. And, odder still, there was nothing in any of the envelopes relating to her father or his side of the family except for Jeanne's marriage certificate and divorce decree.

The bottom third of the box was filled with a thick layer of what looked to be unopened greeting cards. Picking one at random, Rowena saw, with a start, that it was addressed to her. The next was addressed to Claudia; the third to Cary. Cary had been dead for thirty-two years, which meant that this card had been sent prior to his death. Both apprehensive and excited, she upended the carton over the bridge table, and the envelopes fell out in a heap. With unsteady hands she began sorting them. Two were addressed to Cary, twelve to Claudia, and a total of thirty-four bore her name. None of the envelopes had a return address, but she didn't need one. She knew they were from her father.

She set aside the ones for her brother and sister, and, working from the postmarks, put those addressed to her in chronological order, ending up with sixteen years' worth of letters dating from 1963 to 1979. Then, in need of some fortification before daring to investigate further, she went upstairs to the kitchen, put the Barq's back in the fridge, poured a glass of white wine, got her cigarettes and an ashtray. Seated once more at the table in the cellar, she took a sip of wine, lit a cigarette, and gazed at what she knew would be evidence of the deplorable lies her mother had told.

How could a woman not only deny her children the opportunity to be with their father but also turn the truth inside out, repeating time and again that he didn't care, had never given them a moment's thought once he'd left? When Rowena had listened to Kip talk about his father and two half brothers—those "cute little dudes" he'd spoken of with such unalloyed affection—she'd had a sudden, visceral understanding that Jeanne had done to her what Penny had done to him. It was such a wicked and heartless offense that she hadn't wanted to believe it. She imagined her reaction in this instance was the same as that of women who distantly suspected their partners of abusing their children: a deep reluctance even to consider the possibility because it was too terrible. Yet she'd known it was exactly what Jeanne had done, just as she'd known in her bones that her father had not abandoned them. He was a man who loved his children above all else, and he'd have made every effort to remain in touch with them.

Kip might be able to forgive his mother—Penny had, to her credit, been a loving and attentive parent—but Rowena would never forgive Jeanne, who'd been no kind of parent whatever. And why had she kept letters she'd had no intention of allowing her children to see? Why not throw away such damning evidence? One more question without an answer.

Another sip of wine, and she reached for the first of Cary's two letters. It was a birthday card, containing fifty dollars in cash. The message read, "Cary dear, I'm not settled in yet, but as soon as I am, I want to see you and your sisters. I miss you and think of you constantly. Hope your birthday is a happy one. All my love, Dad. PS: Here's enough loot to pay for the flippers and mask you've been wanting. See you very soon."

The second was a Christmas card, with another fifty dollars. Inside, George Graham had written, "My dear, I was so hoping to see you over the holidays but I'm sorry to say your mother and I were unable to work it out. Please use the enclosed cash to buy yourself something you really want. Remember that I love you, Cary, and I think of you all the time. Hope to see you soon, Your Dad."

The cigarette had burned itself out. She lit another and drank some more wine before setting the money apart, then with care returned each card to its envelope. Claudia's letters consisted of six years' worth of birthday and Christmas cards, each with small sums of cash. The messages inside were different—short, simple, and less emotional than those directed to Cary. "I miss you. Love from Dad." Or, "I'm thinking of you. Love, Dad." Claudia would have been five at the time of the first card and almost eleven by the time Jeanne had tossed aside, unopened, the last one. Claudia had been less affected by her father's departure than her older brother and sister. In fact, she'd scarcely seemed to notice his absence and had behaved as always in her self-absorbed and mischievous fashion.

Again, Rowena put the cards back in their envelopes, holding aside the money, and confronted the remaining letters as she drank the last of the wine. Another glass would have been good, but she thought it best to abstain. For the moment. Later she might have two or three more glasses—enough to blur the edges and dull the senses without giving her another vicious hangover.

An ache in her throat, hands now very unsteady, she lifted the first envelope bearing her name. Postmarked Stamford, it was dated July 10, 1963. A card for her seventh birthday, containing fifty dollars.

"Dearest Rowlie, I wish more than anything that I could be with you on your birthday. But I can't be, so I'm sending you all the hugs and kisses in the world. I promise I'll come visit you very soon. For now, buy yourself some new books, sweetheart. And when you read them I hope you'll think of your dad who loves you."

Stricken, eyes burning, she held the card to her chest. How could she possibly have forgotten something as significant as the fact that her father used to call her Rowlie? His words brought so much back: the memory of sitting inside the safe circle of his arm as he read aloud the nightly chapter from *Kidnapped,* or *My Friend Flicka;* the time Claudia wandered off during an excursion to the Bronx Zoo and how he'd tried to hide his panic as they'd backtracked at a run, looking for her, and his great relief when they'd found her gazing, rapt, at a lion who lay calmly licking his paws and gazing back at her; the Easter morning when she'd awakened very early and looked out the bedroom window to see her pajama-clad father hiding foil-covered chocolate eggs in the garden.

He'd done all the things Jeanne claimed she never had time for— outings to the city for a Broadway matinee; outfitting them in make-shift costumes and painting their faces before taking them trick-or-treating through the neighborhood; long walks he called "nature rambles" when they picked wildflower bouquets for their mother who accepted these scraggly offerings with a thin smile that failed to hide her disinterest; and Sunday-afternoon drives upstate to see the "other" grandparents in Avon, his mother and father, Anne and Bickford Graham, who would come hurrying out of the house upon hearing the car pull into the drive. As a toddler Claudia had called them Grandie and Pickle—something else that had been misplaced in her memory.

She had forgotten far more of her childhood than she had remembered, helped along in her amnesia by a vain, egotistic woman who gave top priority to her social commitments. The three children she had were incidental, mandatory luggage that came with marriage. She'd lived up to her part of the marital bargain by carrying those babies to term before expelling them from her body. And no one fully appreciated what an effort it was to regain her shape afterward—months of strict dieting and strenuous exercise so she could once more fit into her clothes. In view of all this, it was hardly fair to expect her to devote her entire existence to the children. They were clothed, sheltered, and fed. "What more do you want?" Rowena could hear her asking her father in memory. "Am I supposed to *live* for them, too?"

God! How *could* she have done that—ruthlessly severing their connection without a qualm? Chilled, Rowena lit a cigarette, took several puffs, then read the cards, one after the other. Sixteen years' worth of consistent caring thrown into a carton and buried beneath the detritus of Jeanne Graham's life. Salvaged treasure.

*   *   *   *   *

"...I'm kind of worried that you're not receiving my letters. I hope I'm wrong about that.... I've finally got a decent apartment, with room for you to stay over. Here are my numbers at home and at the office. Call me any time, honey. I miss the sound of your voice, and I'd love to see you and your sister...."

*   *   *   *   *

"...You're ten years old, Rowlie. I can hardly believe it's been so long since I've seen you. I have a picture of the three of you that I keep on my desk, but you were all just puppies when it was taken.... When I see you I'll have to bring along my camera, take some snaps so I can have a more recent photo to put on my desk...."

*   *   *   *   *

"...I've been thinking for a while now about moving out of state, starting up my own law office, maybe in Vermont or New Hampshire. I kind of like the idea of the countryside, and the quiet. I'll let you know what I decide, Rowlie. And if I do move on, I'll tell you where to reach me...."

*   *   *   *   *

"...my office is in downtown Brattleboro, a nice city, and I'm renting a cabin in the woods a few miles outside of town. There's room for you, sweetheart, if you ever want to come for a visit. It would be so wonderful to see you, Rowlie. It's been such a long time, but I think of you so often. I picture you curled up with a book, chewing on a strand of your hair. Do you still do that?..."

*   *   *   *   *

"...I've been seeing a very nice woman for the past few months. She's a lawyer, too. We kept running into each other at the town hall, and we got to talking. Finally, we decided to go into partnership. So now we share offices, and we've become good friends as well as partners. I think you'd like her, honey. Rosemary likes to read almost as much as you do. She's always got a book in her briefcase.... I've told her all about you and your sister, of course, and she would love to meet you sometime...."

*   *   *   *   *

"...I wanted you to know Rosemary and I are going to be getting married next month. I've been on my own for nearly five years now, honey, and to be honest, until Rosemary came along I was a pretty lonely fellow. It would make both of us so happy if you and Claudia could come to the wedding but I guess that's not going to happen. I have to wonder if you get my cards. My feeling is that you don't, because I know my girl, and I would have heard from you long since if you did get them. But on the off chance one of them might reach you, and because it helps me feel closer to you, I'll keep on writing. Enclosed is a little book money...."

*   *   *   *   *

"...Congratulations on becoming a teenager! I'll bet you're top of your class and the prettiest girl, too. I hope you're enjoying yourself, sweetheart. I try to picture you as you are now, but in my mind you're still a little girl. I'd love to have a recent photograph of you and Claudia. The old one of the three of you is still on my desk.... Well, the big news is Rosemary and I are expecting a baby. We're very excited. Maybe you could help us out with names. You always did have such a fine imagination. Any and all suggestions would be welcome...."

*   *   *   *   *

"...Here's a picture of Rosie, little Gwyneth, and me in front of our new house. The roof leaks and there's a family of raccoons who are putting up quite a fuss about being evacuated from the attic, but it's a good old place, with lots of potential. We've got a full acre of land and I plan to start a garden in the spring. I've started ordering a few things from catalogs.... The house has four bedrooms and we'd love to have you come visit, Rowlie. Gwyneth reminds me so much of you at her age. She loves to be read to, and I'm sure it won't be long before she's curled up in a corner with a book. Please write when you get a chance, or phone. The new address is..."

*   *   *   *   *

"...We're expecting again, and just tickled. Gwynnie's excited about having a new baby brother or sister, and she's been playing big sister with her dolls, practicing for the real thing. A friend of mine in Norwalk sent me a clipping from the *Hour* mentioning your name on the honor roll at Brien McMahon. That's wonderful, sweetheart. I'm so very, very proud of you. Sometimes it doesn't seem possible that so much time has gone by. But you're in my thoughts, and in my heart, and I know one day we'll see each other again. Remember, Rowlie, I'll always be your father, and I'll always love you...."

*   *   *   *   *

"... I imagine you're off at college now, and I wish I could write to you there, confident finally that you'd receive my letters. I picture you a young woman, away from home and on your own, and I hope you're enjoying all these new experiences. The friends you make at college usually go on to be friends for life. And the independence you discover now is a splendid and heady thing that can make you pretty giddy the first semester, before you settle into it. Savor it all, Rowlie, and know that I'm thinking of you. I actually miss you more and more as time passes.... Enclosed are some recent snaps of Rose and me with Gwyneth and Derek. And here's a little something for you to spend on yourself...."

*   *   *   *   *

"... Rose and Gwynnie are stringing cranberries and popcorn to decorate the tree and Derek's fallen asleep in his playpen, so I thought I'd take this opportunity to write. Funny, but every year at this time I find myself remembering you and Cary and Claudia, and those early Christmases when the three of you came tumbling down the stairs in your Dr. Denton's, in a rush to see what Santa had brought you. I guess it's the season for being sentimental, but I wanted you to know I've been thinking of you, just a little more than usual...."

*   *   *   *   *

"... You've probably finished college by now. Amazing to think of it! It seems I finished law school a hundred years ago, and three months later your mother and I were married. A year after that Cary was born. Looking back, I didn't think so at the time, but I was awfully young and maybe a little cocky, married at twenty-two, a father at twenty-three, and in way over my head without knowing it. Take your time, Rowlie, and don't rush into anything before you're ready. . . .

"Having given the matter a great deal of thought, I've decided this is the last time I'll be writing to you. I don't believe you've received a single one of my cards over the years, and since you'll undoubtedly be going out on your own now there seems little point to continuing. That doesn't mean I won't be thinking of you, because I will be, always. Perhaps one day you'll find these letters and then you'll know that I never stopped caring, not for a minute. I hope life is good to you, honey. And if there's ever anything you need, I'll be here, waiting for the day the telephone rings and the voice on the other end of the line is yours. . . ."

*   *   *   *   *

For a while, she sat looking at the photographs of her father and his new family, happy for him, and deeply moved by all the time and thought and love he'd put into the letters. It would have meant so much to both of them if she'd received even one of his birthday or Christmas cards. But she had them now and maybe it wasn't too late to make a long-delayed visit. If he was still there. She copied down the Vermont address and telephone number, then collected her glass and cigarettes and, drained, went up to the kitchen.

No longer interested in having more to drink, she left the wineglass in the sink and lit a cigarette, then went over to the window to look out at her father's garden, restored to a close approximation of what it had once been. She sniffed, and reached into her pocket for a tissue, telling herself George Graham would be pleased by the results of her hard work.

Twenty-Two

For a second night she went up to bed, read *Heart of Darkness* until the words turned fuzzy on the page, then fell asleep and found herself awake three hours later. Going back to sleep was out of the question. Her brain was up and running, and she fretted that after so many years her father might have retired and moved away—escaping from the harsh Vermont winters to somewhere warm all year round. And if that was the case, she'd have to hire private detectives to try to track him down. Along with the fear that she might finally have found her father only to have lost him again was her continuing need to know the specifics of Claudia's death. Regardless of all the admittedly good advice she'd been given, she couldn't let it slide. Altogether, she had few answers, and more and more questions, which were steadily grinding her down. It felt as if she'd climbed onto a treadmill and was unable to climb off.

Heading through the darkened house to the kitchen, she drank some apple juice, then went to the living room to run the tape again. Watching it had become something closely approximating homework, and she'd never minded extracurricular studies. They had provided a legitimate reason to shut herself away—from everything. With the bedroom door closed and a warm circle of lamplight cast over her textbooks, she had gladly plunged into the imagery and nuances of Shakespeare's plays, the dryly documented facts and dates of world history, the clinically cool precision of mathematics, and the wonders of elemental science. She had avidly sought knowledge, having heard or read somewhere that it could set one free. Throughout her teenage years she had yearned to be free and, ironically, all these years later, she still did. Back then she had believed that in moving away from home she would be leaving behind the small sorrows and private miseries that had come in the wake of her father's departure and Cary's death. Time had shown her how naive she'd been in that belief, and she'd ultimately settled for far less than she'd wanted but a fair amount of what she'd needed. What she longed for now was a freedom of the mind, to have the attic of her brain swept clean of its accumulated clutter—those dusty, irregularly shaped packages of unresolved matters and emotions.

Sitting with a cigarette in one hand and the remote control in the other, she no longer focused on the two players in the silent performance but rather on the space around them, on the details of the bedroom, on the very atmosphere of the encounter. Yet, maddeningly, whatever was off-kilter about the tape continued to elude her. It was there. She was certain of it. She just couldn't *see* it.

During a second viewing, she fell asleep on the sofa and awakened more than three hours later to see a fresh-faced, unbearably perky pair who were, mercifully muted, delivering the early-morning news. Groping between the sofa cushions, she found the remote, turned off the TV, and got up to begin her day.

Once the *Times* had been collected from the front doormat and the coffee maker was going, she shut down the alarm system and went out into the back garden in pajamas and slippers to water the flowers. As it was a day when the gardener and his crew weren't due, she repositioned the sprinkler to give the grass a good soaking, and for a time stood mesmerized by the silvery streams arcing back and forth in the cool dawn air.

Later there was ample time to watch the tape once more before she went out to turn off the sprinkler on her way to the car. As she was fitting the key into the ignition that tantalizing fragment of memory flickered on and off, but, infuriatingly, wouldn't allow closer examination. As the engine settled into its almost inaudible idle, what suddenly did come back to her with absolute clarity was an altercation she'd overheard when she was almost five years old.

She saw herself squatting just inside the dining room, concealed by the paneled sliding doors that once had separated the two rooms. Cary was at school. The housekeeper had taken Claudia upstairs to change her diaper. And in the living room her mother and grandmother were talking. Rowena planned to pop out from behind the doors and go running over to her granny who'd clap a hand to her chest, exclaiming as always over what a shock Rowena had given her. Then, smiling, she would open her cavernous purse, the inside of which always smelled of Chiclets and Granny's Shalimar perfume, and produce a bag of candies that she'd exchange for a "good big hug."

But as she was about to spring into the doorway her grandmother said, "It's not the least bit amusing, Jeanne," and the tone of her voice warned Rowena to stay where she was. Sometimes, when she was mad and sounded the way Granny did then, Mama would shake Rowena and say little pictures had big ears. It made no sense, but Rowena didn't want anybody to be mad at her, so she remained hidden and listened, waiting for a chance to jump out and surprise her granny.

In memory, she could feel a breeze flowing between the rooms; she could smell something cooking in the kitchen; and, squatting so close to the floor, she could see that the wood had different patterns in every strip. She wondered how a floor was made so it came out that way. Her daddy would know, and she'd ask him when he got home later. Daddy knew the answers to everything.

"Oh, for God's sake, Mother. It's only a glass of wine. You make it sound as if I'm shooting myself full of heroin."

"Surely you realize the alcohol goes right into your milk."

"Where do you *get* this nonsense from?" Her mama gave a laugh like glass breaking, a laugh that made Rowena scared whenever she heard it, and she'd been hearing it a lot since her baby sister got born. "I had a drink or two every evening of the entire pregnancy, and you can see for yourself the baby's perfectly fine."

"If you insist on drinking, you should put Claudia on a bottle. It's time you weaned her anyway. She's old enough."

"I don't happen to agree. I breast-fed Cary until he was two and a half, and Claudia's just turned two. Naturally, Rowena being Rowena, she was never satisfied, no matter how often I nursed her, so I gave up after three weeks and put her on a bottle. Then she was happy as a clam. Anyway, you can see for yourself there's not a thing wrong with any of the children."

"You weren't drinking with the first two the way you are now, and I have to tell you, Jeanne, I'm very worried. I know you and George have been going through a rough patch, and I realize you didn't want another baby, but that's beside the point...."

"What *is* the point, if I may be so bold?" Mama asked in a sharp voice.

"It's the middle of the morning, for heaven's sake. You haven't had *lunch* yet, and you're already drinking. It's simply not healthy—for you or for the baby."

"I won't finish it. All right? Look, I'm putting it down. Okay? Are you satisfied?"

"Frankly, no. What *would* satisfy me is to see you stop riding roughshod over poor, dear George, and to have you get your drinking under control."

"Poor dear George, for your information, has become too boring for words. All he ever does is work, and when he *is* home, he's not interested in doing anything *fun*. He wants to play with the children, have his dinner, and go to sleep. That is *not* what I had in mind when I married him. I have a *right* to enjoy myself. But, never mind *me*. Whatever you want, Mother. I'll be nicer to the *poor, dear* thing. It won't help, but I'll do it if it'll make you happy. All right? Now could we change the subject, please? This conversation is beginning to get on my nerves."

"I thought you weren't going to finish that."

"God!" There was the sound of a glass being set down hard. "Stop treating me like a *child!*"

"You're *my* child, Jeanne, and I'm your children's grandmother. I have a certain responsibility—"

"You have *no* responsibility for *my* family."

"I think I do. I believe you have an alcohol problem, and that you may be harming the baby, drinking as much as you do and continuing to nurse her."

"The *baby* is *fine!*"

"I'm afraid the harm may already have been done. I admit she *seems* all right, but there's something . . . ?"

"I'll wean her. Okay? I'll put her on a bottle today, right now, this minute. Okay? Are you *happy?*"

"I wish you wouldn't take this attitude—"

"If you don't drop this right now, I'm walking straight out of here. I'll go have lunch by myself at the club. I'm sick to death of you sticking your nose into what doesn't concern you. And I'm sick to *death* of George and these goddamned children, and of everybody volunteering their opinion of what's good for me. What about *me?* What about . . ."

Alarmed by the escalating volume of her mother's voice, and afraid of being caught, Rowena had crept away to her hiding place in the small sloping closet under the stairs, and stayed there, sitting in the dark, trying to understand what she'd overheard, until the housekeeper came to fetch her for lunch.

When she clicked back in to the present, she saw that she'd managed to get to New Canaan on automatic pilot. It was the second time this had happened, and it was very disconcerting. She was going to have to be more careful from now on. But still, what she'd remembered felt like gold. It tied in with something she'd read recently, something significant.

Pulling into a free space in the parking lot, she turned off the radio and sat with her elbows propped on the bottom of the steering wheel, massaging her forehead and trying to think what it was that she'd read. Nothing came, and she felt a flaring of angry frustration. She couldn't see what was wrong with the damned trophy tape, and now she couldn't remember whatever it was she'd read. Added to the fact that she'd driven, unaware, for a good twenty minutes, she couldn't help wondering if her brain had gone on vacation without bothering to let her know. Maybe this was how people quietly went bananas. She didn't *feel* crazy, but popular wisdom had it that crazy people were always the last to know they were a few cards shy of a full deck. So it was not impossible that she'd begun operating on a supraliminal plane.

Ian was writing on a message pad when she walked into the office. Upon seeing her, he said, "Oh, good. You're here. Saves me the bother' of writing this down." He tore the page from the pad and dropped it into the wastebasket. "Your friend Penny's been burning up the telephone wires." He handed her several message slips. "She rang soon after you left yesterday, and three times already this morning." He was very annoyed, spine stiffer than usual, eyebrows lifted and lips thinned.

"Why is she hounding me?" Rowena asked rhetorically, reading the messages which all said, "Please call."

"Why, indeed?" Ian echoed archly. "Perhaps you could persuade her to cease and desist. Her calls have become a nuisance. His mother patently has none of Kip's sense of propriety. The woman doesn't seem to understand this is a place of business."

"I'll take care of it." She was cowed as ever by his, or anyone's, displeasure. When angry he had the aura of a clever, slightly caustic headmaster, and at these times she found him more unapproachable then ever.

"That would be good," he said, with a crisp bite to his consonants, and went off to perform his preluncheon inspection of the tables.

It was ten past eleven. She dialed Penny's home number, knowing she'd be at work, and waited, breath held, for the answering machine to come on. When it did, she exhaled in a rush, waited for the tone, and said, "It's Rowena. I don't know when I'm going to be ready to talk to you, Penny, but it definitely won't be for a while. So I'd appreciate it if you'd stop calling the restaurant. It's disruptive, and it really isn't helping matters. Thanks. Bye."

She hung up and went to check the reservations book, then got some coffee from the carafe at the service area. Wondering if her message hadn't been a bit too cold, she returned to the office to have a cigarette while she drank the coffee. Cold words or not, with any luck, Penny would back off and stop trying to force matters. Now if only Reid would do the same, she might be able to concentrate and get a few things settled.

It was another day when the temperature was in the high nineties and by twelve-thirty the patio was full and most of the inside tables were occupied. She was about to seat a party of four when the telephone rang. The ID box showed Reid's office number. Panicked, she looked around to see who could take the call. The foursome was waiting. Ian was out of sight. Terry was busy behind the bar. The staff were hustling, serving, busing, everyone on the move. The phone went on ringing as she reached for menus and asked the group to follow her. The ringing sounded extraordinarily loud and shrill, going on and on. Then, all at once, to her immense relief, it stopped mid-ring.

The group seated and given menus, she moved back to the reservations stand. Perspiring, she reached into her pocket for a tissue to dry her hands as the door opened and a threesome entered, one of whom was the man she'd encountered in the bookstore doorway the previous day. The bottom of her stomach seemed to fall away and for a second time she looked around in vain for help. Ian was still out of sight. Terry had the blender going, making frozen daiquiris. The trio approached, and the most senior of the three asked with a smile if she had a table.

Drowning in the wet heat of her body, a headache threatening at the base of her skull, she looked at the book. "We have a table in the non-smoking section," she said, hoping they'd declare themselves smokers and go off to some other restaurant. But no. Non-smoking was fine. She smiled and collected menus, aware of Mr. Spain's attempts to catch her eye, but she pretended not to notice as she led them to the one free table left.

As the other two seated themselves, Spain hung back and, with a smile every bit as dazzling as the one he'd given her the day before, said, "So, we meet again."

"Yes we do. Good to see you." Affecting a casual air, she said, "I hope you enjoy your meals, gentlemen," and turned away to walk at what she deemed a reasonable pace past the bar, and out to the patio. She wanted to ask Ian to cover the front for a few minutes but he was probably in the cellar filling a wine order. She sighed, went back inside, and almost made it to the office when she heard footsteps behind her.

"I wonder if I could have a quick word with you," Spain said quietly.

Resigned, the headache developing now in earnest, she turned and said, "Please come into the office. We can talk in here."

Settling behind the desk, she invited him to take a seat as she got a cigarette lit. She dreaded what he might say, fearing another painful confrontation.

"You're Claudia's sister, am I right?"

"Yes, you are."

"I was a bit slow putting it together yesterday. I heard she died not long ago."

"February."

He shook his head. "Such a young woman. I'm very sorry. It must have been difficult for you." He gazed at her for a moment or two and when she didn't say anything, he went on. "Yesterday you thought you knew me. You were familiar to me, too, because—I later realized—you have a strong resemblance to your sister. Anyway, I had to wonder why. I mean, why you thought you knew me. I haven't been in the restaurant in a couple of years, not since I moved up to Westport. I do have clients here in town—which is how I met Claudia; I often brought people here for business lunches. The point is, I haven't been around for quite some time, yet you recognized me. My question is, how?"

"I suppose I must've seen you somewhere. I really don't know." God, but she hated lying. She felt like a complete fraud every time, positive she'd be caught. Her head was throbbing, sending out rays of pain that interfered with her vision.

Disarmingly, he smiled and said, "You're an honest woman. I thought that yesterday when you realized you'd made a mistake and weren't sure how to handle the situation. So I hate to contradict you, but I think you do know. My guess is there were pictures or something, and that you've seen them."

Her heart lurched, and she was suddenly overheated. "Pictures? Why would you think that?" She took a drag on the cigarette then carefully tipped off the ash. The inhalation seemed to heighten the intensity of the headache.

Making himself comfortable in the chair, he unbuttoned his suit jacket and crossed his legs, saying, "I had an affair with your sister. Not a very long one, and not a very good one. I couldn't connect with her somehow, not even in the most intimate of circumstances. The couple of times we were together at her house, I had the feeling things were a little—staged. It gave me a hinky feeling and I wondered if maybe someone was watching or taking pictures. You see, it was as if she was giving a performance for an audience she knew about but that I couldn't see. And the posturing, the gestures and little moans, the faked orgasms were all for the benefit of the camera. I'm sorry if I'm embarrassing you. That's not why I came today. I wanted a chance to talk to you, and maybe satisfy my curiosity."

"Of course," she said softly. "I can understand that."

"I hoped you might. The thing is, my marriage broke up about six months before I met your sister, and, to be frank, I was kind of wild for a while, drinking too much and seeing a lot of women. Claudia was one of them. But there was something about her that honestly scared me— the difference between the way she acted in bed at my place and the way she acted in bed at hers, the way she talked, even the way she took off her clothes. I was pretty well convinced pictures were involved, but when we stopped seeing each other I put the whole thing out of my mind. After all, what did it matter? If she had pictures, they couldn't be used to damage me in any way. Then, running into you yesterday brought it back, started me wondering again."

She took a last puff of the cigarette but said nothing. For a moment her attention was taken up by the headache. It felt as if some tiny feral entity had attached itself to the back of her skull by its claws, which were sinking past the bone, sliding deeper and deeper into her brain.

"I can tell this is awkward for you," he said. "Just satisfy my curiosity and that'll be the end of it. I'll be on my way. *Were* there pictures?"

"A tape," she admitted almost inaudibly. "She had a video camera set up with a timer."

"I *knew* it! And that's how you recognized me, right?"

She nodded, her face burning.

"You watched it not knowing what you were going to see, right?"

"Them," she corrected him. "There were a fair number. When I realized what they were I destroyed them."

"Must've been a whole lot of fun for you, finding those. What kind of woman *does* a thing like that?" he wondered aloud.

"Since she died I've been trying to figure that out myself, Mr....?"

"Delgado. Simon. You never did tell me your name."

"Rowena."

He gave her another of his glorious smiles, and said, *"Ivanhoe.* Man, I loved that book when I was a kid."

"So did I." She was able, finally, to offer him a smile in return. Then, trying to ignore the increasing pain in her head, she said, "I'm sorry if I caused *you* any embarrassment, Simon. I didn't handle it very well yesterday, but I had no idea what to say." She shrugged. "You have my word the tapes have been destroyed, and I'm the only one, aside from my sister, who saw them." Was that true? Or had Claudia shared her trophies the way she'd shared certain edited telephone messages? A terrifying thought, one that should have occurred to her sooner. Now, along with the headache, she was sweating again.

"Let's both forget it," he said magnanimously. "I've got my answer, and I'm satisfied. I'd better get back now or my partners'll wonder what's happened to me." Getting to his feet, he held out his hand to her, saying, "Thank you, Rowena. I appreciate your telling me the truth. You really are sweet, and I'll stop in again, if I may, next time I'm in town."

"Please do. I'd like that."

He walked out of the office and she sat there, silently thanking the powers-that-be that Delgado had turned out to be a fair-minded and reasonable man.

Ian, however, seemed most unreasonable when he came charging into the office only moments later, demanding to know why she wasn't covering the front and why she had allowed the telephone to go unanswered.

"Have you any idea of the negative impression that sort of thing creates?" he demanded. "This is simply *not good enough!* On top of which, it was the doctor again." He slammed a message slip on the desk saying, *"Please* ring these *damned* people *back,* Rowena! The whole thing's becoming *much* too *much!"*

To her chagrin and his obvious horror, she opened her mouth to speak but instead broke into tears. Bending her aching head into her hands, she felt a fool and a failure. Unnerved by the arrival of Simon Delgado, she'd neglected her responsibilities.

"Oh, bloody hell!" Instantly softening, he pushed his handkerchief into her hand. "Please don't do that. I had no right to carry on at you. I'm sorry." Grabbing his pack of Silk Cuts off the desk, he fell into the chair Delgado had just vacated and lit a cigarette.

"No, no, you're right," she croaked, blotting her face with the freshsmelling, monogrammed linen square. "I should've answered the phone, and I should've been covering the front. Things seem to be piling up on me.'' Maybe she was having a so-called nervous breakdown, and if so, it wasn't the cataclysmic event she'd always imagined but more a steady, stealthy crumbling of one's control. It was being unable to remember things, and driving from one place to another in an oblivious state; it was falling victim to unseemly emotional displays; and it was spending every free moment trying to piece together a lifetime's worth of fragmented memories that probably could never be made into a cohesive whole.

''You'll think I'm a complete tyrant at this rate,'' he said remorsefully. ''But please understand. It's rather like a frightful case of déjà vu. Claudia positively *thrived* on having the lot of us taking messages for her, turning away jaundiced suitors, running her errands, fetching and carrying, dancing to her tune. I'm aware you've been experiencing some, ah, difficulties the last little while, and it was wrong of me not to make allowances. Unfortunately, my dear, it's bad for the image when a telephone goes unanswered in an establishment of this caliber.''

''I know that, and you're right. I let personal matters interfere with business.'' Maybe she didn't belong here. At least at the library she'd understood the rules. Or perhaps she'd created her own there and had abided by them. But since her first evening here she'd been freefloating, periodically bumping up against unwritten guidelines no one had taken the time to define for her. ''It's okay, Ian.''

''No, it isn't, actually. I do most sincerely apologize for my outburst.''

''It's not necessary, but thank you.''

''Could we come to an agreement regarding the telephone? If it's a call you don't wish to take and I'm unavailable, let's have Terry answer on the bar extension if no one's picked up by the third ring. Will that suit?''

''Yes, of course. And I've already left Penny a message telling her not to phone me here again.''

''Good.'' He finished his cigarette, then looked directly into her eyes. ''You know, Rowena, I expect we could both do with a bit of time off,'' he said with admirable diplomacy. ''It's been ages since I, for one, had a vacation. And you've scarcely taken any time to yourself in the months you've been here.''

''Why not take a couple of weeks off, then?'' she suggested.

"If you feel you could manage on your own, I might well do that. Perhaps at the end of August, before the Labor Day weekend. It's usually quiet then."

"That would be fine."

"And what about you, my dear? When will you take some time to yourself?"

"I'll have to give that some thought."

He reached across the desk to cover her hand with his. "Even in the very best of relationships people find themselves disagreeing from time to time. It doesn't mean they don't care about one another or that they're no longer friends. I do care and I'm sorry I upset you."

"I'm sorry, too."

His fair brows drawing together in perplexity, as if unsure how to interpret her remark, he withdrew his hand, saying, "I'd best get back out there now."

"Yes. I'll be along in a minute or two."

"Take your time." He gave her a conciliatory smile before leaving.

The message slip read, "Dr. Reid rang. No need to ring back."

She lowered her pounding head to the desk and sobbed into Ian's handkerchief. Then she went down to the women's room where she swallowed two Tylenol caplets with a handful of water, repaired her makeup without daring to look at herself fully in the mirror, and returned to work.

Arriving home two hours later, she fixed a weak vodka and tonic and carried it upstairs to drink while she soaked in a tub of hot water. The bruises, she saw, were turning yellow. Gazing down the length of her body, she ran a hand lazily over herself, remembering one evening when Claudia had come bursting into her room as she was undressing for bed. "It's really not *fair,*" her fifteen-year-old sister had declared, looking her up and down. "You got the brains *and* the breasts."

Rowena had been yet again amazed at the vast difference between what she and her sister considered important. But she'd been touched by what she recognized as Claudia's longing for her own kind of freedom—a physical perfection that would bring her the admiring attention she seemed to require like a drug. Rowena had quickly pulled on her pajamas before giving her sister a hug, and telling her, "If you want them badly enough, someday you'll be able to buy any size and shape you want." In due course Claudia had—along with a few other minor alterations—purchased a new, improved set of breasts that pleased her inordinately. And they'd turned out to be a better investment than most, because those breasts would sit, for all eternity, unalterably high and proud upon her sister's chest.

As she sipped her drink, the hot water easing some of the residual tension in her neck and shoulder muscles in the aftermath of the headache, she considered Ian's suggestion. Maybe she'd take a week off in September and drive up to Vermont to find her father. She wanted so much to see him, to meet his children—her half brother and sister who were both now in their twenties—and her stepmother, the woman who'd given her father the love and respect he so deserved but had gone for so long without.

The water cold, the drink finished, she put on baggy Bermudas, a T-shirt, and moccasins, then switched off the ringers on the telephones and turned down the volume on the answering machine. While the kettle was boiling for tea she made a sandwich with baked ham, Muenster cheese, lettuce, tomato, and champagne mustard on pumpernickel bread. Then, with a Vivaldi woodwind concerto playing on the radio, she ate half the sandwich and slowly reread every word of her father's cards. Finishing the last of them with a second cup of tea and a cigarette, she put the cash in an envelope and slipped it into the odds-and-ends drawer, not sure what she'd ultimately do with the money. The cards she left on the counter, planning to read them again before bed. Finally, she went outside with the idea of settling on the chaise with the Conrad book, but in less than ten minutes she was back inside, unable to stop herself, on her way to the living room and the VCR.

By nine o'clock she'd been through the tape five times, and was almost halfway through it again when an angry voice said, "So *this* is where you are. What the *hell* is going on, Rowena?"

Starting violently, she turned to see Mark standing, hands on hips, in the doorway. Profoundly ashamed, her pulse frenzied, she grabbed for the remote, desperate to stop the tape.

"No, don't," he said in a frosty tone, walking over to drop down beside her on the sofa and take the remote from her hand. He glanced at the screen then back at her, and pressed the Pause button. "I've been calling every ten minutes for over an hour. I knew you were home, and when the machine kept picking up, first I thought you were in the shower, then I started getting scared. I had visions of you lying dead in here. So I let myself in to make sure you were okay."

"Why didn't you knock?" she asked, at last able to speak. "And why would I be dead?"

"If you weren't answering the phone," he said reasonably, "why would you answer the door? Maybe you slipped in the tub and concussed yourself. Maybe you stuck your wet finger in a socket. I don't know! I *thought* something was *wrong.*"

"Nothing's wrong," she whispered, lighting a cigarette.

"Don't bullshit me, darling," he said mildly, glancing over at the frozen picture on the screen. "Something's wrong big time. You didn't get rid of the tapes, after all. I was afraid of this."

"No, I did, Mark. I did. I just found this one...." Her entire body was shaking. And the shame seemed to be shrinking her fasciae, which in turn were strangling her organs, cutting off the air to her lungs so that she could barely breathe, could scarcely get the words out.

"Ro, please be straight with me."

"*I am!*" she insisted. "*I am!*"

"Let's have a look at this," he said, preparing to release the Pause button.

"Mark," she pleaded, "I don't want you to see it." But it was too late. The tape was running.

"Ah, shit, shit, shit!" he said sadly. "It's the shrink." He paused the machine again and turned to her. "You found this, and now you're brokenhearted, because you cared for him. And please don't try to say you didn't, because I know you did."

Overcome by a sense of futility, she averted her eyes and put out the just-lit cigarette.

"Don't be embarrassed, Ro. I understand. I really do."

"I already feel like a fool, Mark," she said thickly. "Don't make it worse."

"I'm not going to go home and pretend I didn't find you here, sitting like a hit-and-run victim, watching your sister's sexual home movies."

"Why can't you? If it was what you wanted, I'd do it for you."

"But I'm *not* you, honey. And I can't play dumb because that wouldn't help you."

"Please give me the remote."

"Ro, you need help, and I can't give you any if I don't know what we're dealing with."

"I don't *need* any help!"

"You *do!* Okay? You've been messed up ever since Claudia died. I'd like to see what's making you crazy and maybe then we can talk."

"You think I'm crazy?"

"No, but you're close, babe. This is me, Ro. I *know* you, and you're about an inch away from the edge." His eyes filling, he said, "I love you, Rowena, and no way am I going to stand by quietly and watch you go over. Tim's gone. Half my friends are gone or dying. I can't lose you, too. I *won't* lose you without a fight!"

"You're not going to lose me," she argued tearfully. "I've got a lot I'm trying to deal with, and I admit I'm upset about Reid, but please don't say things like that."

"Ro, you're disappearing in front of my eyes. You've lost so much weight there's practically nothing left of you. You're all hard angles, and a coat-hanger clavicle. You've got this harried look lately, and now you're turning off the phones so you won't be disturbed while you repeatedly stab yourself in the heart watching this fuck tape your rotten sister made. So please don't tell me I have nothing to worry about, because I can see it, plain as day. We're going to *watch* this tape, and then we're going to *talk* about it!" He took firm hold of her hand and released the Pause button.

After several minutes he said, "I've heard about that, but I've never actually seen anyone do it."

"Do what?" she asked dully, mired in self-hatred and held captive at his side.

"The condom trick," he explained, rewinding the tape so he could show her. "See there, she grabs it off the table and pops it in her mouth. Now she's down on her knees, and she puts it on him without using her hands. An interesting talent."

"I can't *do* this." Yanking her hand free, she jumped up. "I'll go make some coffee."

"Coffee would be good. It's gonna be okay, Ro," he said, not taking his eyes from the screen. "I promise."

Wanting to scream, the headache back, she fled to the kitchen where she mechanically poured water into the well, spooned coffee into the basket, and turned the machine on. Unwilling to go back to the living room for her cigarettes, she opened a fresh pack, lit up, and began pacing back and forth, chewing on the inside of her cheeks.

"Hey, Ro?" Mark called after five minutes or so. "Who shot this?"

"Claudia," she called back, her voice scratchy.

"No way, my tiny Tasmanian devil. C'mere and check this out!"

Deeply reluctant, she went back to the living room.

"Sit down and look at this!" He hit the Play button, saying, "Watch!"

On the screen Tony Reid climbed off the bed, hastily pulled on his clothes, then walked out of the room.

"See?" Mark asked her.

"See what?"

"Somebody else had to be there, Ro. Cameras don't move by themselves."

"Oh, my God!" At long last she knew what had disturbed her about the footage all along: When Reid stormed out of the room, the camera panned to follow him. "I knew something was wrong but I couldn't figure out what. That's why I kept watching."

"When it comes to movies and television, we become the eye of the camera. We accept images without thinking, because we're so accustomed to camera movement." He stopped the tape and shut off the set before turning to her. "Did that happen on any of the other tapes?"

Thinking back, she had to say, "No."

"So, on at least one occasion, Claudia had a partner in crime."

"Oh, my God!" She sat, mouth agape, as more pieces of the puzzle fit themselves neatly into place.

Twenty-Three

Huddled inside Mark's embrace, she cried like a child, on and on, until the tears ran out. He held her close all the while and soothed her with soft murmurs and a hand stroking her spine. When the worst was past, he asked quietly, "What're we gonna do about this, Ro?"

"About what?" She shifted away and used the bottom of her over-size T-shirt to dry her face.

"The tape, my love. What d'you want to do with it?"

"Get rid of it," she said hoarsely. "I told you I only kept watching because I couldn't figure out what was wrong with it."

"And maybe because it reinforced your already-low opinion of yourself?"

She tried to think of some rejoinder, but couldn't because what he'd said was the truth, and instead looked away, drawing her lips inward between her teeth.

"That's attractive," he teased.

Letting her mouth relax, she wished she could go off and hide somewhere. But he wasn't about to permit that.

"Let's discuss this," he said, leaning forward to pour himself more of the now-lukewarm coffee. He held out the carafe inquiringly, but she shook her head and he put it down. After several quick sips he set the mug on the coffee table and shifted to face her squarely. "Okay. What occurs to me is you have no way of knowing when the tape was made. To keep things simple, we'll say it was last fall. When it was made really doesn't signify much. *But.* All the tape proves is that the man had sex with your sister once. It was patently *not* one of the high points of his life, so it's extremely unlikely this was an ongoing affair. Will you concede that much?"

"So what if I do concede that, Mark? It doesn't alter the fact that he *lied* to me."

"Dear heart, I know you're hurt and angry, but think for a minute, please. If you were a man Claudia practically dragged into bed with her, would you admit to it? I sincerely doubt it. What comes across clear as day on the tape is that the doc didn't want to be there. What occurred was your basic mercy fuck. And he was a lot nicer about it than I think most guys would've been. He didn't get rough with her and he didn't humiliate her either. I'm sorry, but I find his behavior completely understandable. What's relevant here is, number one, that you fell for him and now you hate yourself because all you can focus on is the one lie you know he told you. And, number two, she dragooned someone into taping the session for her—probably because she couldn't be certain when, or how, or even if, she was going to be able to carry it off. So, got any ideas on who she might've roped in to do it?"

"I don't want to get into it now." She lit a cigarette and inhaled, the smoke biting the back of her throat. "If I do, I'm going to fall apart again."

"Why? Because it's a pretty good bet it was Ian?"

She looked over sharply. "What makes you say that?"

"Who else *could* it have been, Ro? She was juggling way too many balls so far as her other pals were concerned to risk asking one of them. She would've gone after someone she knew she could trust, who wouldn't give the game away. He's already admitted to you that he knew about the tapes. So, who else could it have been but him?"

She sat holding her head for a time, then straightened and took another drag on the cigarette. "Okay, since you insist, let's look at Ian as a candidate. Why would he go along with such a sordid scenario?"

"That's the big question. Why *would* he?"

She stared at him, at a loss for an answer.

"Blackmail?" he suggested.

"It's possible. I don't know."

"I think it was some kind of blackmail. Why else did he put up with her crap for so many years? He's a highly competent, well-educated man with expensive taste in clothes, an upper-class accent, and, I'd bet, credentials from a top-ranking hotel school. He could probably pick and choose his jobs. There had to be a pretty cogent reason why he didn't leave. It sure as hell wasn't the *gemütlichkeit* of Le Rendezvous that kept him there."

"And he stayed on after . . ." She trailed off, not sure where she was headed.

"After what?"

"After Claudia died. Maybe he couldn't take it anymore and that's why he killed her."

"*Yo!* Wait a minute! Did I miss the first reel of this flick? Who said anything about *killing* anybody?"

"She would *never* have killed herself, Mark. Never! Suicide was the *last* thing Claudia would ever do."

"Dearest, it *was* the last thing she ever did. You are way, way off base here. Nobody killed her."

"My sister did *not* kill herself!"

"So all these months, that's what it's been about—trying on Claudia's life, obsessing over the tapes after you found them, working at the restaurant so you could figure out who knocked her off."

"I have not been 'trying on' her life, and it so happens I enjoy the restaurant a hell of a lot more than I did the Mag. But yes, I have been trying to find out who killed her."

"*Nobody killed her!*"

"You're wrong. Ian and Reid both had motives."

"Oh? Care to enlighten me?"

"Obviously I can't."

"Fine. Motives unknown. Excuse me, but don't you think the medical examiner would've insisted on an autopsy if he'd found anything the least suspicious about her death?"

"The man spent ten minutes tops upstairs with her body."

"Plenty long enough for someone experienced to decide if a death doesn't look or feel right."

"I disagree, Mark."

"You can disagree till the cows come home, that still doesn't mean we're talking murder. And are you trying to tell me you're working every day with one of your prime suspects, and the other is romantically inclined toward you?"

"Maybe."

"Well, all Reid knows right now is that for some reason you've decided to play hard to get, and you're not returning his calls. And Ian's pissed off because you're starting to pull stunts too reminiscent of Claudia for his liking. So, neither of them knows you're suspicious of him. What's your plan?"

"I don't have one. And I am not pulling stunts. I had Caller ID installed so I wouldn't have to talk to Penny or Reid just now."

"Rowena, do you hear how nutty this sounds?" He reached for her hand. "Maybe you need to take a break and go off on one of your big trips. Things are getting very out of control around here. Seriously. You don't believe for a moment that Ian's a murderer. If you did, you'd be too scared to go to the restaurant. And do you actually think Reid's a violent man?''

"He could be. How would I know?''

"You don't know,'' he repeated. "Well, I watched that man getting the treatment from your sister and he came across to me as very tenderhearted. I don't think he has a violent bone in his body. What're you *doing,* Ro? What're you *saying?* On the one hand you think both these men are capable of murder, but on the other hand they're not?''

"Ian has a terrible temper. And Reid lies at the drop of a hat. I'm trying to figure it out.''

"Big deal. Ian gets a mad on now and then, and Reid's been known to bend the truth. That doesn't make either of them a killer. Please tell me what it is you're trying to figure out.''

"About Claudia ... and my mother. I'm ... starting, uhm, to remember things.''

"What things?'' he asked gently.

"Things.'' She pulled her hand free, put out her cigarette and at once lit another. A snippet of that other memory that was still eluding her was illuminated for a moment in her mind, then went dark.

"Will you *please* talk to me? Don't you know how worried I am about you?''

"I do know, and I *am* talking to you. But you don't seem to want to hear what I'm trying to say.''

"You have no idea how wrong you are. I wish, for maybe ten seconds, you could be me, listening to my dearest friend saying some of the looniest stuff I've ever heard, and behaving in a way that bothers me more than I can say. You've dropped all your old friends and don't go anywhere anymore except back and forth to the restaurant. Everybody at the Mag's been asking about you, especially Marcia, and I don't know what to tell them.''

"You don't have to tell them anything.''

"I'm going to make like you didn't say that. I don't want to get off topic. You're sitting here saying somebody killed your sister, and you've got two suspects but you don't *really* suspect either one of them. Ro, I love you dearly, but you need to get a grip on. Why not talk to Reid, hear what he has to say? And why not come right out and tell Ian you'd like to know what was going on with him and Claudia? What's it going to cost you?''

"You know I loathe scenes,'' she lamented, breaking into tears. "Why can't you leave me alone and let me handle this in my own way?''

"Because, for the hundredth time, you're *not* handling it."

"You really do think I'm cracking up, don't you?"

"I'm afraid of that possibility," he said cautiously.

"She *didn't* kill herself, Mark. Maybe I *am* losing my marbles. Lately, it feels as if I am. But you're going to feel very foolish when you find out I was right all along."

"If you are right, my tormented tamale, I will sit at your kitchen table and eat as much humble pie as you can dish up. And speaking of eating, you haven't had anything, have you?"

"I had a late lunch."

"I had an early dinner." He looked at his watch. "It's almost eleven and I'm hungry. I'm going to whip up a salad and some omelets and we'll continue this discussion while we eat."

She wanted to refuse but knew he'd misunderstand, so she shrugged and said, "I'm not really hungry, but okay."

For a second time he took hold of her hand, saying, "I know you'd love to tell me to blow it out my ear right now, but I also know how much you hate confrontations, so I'm not fooled, cupcake. I know agreeing to eat is by way of a compromise. Be aware that I do know, and that I intend to hang in until we can somehow get you to the point where you're making sense again. All right?"

Feeling defeated and not trusting herself to speak, she nodded her agreement.

After they'd eaten and argued back and forth about her suspicions without either of them gaining or losing any ground, he insisted on putting her to bed.

"The tape's going home with me and I'm going to dispose of it. Now you get into your jammies, then I'll tuck you in."

He sat on the foot of the bed to wait, and she left the dressing room door ajar while she changed.

"What're you going to do about this situation, Ro?"

"Speak to Ian, I suppose."

"I think that's a good idea. And what about the shrink? Are you going to give him a chance at least to state his case?"

"I don't think so." She turned off the dressing room light and went into the bathroom to brush her teeth. When she came out, he had the blankets folded back and stood waiting for her to climb in.

"You look so little and cute I feel as if I should read you a bedtime story."

"I may be little, but I've never been cute."

"You've *always* been cute. Get *over* this ugly stuff, would you? Okay if I stretch out beside you?"

In answer, she patted the space beside her. He stepped out of his loafers and lay down, leaning on his elbow facing her.

"I'm gonna tell you a bedtime story anyway. So turn out the light and settle down."

She did as he asked and curled up on her side, hands tucked under her cheek.

"Once upon a time," he began, "there were two princess sisters. They lived in a castle with their mother, the queen. The three of them should have been very happy because they had everything in the world, but they were not. The older princess was unhappy because her father, the king, had gone away and left her and she believed in her heart it was her fault that he'd left them. The younger princess was unhappy because that was her nature. She could only be happy when everyone paid attention to her and told her over and over again how beautiful she was. But even though she really was quite pretty she was such an unpleasant girl that people in the court rarely complimented her or paid her very much attention. Mostly they tried to stay out of her way. The older princess sister was clever and beautiful and kind, and this made her mother the queen unhappy because she was no longer young and beautiful and because she had never been clever or kind. By reflection the older princess made the queen look bad. So to punish her beautiful daughter, the queen told the child at every possible opportunity that, clever though she might be, she was ugly and unlovable and therefore no prince would ever want her for his true love. And because the younger princess was jealous of her lovely older sister, she too was unkind and tried to steal away all her sister's friends...."

"Mark, don't please." A tear trickled down the side of her nose.

"Okay, I'll stop. C'mere." He eased her over so her head was resting on his chest. "Now close your eyes and I'll stay with you until you fall asleep."

"I love you," she whispered.

"D'you wish I was a straight guy who'd make love to you, Ro?"

"No, do you?"

"Sometimes. But I think it'd wreck everything. Sex has a way of doing that."

"It's not what we're about. You're my family, and I love you exactly the way you are."

"Me, too, you. Tell me the truth. You were in love with the doc, weren't you?"

"You already know the answer to that."

"Yeah, I do. Okay, close your eyes and go to sleep now. Things'll look a whole lot better when you wake up."

"That would be very nice." Her arm across his waist, she shut her eyes and listened to the slow, steady beating of his heart, breathing in the scent of Canoe, until she felt herself slipping down and away.

She did feel better, less frazzled, the next morning as she went out to the car to drive to work. Setting off, she had to admit she really didn't believe Ian had killed her sister. But he was the only person she could think of who might have shot the tape of Claudia and Reid. She also couldn't picture Reid as a murderer. All she had was the continuing conviction that Ian knew more than he'd so far been willing to say, and her ongoing sense of betrayal by Reid. She would have to circumvent her reservations and ask Ian point-blank today to tell her what he knew. What she'd do about Tony Reid she just didn't know.

She was on the Post Road, headed for Route 124, when that elusive memory flashed once more on her mental screen. And this time, through sheer force of will, she was able to nail it down, to fix the time in her mind: her junior year of college. And the circumstances: a spur of the moment decision to drive home for an unannounced weekend visit.

Energized and made oddly homesick by the crisp air and the sunlit glow of the blazing autumn foliage, she had set off very early on a Saturday morning. Arriving home near noon, she went from habit to the back door, and opened it in time to see Claudia shove a cringing Jeanne into the refrigerator, then slap her several times, hard, across the side of her head.

Rowena's horrified cry startled the other two into frozen attitudes that reminded her of the game of statues that she and Cary had played as kids.

Her ugly expression instantly transformed into one of delight, Claudia exclaimed, "Ro! This is great! Are you home for the weekend?"

Astonished as ever by her sister's speed-of-light ability to shift moods, Rowena asked, "What's going on?" Her pulse fluttering fearfully in her throat, the understanding had crystallized in her mind that on a certain level she was afraid of her sister, and always had been.

Something about Claudia was beyond the realm of her comprehension; it was something primal and untouched by the concerns that governed most other people's behavior. It had showed in her as a small girl when she'd blithely destroyed an entire flower bed, or when she'd jumped up and down the back steps over and over and over, never tiring, thoroughly engrossed in her mindless activity. As she'd grown older, it had showed in her utter disregard for the feelings of the rest of the family as she'd repeatedly ransacked their bedrooms, making off with whatever took her fancy. It had showed in her casually taking over Rowena's friends, both male and female; and in her intense depression when compelled to attend Brandon Prep. "What's happening here?" Rowena asked again.

"Oh, nothing," Claudia answered cheerfully. "Hey! Let's all go to the club tonight for dinner. I've got a fabulous new dress. Wait'll you see it!"

"Why were you hitting her?" Rowena asked, aware that her mother had also undergone a transformation—from cringing fear to the typically benign interest she'd always displayed when her daughters appeared to be communicating in a reasonably civilized fashion. Her expression seemed to say, Play nicely now, girls. And for years, Rowena had wondered why Jeanne imagined her daughters ever could or would get along. "Play nicely" wasn't an idiom that meant anything to Claudia. And to Rowena what it meant was, Shut up and try to look pretty—a command that infuriated her and made her insides shrivel.

In a blink, Claudia's mood shifted again. Assuming an aggressive posture, eyes slitted, chin outthrust, and hands on hips, she asked, "What're you doing here anyway? You're supposed to be at college, not sneaking around, spying on people."

Rowena moved closer to her mother, saying, "Don't be ridiculous. No one's spying. What was that about, Mother? Why were you letting her hit you?"

"Go ahead and talk, the two of you. Pretend I'm not here."

"Claudia, be quiet a minute," Rowena said in the neutral tone that seemed to work best with her sister. "Mother, answer me please. What's been going on around here?"

"Christ Almighty! I hate the way you always do this!" Claudia ranted. "You come barging in and start taking charge. Me and Mummy do just fine when you're not around."

"I can see that," Rowena said bitingly.

"Settle down, dear," Jeanne addressed her younger daughter with a tremulous smile.

"Settle down, dear," Claudia mimicked her. "You are *such* a fucking moron!" Glaring, she turned and stormed off, her footsteps heavy and rapid as she raced up the stairs.

Jeanne sank into one of the kitchen chairs, with a quivering hand smoothing her hair. Then, as if remembering she had a part to play, she smiled brightly and said, "What a nice surprise, Rowena! Will you be staying for the weekend, dear?"

"Why was she hitting you? And why were you letting her?" Rowena asked, for a moment wondering if she had actually witnessed that vicious scene, or if perhaps her mother had a hearing problem. Were her mother and sister crazy, or was she?

Eyes on the doorway through which Claudia had gone, Jeanne gave a small shrug and, still smiling vaguely, said, "It was nonsense. You know your sister."

Not sure she knew either one of them, Rowena persisted. "*Why* did she hit you and *why* did you let her?"

"You must be hungry." Jeanne diligently ignored the question. "I'll get Hilda to fix lunch. And tonight the three of us will have dinner at the club. Where *is* Hilda?" She looked around. "Oh, that's right. She's doing the marketing. Yes, we'll go to the club. You know how Claudia loves to dress up. And you must be dying for some decent food. You're getting awfully thin, dear."

Rowena pictured it: The sycophantic maître d' and his crew of waiters would swarm around their table, bringing Jeanne a manhattan the instant she was seated, complimenting Jeanne and Claudia on how well they looked. And her mother and sister would preen, eating it up, their heads tilting toward the compliments like flowers following the sun.

"I can't stay," Rowena said, changing her plans on the spot. "I just came to pick up a couple of things I need."

"You drove for four hours to get here and you're not even going to stay the night?" her mother asked, as if genuinely disappointed. Perhaps she was. If Rowena stayed Jeanne would be safe for a time because Claudia wouldn't dare attack her again while Rowena was in the house.

Feeling unequal to the task of deciphering the complex dynamics between her mother and sister, yet sympathetic too, Rowena was on the verge of changing her mind again and saying she'd stay after all when Claudia spoke scathingly from the doorway.

"You are *so* stupid! She doesn't *want* to stay here, Mother, darling. She *hates* it here. She *hates* you, probably because you're a pathetic lush who's forever falling over her own feet. Any time we go to the club for dinner, everyone's holding their breath, waiting for Mummy to go ass over teacup on her way to the ladies' room, or as we're leaving. You should see them, waiting to see if she'll make it down the front steps this time without breaking her neck.''

"That's not true," Rowena said hoarsely, shocked by her sister's almost casual vehemence, and by her mother's steadfast refusal to defend herself. "I do not hate you," she told Jeanne and, for an instant, she saw something soft and broken in her mother's eyes.

"I know you don't," Jeanne said, mouth trembling slightly.

Turning to Claudia, Rowena said, "You have no right to talk to her that way, and you have no right to hit her."

"You mind your own business! What goes on here is between Mummy and me. And what would you know anyway? You never want to *see,* even when things are staring you in the face."

"This *is* my business," Rowena argued hotly, while the voice inside her head said, *That's true. I never do want to see. I don't want to see what's happening here right now.* She took a menacing step toward her sister, feeling alarmingly close to the edge of herself—as if she'd only just then realized that there were invisible walls that contained her. "You have no right to hit her," she repeated more strongly.

Claudia moved to stand behind Jeanne's chair, as if for protection. "You don't tell me what to do! *Nobody* tells me what to do!"

That's true too, Rowena thought. *No one's in control here. They need each other because neither of them can survive alone, without the other.*

Her hand now on her mother's shoulder, Claudia said, "You're always trying to come between Mummy and me, because you're jealous. You've *always* been jealous of me. And that's just *sad,* Rowena. You're sad. Boring and ugly and sad."

"Why on *earth* would I be jealous of you?" Rowena asked her with surprise.

"Because I'm better-looking and sexier. Because you couldn't draw *flies,* and I can have *any* man I *want.*"

Involuntarily, Rowena laughed. But inside she was quaking. She was confronting a form of madness in which both her mother and sister actively participated. It wasn't the sort of uncontrolled dementedness that got people locked up in rubber rooms, but rather an insidiously subtle and complex joint lunacy, with each partner requiring the presence of the other in order for both to perpetuate the pain and the rage, and to have companionship. They were, on a certain level, a perfect match because no one else would, or could, tolerate either one of these women for the long term. In some ways they understood each other completely, and in other ways they failed utterly to know one another. They were, Rowena thought, like blind and hobbled primates with an instinctive animosity toward one another, grappling from habit and necessity.

"Girls, please," Jeanne said weakly. "Don't fight."

Fight? Rowena looked with curiosity at her mother, viewing her as she might a stranger. And what she saw was a woman with long, exquisitely shaped legs—in dark hose and high heels, as always, to draw admiring eyes—a thickened torso and sticklike arms an expensive, well-cut black suit couldn't conceal, and a bloated but still beautiful face. Portrait of an alcoholic mother, painted in shades of gray. *It's because she drinks, because she's been drinking too much for years and years.*

In the few moments she took to study her mother and come to this realization, Claudia's mood had altered yet again. "Well, I've got to get going," she announced cheerfully. "I have a lunch date. I'm taking your car, Mummy." She bent to touch her cheek to Jeanne's. "You staying or heading back?" she asked Rowena.

"Heading back," Rowena replied, dazed.

"Okay. See you soon." Claudia touched her cheek to Rowena's and flounced off down the hall, leaving Rowena enveloped in a cloud of Joy. "Bye," Claudia sang out. Then the front door opened and closed.

Rowena sat down openmouthed, once more wondering if she was crazy or they were. Did other families behave this way? Was it possible Jeanne and Claudia were quite normal and that she was the one with the skewed take on the situation? For such a long time she'd felt different, an outsider cut off even from the people to whom she was closest, like Penny. But no, her take was objective. Her mother and sister were engaged in complicitous combat, warring against each other, yet immediately joining ranks if threatened by outside forces. And she, Rowena, was an outside force. Astounded, she took one of her mother's cigarettes without bothering to ask if she might, and lit it.

"She doesn't mean the things she says," Jeanne said. Her hand shook badly, Rowena noticed, as she too lit a cigarette.

"Maybe, and maybe not," Rowena said, finding it difficult to breathe in the tainted atmosphere of the house. The air seemed thick with the spilt blood of too many battles, of secrets, and of years of things left unspoken that hung like gluey spiraling coils of flypaper suspended from the ceilings.

With the flapping motion of one hand, Jeanne tried to brush it all aside. "Claudia's temperamental. You know that, dear. She has such awful mood swings, poor girl." That soft, broken thing in her eyes, like some caged and starving creature, regarded Rowena pleadingly, begging her to play the game, keep the deceit intact. And because there was a part of her that loved her mother no matter what, Rowena had tacitly consented to put the truth from her mind.

And for more than twenty years she had kept her promise, denying her mother's alcoholism, even going so far as to omit any mention—or even private acknowledgment—of its being the cause of the liver cancer that eventually killed Jeanne at the age of fifty-five. But now it was again in the forefront of her mind, and she was within touching distance of an explanation for Claudia's . . . .

Her attention was pulled forcibly back to the road by a car ignoring the stop sign at the T intersection perhaps fifty yards ahead. Christ! Where was she? On Route 124, and she couldn't remember even making the turn. Oh, God! The other car made a lazy, low-speed left turn, narrowly avoiding a collision with a Jaguar traveling in the opposite direction, and putting it squarely in Rowena's path. Oh my God! Time both sped up and slowed down so that she saw the look of fright on the woman in the Jaguar as it passed, and she had a glimpse of an elderly man in the driver's seat of the slow-moving old Cadillac. God! Fear sending its adrenal message through her entire body, she was spinning the wheel of the Mercedes hard to the right to avoid rear-ending the Cadillac while at the same time stomping on the brake. She was going to die without seeing her father again, without knowing why Claudia died. *Mark, I'm sorry.* The massive trunk of an ancient copper beech seemed to come flying through space at an extraordinary speed to meet her, and as she spun the wheel to the left, trying not to hit it, she realized she'd forgotten to put on her seat belt. The passenger side of the Mercedes slammed into the tree with a great, deafening crash and she flew sideways across the front seat, colliding headfirst with the passenger door. An amazing sensation, as if her skull had been driven down into her shoulders. She heard glass shattering and metal grinding on metal, smelled the sweetish reek of gasoline as the car rocked and then slowly settled. She stayed very, very still, doubting she could move even if she wanted to. *This is how it is, how it ends, how I die. It's okay, not so bad. No pain. No pain.*

*   *   *

Someone was speaking to her and she opened her eyes to see a woman with an anxious expression leaning in through the driver's door, asking in a soft, low voice, "Are you conscious?"

"I'm not sure." She wasn't dead. And there didn't seem to be any pain.

"What's your name?"

"Rowena."

The woman knelt in the well of the driver's seat and took hold of her hand, saying, "I've called 911. An ambulance will be here soon."

"I'm sleepy." Her eyes wanted to close. It was hard to stay awake, hard to pull things into focus.

"Come on, now. Don't go to sleep, Rowena. Talk to me. Is there someone you'd like me to phone for you?"

"Mark. He's at the Mag."

"What's the Mag?"

"The library. Stamford."

"Oh, okay. What's Mark's last name, Rowena? Don't close your eyes. Keep them open now. What's his last name?"

"Who?"

"Mark at the library."

"Daley. My best friend. I should get up."

"No, no. Just stay still and talk to me."

"But I'm all right."

"We'll talk until the ambulance gets here. It won't be long. Open your eyes, Rowena. Are you married?"

"No. Are you?"

The woman smiled. "Divorced."

"You're very pretty." It was true. The most beautiful eyes, large and deep-set, and the most unusual blue. Cornflower blue.

"Thank you. Don't go to sleep, Rowena. Come on. Open your . . . eyes . . ."

She came to in the ambulance and tried to move but found she couldn't. It scared her. She tried again.

"We've got you in a cervical collar and on a backboard till we can get some X rays," a soothing voice told her. "Lie still and relax now, honey. Okay?"

"Okay," she murmured, and closed her eyes.

She awakened again in the emergency room because someone was saying her name over and over. "Hey! Stay with us now, Rowena. Okay?"

"Okay," she agreed, and then plummeted deep into darkness.

Twenty-Four

She dreamed she and Cary were on the beach at the Roton Point club. A storm was forecast and the Sound was too choppy for sailing, so while the housekeeper sat nearby reading a copy of *Redbook,* they were building an elaborate sand castle, with towers and drawbridges and moats. Cary was the architect, directing where Rowena should deposit the next pailful of damp sand, or the next Popsicle stick drawbridge. They'd been at work on the castle for quite some time when Cary announced, "It's finished," and sat on his knees beside her to admire what they'd created.

"Pretty good, huh?" he said with a satisfied smile, then turned to look at the water. "Uh-oh. Here comes the rain."

She too turned and saw the rain slanting down some distance out in the Sound. When she turned back Cary was gone and so was the housekeeper. Frightened, she stood up, not sure what to do. The beach was completely empty; even the snack bar was closed. Where had everyone gone? The storm was blowing in fast, the wind rising, and she was cold. If she didn't do something the castle would be washed away.

Spotting a sheet of plastic near the snack bar, she ran and got it, then laid it carefully over the castle, using twigs to keep the plastic elevated and rocks to hold down the edges. The rain began to fall, lightly at first, then more heavily, while the wind kept finding its way under the plastic so that she had to run here and there, finding more rocks to weight down the protective cover.

Finally, there was nothing more she could do and she sought shelter under the overhanging roof of the snack bar. Squatting in a corner, shivering, she gazed through the curtain of rain, waiting for Cary to return to get her. Teeth chattering, she began to rock back and forth, trying to get warm.

When she opened her eyes again she was an adult. It was winter. The shoreline was icebound and snow covered the sand. She was still squatting in the corner near the snack bar but now she was wearing heavy boots and Claudia's mink coat. Underneath it she was naked and the silk lining was cold against her bare skin. Gazing out at the gray-green water, she got to her feet and started toward the parking lot.

Emerging from the lee of the stand, the wind pushed against her. Icy, wind-driven snow particles stung her skin and, head down, she trudged on, anxious to get home, to put some clothes on and get warm. As she was passing the clubhouse, the pay phone began to ring and she stopped to pick up the receiver.

It was Cary, saying, ''Ro, you've got to come home. I know you're mad at me for leaving you, but please get home.''

''Cary, where did you go?''

''That doesn't matter now. Just get home, Ro.''

''I'm trying to, but there's a terrible storm. I can hardly see where I'm going.''

''You'll find your way. The important thing is to keep trying, okay?''

''Okay. Will you be there, Cary?''

''Don't think about that now.''

He hung up and reluctantly she did too. Then she set off again, her exposed legs becoming numb, her face burning. The parking lot was up a slight, slick incline and she kept slipping, but managed to prevent herself from falling by grabbing hold of some prickly bushes, hanging on until she regained her balance and could continue forward.

At last she got to the top and could see the car sitting alone in the lot. The keys were in her pocket and she held them tightly in her fist as she worked her way toward the Mercedes. Praying the lock wasn't frozen, she pushed in the key and turned it. The lock rose slowly; she pulled open the door and climbed inside. The car started right away and while she waited impatiently for the engine to warm up, she closed her eyes, thinking how wonderful it had been to hear Cary's voice again.

She and Mark were at the old boathouse that used to be situated at the edge of her granny's property in Greenwich before it caught fire under mysterious circumstances and burned down. The two of them were sitting on the side of the small, sun-bleached, splintery dock, their legs hanging over the edge as they watched gulls swooping near the shoreline and sailboats far out in the Sound.

Mark was saying, ''If you'd been wearing your seat belt you probably would've walked away without a scratch. And that's the part that bothers me most, because I've never known you not to buckle up.''

''Listen, Mark, there's something important I have to tell you.''

He went on as if she hadn't spoken. ''This business with Claudia has turned you inside out, and I *wish* you could let it go, get past it.''

"I've got the important part figured out now, though. It'll be finished very soon. I only have a few questions left."

"You hurry up and get better so we can get you the hell out of this place."

"I will, I promise." She looked at the surface of the water and said, "Come on. Let's go for a swim!"

Without waiting for his response, she stood up, the bleached decking warm beneath her bare feet, the sun drilling into the top of her head and shoulders, and dived straight in. The water was so cold it made her heart stutter and pause, as if it might stop beating altogether. Using her arms in powerful sweeps, legs kicking hard, she went deeper and deeper, where the water was colder and darker. There was something down there she had to see and her eyes strained, trying to define what it was.

Arriving at the bottom, almost out of air, she drew closer to the shape she could now see was Claudia. Her sister was naked, laughing. *Come play with me, Ro.* Her hand reached out and closed around Rowena's wrist.

I can't! I'll drown! Let me go! I'll come back when I've got more air.

You won't, Claudia insisted, her grip tightening. *You always say you will, but you never do. And it's lonely here.*

Her lungs burning from lack of oxygen, Rowena begged her to let go. *If you don't let me get back to the surface, I'll die, Claudia. You don't want me to die, do you?*

No, I don't. Do you love me, Ro?

Of course I do. You're my baby sister. Please, I'm drowning. You've got to let me go.

I love you, too, Ro. I couldn't help any of it. You have to believe that. It was like a game. It got more and more complicated and I kept playing but I could never win. Can you understand?

I'm beginning to. Please!

Okay, go! Bye, Rowlie. Don't forget me!

Claudia released her, and she began shooting toward the surface.

Breaking into the light, she gulped down air, filling her starving lungs as Mark, hanging over the edge of the dock, cried, "Where *were* you? You were down there so long I started getting scared. I was about to dive in after you."

She smiled to reassure him. "Sorry I scared you, my darling, but I'm all right. Really, I'm all right."

* * *

Reid was sitting on the side of her bed, watching a woman undress, and Rowena was watching both of them, fascinated. The woman wasn't young but somehow the signs of age—fine lines about the eyes and a softening of the flesh—only heightened her appeal. Small, with boyishly cropped hair, and large vulnerable eyes, her slender legs and delicate bone structure gave her an oddly potent sexuality to which Reid was clearly responding. Extraordinary! Rowena thought, watching as this woman almost impatiently revealed herself. Her movements were agitated, as if she could scarcely contain her immense appetite. Rowena sympathized; she knew how that felt. Reid was a powerfully attractive man.

Look carefully! You'll never have another opportunity to see as clearly as you do at this moment.

The woman shed the last of her clothes and stood for a moment, arms at her sides, allowing herself to be studied by the avid Reid who seemed fairly stricken by the sight of her. Rowena thought she was lovely, with skin that looked polished, and rather heavy breasts for so delicate a rib cage. As if unable to wait another moment, Reid held out his arms and the woman walked into them, emitting a deep, shuddering sigh as she held his head to her breast.

Unlike the trophy tapes which had filled her with a harrowing sense of perversity, watching these two gave her a feeling of profound rightness. It was an experience as gratifying as a fine production of a classic ballet, instilling only appreciation and approval. There was a fluid spontaneity of one caress leading inevitably to another, with no hint of premeditation. Reid remained seated, the woman remained standing, yet there was a steady intensifying of the contact—his hands curving over the backs of her thighs, a slight arching of her spine, the muscles in her shoulders growing taut. A shimmering heat haze seemed to enclose them, yet the woman shivered when the cool air came into contact with her damp breast. Reid effortlessly lifted her onto his lap and she closed her arms around him, her eyes fluttering shut.

Suddenly Kip appeared in the doorway, and Rowena slid back into her body—an instant of astonished recognition, realizing that *she* was the comely woman she'd been envying and admiring. There was the briefest fragment of time before her marvelous physical acceptance and self-possession were, so sadly, lost. She signaled frantically to Reid to release her. Misinterpreting the signal, he maintained his hold.

"Let go of me, for God's sake!" She pushed at him. "I can't do this with someone watching. I don't want Kip to see."

Finally Reid released her and turned to look over at the young man, asking, "Are you upset, Kip?"

"Oh, yeah, big time." Kip grinned. "Bad girl, Auntie Ro, doing the old shag-nasty with the shrink," he teased.

"Kip, I'm sorry." She reached for her slip and turned her back while she got it on.

"Don't be, Auntie Ro. You've got a right, like everybody else. It's no biggie."

"But for you to *see* me this way...."

"Don't go being bummed, Auntie Ro. It was beautiful. And I shouldn't've come charging in like that. *Bad* action, a major no-brainer. *I'm* sorry. You shouldn't be."

"Listen to him, Rowena," Reid said softly. "Why do you judge yourself so much more harshly than anyone else ever would?"

"I have to. I'm the so-called normal one in this house. Someone has to be in control."

"Not all the time. You could trust me to hold the fort for a few hours. I'd be happy to do it for you."

"How do I know that's the truth?"

Kip came across the room and sat down on the side of the bed next to Reid. "Sounds like a good offer, Auntie Ro. What's the worst that could happen?"

"He *lies,* Kip. You can't trust someone who lies."

"I don't know. It depends on what kind of lies they tell, and why they're telling them. The doctor here seems like a pretty cool dude to me." He and Reid gave each other a high five. "Lots worse people you could be with, Auntie Ro. I mean, what's one lie in the overall scheme of things? Not a whole lot. The way I see it, it's major good luck you're alive. So you should go for whatever makes you happy."

"Surely you have to think less of me, Kip, finding me this way."

"Why, 'cause you're human? Sex is okay. Sex is *good.* You're the one who told *me* that. Don't you remember? You told me every-thing—about not rushing but taking it slow and gentle, and not being afraid to let my feelings show; about contraception and being a re-sponsible person. All the important stuff. My whole life you've been telling me the things I needed to know when my mom couldn't, or was too embarrassed, or whatever. How I feel about you wouldn't go changing just 'cause I saw you without your clothes on. You've got something you want, a situation that's good for you. That would only make me happy for you, Auntie Ro, because I want you to have what-ever you want. Don't you know how much I love you? In lots of ways I'm closer to you than I am to *anybody* else."

Her heart seemed to surge in her chest and it occurred to her that emotions were weighty things, big and hefty, and when they were aroused they could swell to take up a considerable amount of space.

"I've loved you, sweetheart, since the first time I saw you, when you were seven hours old. I knew you were going to be my only chance at a child, and I wanted to give you all the things I lost after my father left. I wanted you to know there was someone in your life who loved you without reservation and always would; someone who would always tell you the truth, even when it was painful—to say and to hear; someone who would celebrate your every success, big or small, and who would be there to comfort you when there were disappointments. I wanted you to know that, to me, you were magical and always would be. The very fact of your existence, the sight of you gave me joy, and when I held you in my arms that first time, I knew there was such a thing as a miracle."

"All that shit Mom told me about my dad, the only reason I could deal was because when I was a little dude and came to you, Auntie Ro, asking could it be true he'd go off and never give a care about me, you said that no matter what happened he'd always be my dad and someday it'd all get straightened out. I believed you because you never played head games with me. And it took way longer than I thought it ever would, but it did get straightened out. So you were right. When Mom hated my girlfriends but would never tell me why, I'd swing by the library so you could scope 'em out, and later on you'd say who you liked and who you didn't, and why, without coming on all harsh and judgmental. Like, remember Jodie, with the green Mohawk and pierced nose? Mom had a full body spasm. But when we dropped in here, you gave Jodie Red Zinger tea and let her braid your hair, and we had a good time, the three of us. After that we used to drop in a couple of times a month the whole year we went together. She was crazy for you, and whenever I run into her at school, Jodie still asks about you.

"And remember what a complete tool I was about Jenny McCall? Man, that was majorly bad. No one, but no one, could stand her, but I had the hots so bad for that wench. I tried not to, but I couldn't keep away from her even though every time she opened her mouth I was embarrassed because she was such a complete subnormal. We dropped in one night, and a couple of days later you asked me to tell you what was so special about her, and I couldn't. Remember? Finished that off in a big hurry. What I'm saying is, you've been pretty magical for me, too, Auntie Ro. So don't get fussed. Things're cool. I'm here for you now. I'll always be here for you."

She was back in the cold water, trying to convince Claudia to release her before the last of her precious air supply was gone. But her sister didn't seem to want to listen, and she was growing tired, her arms and legs beginning to cramp.

I can't keep begging you. If you don't let me go now I'll drown.

If you're so afraid of dying, why do you keep coming back?

Why *did* she keep coming back? She didn't want to.

Suddenly she was free, but her energy was depleted so her ascent to the surface was slower this time. Her heart was in a frenzy, fighting for oxygen, and she broke through into the air just as her mouth was readying itself to open and fill her lungs with salt water. She had to float on her back for quite some time before she had sufficient strength to swim back to the dock where Mark sat waiting, his face a mask of anger and fear.

"You have to give this up," he warned. "It's too goddamned frightening."

"I'm sorry," she gasped. "I am so sorry."

Someone was at the front door and she opened it to find her father standing on the porch.

"Hi, Rowlie. How are you, sweetheart?"

"Daddy!" She threw her arms around him, and held on hard, able only to say, "Daddy, Daddy," over and over as she laughed and wept, happier than she'd been since early childhood.

He held her away and took a long, slow look at her. "I knew you'd grow up to be a fine-looking woman. It's so wonderful to see you, honey."

She shook her head in automatic denial, unable to stop crying or to stop smiling. "How did you know where to find me, Daddy?"

"Your friend Mark."

"Mark?"

"Yup. He phoned and told me you'd been going through boxes of your mother's papers and found my letters. I *knew* you'd never received them, otherwise I'd have heard from you long since."

"It's wonderful to see *you*. You look the same, Daddy. You haven't changed at all."

"Oh, honey, I've been riding in the time machine. Damned thing goes so fast I've got whiplash. But look at you! You still look like a kid. Hard to believe so much time has gone by."

"Jeanne said you didn't care about us, but I never believed her."

"At least she didn't throw my letters in the trash. If she had we might never have found each other. And that would've been an awful pity."

"People get lost. It's awful to realize that, but it's true, isn't it, Daddy? We lose so many people in the course of a lifetime—some we were close to yet we can't even remember their names or what they looked like. They're like phantoms in the dark corners of our minds.''

"We never lose the people who love us, Rowlie. They might not be nearby, but they keep on caring no matter what, just the way I kept on caring about you.''

"Why did she have to lie and keep us apart?''

"Let's not dwell on the past, sweetheart.''

"No, let's not. I'm so happy to see you.''

"You'll never know how happy *I* am to see *you,* Rowlie. I've missed you so much. Do you forgive me?''

"There's nothing to *forgive.* Nothing!''

"There's an awful lot I need to be forgiven for. I could've tried harder, put up more of a fight to see my children. The thing is, I knew I couldn't win. And that was one more bitter pill to swallow. I loved your brother and sister, but you were my joy, Rowlie, literally the light in my life. You were the dearest, the brightest little girl. The very sight of you made me happy. To tell the truth, I never forgave myself for the way I handled things, or your mother for her cruelty. She knew that the one sure way to hurt me, to pay me back for leaving her, was to keep me from seeing you. It didn't matter that she'd been wanting out of the marriage for years. I had the audacity to be the one to go, and by God, she was going to make me pay for that. And she did.''

"Why are we always expected to forgive people when they've done the most terrible things to us? Why is that?''

"I honestly don't know, Rowlie. Supposedly it's the Christian way. Some things, though, are beyond absolution. Time does its job and deadens the pain, lets you forget for longer and longer periods, but forgiving is out of the question. But let's put that behind us now, sweetheart. We're together and that's what counts. I always believed we'd one day find each other again.''

Again she was in the depths of the dark, frigid water, held captive by her sister. Why, oh why couldn't she be free once and for all? Why was she forced each time to beg for her life? She was tired, so terribly cold.

It's my nature. Mark tried to tell you, but you didn't want to hear. He was telling the truth, though. And you know what else, Ro? I think Mummy wanted to make herself feel better about me by trying to keep you in my shadow. You know? Giving me whatever I wanted, building me up at your expense, because she felt guilty. She knew she'd made me the way I was. And in a way I kind of knew it, too. You should've listened to your friend, Ro.

I can't fight you anymore, Claudia. I'm too worn out.

Then don't come back here anymore! Nobody made *you. But every time you do come back, I have to hold on to you. You're all I ever had. You were the only one I knew for sure was real, the only one who really loved me.*

I still do and always will. If you let me go this one last time, I won't be back.

That's okay. But you better go right now, before it's too late. You're starting to die and I don't like it.

Her body didn't want to obey. Her legs wouldn't kick and her arms hung limp at her sides; her mouth was loosening, ready to fall open and swallow the Sound. The surface and daylight seemed too far away. She didn't think she could make it back.

Then, as she was beginning to grow heavy, Mark leaped into the water and began swimming down to her, shouting, DON'T YOU DARE GIVE UP! DON'T YOU DARE! JUST STAY WHERE YOU ARE AND I'LL COME GET YOU!

It took every last bit of strength she had but she managed to kick just enough to stay in place until she felt Mark's hand close around hers and begin pulling her up.

KEEP HOLD OF MY HAND! WE'RE ALMOST THERE, RO. DON'T LET GO. I'LL GET YOU THERE.

The air was soft and tasted sweet; the sun took the chill from her bones, eased the cramping in her legs. She wanted to open her eyes but it took considerable effort. And when she did get them open, everything was grotesquely distorted as if she was still trying to see under water. Perhaps if she sat up. But when she tried to lift her head a bolt of pain drove directly down through the top of her head right to the base of her skull. At once she abandoned any idea of attempting to move. Her whole body pulsed with pain and her mouth was so parched she couldn't swallow.

Moving only her eyes, she saw Mark in a chair by the side of her bed. She was jarred by the look of him—rumpled and unshaven, he sat with one hand holding hers, his other arm propped on the bedside table, head in hand. She tried to speak but couldn't. Her tongue seemed to be welded to the desiccated floor of her mouth. Instead she gave his hand a little squeeze.

He straightened slowly and rolled his head to ease his stiffness. Then he looked at her and with a start came off the chair to bend close to her. She squeezed his hand again, then felt herself slipping away.

Twenty-Five

"Rowena? Come on now, wake up, hon. It's time to wake up."

The voice was a mellifluous one but it irritated her, repeating the same thing over and over. She wished it would stop so she could remain in the pain-free silence at the bottom of what seemed to be a lightless spiral.

"Come on now, hon. Open your eyes. Rowena, I know you can hear me. You have to wake up now."

At last she had no choice but to fight off the sticky tentacles of sleep, climb to the top of the spiral, and open her eyes.

"Good woman. Keep 'em open now, Rowena. We want you to stay awake for a while."

The musical voice belonged to the good-humored face of a round middle-aged nurse who was standing patiently by the side of the bed. "Woulda thought you'd had enough of sleeping by now," she said with a wide smile. "You know where you are, hon?"

Rowena used her eyes to indicate that she didn't.

"Norwalk hospital. You remember the accident?"

A slight nod.

"That's good. You had us all thinking you were gonna sleep forever. Dry?"

Another slight nod.

The nurse poured a glass of water from the carafe on the bedside table, inserted a bent straw, and held it to Rowena's mouth. "Drink a little. You'll feel better."

Gratefully, Rowena took a sip, then another, and did feel better as the water seemed to cut a thin path through the dust in her throat. "Where's Mark?" she asked, her voice a raspy whisper. "Here, or a dream?"

"Oh, he's here all right. I sent him to the cafeteria to get something to eat. Practically hadda use a crowbar to get him outta that chair there. Man's been here night and day, watching over you. You drink a little more now, then I'll take your temperature and blood pressure before the doctor comes." She checked Rowena's vital signs gently, with quick efficiency. "Bad headache, huh?"

Rowena nodded.

The nurse gave Rowena's arm a light reassuring pat. "You'll get some pain medication after the doctor's been to see you, so hang in a couple more minutes. Stay awake now. Okay?"

She must have dozed off because she was startled by a male voice and opened her eyes to see a man who looked far too young to be a doctor. Short, bouncy and balding, he reminded her of Bobby Engles, Cary's best friend, who used to live three doors down. Chubby Bobby Engles had always worn high-top sneakers, had a unique toe-to-heel rolling walk, and an agreeable, sunny nature.

"Hi, I'm Len Rothbart, your neurosurgeon. It's good to see you awake at last. How're you feeling, Rowena?"

"Head hurts."

"I'm sure it does. You took one hell of a knock on the noggin, got yourself a fabulous concussion. Luckily not too much else, some cuts and bruises. You're going to have a rotten headache and feel generally lousy for a couple of weeks, until the subdural swelling subsides completely and the various lacerations and contusions heal. You'll experience some nausea, a bit of vertigo, so we're going to want to keep an eye on you for at least another week, possibly more."

"Another week?"

"At least," he repeated, using a light to look into her eyes, then examining her ears with an otoscope. "You've been in a coma the better part of eight days."

"Eight days?"

"Unh-hunh. Had us all pretty worried, Rowena. How many fingers d'you see?"

"Three."

"Now how many?"

"Two."

"Good."

He lifted the bottom of the bedclothes and ran something prickly along the soles of each foot, then again said, "Good."

"Why worried?" she asked.

Coming to stand beside her, he said, "A couple of times your respiration and heart rate got awfully sluggish and it started to look as if you were going to quit on us. We debated surgery, which I was frankly reluctant to do, to relieve the intracranial pressure. I felt a noninvasive approach was safer. Happily, you rallied both times and now here you are, proof I was right. As I said, the next week or two'll be kind of rough. You definitely won't want to listen to any acid rock or go out dancing"—he smiled at her—"but in no time you'll be good as new, except for an interesting scar on your scalp, which can be a secret between you and your hairdresser." He made some notes on her chart, then asked, "Any questions?"

"Scar?"

"In the contest to see which was harder, your head or the door panel of your car, the panel won."

She laughed, then winced. The pain was instant and overwhelming.

"Sorry about that." He patted her on the arm as the nurse had done. "You have nineteen stitches in the wound which will come out tomorrow or the next day. And I should warn you, you are not looking your best, so I'd resist the temptation to ask for a mirror. I'll have the nurse bring you something for the pain right away," he said with a commiserating grimace. "You're going to want to sleep a lot. That's natural after head trauma, so don't let it scare you. Okay?"

She managed to nod.

"Good to have you back, Rowena." He smiled, patted her arm again, hooked the chart back over the foot of the bed and went on his way.

A few minutes after she'd been given the pain medication Mark appeared in the doorway, breaking into a smile at seeing her awake. Pulling one of the chairs close to the bed, he sat down and laced the fingers of his hand through hers, saying, "Hiya, cupcake. How're you feeling?"

"Not good."

"They give you anything for the pain?"

"Waiting for it to work."

"Do you remember the crash, Ro?"

"Twenty-nine, or mine?"

He laughed. "You're definitely going to live. *Do* you remember?"

"Old man pulled out . . . in front . . . I hit a tree."

"Old *woman*," he corrected her. "The woman who called 911 saw the whole thing. She got the plate number of the Caddy—which kept right on going, by the way—then stayed with you until the ambulance came."

"She talked . . . held my hand . . . don't even know her name."

"It's Jenny. When she called the Mag to tell me about the accident, my heart stopped. I ran out of there like a madman and got here maybe five minutes after you did. And Jenny, bless her heart, followed the ambulance. She's quite a lady, Ro. She's been here almost every day to see you." He sniffed and shook his head. "I know you're hurting and it's hard for you to talk, but could you *please* tell me why you weren't wearing your seat belt?"

"Forgot," she confessed, her hand clutching at his as, suddenly, she found herself reliving those few seconds when the tree seemed to fly forward to meet the car and she was frantically spinning the wheel, trying to avoid hitting it. She heard again the shattering noise of the impact and felt the weightlessness as she went hurtling sideways, headfirst into the passenger door. "Sorry...forgot," she repeated, feeling once more the consuming fear of knowing she was going to die, the shriek of tearing metal and the rain of broken glass echoing inside her head.

"It happens," he said generously.

"I had dreams . . . you . . . Reid . . . Kip . . . my father."

"They've all been here, Ro."

It took a moment for that to register. When it did, forgetting herself, she moved to sit up. The pain in her skull exploded. She lay back and kept her eyes closed for a few moments, battling nausea. Then, opening her eyes again, she asked, "My father here?"

"Unh-hunh. He's in the cafeteria with Kip right now, grabbing something to eat."

"*Here?* How?"

"I found the letters in the kitchen and called him. I called everybody, Ro. A zillion people have been by—half the people from the Mag, including Penny, and, at one point or another, every single person from the restaurant. The hard-core group—me, Tony, Kip and your dad—we've been taking shifts every day, sitting here, talking to you. We all believed you could hear us."

"I thought dreams." Tears leaked from the corners of her eyes as, for the first time, she noticed the flowers covering every available surface and the entire width of the window ledge. *Reid* had come every day? And her *father?*

Mark grabbed a tissue and dried her face.

Not dreams, she thought, aware of the darkness creeping in at the edges of her vision. She wanted to stay awake, to see her father. He was right there in the same building. "Pills working," she managed to say, unable to focus any longer.

"Rest now," Mark said, holding her hand to his cheek. "Rest and get better. I'll be right here."

* * *

The next time she awakened it was her father sitting in the chair beside the bed. Made sluggish by the painkillers, she blinked several times to be sure she wasn't dreaming, then held her hand out to him, whispering, "Dad."

"Hi, Rowlie. How's my girl?"

"So happy to see you." Helpless tears ran from the corners of her eyes.

"Want some water, sweetheart?" he asked, tenderly drying her face with a tissue from the box on the bedside table.

She nodded, and he held the glass with the straw to her mouth. She took several sips. "You look wonderful, Dad." At sixty-six, trim and in obvious good health, he looked a good ten years younger: his hair silver but still abundant, his eyes the same gray-blue as her own, his face scarcely lined. "How is your family?"

"They're just fine, Rowlie." He sat down and took hold of her hand again.

"Tell me about them."

"Well, let's see. Gwyn's twenty-seven now, teaching second grade at a school in Boston. Derek just turned twenty-five. He's working toward his Ph.D. in economics at Yale. Rosie and I are still practicing, but we're thinking about closing the office in another year or two. The old house is still standing—just—and there's a guest room ready and waiting for you."

"I'd love to come, meet everyone."

"And you will, you will. They're anxious to meet you, too, Rowlie. They all send their love, and want you to be well soon."

"Jeanne lied, but I found the letters."

"I know. Mark filled me in—on poor Claudia and what's been going on the last little while."

"She didn't kill herself."

"Maybe not. But I don't think it's a good idea for you to get worked up about that right now."

"Tell me about Jeanne, Dad."

"What do you want to know, sweetheart?"

"Everything."

He chuckled and shook his head. "That'd take days."

"Did you know about her drinking?"

"Sure. But we all drank. It didn't seem like a problem. Of course it *was*, but it was a long time before I understood. Your mother had problems from the start, but I was too young to recognize that. And too young to know how to deal with them. She always did like her cocktails, and could hold her liquor, but after you were born the booze seemed to get a stranglehold on her. Her father's side of the family was filled with alcoholics. Old DeVilliers, your grandfather, died of cirrhosis, and so did one of his brothers and a couple of the sisters. Jeanne's older sister Genevieve was a falling-down drunk by the time she was eighteen. She probably wouldn't have survived as long as she did if she hadn't had the means to support herself, thanks to a lifetime trust DeVilliers set up for her.''

"How *did* she die? The obituary only said 'after a short illness.'''

"Genevieve was emotionally fragile and apparently almost anything could set her off. Anyhow, according to your grandmother, poor Genevieve went on a serious bender one winter. She got so blind drunk she forgot to turn up the thermostat in her house. There was a terrific storm and while she was out cold the pipes froze and burst, flooding the place. Evidently she came to long enough to go downstairs, barefoot and half-dressed, looking for more booze. She got herself well and truly soaked. They found her on the sofa with an afghan over her, an empty bottle of J & B in her arms. She froze to death right in her own home. Awful.''

"Why did you marry Jeanne?''

He looked off into space for a second or two. "She was beautiful, sweetheart. Sophisticated and a little—dangerous, I guess. I was young and impressionable and just nuts about her. Her mother tried to warn me off—she was a good woman, Leila. But naturally I didn't listen. No one ever does, even when we know what we're hearing is the truth. And I knew it was the truth. Sitting there with Leila in the house in Greenwich, listening to her tell me I was making a mistake marrying Jeanne, I knew she was right. I also knew I was going to go ahead and marry her no matter what. Because I thought she'd change; I thought I could change her. Youthful arrogance maybe, or simple foolishness. I couldn't change anyone or anything, and your mother wasn't about to. She just gradually got worse. In the end I had to get out because the one thing I did know by then was that if I didn't we'd all be destroyed.

"I loved your mother, Rowena. It was a reckless, heedless kind of thing. I loved that woman the same way I imagine race car drivers love the race, knowing they could get smashed to smithereens at any moment. Or the way drug addicts love their drug, knowing they could OD and die from it. It's narcotic and dangerous as hell and no basis for family life, no basis for anything healthy. As long as it was only the two of us, it was the most exhilarating experience of my life. Nothing could ever duplicate what we had—for a while. Then we started having babies, and I loved the three of you kids. *You* were my family life, my health. What it finally came down to was my having to choose between my children and my own future. Leaving you behind was the hardest thing I've ever done, but I was still relatively young and I wanted my life. I'd had the big highs, the way-down lows, and I wanted something quiet and peaceful. That sounds pretty selfish.''

''No, it doesn't.''

''Oh, it was, honey. But all I could see was the future stretching off into an infinite sameness, with Jeanne drinking more and more and becoming uglier, nastier, while I grew more and more desperate, feeling more and more trapped. I couldn't keep on with it. It was as if I'd started off for some easy skiing down a gentle snow-covered slope that turned into an Everest of sheer black ice. I had to get off before I was going downhill so fast that I'd crash when I reached bottom.''

''I understand.''

''Do you?'' He searched her eyes.

''I do,'' she said strongly.

''You were a kind-hearted little girl. That hasn't changed.''

''What happened after the divorce?''

''We had joint custody, but she'd never let me anywhere near the three of you. My folks offered to back me if I wanted to take it to court, but I knew Jeanne too well by then. No matter what any judge said she wasn't going to let me see you. It was her primary weapon and she meant to use it as long as she could.''

''And she did.''

''She surely did. She never forgave me for refusing to join her in the bottle. And she couldn't forgive me for finding her resistible, after all the years of being so addicted. I was obsessed, but got over it, and she construed that as meaning she'd lost her allure.''

''Which was true.''

''Which was true,'' he agreed. ''I should've fought harder, made more of an effort to try to see the three of you, but I was afraid it would end up with Jeanne taking her anger with me out on you kids. She'd always left you in the care of housekeepers—some of them rotten, and some not so bad—and I told myself you'd be okay. I had to believe that. If you'd been left solely in your mother's care, I'd have waged all-out war to get you three away from her. But I knew she wasn't going to change the setup. She was too lazy, too self-indulgent. I just had to hope the housekeepers kept on being not so bad.''

"They were okay. We managed."

"I'm relieved to hear that. You know, Rowlie, for years I've been picturing you married with a bunch of kids. Maybe I didn't set too good an example."

"Not you, Dad. Jeanne and Claudia. They were the example."

"Well," he said brightly, "you've got yourself one hell of a nice fella now."

"Mark's my dearest friend."

"He's a great guy, absolutely adores you, but I was referring to Tony."

She was about to ask him how he'd arrived at that conclusion when she remembered Mark had told her about their taking turns, keeping watch on her. "We're not . . . I don't know what Reid and I are."

"Well, listen, sweetheart. You've had a rough time of it and I don't want to wear you out. You take it easy now, get some sleep, and I'll come back in the morning." He paused, then said apologetically, "Rowlie, I'm afraid I've got to head home tomorrow. I have a court date I can't miss. We've already had two postponements and the judge won't go for another. Maybe when you're back on your feet you could come up to visit."

"I'd love that, Dad."

"Wonderful. We'll have Gwyn and Derek there so you can meet everyone." He got up and bent to kiss her on the forehead. "Sleep well and I'll see you in the morning. I love you, Rowlie."

"I love *you*, Dad."

"Why hasn't he come to see me? It's been three days."

"Disappointed?" Mark asked.

"No," she lied. "I just wondered."

"He wasn't too sure of his welcome, Ro. Can you blame him?"

"No," she answered. "I can't blame him."

"He cares about you for real, cupcake. Not a lot of guys would've been here day and night the way he was."

"I suppose that's true."

"Damned right it is. Once he knew you were out of the woods, he backed away. For the record, Ro, I think he's a good man, and I like him a lot. But I'm not about to tell you what to do. You probably wouldn't listen anyway."

"I might. I usually take what you have to say seriously."

"Usually, but not always."

"No," she admitted. "Not always. But that doesn't mean I thought you were wrong. It means I'm not too smart sometimes."

"You're always smart, kiddo. It's self-confidence you lack from time to time."

"More like most of the time. Mark, would you do something for me?"

"Anything. Name it."

His willingness moved her, and she had to push back the tears that seemed, since the accident, to be too ready to spill over. "Will you pull anything you can find in the system on Fetal Alcohol Effect?"

"Sure. Am I allowed to ask why?"

"It's about something I remembered. If you have time, read what you find and see if it doesn't sound like Claudia."

"Rowena, I was hoping this business was finally behind you."

"It's never going to be behind me until I've got the answers I need. And some of them concern FAE. Please do this for me, Mark."

"I'm not happy about it, but okay," he relented. "I'll do a search and bring you the results when I come back this evening." He glanced at his watch, saying, "I've gotta scram. Marcia's covering for me again and I promised to bring her back a sandwich."

"Send her my love."

"Done."

"One more favor?"

"What?" he asked warily.

"Could you give me my handbag?"

"Your wallet, jewelry, and what-have-you are at the nurses' station."

"That's all right. I'd just like my bag."

"You want the mirror. Right?"

"I want to see how I look."

"Okay. But be warned, it's not good."

"So I've been told."

"It's *really* not good, Ro."

"I want to see anyway. Wouldn't you?"

"Yeah, I would." He went to the closet, got the bag from the shelf and set it on the bedside table within easy reach. "They're bringing the lunch trays. You start on light foods today, you lucky little thing. Hungry?"

"Unh-hunh."

"Good." He gave her a quick kiss on the lips, said, "Love you. See you later," and hurried away.

Feeling like a naughty child, she took a deep breath and held up the mirror, horror-stricken by what she saw. Mark hadn't exaggerated. Both eyes were blackened, the whites of her eyes completely red. Her face was battered, discolored, and grossly swollen. There was dried blood in her ears and nostrils and all around her hairline. Above her left eyebrow was an inch-long cut, spiky with black sutures. Her skull was hidden by a turban of white gauze and she touched her fingers to the bandage as Lorene, the nurse, came bustling in.

"Not pretty, is it?" she said, sliding a thermometer under Rowena's tongue, then placing cool fingertips on the inside of her wrist while a uniformed figure darted in and out, leaving lunch on the tray table. After a blood-pressure check, Lorene made notes on the chart, then lifted the lid from the tray, saying, "Let's see what we've got. Oh, yummy. Chicken broth, some crackers, apple juice, and cherry Jell-O. You up to feeding yourself, Rowena?"

"I'll try. Are you going to unhook me from this?" She indicated the IV pole.

"We're gonna wait and see on that. Lemme raise you up a bit here. How's that?"

Unbelievably, elevating the head of the bed induced immediate nausea.

"No good, huh?" Lorene at once lowered the bed to half the height. "Better now?"

Eyes closed, Rowena swallowed several times, willing away the sickness.

"Guess I'm gonna play momma," Lorene said. "Lord knows, that's nothing new."

"You have children?" Rowena asked, at last opening her eyes as the cheerful nurse unfolded a paper napkin and positioned it under Rowena's chin.

Lorene laughed and said, "Four grown-up, gone-away children. Youngest is twenty-four. Five grandchildren. Okay now, let's get you going on this soup."

After two spoonfuls Rowena began to retch. Lorene grabbed a basin.

"Let's try the Jell-O," the nurse said when the spasm had passed.

The sweet synthetic cherry dessert tasted remarkably good, and Rowena was able to eat all of it and to drink half the apple juice as well.

"If it stays down, I'll come back'n unhook you," Lorene promised. "I'll be back with your pain meds in half an hour anyway. Say, how come your fella hasn't been back to see you?"

"Reid's not my fella," Rowena said, drowsy now and wishing everyone would stop trying to push the two of them together. "He's just . . ." What was he? A friend? Not really. And not her lover, even though she'd made love to him a few times in her dreams. She fell asleep before she could think of a suitable reply.

Twenty-Six

Mark returned, as promised, with an envelope containing printouts of a number of articles. "I didn't have a chance to go through them," he told her. "It's going to have to wait until after you get home. Okay?"

"Of course. And then we'll be able to discuss them—if, of course, you're willing." She hesitated, then said, "Mark, about Reid."

"What about him?"

"The two of you spent a lot of time together the last little while, and I wondered—"

"Ro," he interrupted, "I'm not going to tell you what he and I talked about, so please don't ask. It wouldn't be right, or fair of me to repeat any of it."

"Just answer one question. Does he know I know about the tape?"

"No, he doesn't. The subject never came up and I certainly saw no reason to introduce it."

"Good. That's all I wanted to know. So, how is Richard?"

After he left, she got the first of the articles out, but trying to read made her so dizzy she had to quit, and replaced the envelope in the drawer of the bedside table. By the fourth day she could sit up in bed without the room starting to spin, but she still couldn't read more than a line or two before becoming queasy. On the morning of the fifth day as she was planning to give it another try, Lorene came in to say, "We're gonna let you sit in the chair for five minutes while your bed gets changed. Isn't that exciting?"

Appallingly, she had no strength and had to rely on Lorene's support to get from the bed to the chair. Once there, it was as if sitting was something she'd never done before, so odd and perilous did it feel for the first minute or two. Her body was like a jumble of ill-connected, barely functional parts, and it required her complete concentration to adjust herself to the chair's unyielding structure and remain upright. She felt giddily top-heavy and insubstantial, and was glad when Lorene announced, "Okay, all done." Exhausted, she would gladly have climbed back into the bed and gone to sleep at once.

"Got another treat for you, if you're up for it," Lorene said. "Thought you might like a bath."

"God, Lorene, I would *love* one! I must be reeking by now."

"Figured you might be interested. You rest there a minute or two more while I get things organized."

Once undressed, Rowena was so dismayed to discover that most of her body was in the same battered condition as her face that she simply forgot to be embarrassed.

Lorene clucked and said, "Lord, girl, you sure did take a beating, but you think you look bad now, you should've seen yourself when they brought you in. You okay there?"

"I'm fine. This feels so good." She would never have believed that being seen naked in a tubful of hot water by a relative stranger in a starkly white, unadorned hospital bathroom could bother her so little. But a great many of the things that had bothered her prior to the accident now seemed self-indulgent and inconsequential. Merely being alive, regardless of how decrepit her condition, mattered far more than any slight assault on her sensitivities.

"Can't wash your hair yet but let's get some of this blood off." With a soapy washcloth and her usual gentle hand, Lorene cleaned Rowena's nose and ears and along her hairline. Humming softly Lorene then washed her from head to toe. It was like being bathed by a mother—something Jeanne had always delegated to the housekeepers.

"I'll bet your children loved having you give them a bath," Rowena said, feeling drowsily content and very safe in this woman's care.

"All four of them were bigger by age ten than you are right now, and that's a fact. Don't you ever *eat,* woman?"

Amused by her directness, Rowena admitted, "Not a lot lately. Which is funny, really, because not only do I love food, I also happen to own a restaurant."

"That right? What's it called?"

"Le Rendezvous, in New Canaan."

"Don't know it, but we don't get over that way much."

"Before I go home, I'll give you my card. I'd like you and your family to be my guests for dinner one night."

"Yeah?" Eyebrows lifted, Lorene looked both pleased and disbelieving.

"Any time. Just call and let me know when you want to come."

"That's real nice of you."

Rowena could see that the nurse didn't believe her and undoubtedly thought she was merely being polite. "I like you, Lorene, and when I say I want you to come for dinner I mean it. You've been very kind to me."

Lorene looked into her eyes for a long moment, then said quietly, "It's easy being kind to you, Rowena."

The damned tears started again, and Rowena said, "I'm sorry. Everything sets me off lately."

Lorene laughed. "Seems as if that concussion went'n shook loose all your emotions. C'mon now, hon, let's get you outta there." Drying her as if Rowena were indeed one of her children, Lorene said thoughtfully, "I like you, too, Rowena. And I'll tell you something. My mama used to say God is love. But me, I think God is how you treat other people. And the ones who act decently, even when things're bad, they're the ones make life worthwhile."

Rowena said softly, "I think so too," and, going with the impulse, hugged her.

Surprised, Lorene laughed again and hugged her back, saying, "We have *got* to get some meat on these poor bones, woman! Taking hold of you's like grabbing a sack of doorknobs."

The moment she was back in bed she fell asleep and was awakened close to an hour later by the telephone. Assuming it was her father who had called each afternoon since he'd left, she lifted the receiver.

"Hi, Auntie Ro. How're you doing? I hope I'm not calling at a bad time."

"Not at all. I'm doing well, sweetheart. It's good to hear your voice."

"You, too. I was going to come see you but I figure what you don't need is a gazillion people visiting and wearing you out, so I thought I'd check in and say hi. Hey, guess who's covering the front for you?"

"Who?"

"Me! Is that outrageous or what? Ian goes to me he needs someone on the front more than he needs a busboy, and do I want to give it a try. So I go sure. Now every day I get all duded up in like a jacket and tie, and do your gig. It's way cool, Auntie Ro. Couple of guys actually tipped me."

"That's terrific, Kip. Nobody's *ever* tipped me. I'm so proud of you."

"I'm kind of proud of me, too. I guess I should probably be going now. I just wanted to hear *your* voice. When're they letting you go home, d'you know?"

"With luck, the day after tomorrow."

"All *right!* If it's okay, I'll swing by the house to see you."

"Make sure you do. And thanks for calling, sweetheart."

"I'm so psyched you're gonna be okay. I love you big time."

"Me, too, you," she said thickly.

"Take care, Auntie Ro."

Following the call she got the envelope from the drawer, tipped out its contents and made another attempt to read. This time she had no difficulty, and began going through the printouts, reading slowly and with care.

* * * * *

...these children may become abnormally active, detached, rash and fearless, undiscriminating in their reactions to family or to strangers... In milder cases, FAE may be indicated by a consistent failure to adjust to patterns of behavior that depend on a comprehension of long-term consequences or of a socially-accepted code of behavior.

* * * * *

...FAE children may display faulty judgment and may repeat behaviors that have had negative results in the past... Some of these children have been known to use broad vocabularies while failing to understand what they are talking about, so that they sound more competent than they actually are... They fail to learn from their mistakes, and have no real grasp of what they're saying.

* * * * *

...studies made with social drinkers have shown subtle offspring effects, including decreases in IQ and in academic performance (particularly mathematics), as well as attentional and memory problems... There are also disruptions in sleep patterns...problems of attention deficit disorders, of speech and language difficulties, and of hyperactivity. Fetal alcohol exposure is often connected to general failure in school.

* * * * *

... problems with coordination and with motor skills in drawing or handwriting may result ... Even children of normal intelligence may experience disabilities and have faulty attention spans ... There is evidence to indicate that minor aspects of these difficulties might occur as a result of social drinking.

* * * * *

... Behavioral problems, such as lying and bold resistance to authority, also was displayed by many of these patients ...

* * * * *

... Perhaps with early diagnosis appropriate intervention could have lessened some of the secondary behavioral disorders. However, the possibility of early identification appears remote, given that a recent report documented a 100% rate of failure in diagnosing FAE at time of delivery.

* * * * *

... Exposure to alcohol during gestation can result in a broad spectrum of disabilities that have lifelong physical, psychological, and behavioral intimations.

* * * * *

... Studies with both animals and humans reveal that the consumption of alcohol during pregnancy can alter the fetal brain and affect both infant and childhood behavior—even when no evidence of physical damage is present. The children of moderate drinkers may demonstrate extreme nervousness ... and abnormal sleep patterns.

* * * * *

... It is not known precisely how little alcohol is required to endanger a fetus. A pregnant woman who consumes 3 or more ounces of alcohol daily risks harming her unborn child ... A study involving 31,604 live births revealed that even women averaging less than one drink a day had a slightly increased risk of giving birth to a low-weight baby ... There is evidence indicating that even a single episode of heavy drinking may result in serious damage to an unborn child.

*   *   *   *   *

Her reading completed, it was very clear in her mind what had happened. Jeanne had done just enough drinking during and after her pregnancy to produce a child with a range of disorders, from her inability to do more than rudimentary arithmetic and her ragged handwriting, to her frequent sleeplessness and her peculiar lack of affect. There could be no doubt that Claudia had suffered from Fetal Alcohol Effect.

Rowena was intensely gratified to find confirmation of her deductions, and this confirmation cast Claudia in a new light, one that made her entirely forgivable. Her sister had come into the world impaired, but in so subtle a fashion that no one would have been likely to see that, cumulatively, her disorders were all part of a larger, more insidious, problem. And no doubt, somewhere along the line, Jeanne had figured it out, accepting belatedly the truth of what her own mother had told her so many years before in the conversation Rowena had overheard as a little girl. It was why, she now believed, Jeanne had silently tolerated her daughter's total dependency, as well as the abuse Claudia had heaped upon her right up until the day she died—because she'd felt guilty. And it was why, very near the end, she had begged Rowena to understand. At the time Rowena had thought that she did, but she hadn't really understood. Now she did. Jeanne had left the bulk of the estate to Claudia because without the money and the house, Claudia would have been incapable of providing for herself. She had never been able to learn anything that would have equipped her to hold down a job and earn a living.

She was returning the printouts to the envelope when there was a knock at the open door and she turned to see Ian poised on the threshold.

"Have I come at an inopportune time?" he asked.

"No, no." She smiled. "Come in, Ian, please."

He was, as ever, immaculately dressed in a navy suit of lightweight wool, a blue and white striped Sea Island cotton shirt with white collar and cuffs, and a clear red silk tie. Smelling pleasantly of a cologne redolent of apples, he approached carrying several take-out containers.

"Knowing how truly vile hospital food can be, I had Philippe prepare a light lunch for you. I hope that's all right."

"It's more than all right. I've been longing for some decent food. Thank you so much."

He set the foil containers on her tray table, along with several napkins and plastic utensils, then asked, "May I sit for a moment?"

"Of course."

Seating himself, he asked worriedly, "How *are* you, Rowena? Everyone's been most concerned. I hesitated to come any sooner, for fear of disturbing you."

"I know I look terrible, but I'm much better. I may be able to go home the day after tomorrow."

"That *is* good news! In the meantime, is there anything you need, anything I can do?"

"Not a thing. I spoke to Kip a little while ago and he was telling me you've got him covering the front. That was an inspired idea."

"He's an able and most affable young man, as I'm sure you're well aware. And he's doing a bang-up job. I took the liberty of giving him a small rise in salary. I didn't think you'd object."

"Absolutely not. Things are going well at the restaurant?"

"Oh, yes, very." He couldn't seem to stop staring at her. "I am so sorry about the accident, Rowena. We were all frightfully worried about you."

"It's lucky I was driving the Mercedes," she said, made aware by the rigid way he sat that he was highly uncomfortable. He was, she realized, one of those people for whom a hospital visit to an ailing friend was a painfully unpleasant experience. "If I'd been in the Honda, I probably would've been killed."

"Very lucky indeed," he agreed. "Well, I really must get back," he said, rising to his feet. "Just wanted to pop in and bring you the meal."

"It was very thoughtful of you, Ian." She held up her arms, and caught off guard, Ian hesitated for a moment before bending to receive her embrace and to kiss her cheek. Straightening, he said, "I expect we'll talk at more length once you're home."

"Yes, please. Thank you for this." She indicated the containers. "And give everyone my love."

"Happy to. I hope you enjoy Philippe's concoction." He smiled, turned, and sailed out the door.

Len Rothbart came in as she was finishing the last of the poached chicken breast in a light tarragon cream sauce with wild rice.

"Don't care for our food, huh?" he observed with a smile.

"Not a lot, no." Returning his smile, she put down the plastic knife and fork.

"Can't say I'm surprised. How are you feeling?" he asked, taking a look at her chart.

"Much better. I was able to do some reading today without feeling sick."

"Good, that's good." Placing the chart on the foot of the bed, he came closer to examine her head wound. "Healing very nicely." He checked her eyes before pulling out the otoscope to look into her ears. "Know what I think? I think we're going to let you go home tomorrow, Rowena."

"Really?" It was good news, but given that she could scarcely stand unaided, she had to wonder if she wasn't being released somewhat prematurely.

"Think it's too soon?" he asked, tucking his hands into his lab coat pockets and rocking back on his heels—so like bouncy Bobby Engles all those years ago that she had to smile.

"I don't seem to have much strength."

"It'll come back fast once you get home. Hospital policy is to get patients out as quickly as possible. And I think you're ready to go. You do have someone to help out, don't you? Because if you're going to be alone, I'll keep you in a couple more days."

"No, Mark will be there to help."

"Then we'll turn you loose, let you go home where I'm sure you'll be more comfortable. Will Mark be able to come pick you up tomorrow afternoon?"

"I'm sure he will."

"Great. So you'll go home and eat food you enjoy and get your strength back. I want to see you in my office in a week's time. Otherwise, I'll trust you to use your native intelligence and take things nice and slow. I doubt you will but if you experience any difficulties call the office immediately." Offering his hand, he said, "Take care of yourself, Rowena. And please don't go forgetting a second time to wear your seat belt." He turned to leave then swung back. "What's the name of your restaurant again?" She told him, and he said, "I'll bring my wife by one evening."

"Do that, please, and I'll take good care of *you*."

"Later," he said, and continued on his way.

* * *

With Lorene's help she got into the clothes Mark had brought over the previous evening—everything she'd been wearing at the time of the accident had been cut off her in the emergency room—and into a wheelchair.

At the hospital entrance, she and Lorene embraced and Rowena said, "I'll be expecting to see you at the restaurant, so don't disappoint me."

"We'll be there. Go easy, Rowena. Don't let her go doing too much, Mark."

"Believe me, I won't."

"I believe you," Lorene said laughing. "Her, I'm not so sure about."

With Mark's help Rowena got into the passenger seat of his car and they were on their way. She felt as if she'd been gone for months.

"I've stocked up on food for you," Mark said. "And being the soul of efficiency I also notified your insurance company of the accident. They've already had an adjuster out to the wreckers. The Merc's a write-off. All you'll have to do is sign a couple of forms, send back the Proof of Loss when it comes in and they'll send you a check for the book value less the deductible."

"You are a wonder, my darling. Thank you for doing all that."

"You're welcome. If you're a good little pollywog and promise to stay put, I'll let you play invalid on the living room sofa."

"I'll be a good little pollywog." She reached over to caress his cheek. "I'm so glad to be going home."

"Me, too. If you think you'll be able to manage on your own until noon every day, I've arranged to work half days until you're back on your tiny tootsies. And in the afternoons, we can watch the soaps and play Scrabble. Does that sound like fun or what?"

"I can hardly wait."

He looked over, saying, "It's going to be a couple of weeks before you stop looking like the victim of a crazed hairdresser wielding a straight razor."

She laughed, and turned to look out the window, murmuring, "It's good to be alive." Very soon now she'd have the rest of the answers. It would be over and she'd be able to go forward into her future.

Twenty-Seven

The next morning, Penny called.

"Don't hang up on me, Ro. I just wanted to say how glad I am you're going to be all right."

"I'm not going to hang up. How are you, Penny?"

"A lot saner than I was a few weeks ago."

"Well, that's good."

"I apologize for the way I acted. I know I behaved like a complete lunatic."

"I can't argue with that." Rowena laughed.

"I also know I destroyed our friendship, and I'm going to regret that for the rest of my life. But I'll always care about you, Ro, and I won't try to come between you and Kip. You're very important to him."

"He's very important to me, Penny. There was never any question of my trying to usurp your position or to influence him."

"I know, I know. I was way out of line. Anyway, take care of yourself. Okay?"

"You, too. Thanks for calling."

She had no sooner put down the receiver when the phone rang again and she picked up thinking it must be Penny calling back. She almost hoped it was. It felt as if there was more they had to say to each other. But it wasn't Penny.

"Is that Rowena?" asked a soft, low, familiar voice she couldn't place.

"Yes."

"Hello. It's Jenny Nichols."

"I thought I recognized your voice. How are you?"

"I'm very well. More importantly, how are *you?*"

"Much, much better. It's good of you to call."

"I was very scared for you, Rowena. While we were waiting for the ambulance, all I could think to do was keep you talking. I must have read that somewhere. But there was an incredibly unreal aspect to the situation, and we seemed to make a connection—one of those experiences that transcends the moment...."

"Yes. I felt it, too."

Jenny Nichols exhaled audibly and gave a relieved laugh. "I was afraid you were going to think I was one of those new-age nuts or something. You see, while we were waiting, it seemed to me you were going to die, and somehow it was my responsibility to keep you alive."

"You probably did."

"I truly doubt that. But the thing is, I couldn't be satisfied until I knew you were going to be all right. Now you are, and I can let you go. I hope that makes sense."

"Yes, it does. Before you let me go, though, would you come to Le Rendezvous for dinner one night, as my guest?"

"Please don't think me rude, Rowena, but I'm very superstitious. I think you and I have completed our—contract, for want of a better word, and it would be a mistake to try to make it more than it was meant to be. So let's wish each other well, and say goodbye."

"All right," Rowena agreed, starting to choke up. "I wish you well, Jenny Nichols."

"And I you, Rowena Graham. Goodbye, and God bless."

"Goodbye."

"It's very Zen," Mark was saying over lunch in response to Rowena's relating of her conversation with Jenny Nichols. "I like it," he declared. "A very classy woman."

"Then my father called," she continued, between mouthfuls of Mark's homemade mushroom soup. "I told him what I'd learned about FAE, and he agreed it seemed to apply perfectly to Claudia."

"I'd have to agree, too, now that I've read the material. Makes you wonder why nobody ever put it together."

"That's the awful thing about FAE—it can be so subtle. I think you would've had to have lived with Claudia to see it. It wouldn't have been obvious to anyone who hadn't been exposed to her over the long term."

"All those years of psychiatrists. What a colossal waste of money." He took another piece of the fresh, crusty baguette and buttered it.

"They were treating her one symptom, or one problem at a time. No one had the full picture. No one outside the family *could* have had. Let me give you some examples. As a small child her attention span was so short she'd be squirming to get away almost before you started trying to tell her something. If they hadn't invented calculators, she'd still be stuck trying to add a pair of double digit numbers. And her handwriting was atrocious. The biggest thing, though, was her absolute inability to empathize. She had no idea how other people might feel. On top of that, she didn't care. I now believe the majority of her actions were learned, not innate. She wasn't in the least stupid but there were quantum holes where her emotional responses should've been. Plus, she was categorically incapable of denying herself anything pleasurable."

"And your father confirmed your mother's alcoholism?"

"Definitely." She paused to finish her soup. "This is fabulous."

"Thank you. More?"

"Not right now, thanks."

"You think Jeanne knew what she'd done to Claudia?"

"Not specifically. Initially, I think she felt guilty because she hadn't wanted another child. Claudia was the accidental by-product of Jeanne's attempt to rekindle my father's interest in her. Later on, though, she had to be aware there was something wrong with Claudia, and then she felt even guiltier, overcompensating like crazy. I think Claudia also knew there was something wrong with her—and she blamed Jeanne. After Dad left, the two of them played this pathologically complicated love-hate game that was so ugly and vicious, yet so mutually dependent, that I couldn't bear to be around them. I know I blocked out a lot of what went on, and refused to see the rest."

"So do you accept her suicide now?" he asked.

"Of course not. This is something incidental to that. It probably has some relevance to her death, but no, I do not accept it was a suicide."

Impatiently, he asked, "Is this *ever* going to end, Ro?"

"Oh, yes. Quite soon now. I'm nearly there."

"Well, if you're finished eating, it's time for the soaps. Then the cupcake has her bath and a nap."

"Right, chief."

She was almost asleep in the tub when Mark spoke from outside the door. "Time for you to come out now. You need help, or can you manage?"

"I think I can manage."

It took a minute or two but she was able to climb out of the tub. She had to sit down to dry herself and pull on clean pajamas.

"You okay in there?" Mark asked anxiously.

"Depends on your concept of okay," she answered. "But I'm finally out and dressed."

"Right." He pushed in, lifted her off the small enamel stool and carried her to the bedroom. "In we go," he said, depositing her in the bed.

"I feel like an infant," she complained.

"Enjoy it, because it's strictly temporary. Have a nice nap."

When she awakened, she automatically looked at the clock and saw the note he'd left propped in front of it. "Gone home. Back in time for din-dins."

She smiled, moved the note and saw it was a quarter past five. She thought she'd close her eyes for a few more minutes, and slid back into sleep.

When she awakened the second time, it was because Mark was tapping her on the tip of the nose with his finger. "Time for you to relocate downstairs. We're having some nice pasta with fresh mozzarella and smoked chicken for dinner."

"Why don't you let me sleep until it's ready?"

"What d'you think you are, a teenager? Up!" He threw back the bedclothes and waited.

She insisted on making her way down the stairs without his help.

"I could've knitted a sweater in the time this is taking," he said, hovering close by.

"I didn't know you could knit."

"I can't, but I could've learned how *and* knit a sweater in the time this is taking. You fall and I'll kill you."

She laughed and said, "I'm not going to fall."

"Oh, sure," he scoffed. "You'll just give me a heart attack by *looking* as if you're going to fall."

"Will you *stop!*" She was laughing so hard she had to hold on to the banister with both hands.

He went on ahead and sat tailor fashion at the foot of the stairs to wait for her, looking at his watch and faking yawns.

"You're distracting me. Quit that!"

"Fine." He folded his arms over his chest and gazed up at her.

She managed to make it to the bottom and into the living room, where she swatted him on the head before at last lowering herself onto the sofa.

"I'm worn out from all this caretaking," he said, as the doorbell rang.

"Who could that be?" she wondered.

"Here's an idea. Why don't I go see?"

She heard him open the door and exchange a few words with some-one. Then, to her consternation, Tony Reid appeared in the living room doorway, with Mark behind him.

"How about some coffee, or a drink, Tony?" Mark offered.

Somewhat uncertainly, Reid said, "I could use some coffee. How are you, Rowena?"

"I've had better days," she answered, her heart racing, in no way prepared for this meeting.

"Sit down, Tony," Mark said, giving Rowena a look that said Be-have! "Want something to drink, Ro?"

"Look," Reid said, half-turning toward Mark, "maybe this isn't such a good idea."

Disregarding that, Mark asked with a smile, "How do you take your coffee?"

Bemused, Rowena followed the exchange.

"Black would be fine, thanks, Mark."

"Coffee, Rowena?" Mark asked her.

"Sure. Why not? But could you help me into the bathroom first?"

"Okeydokey." He sailed over to her.

"Please sit down, Reid," she said. "I'll be right back."

"This could wait till some other time," Reid said.

"No, no. Sit down. I'll only be a couple of minutes."

Looking unconvinced, Reid was moving toward a chair as, with Mark's arm around her waist, she hobbled as quickly as she was able along the hall toward the downstairs bathroom.

"How could you *do* this?" she asked Mark in an angry whisper. "I'm not ready to see anyone, let alone him."

"Don't be a jerk, Ro," he whispered back. "*He* doesn't know you know about his flingette with your sister. He also doesn't know you've cursed him out and wished him dead—none of which you meant for a single moment."

She had to fight off a smile. "You had no *right* to do this without consulting me."

"Grow up! He's a good guy and the two of you care for each other. Now stop this twaddle! Flush the toilet and pretend you've had a whizz, then get back in there and be nice!"

"We will discuss this later," she warned. "*If* I let you live."

"Oh, look! I'm *so* scared! Minnie Mouse is threatening to kill me. Oh, help!" Smirking, he went off to the kitchen.

Reid was still standing and looked as if he wanted to help when she came shuffling back.

"I'm okay," she said. "My motor skills are just a little rusty. Reid, sit down, for heaven's sake." She made her way back to the sofa and sank onto it, huffing, out of breath. Nervous, she took a cigarette from the pack on the table.

"That's probably not a good idea," Reid said.

"You're right. It's probably not. But I'm going to have one anyway." She lit up, took a drag, and instantly became so dizzy and nauseated she thought she might pass out.

"I did tell you." Reid came over, sat down beside her and put the cigarette out. "Put your head back and close your eyes for a couple of minutes."

Too weakened to argue, she did as he suggested, and thought perhaps she had fallen asleep because the next thing she heard was Mark asking Reid, "What's wrong?"

"Nothing, really. Rowena thought she'd have a cigarette."

Opening her eyes, she said, "He said it wasn't a good idea, and it wasn't."

"You're such a jerk, Ro," Mark said fondly. "You guys have your coffee. I'll be in the kitchen, if you need anything."

Reid picked up one mug and handed it to Rowena, then sat cradling the other in his big hands for a few moments after Mark had gone, before asking, "Why are you so angry, Rowena?"

"I don't like surprises. I wasn't expecting any visitors."

"If you had a change of mind, why didn't you say so instead of avoiding me day after day? I don't enjoy being made to feel stupid."

"I don't enjoy being lied to."

He took a sip of coffee then set the mug down on the table. "Lied to? About what?"

"About Claudia. About your involvement with her, and about your diagnosis."

"A diagnosis is basically skilled guesswork. It's eminently possible I was wrong, but I most certainly didn't lie about my conclusions."

"You were involved with my sister. Please don't try to deny it." As the words left her mouth and she looked into the incomparable blue of his eyes, she had to ask herself why she was doing this. It really no longer seemed important, and she didn't want to hurt him.

"What makes you think that?" He sat up a little straighter, a new alertness overtaking his eyes.

"My sister had a little hobby, Reid. She liked to make home movies of her encounters."

His already-pale complexion actually went paler. He gazed into space, as if mentally attempting to reconstruct the event and see where this new information might fit. "She made *tapes?*" He turned back to her wide-eyed, horrified.

He was so stricken that she felt sorry for him and ashamed of herself.

"Jesus!" He was sitting now on the edge of the sofa, as if prepared to jump up and rush off. A pulse throbbed visibly in his temple. "Obviously you have this tape, and you've watched it."

"I watched it," she admitted. "It's since been destroyed."

"Well, this explains a lot." He ran a hand over his hair, then rubbed his eyes.

"You lied to me," she said, thinking she sounded petulant and fatuous. But having started this, she couldn't simply drop it.

"Don't be childish. *Everybody* lies, Rowena," he said tiredly. "Everybody," he repeated, glancing at her then away again. "I wasn't about to broadcast the fact that I'd made a stupid mistake. Which, it now turns out, was an even stupider mistake than I'd thought."

He was taking it so badly she found herself wanting to comfort him, and put a hand on his shoulder, saying, "Don't you think I deserve to know the truth, finally, Reid?"

"I suppose you do." Retrieving his mug, he took another swallow of coffee then sat holding the mug between his knees, staring down at it.

She pulled back her hand and drank some coffee herself, waiting to hear what he'd say, and thinking she'd screwed this up badly.

"It was a setup," he said at length. "But I didn't realize that until later." He shook his head in dismay. "She put in an emergency call to my service late one night last fall. When I called back she said she was deeply depressed. She needed to talk to someone or she was going to kill herself. Even though she was no longer my patient, I agreed to come over and talk to her." Again he looked at Rowena, but this time he didn't look away. "I *believed* her. She sounded genuinely suicidal. She told me the names of all the prescription medications she planned to wash down with gin or vodka. I don't remember what precisely she said she was drinking. It's irrelevant. She had everything ready, she said, and couldn't think of a single reason not to go ahead. There was a deadness to her tone that got to me, and I came on the run."

Rowena shivered. This wasn't what she'd been expecting to hear. "Go on," she said quietly, captured by his expression of self-disgust.

She knew that feeling all too well and wanted to tell him so. But it would have to wait.

"When I got here, the front door was ajar, and that struck me as strange. I called her name. And in a voice I could barely hear, she said she was upstairs. So I went running up. And there she was, stretched out naked on her bed, giggling merrily, delighted with herself at having lured me here. I was absolutely furious. I started to tell her what I thought of her, but she threw herself at me." He shook his head and again stared into the depths of the mug. "Even while it was happening, I was pissed off with both of us—her for pulling this stunt and me for falling for it and for responding. I kept telling myself to get the hell out, but . . . I responded."

He sighed and shook his head. "When it was over, I warned her *never* to call me again, then I got the hell out of here. The following week the calls started. İt turned into a nightmare. She would *not* stop. Twenty, thirty times a day she called the office. She phoned the house all evening, every evening, and even had the service page me if I went out to get away from the phone. It continued for weeks, until I decided I'd have to get a restraining order to get her to quit. Then, suddenly, it was over. At first I couldn't believe it. But days and then weeks went by and there were no more calls. It was like being in prison and having my sentence commuted. Just like that, I was free of her. I tried to forget the whole damned mess, put it right out of my head. And that was the end of it, until I got your message that she'd died."

Rowena didn't know what to say. She'd finally heard the truth, but there was more, and not only had she no idea how to tell him, she also wasn't sure she wanted to.

Looking and sounding worn out, he said, "Why have you taken the position of injured party without actually having been involved, or harmed?"

"It's not a *position,* Reid. *You* were acting under false pretenses."

"Why? Because I made an idiotic mistake and had a single, unpleasant, sexual encounter with a woman who happened to be your sister? And what lie did I tell about my diagnosis? While you're venting, you might as well get it all out."

"I misspoke regarding your diagnosis. You didn't lie about that. You were wrong, but that's a recent discovery."

"Care to tell me about it?" he asked sourly, loosening the knot of his tie.

Mark reappeared, this time carrying a tray with cheese and crackers. As he set it down on the coffee table, he said, "I've decided to play referee. If I don't, you two are going to keep spinning your wheels, and wind up missing the whole point.''

''I wish you wouldn't interfere,'' Rowena began.

''No,'' Reid cut her off. ''I think it's a good idea. Mind if I help myself to a refill?'' He held up his mug.

''Please help yourself,'' and ''Go ahead,'' Mark and Rowena said simultaneously.

The moment he was out of earshot, Rowena asked, ''What're you *doing?* Why are you getting involved, Mark? I would *never* do something like this to you.''

''I know that,'' he replied placidly. ''But then I wouldn't need the kind of help you do.''

''Which means what?''

''It means you're in over your head and have been since Claudia died. It means you two need a moderator to keep you on track. It *means* neither one of you is any good at dealing with emotional issues. So I'm going to referee.''

''It's a good idea,'' Reid said for a second time, returning.

''Take off that jacket,'' Mark told him. ''Relax.''

With a smile, as if the idea of relaxing was preposterous under the circumstances, Reid draped his jacket over the back of one of the chairs, but remained standing.

''Have some cheese,'' Mark invited.

''Thanks. I'm hungry.''

''I figured you would be, so I'm making dinner for the three of us.''

Rowena groaned and rolled her eyes. ''Mark, you are taking advantage of the situation!'' she accused.

''Yes, I am. Go ahead and sit down, Tony,'' Mark said, standing with his arms folded across his chest like a sorely tried, but devoted teacher. ''Here's how it goes,'' he said, once Reid was back sitting on the sofa. ''The two of you need to talk, and you need to do it now. Rowena, you've let this business with Claudia blind you to important things. And Tony, you may be a shrink, but it sure hasn't helped you much in handling this situation.''

Reid laughed. ''Most of us go into psychiatry because we're better at handling other people's problems than our own. We were talking about my diagnosis,'' he remembered, turning to Rowena. ''I'd like to hear your recent discovery.''

''It's good stuff,'' Mark put in.

''Could you please not editorialize?''

"Ro, simmer down. It *is* good stuff. Are you going to waste your energy fighting with me, or are you going to talk to the man?"

"This is weird. What's going on here?" she asked, looking first at Mark, then at Reid.

"Nothing's going on," Mark said.

"I'd like to hear what you've come up with," Reid said, helping himself to a chunk of white cheddar and washing it down with a mouthful of the fresh coffee.

"The two of you are up to something," she insisted.

"Tell him about your research, Ro."

She wanted to pursue her suspicions but decided it would be a waste of time. Neither of them was going to confess to having set this up. She sighed, sank into her corner of the sofa and said to Reid, "Ironically, I first read about it in your waiting room, in a back issue of *psychology today*. Does FAE mean anything to you, ring any bells?"

"I'm aware of it. Tell me why it rings bells for you."

"I can't do this! You're talking to me as if I'm one of your patients."

"No, he isn't, Ro," Mark disagreed.

"I do want to hear what you've got to say," Reid said. He looked over at Mark, back at Rowena, then at Mark again, saying, "Rowena's right. This *is* weird."

Rowena laughed. "I give up. Mark, would you please get the printouts?"

"Sure. And while I'm doing that, why don't you tell Tony your theory about Claudia's suicide."

"A theory? Mind if I take off this tie?" Reid asked.

"I don't mind," she said, and lost track of what she'd intended to say as she watched the way he further loosened the tie and pulled it over his head without undoing the knot. She remembered Cary dragging his shirt and sweater off over his head in one go, then pushing his jeans, shorts, and socks off all at the same time. Two moves and he was ready for the shower. He stood in her mind—small, sun-golden, and sturdy—and she missed him intensely, as if he'd died only days, not decades, ago.

"What?" Reid asked.

Such beautiful eyes, and he picked up on the slightest alteration in her mood. She recalled his start of surprise and the feel of his mouth when she'd kissed him that rainy afternoon under the canopy. He'd been at the hospital every day while she'd been in the coma; he'd met her friends and her father. Mark had invited him here this evening, and he had come. They were separate beings, yet he was already well inside her life. And, astonishingly, the sight of him no longer made her feel ugly because she knew at last that this had nothing to do with surfaces.

"Are you all right?" he asked, leaning closer, concern edging into his features.

"You *do* care about me, don't you, Reid?"

"You just figured that out?"

She nodded.

"Anyone ever tell you you're a little slow?" He came closer, smiling.

"No, but maybe they should have."

He took hold of her hand. She watched, feeling drugged. "Your theory about the suicide," he prompted.

"I don't think it was a suicide."

"What, then?" he asked.

"Maybe one of her subjects found out about her little hobby and objected."

"Murder's a pretty strenuous form of objection, Rowena."

"That's what I've been telling her for months." Mark came in, handed the printouts to Reid, then helped himself to a wedge of Brie. "Want some cheese, Ro? Dinner'll be ready in about half an hour."

Slipping her hand free, she wound her arms around her drawn-up knees. "I ought to be angry with both of you for conspiring to set this up, but since you're both probably angry with me, too, let's call it even and talk about Claudia."

"I can't tell you how much I *don't* want to talk about your sister," Reid said. "But if this'll put an end to it, let's do it. First, regarding FAE. In my own defense, unless you've got a patient's history from the time of conception, it's a tough call to make. I thought she had de Clérambault's. Everything fit, and still does. But for the sake of argument, let's say you're right. How do you get from FAE to murder, Rowena? That's a quantum leap."

"Hey," Mark interjected, "just be grateful you're off the suspect list."

"What? You actually thought I killed Claudia? You think I'm capable of *that?*"

"When I found the tape, I thought maybe you were."

"It's nice to know I made such a positive impression on you," he said, scowling.

"I still don't buy her death as a suicide. I never will."

"Based on what?" Reid asked.

"Based on the fact that I *know* categorically she would never, ever have killed herself."

"See what I mean?" Mark said to Reid.

"Don't you two try ganging up on me!" she warned. "Just because I'm willing to overlook your conspiracy to set up this confab, doesn't mean I'm willing to sit here and let you humor me. I'm not crazy."

"Okay, then," Mark challenged her. "Who killed Claudia?"

"Whoever shot the tape," she fired back.

"I'm lost. Which tape?" Reid asked.

"Yours," Rowena explained. "All the others were done using a timer. But someone actually ran the camcorder for yours."

Again, he paled. "Are you telling me there was a *third party* involved?"

"Afraid so," Mark said.

"You saw the tape, too?" Reid asked him.

Mark nodded regretfully.

"Jesus! This gets worse and worse." He sat with his head in his hands.

"I'll go fix the food." Mark hurried back to the kitchen.

"I'm sorry," Rowena murmured. "I never intended it to come out this way."

"Oh? What were you planning, a full-page ad in the *New York Times?* Or maybe one of those light aircraft with a banner?"

"Don't go overboard, Reid. You got suckered by my sister. I know how that feels, and I'm sympathetic. It doesn't alter the fact that you weren't honest with me."

"I wasn't dishonest, either. I admit I didn't turn around and walk away from Claudia when I had the chance that night. But it doesn't really have anything to do with you."

"She was my sister."

"So what?"

"So. . . I don't know."

"Mark has a valid point, you know. I'm not good when it comes to dealing with my own emotional issues."

"Something we have in common."

"Are we going to be able to get past this, Rowena?"

"I think we probably already are."

He sat back up asking, "Am I expected to do heavy penance?"

"I wouldn't think so, no."

Starting to smile, he said, "So in future my calls might be re-turned?"

"I'd say there's every likelihood they will."

"Because I've come clean?"

"That, and because I've decided it's a waste of time being afraid of what might or might not happen. I don't want a half-life. We get to be dead for a long, long time."

"Very true," he agreed.

"My father's assured me that Jeanne hardly drank at all when she was pregnant with me, so there's almost no chance of my having FAE too. I was kind of worried about that."

"You must be relieved."

"Very. So, before I get dead, there are a few things I want to do."

"Such as?"

"Come over here, and let me whisper in your ear."

Grinning, he moved down to her end of the sofa.

Twenty-Eight

They'd finished eating and were back in the living room. At one end of the sofa, Reid was finishing his wine. Curled up at the other end, Rowena was trying hard to stay awake. And Mark was sitting cross-legged on the floor behind the coffee table, facing them.

Rowena yawned and said, "The two of you stay and finish your wine. I've got to go to bed."

"I should probably get going," Reid said with a quick look at his watch. "I have some case notes to finish."

"It's not even nine o'clock," she said apologetically.

"Ro, go to bed," Mark ordered. "Your system's still in shock from the accident. Nobody's going to give you a hard time for pooping out on the party." He got up and offered Reid his hand. "Good to see you again, Tony."

"Maybe you and Richard would like to come out on the boat one Sunday soon."

"Hey! That'd be great. I'll ask him." To Rowena, Mark said, "I'll go load the dishwasher. Give me a shout when you're ready to go up."

"So," Reid said after he'd gone, "when will I see you?"

"When would you like to see me?"

"How about a boat ride Saturday afternoon?"

"I'd love it."

"Okay. We'll talk tomorrow."

"Reid, I'm very graphic about certain things. Please don't say you're going to call if you don't mean it. Because if I don't hear from you, I'll read all kinds of things into it."

"Okay. I won't not call you tomorrow," he said with a smile. "Is it safe to kiss you good-night?"

"Probably not, but don't let that stop you."

"That'll teach you to go whispering things in my ear." He slid over and put an arm around her. "I'm fairly graphic myself," he murmured, his other hand slipping under her pajama top to slide slowly up, then down the length of her spine.

"It's not fair to molest a woman in a weakened condition."

"You're graphic, and I don't like to play fair."

"Wonderful." She let her forehead come to rest on his shoulder. "So I'll come out on your boat and you'll take complete advantage of me."

"Count on it." The hand now traveled around and came up over her breast.

Struggling to draw breath, she stilled the movement of his hand, covering it with her own. "I'll be waiting on Saturday with a gross of condoms. Go home," she whispered.

"I haven't had my good-night kiss yet."

With an effort, she lifted her head. "Better do it, then." Flushed, she smiled at him.

"Guess I'd better." He kissed her on the lips, then on the forehead, withdrew his hand, and said, "Maybe you'd better bring two gross."

She laughed, with one finger tracing the shape of his mouth. He kissed her again, and got up to retrieve his jacket. "I'll talk to you tomorrow."

"Okay. 'Night, Reid."

He waved, called goodbye to Mark, and let himself out.

She remained where she was, cooling down for a minute or two, then went to the kitchen and sat at the marble table, waiting for Mark to finish loading the dishwasher.

"Need help getting upstairs?" he asked.

"In a minute."

He wiped down the countertop, threw the sponge in the sink, and stood drying his hands on a dish towel. "Want some tea?"

She shook her head.

"What? Are you mad at me, after all?"

"No, no. I'm just amazed you'd do that. You take risks for the people you care about. I've never in my life taken a risk. I've either accepted things at face value, believing what people told me, or I hid out and tried not to see, all the while wishing to God I could run away."

"So what?" he said, sitting down opposite her. "At least you're real, and you actually feel things. So does Tony. But I guess you've finally clued in about him. You know what really spoke to me, Ro?"

"What?"

"When I called him about the accident, he dropped everything and came running. Not too many people who'll come on the run."

"I know. Hardly anyone."

"Sure you don't want tea?"

"I'm sure. I'd better go to bed now."

"Okay. Come on."

He helped her up the stairs and before climbing into bed, she hugged him hard and whispered, "Thank you for tonight."

"In you go," he said, folding back the bedclothes.

She got into bed and he sat down beside her.

"Listen to me, dear heart. You hung in and helped with Tim right to the very end. His stinking *family* didn't want to *know,* but you were there. When we were down to the home care and I was scared to leave the room for a minute in case he died when I wasn't there, you came and held his hand and read to him; you fed him and cleaned him up, and gave me time to go hide out in the bathroom and cry. And later, when it was all over, and I needed to get out of that apartment or lose my goddamned marbles, you gave me a new home. So, please, don't thank me for setting it up so you and Tony could clear the air. It's the least I could do. Now go to sleep, have nice little-person dreams, and I'll see you in the morning."

After eleven on a Saturday night two and a half weeks later, Ian walked into the office at the restaurant. He was so startled when he saw Rowena sitting behind the desk that he dropped his cigarette.

"You gave me quite a turn," he said, bending to retrieve the burning Silk Cut from the floor.

"Sorry. I've been waiting to talk to you in private."

"Are you feeling better? You're looking much improved."

"I'm getting there. Come sit down, Ian."

"Actually"—he looked over his shoulder toward the door—"I haven't yet locked up."

"I'll come with you. I was starting to feel kind of claustrophobic in here." She followed him out, opting to sit at the bar as he locked the front door.

Going behind the bar he asked, "Care for anything? I thought I'd have a brandy before I go."

"No, thank you," she answered, understanding that he was going to remain back there, keeping some distance between them.

He got an ashtray, put out his cigarette and at once lit a fresh one. "Sorry. Care for one?" He offered her the pack.

"No, thank you. Wouldn't you like to sit down?"

"I'm just as happy standing. What was it you wanted to talk about?" He regarded her over the top of the snifter as he took a sip of the brandy.

"I think it's time you told me what happened, Ian."

A police cruiser drove slowly past outside and they both turned to watch it.

"Why couldn't you leave it alone?" he asked sadly. "I did try to warn you."

"How could I? Regardless of whatever else she was, Claudia was my sister."

"A fact I will always find nothing less than astonishing."

"Did you have something to do with her death?" she asked quietly.

If he was thrown by the question he didn't show it. He drew in a deep breath and said, "In a manner of speaking, you could say so."

"It was you who taped Dr. Reid, wasn't it?"

His eyes were on the window as he nodded slowly.

"Why did you do it?"

He shrugged and took another sip of the brandy, then drew on his cigarette. "It was rather a black comedy, in a way. I was for a time very fond of Claudia, you know. A great and terrible lapse of judgment on my part. But there you are." He met Rowena's eyes and offered her a self-deprecating smile. "No sense, no logic. I left a stifling marriage in England, to a woman whose primary goal in life was to wangle an invitation to any event attended by one of the royals. Silly damned woman, but it took me close to ten years to break free. Never have been very quick on the uptake, I suppose. I came to America looking for something, didn't find it in New York, then decided to settle for a bit of peace in the countryside instead, and accepted the offer of managing this place. Right up my alley, you see, since I'd literally grown up in the hotel business. My family owned several hotels, and I went to the Swiss schools, the lot. So this was bound to be a piece of cake.

"I signed on because of Claudia. She was like no one I'd ever encountered—all flash and glamour and, underneath, slightly evil. Not a clue how to run a restaurant, of course. But I admired her nerve, so I took it on. I became her confidant from the outset. She assumed I was gay, which didn't bother me, and loved to regale me with gossip and details of her conquests. Initially, I came in every day eager to hear what she'd got up to the night before. I'd listen and refrain from comment, so she, again, assumed I approved of her. The truth was I neither approved nor disapproved. I simply accepted that she was what she was. And for quite some time, we got on like a house afire. I had daily entertainment, as it were, and she had someone to whom she could confide her endless plots. I was enjoying myself. Makes me sound a right nana." He paused to take another drag on the cigarette and leaned against the back bar.

"Inevitably, a few years down the road, it started catching up to her. One can't mess about with people in a small town without repercussions. There was the odd scene or two. Canny creature, she usually managed to disappear at the crucial moment, and turn up again after the fact, tittering like a schoolgirl. A few more years on, I was having to deal fairly regularly with people who were well and truly shattered; trying to console them with the offer of a drink and a word or two of advice. It had a cumulative effect, and I'm afraid my tolerance began disintegrating. There were the telephone calls she didn't want to take, the people she didn't want to see—more and more of both.

"Hearing about the tapes was rather like another of her exotic fantasies. One never knew with Claudia what was real, had actually occurred, and what she'd merely dreamed up."

"I know," Rowena said. "She was always that way."

"Well, then, you'll understand that when she came into the office to show me her latest video camera, I saw that it was real enough. But when she talked of the tapes she'd made, it struck me as somehow too cold-bloodedly clinical to be real. I was fairly convinced she fabricated these stories merely to entertain me. As time passed, however, I came to realize two things: that the stories were indeed true, and that her pleasure in these conquests was derived from the seductions themselves, and in possessing proof in the form of the tapes. She derived no satisfaction whatever from the actual sex. That was merely what had to be done in order to claim another victory. Soon I began to find it tiresome in the extreme. I began finding *her* extremely tiresome. I was caught in a frightful ambivalence, disliking her intensely on the one hand, and, irrationally, continuing to have this baseless fondness for her on the other. It sounds mad."

"No," she said, looking into his hazel eyes, able to see the injury there. "I understand completely. I never liked her, but I always loved her. She was addictive."

"Precisely! I had no idea your view of her was so...objective."

"We've never really talked about her. You wouldn't give me an opening."

"That's true," he said regretfully. "But I felt I was on very shaky ground."

"How did she get you to go along with her?"

"Actually, I think I would like to sit down. I'm rather tired. I've been dreading this for months, gearing up for it, expecting...I don't know. A frightful scene, I suppose. I should've known it's not your style.''

They shifted to one of the tables for two by the entry.

''We took great care to be discreet,'' he said after a time, ''but somehow Claudia guessed that Mae and I were involved.''

''You *were?*''

''Are,'' he informed her. ''Have been for a good five years, now. It's an arrangement that works well for both of us. Mae's divorced and has a delightful young daughter. She had a dreadful marriage and has no interest in marrying again. I too had a bad marriage, and also have no interest. So it's been an ongoing, committed sort of thing that satisfies needs we both have while allowing us to maintain our freedom. We kept it very much to ourselves, but Claudia guessed. And she suggested that I might want to do her this one favor or she'd have to cut back on staff and let someone go. Now while I don't need this job, or any other for that matter, Mae does. Her former husband rarely makes his child-support payments, and she's dependent on her job here. Also, she's a proud woman and wouldn't dream of accepting money from me—even as a loan. So, once again, as I'd seen and heard her do countless times to others, Claudia unerringly went for my most vulnerable spot. What, I asked her, did she want?

''Oh, it was nothing, she said. She'd made up her mind to add the doctor to her shelf, as it were. It was a great challenge, and there were problems. She couldn't simply set the timer and work to a schedule as she usually did, because she was going to have to use some sort of ruse to get the doctor to the house. I was to be there, in the dressing room, at the ready with the camera, if and when. 'Just this once, Ian, and I'll never ask you for anything ever again.''' He shook his head and stopped. ''If you don't mind, Rowena, I think I'd like a refill.''

''I don't mind.''

''Thank you.'' He got up, poured another splash of brandy into the snifter, then returned. ''You're very generous,'' he said, searching her eyes. ''I *am* sorry about this sordid business. I had hoped no one would ever have to know.''

''No one else will, Ian. It's just that *I* need to know.''

''I should've realized that. Well, where were we? Ah yes, in the closet, so to speak.'' He gave a brief bitter laugh, took a hard drag on his cigarette and looked into the darkened depths of the restaurant. ''That bloody woman. She rang Reid's service and insisted it was an emergency; she was desperate. He rang back quite quickly, and she put on an astonishing performance. From moment to moment she actually had me convinced she was bent on suicide. Then she put the phone down and let out a triumphant shriek. She'd done it. He was on his way.

"She ran about like a mad thing, setting the scene. Left the downstairs door open, came flying back upstairs to touch up her makeup, fixed her hair, then stripped off and arranged herself on the bed. It was all I could do not to laugh. But then he arrived, and suddenly, I was terribly afraid. Can't explain it, really. I had a dreadful feeling of guilt at having consented to assist her in this. I kept asking myself, was I mad? What was I doing, hiding out in a damned dressing room with a camera? I hoped he'd take umbrage, give her a good talking-to, and go. But the poor bastard never had a chance, really. You've seen the tape, so you know. Well." He sighed, and drank more brandy. "As fate would have it, she had one of the rare, if not the only, unfeigned orgasm of her life. The poor doctor left as quickly as he could, and so, by God, did I. I've never *been* so ashamed. I couldn't look at her, let alone speak to her. I simply shut down the camera and got the hell out. Went home and drank myself blind, told myself it was done, that was the end of it.

"But no one ever got away from your sister scot-free. I'd been naive to imagine the blackmail wouldn't continue. The very next day she was on fire with the idea of doing it again. Having a witness, you see, was what got her turned on. I wouldn't have to do a thing, just be there in the dressing room while she lured the doctor back for another round. It was out of the question I told her, and she was mad if she thought the doctor would ever come anywhere near her again."

"But she wouldn't listen," Rowena filled in. "And she started calling him day and night."

"Exactly."

"Then, all of a sudden, she stopped. Why? What happened?"

"One day, after harassing the poor bugger for weeks, it occurred to her that it didn't have to be him. It could be anyone, so long as I was there, hidden in the dressing room, watching. First she threatened. It would be Mae's job if I didn't capitulate. I said fine, do what you will. I was giving my notice and she had a month to find another manager. No, no. Of course she wouldn't fire Mae. Just a joke, Ian. Would I do it for money? She'd give me a thousand dollars, two. She was shocked when I said I had no need of her money. In fact, I was giving my notice regardless, because I couldn't take any more. The restaurant was suffering. The staff were on edge because she'd attack them individually or collectively on the slightest pretext. I put my resignation letter on her desk, said I'd help hire a replacement and get him or her started in the job, but I'd made up my mind and was going. I'd already begun asking around, looking to find Mae another job. I thought if I could present her with a new situation as a fait accompli, she'd very likely be happy to get away from Claudia. All the staff felt much the same way. We were on the verge of mutiny. Terry came to me saying he'd had another job offer and was seriously considering leaving. Philippe had had it up to his eyeballs with her; Doug was already applying at other restaurants. Even the busboys were grumbling.

"Now Claudia became frantic. I *couldn't* leave. She couldn't run the restaurant without me. She couldn't possibly work with anyone else after so many years. She'd never again ask me to do *anything,* but I had to stay. No. I held firm. Sorry, but I'm off at the end of the month. I won't leave you high and dry, I told her, but nothing could persuade me to stay on.

"So what did she do?" Again he emitted his bitter laugh. "It was too ridiculous! She simply didn't bother showing up on the Friday evening. We were frantic, shorthanded, with no one to cover the front. And she rings me at the peak of the evening, threatening suicide if I don't agree to stay on. Almost the exact performance, word for word, that she'd used on the doctor. Stop the nonsense, I told her. The restaurant was fully booked, and I was busy. She had pills, she insisted, and was going to take them. 'Take them, then!' I told her. 'I've got no time for this rubbish!' and put the phone down."

"So she did," Rowena finished for him.

He nodded. "I awakened early the next morning and got to wondering if she was mad enough to go ahead and take the pills, believing I'd come along to save her in the nick of time. That had been her original plan with the doctor, you see. But when she realized the pills might make her sick or render her incapable of performing, she abandoned the idea. I rang the house, and when the answering machine came on, I thought I'd best stop by, just to be sure. I wish I could tell you I was sorry when I found her, but I wasn't. God forgive me, I was simply relieved, glad it was over. I checked for a pulse, but it was obvious she'd been dead for hours. She was already cold.

"I went down to the kitchen and stood outside the back door, having a cigarette, deciding what to do. Finally, I came back inside and rang the police, then you. I did what I thought was best. I'd like you to believe that."

"I do," she told him.

"At a certain point, you know, I thought she was evil. But she had no concept of morality, none at all. Trying to reason with her was impossible. She simply failed to comprehend. There was a concept of right and wrong; she'd heard about it, seen it on the telly, perhaps. But it had no application to her life, meant nothing to her. And that was when I became frightened of her. Because I realized she was capable of absolutely anything.

"You see, Rowena, I couldn't be certain it wasn't a family trait. I mean the two of you didn't *seem* in the least alike. When you came to the house that morning after she died, and the first thing you did was hug me, I was tempted to tell you straightaway. Because that gesture was such a healthy, *human* sign—something beyond Claudia's abilities. But then how could I be sure you weren't perhaps a more evolved model, one with more finely honed performance capabilities? It didn't seem safe, so I kept silent.

"When you first came to fill in here, everyone felt the difference at once. And I decided I'd stay on after all. Things would work out. I should've known it wasn't to be." He looked down at the tabletop. "I expect you'd like me to pack it in."

"No, I wouldn't."

Surprised, he raised his eyes to hers again.

"I brought some articles for you to read. I think they'll help." She opened her bag, pulled out an envelope and handed it across to him. "It's a long story, but she couldn't help being what she was. And it wasn't your fault that she died. I thought when you broke into the house—"

"I didn't break into your house," he declared, perplexed.

"But I thought you were looking for that last tape."

He shook his head in vigorous denial. "Why would I, when I had a set of keys? Besides, what earthly good would that tape have been to me? I confess I did have a quick look round before I rang the police that Saturday morning, but the only tapes I saw were the old films in the living room. I mistakenly assumed her personal tapes would never be found."

"She had a secret hiding place, but that was for the camera and the very last tape. The rest of them were right there in the living room, disguised as old films."

"I'll be buggered." He gulped the last of his brandy.

It was a genuine break-in, she thought, thrown. Nothing had been taken, probably because Mark had arrived home and frightened off the burglars.

"Forgive me, but are you saying you'd like me to continue on?" he asked, looking truly fatigued now.

"I intend to keep things as they are. If you'd like to stay."

"I was so geared up to having you send me packing." He shook his head, and asked, "Are you quite sure? It's not a pretty story. Perhaps when you've had time to think it over—"

"I've had most of my life to think it over, Ian. What you've told me isn't quite what I'd imagined, but it coincides with Tony Reid's account. The thing is, I knew Claudia would never commit suicide. What happened was an accident. I can accept that."

"It struck me at the time that you were badly thrown by her death," he said, "but you didn't appear particularly . . . upset."

"To be honest, I felt the way you did. I was glad it was over. I lived most of my life scared of and yet fascinated by my sister, and angry with my mother for catering to her the way she did. I blocked out some things, denied others. Now it's over, and I have the answers I wanted. I think what's in the envelope will give you some, too. It's late, and time to go home. We've both had a rough six months. Let's get on with our lives and forget this."

Getting to his feet, he asked cannily, "Will you forget it all that easily?"

"I'm going to give it a damned good shot." She, too, stood and took a slow look around. "You see, Ian, the restaurant was *my* dream."

"I beg your pardon?"

"Every bit of it, right down to the color scheme, and the vases of fresh flowers. It was what I planned to do with my small part of the inheritance after Jeanne died. I'd even been here to look at the space. When I called the real estate agent three days later to say I'd go ahead, she told me someone else had beaten me to it." Her eyes coming back to Ian, she gave him a rueful smile. "During the reception after our mother's funeral, Claudia overheard me telling Penny my plans. Later, when the place was open and a success, my sister said, 'You'd never have been able to pull it off, Ro. You have no style.'" She shook her head. "But she was wrong. I've got all kinds of style."

"Indeed, you do."

"So, will I forget it? You bet." She went up on tiptoe to kiss his cheek. "And so will you. Let's go now. I've got a date with Tony Reid to go sailing tomorrow, and I want to be rested."

"Good chap, the doctor," he said approvingly. "I'll see you to your car, Rowena."

She waited on the patio while he coded the alarm, then locked the back door. The air was cool, the sky very clear.

"Fine weather for sailing tomorrow," he observed as they started toward the parking lot.

They arrived at the Honda and he stood by while she unlocked the door and climbed in, then rolled down the window. He bent to look in at her, saying, "Mind you fasten your seat belt."

"Oh, I will."

"And thank you, my dear. It's a great relief, having that off my mind."

"For me, too, Ian."

"You'll be back to work Monday, you think?"

"Count on it." With a smile, she put the car in gear and headed home.

ACKNOWLEDGMENTS

My interest in FAS/FAE was aroused by Michael Dorris's extraordinarily moving and important book *The Broken Cord,* (Harper & Row, 1989). Some of the information used herein was derived from it.

Additional information came from "Fetal alcohol syndrome in adolescents and adults," by Ann Pytkowicz Streissguth, Jon M. Aase, Sterling K. Clarren, Sandra P. Randels, Robin A. LaDue and David F. Smith, il v265 JAMA, *The Journal of the American Medical Association,* 17 April 1991, p1961 (7).

Also: *The Addiction Letter,* May 1991, p5 (1).
The Brown University Digest of Addiction Theory and Application, May 1991, p4 (2).
Alcoholism & Drug Abuse Week, 17 April 1991, p5 (1).
The Brown University Child Behavior and Development Letter, v7, April 1991, p3 (1).

"Learning impairment: major risks and suggested preventions," by Lucille F. Newman and Stephen L. Buka, *The Brown University Child Behavior and Development Letter,* v7, April 1991, p1 (2).

"Recommended interventions for fetal-alcohol syndrome children," by Lyn Weiner and Barbara A. Morse, *The Brown University Child Behavior and Development Letter,* v6, Dec. 1990, p1 (2).

I am grateful to the librarians at the South Norwalk library for their unfailing willingness to be of assistance, and also to their counterparts at the Metropolitan Toronto Reference Library.

TELL THE AUTHOR

Dear Charlotte Vale Allen,
I just finished reading Claudia's Shadow *and wanted to tell you what I*
thought of the book.

_____

_____

_____

Sincerely,

name _____

address _____

city, state, zip code _____

(please print)

If you are reading a library book, please copy this page and leave it for the
next reader.

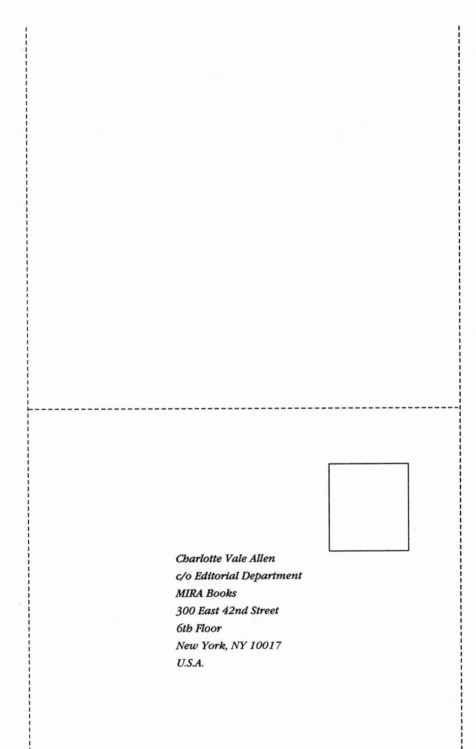

Charlotte Vale Allen
c/o Editorial Department
MIRA Books
300 East 42nd Street
6th Floor
New York, NY 10017
U.S.A.

(seal here)

TELL A FRIEND

Dear _____,

I just finished reading Claudia's Shadow *by Charlotte Vale Allen and wanted to tell you about it because I think it's a book you will enjoy as much as I did.*

Sincerely,

_____

Claudia's Shadow, *published by MIRA Books, is available wherever books are sold.*

(seal here)